AFTER

NINETEEN STORIES OF
APOCALYPSE AND DYSTOPIA

HYPERION

NEW YORK

NINETEEN STORIES OF
APOCALYPSE AND DYSTOPIA

edited by **ELLEN DATLOW** and
TERRI WINDLING

Featuring stories by:

RICHARD BOWES

SARAH REES BRENNAN

CECIL CASTELLUCCI

CAROLYN DUNN

CAROL EMSHWILLER

JEFFREY FORD

STEVEN GOULD

NALO HOPKINSON

N. K. JEMISIN

CAITLÍN R. KIERNAN

MATTHEW KRESSEL

KATHERINE LANGRISH

GREGORY MAGUIRE

GARTH NIX

SUSAN BETH PFEFFER

BETH REVIS

CARRIE RYAN

GENEVIEVE VALENTINE

JANE YOLEN

Introduction © 2012 by Terri Windling
"The Segment" copyright © 2012 by Genevieve Valentine
"After the Cure" copyright © 2012 by Carrie Ryan
"Valedictorian" copyright © 2012 by N.K. Jemisin
"Visiting Nelson" copyright © 2012 by Katherine Langrish
"All I Know of Freedom" copyright © 2012 by Carol Emshwiller
"The Other Elder" copyright © 2012 by Beth Revis
"The Great Game at the End of the World" copyright © 2012 by Matthew Kressel
"Reunion" copyright © 2012 by Susan Beth Pfeffer
"Blood Drive" copyright © 2012 by Jeffrey Ford
"Reality Girl" copyright © 2012 by Richard Bowes
"How Th'irth Wint Rong by Hapless Joey @ homeskool.guv"
copyright © 2012 by Gregory Maguire
"Rust with Wings" copyright © 2012 by Steven Gould
"Faint Heart" copyright © 2012 by Susan Rees Brennan
"The Easthound" copyright © 2012 by Nalo Hopkinson
"gray" copyright © 2012 by Jane Yolen
"Before" copyright © 2012 by Carolyn Dunn
"Fake Plastic Trees" copyright © 2012 by Caitlín R. Kiernan
"You Won't Feel a Thing" copyright © 2012 by Garth Nix
"The Marker" copyright © 2012 by Cecil Castellucci
Afterword © 2012 by Terri Windling

First Hyperion paperback edition 2013
Printed the United States of America
Text is set in 12-point Goudy
Library of Congress Cataloging-in-Publication Control Number for Hardcover 2011034582
ISBN 978-1-4231-4812-8

SUSTAINABLE
FORESTRY
INITIATIVE
Certified Chain of Custody
Promoting Sustainable Forestry
www.sfiprogram.org
SFI-01054
The SFI label applies to the text stock

Visit www.un-requiredreading.com

For Victoria Windling-Gayton and Isobel Gahan,
two young women with indomitable spirits

CONTENTS

INTRODUCTION

BY **TERRI WINDLING** AND **ELLEN DATLOW**

WELCOME TO *AFTER*, A VOLUME OF BRAND-NEW DYSTOPIAN and post-apocalyptic tales for young adult readers by some of the very best writers working today—ranging from best-selling, award-winning authors to rising young stars of the dyslit field.

Before we go any further, however, perhaps we'd better stop and define our terms . . . which is going to put us in dangerous territory; for blistering arguments about what should and shouldn't be labeled dystopian fiction have consumed whole Internet forums, convention panels, and book review columns. There is, alas, no single definition that all of us who love this kind of fiction can agree on.

To some folks (including most YA publishers), dyslit is a broad, inclusive genre of tales that take place in darkly imagined futures: ranging from stories that explore the dangers of repressive governments and societies gone bad to books whose plots unfold in bleak, savage, or oppressive post-apocalypse settings. In this usage, the dyslit label conveys more about a story's overall *tone* than its plotline (or subtext of societal critique): the worlds depicted are *dark* ones, in which protagonists must struggle for physical and/or moral survival.

Others folks (including most literary critics) reach back to the classical definition of dystopian literature, which is far more specific: tales of utopias gone wrong. In this view, post-apocalyptic novels are dystopian *only* if the narrower definition applies— otherwise they are a genre of their own, albeit one that is closely related, and read by many of the same readers. "In a dystopian story," writes John Joseph Adams (editor of *Brave New Worlds: Dystopian Stories*, an excellent collection of traditionally dystopian fiction), "society itself is typically the antagonist; it is society that is actively working against the protagonist's aims and desires." Now, this may true in *some* post-apocalyptic tales, but it's certainly not true in all of them, for many take place in post-disaster settings where human society has broken down altogether. To dystopian purists, such books do not belong on dyslit lists.

As for us, although we respect the purists' view, we've chosen to take a broader road in the creation of this anthology, including *both* dystopian and post-disaster tales (as well as stories that fall on the spectrum between) in order to reflect the wide range of dyslit beloved by teen readers today. As the popular dyslit author Scott Westerfeld has said (in his essay "Teenage Wastelands" for Tor.com): ". . . in the YA universe, the terms 'post-apocalyptic' and 'dystopian' are often used interchangeably. This grates the pedant's soul, and yet is understandable. From a teenager's point of view, a blasted hellscape and a hypercontrolled society aren't so different. Or rather, they're simply two sides of the same coin: one has too much control, the other not enough. And, you may be shocked to hear, teenagers are *highly* interested in issues of control."

Exactly.

Our anthology sprang from a simple idea: to seek out writers who share our love for dystopian and post-apocalyptic tales, and to ask them to please write stories for us about what happens *after*.

After what?

A disaster of any kind: political, ecological, technological, sociological . . . the choice was entirely up to the writer. It could be *after* a nuclear war or a medical pandemic; *after* a scientific discovery that resulted in unforeseen and dire consequences; *after* aliens land, or society crumbles, or the very last drop of oil runs out . . . It could be after *anything* so long as the changes provoked are calamitous, fundamental, and long lasting. "We're not looking for tales focused on the disaster," we said, "but tales that tell us what happens *next*: what life is like for young people who are growing up in calamity's wake, or in 'perfect societies' gone wrong, or in the ruins of their elders' mistakes."

Our intrepid writers went away with this assignment and came back with the amazing stories that follow: frightening, fascinating, mind-bending stories about dark future worlds that could be our own if something (sometimes the smallest thing) goes badly, irreparably wrong.

These stories approach the "after" theme from a variety of directions—some of them straightforward in the telling, and some of them sly, tricksy, and surprising. Like the field of dystopian literature itself, the stories draw upon the tropes of several overlapping genres: science fiction, fantasy, horror, mystery, surrealism, and satire . . . with a bit of romance (*apocalyptic* romance, of course!) thrown in for good measure.

In the worlds conjured by the stories that follow, you'll find floods, famine, and pestilence; you'll find monsters, horrors, despair, and devastation. And also, in the darkness, bright sparks of courage and resistance.

Much like the world we live in.

THE SEGMENT

BY GENEVIEVE VALENTINE

WHEN MASON SHOWED ME THE SCRIPT SIDES FOR THE CHILD soldier, I jumped on it.

"Think about this," he said. "The segment could be huge. Is that how you want to make your career?"

He talked a big game, but this segment was special. He had to know it, too; I was the only one at our agency he'd even talked to about it.

I said, "I'll take my chances."

"All right," he said. He looked serious, but I was pretty sure he was just full of it.

The best gig I'd had so far was the front half of a black bear for a nature documentary. It was on cable.

I'm not complaining—you have to pay your way at the agency, and rent be not proud—but I needed to earn some more, soon, and "bear half" didn't set your career on fire.

Face time was an upgrade. And this wasn't some bit part as a muddy orphan in an establishing shot. This was the big time.

This was the evening news.

That night I walked under our painted motto (Let Those Who Would Be Fooled, Be Fooled) into the dining hall, packed with kids from the Lowers that the agency hired out as sympathetic faces on news segments for the Uppers to go watch when they were feeling generous.

I sat down, grinning, next to Bree.

"I'm in the audition pool for a soldier."

She barely looked up from her vegetable mash. "Oh? Congratulations."

"Yeah," I said. "It's big. Investor backing for the cause, too, so the pay is pretty solid."

"Wonderful," she said. "I was beginning to worry you'd aged out of your best work. It's nice they're skewing older on something."

I was sixteen. Bree was nineteen, and kind of a bitch.

"What's the story?"

"My brother is missing," I said, "and he was the last thing I had left of home. Now I'm fighting the people who took him since I'm dead inside anyway, grenades exploding on us any moment, blah, blah, blah. They wanted someone who can handle a gun, not for crying or anything."

Bree's fork wasn't moving anymore. "Is this for some newspaper?"

I grinned. "The evening news."

Now she was looking up, her head angled by instinct to catch the best light on her face. "What?"

"Yup." I shrugged like it was nothing. "I was handpicked. If the segment breaks big, they'll probably have to retire me."

Bree looked stunned. After a second, she recovered and said, "Dream big."

"I'm going to get it," I said.

She smiled. "I'm sure," she said. "And if that doesn't pan out, there's always a place for you on *Naturewise*."

She was acting like I'd been the *back* half of the bear.

I stood. "I'm going to rehearse."

"Break a leg," said Bree, like she meant it.

When I was still a kid, Bree had gotten a gig as a grieving bride whose husband was killed by government troops on his way up the stairs of the church.

(She was still in the dorms with me, then; she wouldn't be a teacher until after that segment.)

It was supposed to be a small part, a background tableau in the middle of a bigger story, but Bree wasn't a person who played small parts.

In the on-scene segment with the news man in front, she had clutched her veil in her fists as she wept over the body of the guy who'd been her husband.

He was from some other agency. I hadn't seen him since—she'd kept him in the spotlight too long, and his face was too famous after that. She'd taken his career down. Bree played for keeps.

In the grainy newspaper shots (meant to have been taken by a wedding guest), Bree had cradled his head in her lap and lowered her mouth to his mouth, their lips almost touching but not quite.

("You're not supposed to kiss before marriage in that country," Bree told me the night before filming, when everyone else was asleep.

"There's nowhere to go with that," I said.

Bree said, "Watch me."

At the time I hated that we shared a dorm. Our beds were pressed up against the walls, separated except for her voice, and I was trapped listening to her; but there was no question that the advice had done me good.)

The bride segment had been aimed at a regional station, to drum up sympathy for the insurgents in a couple of key cities, that could be pushed over the edge of public opinion by a sob story on the news.

(Stations hired out their news stories now. It was easier and safer than going looking for news, and our stories never went sour on you the way they did if you trusted them out in the wild.

And it's not like audiences knew the difference. To the Uppers, one tragedy on their television was as surreal as the next. Let those who would be fooled, be fooled.)

Bree was paid for a segment on the independent channel, and a picture in the locally edited newspaper.

She ended up on the cover of *Planet* magazine.

("The segment tested so well they're thinking of extending the war," Bree told me. "The Uppers love to watch a cause they can donate to."

Her voice sounded strange.)

She had one of the first editions framed above her bed. It was a close-up, her tear-stained face half hidden by a gold silk veil; her gaze sliding sideways with smeary, kohl-rimmed hazel eyes looking out at the viewer.

The headline: THE WEEPING BRIDE ON THE MOUNTAIN PATH.

The article was ten pages about the plight of the fleeing insurgents. The quotes came from the insurgents, too; *Planet* was classy enough to do research like it was still real. They'd even called the agency to get quotes right from Bree and not from our publicity office, because Bree had done such a good job with the part that they didn't want the performance to be diluted.

(I listened in, of course. I hated her, but I knew when to take notes from a master.)

"I can never kiss him, until we meet in Heaven," Bree had sighed into the office phone, her voice shaking, and on the other end of the line the *Planet* guy muttered, "Holy shit, that's great," and started typing.

(Her hands were shaking, too; Bree never did anything by halves.)

The article won a Pulitzer. Before the year was out, that government fell apart, and the insurgents got the revolution they'd paid for.

At the agency, they treated Bree like she sweated gold nuggets, and added the leader of the insurgents to their list of references for when the next guys called up the agency looking for the kind of story that couldn't happen by accident.

They had pulled Bree out of the audition pool for good after the story faded, because there was no way people would ever forget her face after that.

If you ask me, she was doomed from the beginning with eyes like that, anyway. No hiding those; I don't care how big your crowd shot is.

Now Bree had a look like she thought this was all beneath her. She shouldn't: she was still here, teaching. (The insurgents were good for publicity, but they hadn't paid so great. Wherever the Uppers' money had gone, none of it had made it to Bree.)

She was the only person at the agency who had ever been retired because of success.

So far.

Bree knew how to act above it all, but everybody has their tells, and I knew I'd gotten to her when I saw she'd signed up for phone privileges.

She made a lot of calls; she was a Lower, but she had parents on the outside. They came to visit once a year, and brought books for her (Bree could read), and told her how happy they were that she had done well for herself.

It hadn't made her any friends, but I guess when you have parents, you can take or leave the rest.

I pulled a muscle in calisthenics to get out of the session early. It took some doing to wrench my arm without breaking it, but it was my only option. No good faking anything. The downside of working in a casting agency was that everybody was on to your act.

"Ice that down at the nurse, now," said Miss Kemp, as I headed out. "You'd better look like you know how to carry a gun at the audition tomorrow."

I wasn't worried. I was tall for a girl, and wiry. I could carry half a black bear suit; I could manage a gun.

"Don't worry," I told her, and grinned. (I had all my teeth. My smile was priceless, even on Miss Kemp.)

The phone room was on the office floor, so it was easier for snoopy adults to catch snoopy students. Not that it mattered. With Bree, you never had to get any closer than the landing.

"Mother," she was saying, "you've got to do something about the part they want this girl for."

Bingo.

Her voice, tense and serious, echoed down the hall. "It's not fair. She's sixteen, but she's never done anything! I don't know why they're doing this at all. There's got to be someone else who could use her."

One success can really turn a petty person sour, I thought.

"Yeah, she's good enough," Bree said. "Can't you buy her out? She'll find some other way to earn out of her contract." And a second later, meaner, "Well, decide faster."

I snuck back down the stairs before the call was over. Listening to someone jealous themselves into a heart attack wasn't as fun as I'd thought.

I flew down the hall on stocking feet, and was in the nurse's office before Miss Kemp could even call down to check on me. What took everybody else five minutes, I could do in three.

That night, Bree pulled me aside on the walk back from the dining hall to the dorms.

"Mason told me to help you run lines," she said.

She could read.

"I can get Miss Kemp to do them with me," I said.

"No," she said. "I want to get a look at this part, and you need the help."

I had no idea who she thought she was fooling, but this I had to see.

We went through the script in one of the empty schoolrooms. It wasn't much on paper. I reminded myself that Bree had done more with less, which gave me some courage.

"I'm a pretty good shot," I said, and then I closed one eye and mimicked taking down some scrabbly mammal at a hundred paces.

"Don't worry if you can't hit it," Bree said. "They'll probably hold on you while you shoot, and then just rig one to explode in pickups."

The way she said it threw me, for a second.

The newsman would ask me what had happened to my family,

what I thought about the government and the war, how I felt about being a soldier. I breezed through the lines, the picture of a ruined kid who'd grown up too soon.

(They could have just gone outside, where the city was overrun with Lower kids trying to stay out of the ratcatchers' way long enough to eat, but there was no telling what would happen if someone started in on a story like that. Uppers didn't like being reminded of a problem so hopeless, a problem so close to home.)

When Bree read her lines, her exterior thinned, and the hardened war reporter devastated by what she was seeing sprang to life in front of me.

She shouldn't have been so bitter about what happened after the weeping bride. She was too convincing, too good; whatever role she'd gotten would have been her last.

At the very end, I was supposed to look up at the newsman (cheating my face to the camera) and say, fighting tears: "I miss my brother."

"Wrong," Bree snapped, the first time. "It's not a sandwich, it's your brother. This is the evening news—you have to fool ten million people. Now, picture something you've really lost, and make me feel it."

I closed my eyes. I had a dim memory of being hot and hungry and frightened, from before the agency bought me off the ratcatcher who'd brought me here. But all I had ever really known was the classrooms and the dining hall and the winding upstairs corridors with little dorms on each side, and the overhead signs for pediatric ward, where they dormed the really little kids.

"I can't," I said, opening my eyes.

Bree looked disappointed. "You've never lost a friend?"

"You're one to talk," I said.

After a little silence, she said, "You *have* to nail this line.

There's no point in them keeping you around if you don't sell this, you understand me?"

I didn't understand. I couldn't believe she was so upset; maybe this was the hallmark of an artist.

"Okay," I said. "What am I supposed to do?"

She slapped me.

The pain took a second to reach me; then it pooled where her hand had struck and sent a jolt up my nose like she'd shoved a nail in it. My eyes watered, but I was too scared to close them, in case she tried it again on the other side.

She said, "Give me the line."

I had forgotten to breathe, and when I exhaled it stung my throat.

"I miss my brother."

"Good," she said. "Again."

I got to take the white van to the audition. I pressed my face to the glass, watching as the alleys full of street kids gave way to clean sidewalks and tall buildings and stores that were open for business.

Mason came with me, but in the waiting room of the building (ten full stories up), he sat a little apart, with the rest of the school reps. The kids all sat in one long, silent line, waiting to be called.

The girl ahead of me was fourteen, tops, and she stared at her folded hands like she was about to faint.

I recognized her. Magpie—the puppeteer from the *Naturewise* shoot. She had manipulated the bear's face in the close-ups, hunched under a fur drape, with her arms extended, fingers pulling blindly at a hundred tiny strings.

"Were you a black bear face a few years ago?" I asked.

She looked up, surprised. "Yeah," she said, and a second later, "Poppy, right?"

I nodded. "What are you doing here? There's no puppet stuff, is there?" I was crap with puppets.

Without looking at me, she held up her right hand, which now had only three fingers.

"Infringement," she said.

I didn't understand. I looked at her.

She shrugged, recited as if by rote, "Someone from another agency tried to poach me at my last audition. My agency adjusted my value as a puppeteer."

She folded her hands back in her lap. "They were just protecting their investment, they said. That was all." She took a breath. "I didn't do anything wrong. They weren't angry with me."

When the manager called her name a few minutes later, she slid off her chair and waved to me and walked inside, and I still hadn't said a word.

"I got the part," I said.

Bree had walked downstairs from the teachers' rooms. She was silhouetted in the window at the end of the dorm hall, the only one awake.

"When do you film?"

"Next week," I said. "There's not much left to do. They found some foothills near where they filmed the bear thing, and the newsman's been cast already."

"How did the audition go?"

"I only had to read it once," I said. "They took my picture and booked me on the spot. Mason's already signed." I grinned, willing her to be proud of me, for once.

"Well," she said, after too long, "let those who would be fooled, be fooled."

It wasn't even the insult it should have been; it was the saddest thing I'd heard from her since the weeping bride.

Bree made no sense.

I dreamed about a black bear.

It was real, and close enough that I could smell its wet coat, but when it looked at me it didn't attack, so I must have been wearing my bear suit.

The bear had sharp black eyes and fur that gleamed in the sun, and this close to it, I saw how careful its expressions were: the muscles above the eyes, the flare of its nostrils, and the soft brown lips that curled back a little from its teeth as it smelled the air.

At the shoot, they told us to move deliberately, and I had operated the piston that swung its heavy head to and fro, and they had said, "Good enough."

This bear was real, and looking at it, it seemed impossible that anyone could ever have been fooled.

("What happened to the real bears?" I'd asked.

The director shrugged. "What does it matter why something dies out?" he said, and then pointed to the cameraman. "When you swing the head right, brace the legs and shake the back like you've just seen him. Close cover, watch the angle of the head here for pickups!"

Close cover was Magpie.)

I looked at the real bear, which was so close I could see that its eyes weren't black at all, but brown and flecked with gold.

"You're beautiful," I said.

It grinned; two fingers dropped out of its mouth.

When I appeared in the back hall to the teachers' offices and yanked Bree into the mostly empty pantry, she didn't even seem suprised.

"They cut off Magpie's fingers," I said.

Bree blinked. "What?"

"Magpie," I said. "The puppet handler for the bear. Someone tried to poach her, and her agency found out and cut two of her fingers off."

"Oh, Poppy," she said, "you're so easy to shock, it's like you've never heard of good business practice."

It was a decent act, but her hands had gone white under the nails because of how hard she was gripping her book bag, so I knew better.

I said, "She didn't do anything."

"Lucky for her," Bree said. "She's better off than some."

The hair rose on my neck.

After a beat, Bree looked me right in the eye. "Do you still want to do this part?"

I held her gaze. "Give me a reason not to."

One of the kitchen kids opened the door.

"Frankly, I'm tired of all this insecurity," Bree said, her neck getting longer by an inch. "Either you can do the part or you can't. I suggest you just quit."

She shouldered past me harder than necessary.

The kitchen kid gave me the once-over. He was even thinner than I was; they kept us hungry because it made our eyes shine.

"Break a leg," he said.

All through dinner, I thought about what Bree said.

If you couldn't do the job, the agency expelled you. And now

I knew that before they expelled you, they probably made you useless for other places, too.

If you weren't in an agency, you were on the streets. On the streets the ratcatchers were waiting, and if they couldn't sell you, they just disappeared you and brought in your skullcap for government cash.

(Once, the pediatric acting coach had told me that the ratcatcher had brought me to the agency because I looked so clever. She said it to make me feel better when I was failing some exercise, like the school had taken me for some reason besides my being young enough to be trained. She hadn't lasted long.)

You'd have to be a bigger bitch than Bree to wish the streets on anybody.

And no way would she tell someone to skip out on a contract. Bree was a teacher. Bree made her money when the kids made money. She had the best interests of the agency at stake.

What was so awful about this part that it would be worth telling a student to take a risk like that?

I dreamed about crumbling in front of the camera, about scalding dust coating my lungs as I struggled to speak. I dreamed about my fingers being trapped inside the bear head, about Mason sighing and pulling a hunting knife out of his pocket to do what had to be done.

"I like the dark circles," Mason said, the next time he saw me. "Very soldier. Good work."

Mason didn't come with me to the shoot.

"Today you belong to the director," he said, opening the door to the van. "Do well for the agency, all right?"

I nodded, uneasy, and ducked into the seat.

As the engine roared to life, Bree appeared in the open doorway, her book bag over one shoulder.

"I'd like to go," she said to Mason. "She's been dropping the intensity in the second half, and when I'm there it helps her focus."

"You slapped me," I said.

She shot me a glare Mason couldn't see, and said too calmly, "And it was the only time you've done it right."

Mason looked at her for a second. Then he shrugged.

"I guess if anyone understands a performance like this, it's you," he said. "Be careful not to get in anyone's way on the set."

"Of course," she said, and then she was sliding onto the bench seat beside me, and the van was pulling away, and suddenly she had horned in on my big moment.

I folded my arms. "What the hell is going on? What are you even planning to do when we get there?"

"Wait till we get there, and see," she said.

The guy playing the newsman was from one of the adult agencies, but he was still young, and handsome enough that my palms went sweaty when we shook hands.

Then he looked up, placed Bree, and went wide-eyed. "And you're the weeping bride," he said, grinning as he held out his hand. "This is a pleasure. I'm such a fan of the work you did on that segment."

"Good luck today," said Bree.

When she was gone, he looked me over again. "Well, if she's

your teacher," he said, "then I'm really looking forward to today."

I tried not to blush like an idiot.

We did a run-through with the director, standing in the shade of the trailer, as the cameramen worked on angles and lights for the rocky outcrop where we'd be sitting.

I knew this place; I'd spent four days in these woods filming for the bear. The hazy skyline of New St. Vincent was ahead of us, out of sight; and near the rocks there was enough wilderness to fool the camera into thinking we were in scrub country.

Below us, farther down the rocks where the ground leveled off near the flooded riverbank, was the swampland that seeped into your costume and reeked, and made your legs weigh a hundred pounds more than they told you it would, and looked like a charming springtime meadow when you viewed it through the lens.

"Good," the director said, after the first rehearsal. "Poppy, you're so natural with the gun, that's great, but maybe you could work on the sadness a little? We want the Uppers to really ache for the cause. And Prentis, I like your interest in her—let's play that up on this round, increase the focus."

"Sure thing," said Prentis, and winked at me.

Bree cut in. "I'd like to see you to work on those last few lines, Poppy. Full costume, please."

I slid off the stool, mortified, and sulked over to the edge of the set, where Bree was waiting.

"You have to go," she said, under her breath.

I could have hit her myself. I'd never been so furious. "Are you trying to get me fired? Do you know what's going to happen to me if they drop me from this piece? I don't need help from you if this—"

"They're going to kill you," she said.

I stopped talking, with my mouth still open. My stomach dropped to my boots.

I wanted to scream that she was lying—she had to be lying—but a lot of little things were beginning to make sense in a hurry, as if I had just looked at my stinging arm and seen the ants devouring it.

(Think about this, Mason had said.)

"How do you know?" I asked.

"The grips have been laying wire along the rocks while you were busy. Don't look," she snapped, like I would have.

"But you knew before this," I argued. "You never wanted me to take the segment. You came with me."

She came with me to save me at the last second. That was too strange to think about.

She looked absently across the scene they were building, slid the strap of the book bag through her fists.

She said, "I know what a setup looks like."

I thought how real it had looked on film when the groom fell back from the gunshot; how I had never seen him again. I thought how stunned Bree had looked in the pictures as she bent over the body, tears falling from her wide-open eyes.

Just quit, Bree had told me, and I hadn't understood why she was so upset.

Let those who would be fooled, be fooled.

When I nodded, Bree's shoulders sank with relief.

"What do I do?" I asked.

She slid the strap of her book bag into my hand.

"Hope you're faster than the grips," she said, "and that your memory's good."

I was already looking at the ground, that sloped away beneath us. Down was faster than up, and if I made it to the city, then . . . then . . .

I glanced back at her. "What will happen to you?"

She shrugged, half smiled. "I was supposed to die at the church door, too. I know how to handle myself."

16

Suddenly, I didn't doubt it.

"When you reach the city," she said, "get work on the trains, if you can. By the time you're over the mountains, there's decent work for Lowers, and you'll be too far for us to find you."

When I reached for the bag, I clasped her hand for a second, and she jerked back in surprise before she could get hold of herself. (Everybody has their tells.)

"Can I have a bathroom break?" I asked, loudly enough for the director to overhear.

Prentis raised his hand. "Seconded."

The director checked his watch. "Fine. Meet back here in five."

Bree gave me one searching look; then she was walking back up toward the director. Her face was in perfect light, and as she started talking, he was already grinning.

I swung down behind the first of the outcroppings and headed for the forest.

Five minutes from now, when they realized I was gone, Bree would be as surprised as anyone, and she'd throw a fit and slow them down, but she had nothing to worry about—I'd be under tree cover by then.

What took everybody else five minutes, I could do in three.

AFTER THE CURE

BY CARRIE RYAN

I WAS SHOT WITH THE CURE IN THE DARK. LATER, SOMEONE would tell me it was a Tuesday, but before the tranq dart I didn't know such a thing existed. It was either day or night, hungry or sated, alive or dead.

Then there was the cure and I was hauled to the Sanitation Center to be processed: our identities to be confirmed, and if forgotten, to be assigned a name, a registration number, date of birth, address.

There were so many abandoned kids after the pandemic stormed through that they changed the age of majority to sixteen, so in one fell swoop I became a legal adult female. They gave me my father's house on the mountain outside of town. They hadn't located him yet, and by law I'd have inherited it anyway. They told me it wouldn't matter if he somehow found his way home unrecovered—they'd figured out early on that infected didn't bite those who were cured. Once someone was Recovered, they were pulled back to human again even though they still had the infection in their blood.

At the Sanitation Center there were Reintroduction Classes on everything from basic algebra to civics and manners. I sat off to the side, pulling the old information from the part of my brain that'd never been touched by all of this. Others in the room watched the teacher, rapt, and I swear I saw one or two of them lick their lips or suck their teeth.

I wondered if there was a part of them still hungry or if it was just habit. Sometimes at night, in the darkness of the barracks, I'd hear my own teeth rattle and my stomach grumble.

It was like a secret shared by all of us. We knew that to report the stirring sensations would be to ask for more time locked away. None of us at the Sanitation Center had seen the sun since our first bites. Few of us were willing to give up the possibility of freedom by admitting the truth. I wanted to be back home. Even if my parents weren't there and my sisters were missing, I wanted the familiar surroundings.

I wanted the smell of my old life: Dove soap cooped up in closets with crisply folded sheets.

Like the other Recovered, I suffered through the tests and the bar code tattoo along the back of my ear. Some kept their hair short, at least cut away from the mark. It became a sort of status symbol, like a gang marker, and rumor had it that people who'd never been infected would get similar tattoos in underground parlors or color them on with permanent ink.

Not me. The first thing I did after being released was grow my hair long. I didn't want the reminder of what I'd been. It's enough that in the brightness of the afternoon, sun will reflect oddly through my eyes, creating a faint glow of red.

That's how they recognize us. That's how everyone else knows to shun us.

Monsters, they call us. Cannibals and vampires or zombies. Sometimes there are riots and fights, but I don't see the sense in that. After all, the labels are all true.

I was a monster. I did hunt and kill other people, leaving them to infect in turn when my hunger was satisfied.

To me, vampire seems like too easy of a word for what we were.

For what I sometimes still am.

What was left of the government urged for level heads and acceptance. They handed out grants to public interest groups bent on studying us and integrating us. They introduced laws protecting us and incentives for hiring us.

None of that mattered. One flash of light into my eyes and everyone would know at a glance what I'd once been. It became common for stores and restaurants to install searingly bright bulbs above entrances just to catch us on the way inside.

I tried going back to school for about a week, but it became pretty clear I wasn't too welcome. Classes were segregated, ostensibly to help catch up those of us who'd been "disoriented." When I explained to the principal that none of us—the infected or the pure—had attended a single class for the last five years, so we were pretty much all in the same boat, he just shrugged.

"Legally, I can't treat you any different from them." He was good with his sneers. "But I get extra money for hosting rehabilitation classes, and if that means I get to throw y'all in a different classroom, away from everyone else, all the better."

I walked right out of his office and off school grounds after that. It felt strange just being able to leave. But I was seventeen now, legally an adult, so what could they do?

Half of us—the Recovered—couldn't figure out who we'd once been and where we'd come from. The longer you'd been infected, the more it ate away at your brain until there was hardly anything left. Just gaping holes through old memories so that you might remember half a name, part of a face, a hint of who you were.

They assigned new identities according to the alphabet, the same way they'd once named the hurricanes. If you wanted something different, you had to petition for it and wait.

In the beginning they tried to shield us from the worst of it: what we'd been and what we'd done. But you can't hide something that big for forever, and it didn't take long for us to understand two things: first, the world we'd once known was decimated, and second, we were the cause.

It started as a diet drug and mutated into something else. Transferred with a bite, incubated quickly, it tore fire across the continents.

Not two weeks after I'd been designated as Rehabilitated and released from the Sanitation Center, I saw a video of what it'd been like. I was standing in the little grocery store at the bottom of the hill from my house and they had the television behind the counter turned to the national news. Suddenly, a pirate TV station hacked into newscasts to air footage from raids and attacks, saying it was wrong to just bury something like that in the name of national peace.

The video showed a group of men in battle gear approaching a warehouse. Everything was cast in a greenish tint indicative of night-vision goggles. The feed followed the hunters inside, and that's when I saw the creatures.

They were spread across the floors, lounging in heaps, stuffed into the darkest corners. Each one naked and gray-skinned, bald with patches of stubbornly remnant hair. One of them opened his eyes, the red glow like the sun against the green.

The cameraman didn't see it, but I knew what was coming. I watched the fingers unfurl, long and crooked, tipped with sharpened claws. When the creature ran toward the tiny group, it howled and screeched, showing sharp pointed teeth that glistened with saliva.

Watching that video, I ran my tongue over my own teeth, now ground to a dull flat. My cheeks still calloused against the missing sharpness.

What frightened me most about that video wasn't the horror and disgust I saw on every other shopper's face, but the thrill I felt coursing through me.

I'd done that. I knew it to be true based on my own reactions: the way my mouth watered and my stomach twisted.

I pushed out of the little grocery store while the feed looped around again, and I stumbled home with my arms crossed tight, chin tucked to chest so none of the glaring light of day could reflect in my eyes.

In that moment I wasn't sure where the monster ended and where I began. I know the government just wanted me to go back to the life I'd lived before, but the monster always stretched under my skin as a memory. My nails always a little thicker than before, my hair a little thinner. The taste of animal meat never enough as it used to be.

I wondered why they even bothered curing us. Sure they wanted their world back, but why not kill us instead? If they really thought we were monsters and irredeemable, why go through the trouble and expense?

All they had to do was crash down our buildings, expose us to the light, and be done with it. Killing us by half measures just seemed that much crueler.

He introduces himself as James, and pauses after saying his name as if I should know him. I'd been infected for long enough that there are a few gaps in my memory, and I struggle to place his face in one of them, playing a hesitant smile over my lips to buy time.

"I'm sorry, but I don't—" I start, but he waves his hand through the air to brush away my apology.

"We had a class together in school." He fills in the blank for me. "Back before . . ." He stares off to the side when he says that last word, as if it can somehow offend me—reminding me that the gap between "before" and "now" is filled with monsters and savagery.

I take the chance to glance at the back of his ear, wondering if he tilted his head away for just this reason. No evidence of the bar code tattoo. I force my hands to be still by my sides—they itch to tug my own hair across my cheeks.

"Yes of course." I prop up my smile, trying not to show my unease. A storm hovers on the horizon, signaling that dark will come earlier this evening. I discovered early on that I'm scared of the dark now, which is funny since I'd spent the last two years needing it to survive.

An awkward silence percolates between us until I offer, "How've you been?" and then want to cringe because the answer to that is never very good. Often, in order to stay alive and uninfected, most survivors had to do things more monstrous than the monsters. It's just no one ever talks about that.

"Good." When he smiles, I have to look away because it makes something bright crack open inside me—a lust that tastes as powerful as tearing a human body to strips. I bite my lips, feeling the tension of skin under the pressure of my now-dulled teeth.

He asks to walk me home, up the mountain, and I nod my

head, wondering how I can ever fill each footstep etched in silence. And yet somehow we do, finding conversations that meander through the easy territory, no talk of monsters or pandemics or the end of the world.

I'm sure there are those who figured out how to move on past what they'd been. Just as there were the ones who couldn't—who, even though they were cured, continued to hunt the taste of human flesh. I wondered if the real lucky ones were those who'd gone insane, let the disease lay waste to their brain until they could do nothing but parrot back whatever their rehabilitation coach spat at them.

The scientists think we don't remember. That's supposed to be part of the cure—amnesia of everything during infection.

Except it doesn't work that way. At first I thought I was the only one who, when darkness falls absolute, recalls what it was like to wake standing in the corner, fingers flexed, claws dirty with dried blood. So very hungry that the world buzzes with it.

But then one day I was waiting for my check-in appointment at the Sanitation Center, and I watched another Rehabilitated walk over to pour himself a cup of water from the fountain. It was late afternoon and a storm had blown through, and for the flicker of a moment, the lights in the center blinked out while dark clouds boiled outside.

When the generator kicked in, I found myself staring at the man, at the way his hand shook as he gripped the cone-shaped paper cup. At the hunger in his eyes.

And I knew. We both knew. What we'd been—it's always inside us. Just that some of us bury it deeper than others.

"Is it hard living alone?" James asks. It's the third time I've run into him at the convenience store at the bottom of the mountain and allowed him to walk me home. I grip my fingers around the seat of my bike, propelling it beside me.

"Sometimes." I think about how I used to be so lazy, my room always a mess. These days the house is immaculate. What else do I have to occupy my days? "I miss the noise of people," I admit.

From the corner of my eye I see the edge of his mouth kick up, and it encourages me on.

"I had four sisters. There was always drama. Fights, screams." I realize how bad that sounds, and I temper it back with a laugh. "But it was good in its way. We were crazy about each other."

"I know what you mean." His voice seems indulgent. "I had sisters too."

I turn toward him, to share this moment of similarity between us, and the realization of the meaning of his words is slow to filter through me. *Had* sisters. The bike wobbles under my grip, veering into his path, and he grabs the handlebars, knuckles flaring white.

"I'm sorry," I whisper. I can't look at him. In that moment I feel the monster keenly within. I taste it against the back of my throat.

I could have been the one to kill his sisters. They'd have been young and fresh, almost ripe like a perfect fruit. It doesn't matter whether I did or not; I'd killed someone else's sisters. I'd shredded them open, laid them bare.

And I wonder again why they've let people like me live. Before the pandemic, someone like me—a murderer who tortured her victims—would have been put to death without hesitation.

"I'm sorry," I say again.

His hands clutch at the handlebars, grip pulsing like a heartbeat.

"It wasn't you," he says. And I know what he means is that it was the monster inside me that drove me to such brutality. Ever since the cure, the scientists have embarked on a massive campaign to explain to the Pure how we are not to be blamed for our actions while monstrous.

DON'T BLAME THE VICTIM; BLAME THE DISEASE, is emblazoned across every crumbling billboard.

I don't know how to tell him how wrong he is.

At home, with the bike parked in the garage and nothing but the night surrounding me, I walk through the house and turn out every single light. Before the pandemic we'd had few neighbors—only a couple of properties scattered across the mountain, and beyond, nothing but protected wilderness.

Now the isolation is absolute. The other houses stand barren, their occupants dead or sick. No one's bothered to even vandalize or squat; we're too far from the city to be of much convenience.

Besides, the world is still filled with monsters that like the darkness. Only Rehabilitated would choose to live beyond the civilization compounds, with their artificial lights glaring all night. Sometimes when I walk through a dim room I can see the creatures through the window, racing past the trees searching out their prey.

They speak with a clicking sound that sometimes has the timbre of howling. In the daytime it's easy to spot where they passed, their claws raking divots in the tree trunks.

It's illegal to hunt them, though that doesn't stop most poachers. Back before the Recovery, those with the most kills had the highest designations in many communities.

Now the government hands out the tranq darts filled with the cure, urging hunters to use those instead, but sometimes they "forget" or claim an ambush and . . . Oh, well . . . another pod of monsters killed. What loss, really, is that to the world?

It could have easily been me on one of those piles of burning bodies. Maybe it should have.

At least then I'd have had company.

I've been thinking about James and his dead sisters for a week, but when I finally see him again outside the store, I'm not sure how to approach him, and so I just assume the familiar pose of chin tucked to my chest, stealing glances as I start walking my bike home.

He falls into step next to me.

"I had a boyfriend," I tell him, and the awkwardness of the statement strangles me until I'm compelled to explain. "Before. And he was killed. By one of the . . . them."

Panic lights a fire inside me that this is coming out all wrong. "It wasn't me who killed him when I was one of the . . . them," I'm quick to add, and that's what stops the dribble of words from my mouth.

I want him to understand that I know what it's like to lose someone you know to them. That I've been on both sides, and neither one is bearable. A painful silence settles between us, the click of my bike's wheels counting out the pattern of our steps.

"My mother killed my sisters," he finally says.

I form the word "Oh" with my mouth.

"She wasn't one of them," he clarifies. "It was after the pandemic started. My father kept a gun in the bedside table. She killed him first, then the girls. I heard the last shot. It's what woke me up. She'd ground sleeping pills into instant mashed potatoes." For a moment he pauses. "I hate mashed potatoes, and she didn't remember."

He brushes his hand along my hip, stopping me. The bike

by my side wobbles and then falls against my leg. He's not even tentative as he reaches out, sweeps the fan of my hair aside, and takes the edge of my ear in his fingers as if he can read the bar code through his fingertips.

"There are other kinds of monsters in the world," he tells me.

I want to crawl inside him and never leave.

As I stand in the darkness of my house, I press my hands flat against the plate glass window stretched across the sunroom. There's a pool carved into the patio below, and a body thrashes in the fetid water.

Her claws scrape uselessly at the night. I know it's a she because her body still retains some of the curves, her breasts just breaking the surface as she fights for air. Moments ago I watched a pack of them race past the house, a few of them stopping to sniff the air, as if they could smell me tucked away inside.

The others turned away, kept going once they must have realized my blood contains the same sickness as their own. Except one. She stepped closer and then again. She was staring at the window, and the pool swallowed her whole, ripples easing toward the walls before she broke back up to the surface.

I wonder at how she doesn't realize she could stand if she just moved a bit to the right and stretched her feet down.

I have no idea how long it will take her to drown. I have even less of an idea who she must have been before the pandemic, to have taken such an interest in me standing here.

All I know is that she's a monster. I could call in the hunters, have her shot with the cure and dragged away. I could load my own gun with the cure-tranqs they gave me the day I left the Sanitation Center.

But what kind of existence is that giving her? Who could ever claim my lonely days are anything approaching a life?

"How have you been adjusting since leaving the center?" the scientist asks. White paper crinkles underneath me as I shift on the examination table. The man places his hand on my thigh, casually, as he studies my chart. As if there's nowhere else for him to put it. As if neither one of us realizes his thumb stretches too close to nowhere good.

I try to shift again, and the pads of his fingers press against the edge of my putrid green examination gown that does little to cover the necessary bits. My nails dig into my palm. There was a time only months ago when they were as sharp as weapons.

"Fine." I keep my voice even.

He removes his hand to flip a page in the thick folder documenting my life. Who I was before the pandemic, what I was during, who they want me to be now. His touch then falls back to its familiar place. I'd cross my arms over my chest, but that would only drag the hem of the gown higher up my legs.

"You making friends? Finding a community?"

I think about James. How he's usually waiting for me outside the store after my sessions here. "Sure."

"Pure or Rehabilitated?" he asks.

I lift a shoulder. "I thought we weren't supposed to distinguish between the two."

"Listen, Vail." He sets the chart on the table and shifts so that he's facing me, his abdomen so close that the stray fibers on his white coat tickle my kneecaps. Every time his heart beats, his body barely brushes mine.

There was a time I could have heard that heartbeat from two

hundred yards away. He could have hidden from me, crouched in a closet or trembling in a cupboard, and his fear would have sent his heart soaring and it would sing me to his location.

The music of a terrified heart used to be the most beautiful in the world.

"We've really found community to be key to reintegration here," he says. I'm used to his hands that do nothing but wander idly, never too far, and I keep my thighs pressed tight together. He grips my legs so that his fingers slide into the sweaty crevice at the back of my bent knees. "We have sessions here. The notes show that you used to attend some of them but haven't in a few weeks. I really think . . ."

I tune him out and try to figure out how old he is. His hair's sprayed with white, but still predominantly brown. No glasses, clean shaven. A bit of flab around his middle, that I feel as he shifts against me again in his fervor to see me fully rehabilitated. He's not wearing a wedding ring, but that's not unusual anymore, with gold being so valuable and most other forms of currency useless.

He doesn't look like the type that could easily survive the pandemic. And that's what's always so confusing to me. It was the Pure who holed up in compounds scattered over the country, trying to hold on to memories of what life had been like before. It was in the remnants of one of the government bunkers that they figured out the cure and designed the recovery.

But it was the Infected who ruled the world. Every day the ranks of the Recovered grow, and yet in everyone's eyes, including our own, we're worthless.

As James walks me up the mountain, he tells me about his days at school. "Pretty much like before." He shrugs. "Smaller classes.

And the teachers are a little more lenient. I mean, once you live through the end of the world, getting sent to detention really isn't that significant."

I laugh, and he turns to me. We're at the top of my driveway, where he always leaves me, and he slips his fingers around mine. "I wish you were there." His voice is soft, earnest.

There's an intensity to his eyes, in the stillness, that makes everything inside me unfurl. "You could go again, you know. Those first few weeks, everyone was just trying to figure it all out. There's a rhythm to it now—you wouldn't stand out as much anymore."

I shouldn't stand out at all. That's the thing. According to the government, there's supposed to be no difference between me and James, except after that law there's a footnote as long as a football field about how the Infected are to be Recovered and what we must do to prove our ongoing Rehabilitation.

They're even allowed to kill us under certain circumstances. If they suspect the cure will fail, legally they can do whatever they want to us.

I tilt my head, wishing there were a way to explain to James just how very different we are. "You know, before the pandemic, if you had a male doctor, once you put on the gown, he wasn't allowed to be in a room alone with you. They always called in a nurse just in case."

He frowns. "In case of what?"

"I don't know." I shrug. "It was just one of those rules I always thought was sort of unnecessary. But either way, they don't do that anymore with us. The doctor just comes in when he wants. No nurse."

It's clear James is confused. "Maybe they're short-staffed at the center." And then he smiles as if about to make a joke. "Population isn't exactly what it used to be."

I try to mimic his grin, but all I can think about is the desperation in the scientist's eyes as he gripped his fingers against my pulse, counting out every heartbeat as if it could tell him a secret about the end of the world.

I think it surprised everyone that the cure actually worked. Sure, lab testing seemed positive, but it's different to load up tens of thousands of cure-tranq rounds and go off hunting monsters. Suddenly they had piles of people on their hands, and they rushed to set up the Sanitation Centers to take us all in.

It kept us in one location in case everything failed. Then they could just firebomb the place and be done with us.

They contained us for as long as they could in those centers, but space became an issue, and finally they opened the gate and let us trickle out into the world.

The world went nuts. Enraged communities prohibited Rehabilitated from settling there, vowed to shoot on sight anyone Infected or suspected of having been Infected.

Every time one of us committed a crime, it was because of what we once were. That we shouldn't be saved. They didn't want to see that we were just like them: some of us good, some of us bad.

A few political parties rose up, rumbling about colonizing an island with us, making sterilization part of the cure. Some suggested flat-out murdering us, but of course they never called it that, because we were less than animals. It would be *preemptive self-defense*.

And then one of the self-governing communities by the capital seat dragged a Rehabilitated down to the town square and charged him with murder. He demanded proof; he'd been a model citizen since being Recovered, he claimed. They pointed to the bar code on the back of his ear. He'd been a monster, and the only way a monster could survive was by killing.

The case made it into what was left of the court system, and he was found guilty. The defense took it to one of the remaining four circuits, and the ruling was overturned. It was headed to the Supreme Court, the defense claiming insanity, when the President stepped in and put an end to it.

We were pardoned for any crime committed before we became rehabilitated.

No one ever tried to bring charges against the survivors for what they did.

Her body floats in the pool. She's on her back, arms trailing out by her sides. She'd sunk at first, right after giving up the fight for air, but then sometime later, when I was asleep, she bobbed to the surface and has been drifting through the stagnant water ever since.

I am so so lonely that I consider attempting school in the morning.

In the middle of the night I feel something thundering through me, waking me up in the darkness as though I'd been hit. My breath is ragged, dreams of sharp teeth and succulent skin still clinging to the edges of my vision.

My ears ring, and as they clear I hear the clacking sort of howling that's as familiar to me as my own heartbeat. I push from bed and stumble into the living room, pressing against the cold glass window.

The horizon glows fire, and at first I think it's the sunrise, but then black clouds billow through the brightness. I watch it for a while, the sky undulating as goose bumps spread over my arms and up my neck.

I'm pretty sure I know exactly what just happened, but even so, I reach around the corner and flick on the television. There are only two channels, one fuzzier than the other, but the news confirms what I expected.

An explosion at the Sanitation Center. Clearly on purpose. A purification group has already claimed credit. The entire place ablaze, likely no survivors. The fire engineered to start tearing through the woods, where the monsters sometimes hole up at night.

I watch the inferno boiling in the distance, knowing how dry the season's been and how thirsty the trees are for flame. I'm sure the town will find a way to stop it before it reaches the city proper. But I doubt they'll do much to keep my little mountain unharmed.

Why save a mountain populated by nothing but monsters?

Even though I'd promised James I'd give it another try, I don't bother with school that next morning. There's already the taste of smoke in the air and the television chirps with news of the uncontrolled fire. I sit in the sunroom and watch the clouds billow in the distance, hazing out the sun. Below me, the dead girl bobs in the pool, her skin liquid white and loose, sloughing off to drift across the surface.

There's an uneasiness rippling through me, as if I can sense the distress of the monsters hidden in the woods beyond. Every now and again I'll hear the report of a gunshot. Today, there are no such things as hunting restrictions.

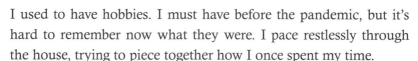

I used to have hobbies. I must have before the pandemic, but it's hard to remember now what they were. I pace restlessly through the house, trying to piece together how I once spent my time.

Most of it was dominated by school, class piled upon class. Bags stuffed with bloated books, lockers smelling like week-old bananas and new-binder plastic. I once took piano lessons, but now my nails are so thick that even when I chew them short they still clack against the keys.

Everything is a reminder of what I was.

My eyes drift closed. We were wretched beasts, but still we felt a sense of community. There were only so many buildings that refused the sunlight and were safe to hide inside. Somehow we'd find our way to them, and we'd find each other in the dark.

When we hunted, we were sleek and beautiful in our unity, calling to each other as we ran, no such thing as an obstacle in the night.

In our own sick way, we all meant something to one another. Each one lost, indistinguishable, to the pack.

Smoke chokes back the light, sending the day skittering into evening faster than usual. The sun's a diffuse ball through the haze, burning the sky a sick orange, when I hear a knock on the door.

I stand in the middle of the living room, listening to the slicing silence that follows. There's a knock again, urgent and pounding, and then I hear his voice.

James calling out, "Vail? You in there?"

A fleeting sensation of joy passes through me at the sound of him. When I throw open the door, he's standing with his hands shoved in his pockets, shoulders curved in a bit.

We stare at each other, me awkwardly trying to smile, until he breaks first. "I was worried," he explains. "After the explosion, and there are reports of hunters and you're up here alone, and I didn't know if they'd come after you, so . . ." He trails off, and his eyes slide to the side. The color of his irises is muffled in the darkness, and it takes me a moment before I taste his unease.

Then it hits me, so full in my chest that I take a step back. His features are blurred because of the darkness on this side of the house, the front facing away from the fires along the horizon. Overgrown shrubbery clings to the decayed porch, plunging the front walk into a gray blackness.

The night's coming faster because of the smoke choking the sky.

Beyond, in the fading trees, I hear the clicking of the monsters gathering.

"Shit," I murmur, balling James's shirt in my hands and tugging him inside. That's when the wailing begins, thick down along my back, as if it could still call me to action. The sound of the monsters calling to the others about their located prey.

I stand mute in the hallway, my steps stuttering as I try to plan the next move. Beside me, James trembles, the edge of my knuckles scraping against his chest as I hold him tight.

At first I start toward the back of the house, thinking about the closets without windows, but then I double around, heading for the stairs into the basement.

It's a risk, I know. If they make it down the stairs, we're trapped. They'll gather around us, bodies so thick there's no such thing as escape.

I start tearing down the blinds over the windows, tossing them to the floor. We just have to make it through the night. In the morning, with the light, they'll be gone. I could coat him with my blood, I think. Hope it masks the scent of his freshness with one of disease.

That's when I realize he's been calling my name. "Vail," he shouts, hands on my shoulders. He forces me to face him.

In that split second, while the monsters wail and chatter and the darkness seeps in, I stare at James's lips. I wonder, for just the barest moment, what they'd taste like. How they'd feel pressed between my own and if I could ever resist sinking my teeth into their tender flesh.

"Maybe we can still make it to the light of the compound," he whispers.

I finally understand that he doesn't hear them. Not yet. His ears aren't tuned to the monsters like mine are. He doesn't know how close they've come. How desperately they want him, and how their need sears through me. "No," I muster. "It's too late for that."

The gun cabinet sits in my father's closet, and I spin the dial, kneeling as I begin to count out the bullets. James reaches for a case on the top shelf, the label wrapped around a bright blue box with orange stripes.

"Cure-tranqs," he says, running his hand over the label. When he looks at me, his eyes are wide.

I lift a shoulder as he pries open the lid. "They gave them to me at the center," I explain. "Sometimes the pack will go looking for the one they lost, and just in case my pack came after me, the scientists wanted me to . . . you know."

"The box is full?" He asks it like a question, as if I need to explain why I've never used them. "So your pack never came back?"

I focus on my hands, sorting destruction into neat piles. What I don't tell him is that I can already hear the pack pushing against the air outside the house. They know there's someone pure inside.

I can already feel the way their mouths water for him.

At night, when they race past the house, is the loneliest I've ever felt. Except for now.

"You shouldn't have come up here." I stand, angry, shoving a box of bullets in my pockets. My shoulder brushes against him as I walk past, and he doesn't even hesitate before following.

It all comes back in my dreams, almost more vivid than my day-to-day life. The first one was probably six years old and plump with her baby fat. She smelled like melted ice cream and tasted like salt and misery.

When we came upon her in the park, she seemed unsurprised, almost as if she'd been expecting it.

"Are you my sister?" she asked calmly when the first of us fell upon her. She asked it again as she whimpered with her last breath, still clinging to the hope that one of us would know her, remember her.

Sister, I thought to myself. *We are all sisters and brothers in the pack*, I wanted to tell her, but I knew that she'd become aware of it soon enough. Once the infection took hold and brought her to us.

And maybe one day she'd be out on a hunt of her own, and a scent would catch the air, and she'd hesitate. *Are you my sister?* she'd be wondering, the clicks of her tongue unable to form the words.

Even as the pool water poured down her throat, that's what she'd be asking. *Are you my sister?*

And I'd stand there mute, wanting to answer "Yes," but knowing it was a lie.

We've gathered every object capable of emitting light and shoved it into the tiny utility room in the basement, but even so it barely creates enough of a glow to sting my eyes.

Which means all we've accomplished is knowing that when the monsters break down the door I'll be able to see clearly as they shred James's flesh, sinking their teeth into his limbs.

I pace back to the door, candle wax dripping from my fingers as I set trembling flames to wicks.

"Have you ever thought about what it would be like to be one of us?" I ask him as I stand with my hand pressed to the wall. I hear the vibrations of them pounding upstairs. Three months before the pandemic, my father replaced all the windows with double-paned glass, which only causes a moment's hesitation in the monsters' assault.

James moves behind me, coming so close I feel the tremor of each exhalation on the back of my ears. "One of you?" he asks, brushing my ponytail aside and pressing his lips to the ridges of my spine.

I close my eyes. "A monster. Creature of the night."

"Have you ever thought," he asks, teeth scraping lightly against skin, "that you're the lucky one? You can live out on the edge, past the compound, in the darkness. You're free."

"Hunted," I tell him. "Alone. Shunned. Hated."

"I can't sleep in the darkness." His hand has been resting on my hip, and now his fingers curl around the bone, pulling me against him until there's nothing separating us. Above, I hear the crash of the monsters, my blood spiking.

Tears begin to edge my eyes. James holding me makes me remember what it was like to mean something to someone else. "I belonged to something before." My voice quavers as I tell him the lie that I wish were truth. "They've been searching for me. Asking me back. No one else has done that. No one from before ever cared."

His hand slips up along my ribs, skimming the edge of my bra until he cups my throat, nails trailing lightly over my jaw. "I came looking for you, Vail."

There's this moment as they pour down the stairs when I think about calling out to them that I am here. That they have come for me at last and that I've been waiting.

Except they've known where I am for weeks. Months. And they have never cared.

I stare at the gun in my hand and the two boxes on the table shoved against the door. Bullets or cure-tranqs. That's the question. Death or salvation.

Except that I can't figure out which is which. It seems worse to damn them to this life, of loneliness and exile. It's taking a part of who they are from them, even if that part is the monster.

But to kill them, the finality of it, seems to make my fingers tremble. All the times I've taken lives without a thought other than hunger and now such cold ambivalence fails me.

I've always wondered if the one who cured me felt righteous. If he left his compound on a Tuesday morning with his pack full of cure-tranqs and thought, Today I will save the world, and instead he found me.

If he could see me now, hesitating, would he think it was worth it? All the monsters' dens he waded into, all the risks he took, just to preserve us.

Thinking he was saving the world when really he was just giving us greater access to destruction. Letting us loose to be despised and cast aside in a manner that absolves humanity of its guilt.

As monsters we were pitiable—it was beyond our control. As

Rehabilitated we are just like everyone else except in every way that matters, which means we could be discarded without a second thought. Alive but only allowed to live among the fringes.

I stare at how James trembles, his chin dimpled with terror, and I wonder if that's what's left of us. We uphold the weak and push down the survivors. He was right: the living sequester themselves in compounds while the rest of us roam the world.

One day, we could own the world if we devised it to be so.

There's a moment when I think about opening the door and letting them have him. Making him one of us. Giving him the ultimate freedom.

The most perfect kind of love.

And then the first creature strips the wood from the frame and they are upon us, and all I can do is shoot, over and over again, as the bodes pile around me. For a moment there is screaming, a painful kind of rage that goes beyond the normal wails in the night. The air fills with the smell of terror and regret, and eventually silence wraps around us both.

They had names once, before, the creatures spread around me. Then they were pack, which meant names became useless. And now we are nothing, lesser than. How many of the bodies lying still at my feet would have chosen this? If they'd had the choice, what would they have wanted?

Will any of them stand in the darkness of a Sanitation Center and listen to the howls of those still out there and feel the tug of their blood, calling them to a home that can never be theirs again?

There were reports shortly after the cure was first administered, of Rehabilitated trying to reinfect themselves. They wanted to go back, they explained; though it didn't take long for them to realize there's no such thing. Once you're cured, you're cured forever.

The scientists locked them in cells deep in their research labs to study their brain patterns, to subject them to endless rounds of therapy, trying to understand why anyone would choose to become a monster.

None of those scientists ever understood what it was to exist in the between of something, and none of us could ever explain it, so we gave up trying. We learned to keep our dreams to ourselves, to swallow back the way our mouths watered when we heard the wail of monsters in the darkness.

We learned to survive alone, with a wanting deeper than hunger.

"I'm sorry." James kneels behind me, vomit pooling around his knees. "I didn't know how fast the darkness would fall under the smoke tonight."

Absently, I shake my head. One glance of sunlight kills the monsters. We knew the turning of the earth in a way more intimate than our own blood. It's what kept us alive, and it's unfathomable that the Pure can't do the same. As if they can't understand true fear and mortality.

"Will they be okay?" he asks, eyes trained on the body of a girl wedged in the door frame, her breath coming in short pants and eyes wavering behind lids.

I have no idea how to answer that question. There are a million definitions of *okay*, and none of them seem to fit this moment. "They'll send someone from the Sanitation Center." And then I remember the fire, and add, "If there's anyone left. They'll all become Rehabilitated. Like me."

James pushes to his feet and skirts the puddle of spreading vomit. Already the cure's finding its way into their systems, fighting against the monster and turning them back to the closest thing to normal we can decipher.

"Did you know them?" he asks.

I shake my head. As human beings, we were as diverse as the days, but as pack, we were one. The moment I was shot with the cure, they became strangers.

He must sense the despair threading through me, because he slips his fingers around my own and holds them tight. "Why did you save me? You could have let them in. Let them take me and then released them back out to the darkness."

For a long time I think about his question: whether I'd have loaded the last cure-tranq into the gun and leveled it at his back as he ran. What it would have been like to lose him to the pack. At night he'd have streamed past my house with the others, and just like them, he'd maybe pause to sniff the air at something passing familiar before pounding on until dawn.

As a human, he knows me in a way he'd never remember as a monster.

"Because you came for me when none of them did."

VALEDICTORIAN

BY **N. K. JEMISIN**

THERE ARE THREE THINGS ZINHLE DECIDES, WHEN SHE IS OLD enough to understand. The first is that she will never, ever give less than her best to anything she tries to do. The second is that she will not live in fear. The third, which is perhaps meaning-less, given the first two, and yet comes to define her existence most powerfully, is this: she will be herself. No matter what.

For however brief a time.

"Have you considered getting pregnant?" her mother blurts one morning, over breakfast.

Zinhle's father drops his fork, but he recovers and picks it up again quickly. This is how Zinhle knows that what her mother has said is not a spontaneous burst of insanity. They have discussed the matter, her parents. They are in agreement. Her father was just caught off guard by the timing.

But Zinhle, too, has considered the matter in depth. Do they really think she wouldn't have? "No," she says.

Zinhle's mother is stubborn. This is where Zinhle herself

gets the trait. "The Sandersens' boy—you used to play with him when you were little, remember?—he's decent. Discreet. He got three girls pregnant last year, and doesn't charge much. The babies aren't bad-looking. And we'd help you with the raising, of course." She hesitates, then adds, with obvious discomfort, "A friend of mine at work—Charlotte, you've met her—she says he's, ah, he's not rough or anything, doesn't try to hurt girls—"

"No," Zinhle says again, more firmly. She does not raise her voice. Her parents taught her to be respectful of her elders. She believes respect includes being very, very clear about some things.

Zinhle's mother looks at her father, seeking an ally. Her father is a gentle, soft-spoken man in a family of strong-willed women. Stupid people think he is weak; he isn't. He just knows when a battle isn't worth fighting. So he looks at Zinhle now, and after a moment he shakes his head. "Let it go," he says to her mother, and her mother subsides.

They resume breakfast in silence.

Zinhle earns top marks in all her classes. The teachers exclaim over this, her parents fawn, the school officials nod their heads sagely and try not to too-obviously bask in her reflected glory. There are articles about her in the papers and on Securenet. She wins awards.

She hates this. It's easy to perform well; all she has to do is try. What she wants is to be *the best*, and this is difficult when she has no real competition. Beating the others doesn't mean anything, because they're not really trying. This leaves Zinhle with no choice but to compete against herself. Each paper she writes must be more brilliant than the last. She tries to finish every test faster than she did before. It isn't the victory she craves, not exactly; the satisfaction she gains from success is minimal. Barely worth it. But it's all she has.

The only times she ever gets in trouble are when she argues with her teachers, because they're so often wrong. Infuriatingly, frustratingly *wrong*. In the smallest part of her heart, she concedes that there is a reason for this: a youth spent striving for mediocrity does not a brilliant adult make. Old habits are hard to break, old fears are hard to shed, all that. Still—arguing with them, looking up information and showing it to them to prove their wrongness, becomes her favorite pastime. She is polite, always, because they expect her to be uncivilized, and because they are also her elders. But it's hard. They're old enough that they don't have to worry, damn it; why can't they at least *try* to be worthy of her effort? She would kill for one good teacher. She is dying for one good teacher.

In the end, the power struggle, too, is barely worth it. But it is all she has.

"Why do you do it?" asks Mitra, the closest thing she has to a best friend.

Zinhle is sitting on a park bench as Mitra asks this. She is bleeding: a cut on her forehead, a scrape on one elbow, her lip where she split it on her own teeth. There is a bruise on her ribs shaped like a shoe print. Mitra dabs at the cut on her forehead with an antiseptic pad. Zinhle only allows this because she can't see that one herself. If she misses any of the blood, and her parents see it, they'll be upset. Hopefully the bruises won't swell.

"I'm not doing anything," she snaps in reply. "*They* did this, remember?" Samantha and the others, six of them. The last time, there were only three. She'd managed to fight back then, but not today.

Crazy ugly bitch, Zinhle remembers Sam ranting. She does not remember the words with complete clarity; her head had been ringing from a blow at the time. *My dad says we should've shoved your family through the Wall with the rest of the cockroaches. I'm gonna laugh when they take you away.*

Six is better than three, at least.

"They wouldn't if you weren't . . ." Mitra trails off, looking anxious. Zinhle has a reputation at school. Everyone thinks she's angry all the time, whether she is or not (the fact that she often *is*, notwithstanding). Mitra knows better, or she should. They've known each other for years. But this is why Zinhle qualifies it whenever she explains their friendship to others. Mitra is *like* her best friend. A real best friend, she feels certain, would not fear her.

"What?" Zinhle asks. She's not angry now either, partly because she has come to expect no better from Mitra, and partly because she hurts too much. "If I wasn't what, Mit?"

Mitra lowers the pad and looks at her for a long, silent moment. "If you weren't stupid as hell." She seems to be growing angry herself. Zinhle cannot find the strength to appreciate the irony. "I know you don't care whether you make valedictorian. But do you have to make the rest of us look so *bad*?"

One of Zinhle's teeth is loose. If she can resist the urge to tongue it, it will probably heal and not die in the socket. Probably. She challenges herself to keep the tooth without having to visit a dentist.

"Yeah," she says wearily. "I guess I do."

When Zinhle earns the highest possible score on the post-graduation placement exam, Ms. Threnody pulls her aside after class. Zinhle expects the usual praise. The teachers know their duty, even if they do a half-assed job of it. But Threnody pulls the shade on the door, and Zinhle realizes something else is in the offing.

"There's a representative coming to school tomorrow," Threnody says. "From beyond the Firewall. I thought you should know."

For just a moment, Zinhle's breath catches. Then she remembers Rule 2—she will not live in fear—and pushes this aside. "What does the representative want?" she asks, thinking she knows. There can be only one reason for this visit.

"You know what they want." Threnody looks hard at her. "They *say* they just want to meet you."

"How do they know about me?" Like most students, she has always assumed that those beyond the Firewall are notified about each new class only at the point of graduation. The valedictorian is named then, after all.

"They've had full access to the school's networks since the war." Threnody grimaces with a bitterness that Zinhle has never seen in a teacher's face before. Teachers are always supposed to be positive about the war and its outcome. "Everyone brags about the treaty, the treaty. The treaty made sure we kept *critical* networks private, but gave up the noncritical ones. Like a bunch of computers would give a damn about our money or government memos! Shortsighted fucking bastards."

Teachers are not supposed to curse, either.

Zinhle decides to test these new open waters between herself and Ms. Threnody. "Why are you telling me this?"

Threnody looks at her for so long a moment that Zinhle grows uneasy. "I know why you try so hard," she says at last. "I've heard what people say about you, about, about . . . people like you. It's so stupid. There's nothing of us left, *nothing*. We're lying to ourselves every day just to keep it together, and some people want to keep playing the same games that destroyed us in the first place. . . ." She falls silent, and Zinhle is amazed to see that Threnody is shaking. The woman's fists are even clenched. She is furious, and it is glorious. For a moment, Zinhle wants to smile and feel warm at the knowledge that she is not alone.

Then she remembers. The teachers never seem to notice her bruises. They encourage her because her success protects their favorites, and she is no one's favorite. If Ms. Threnody has felt this way all along, why is she only now saying it to Zinhle? Why has she not done anything, taken some public stand to try and change the situation?

It is so easy to have principles. Far, far harder to live by them.

So Zinhle nods, and does not allow herself to be seduced. "Thanks for telling me."

Threnody frowns a little at her nonreaction. "What will you do?" she asks.

Zinhle shrugs. As if she would tell, even if she knew.

"I'll talk to this representative, I guess," she says, because it's not as if she can refuse anyway. They are all slaves these days. The only difference is that Zinhle refuses to pretend otherwise.

The people beyond the Firewall are not people. Zinhle isn't really sure what they are. The government knows, because it was founded by those who fought and ultimately lost the war, and their descendants still run it. Some of the adults close to her must know—but none of them will tell the children. "High school is scary enough," said Zinhle's father, a few years before, when Zinhle asked. He smiled as if this should have been funny, but it wasn't.

The Firewall has been around for centuries—since the start of the war, when it was built to keep the enemy at bay. But as the enemy encroached and the defenders' numbers dwindled, they fell back, unwilling to linger too close to the front lines of a war whose weapons were so very strange. And invisible. And insidious. To conserve resources, the Firewall was also pulled back so as to protect only essential territory. The few safe territories merged, some of the survivors traveling long distances in order to join larger enclaves, the larger enclaves eventually merging too. The tales of those times are harrowing, heroic. The morals are always clear: safety in numbers, people have to stick together, stupid to fight a war on multiple fronts, et cetera. At the time, Zinhle supposes, they didn't *feel* like they were being herded together.

Nowadays, the Firewall is merely symbolic. The enemy has grown steadily stronger over the years, while tech within the Firewall has hardly developed at all—but this is something they're not supposed to discuss. (Zinhle wrote a paper about it once and got her only *F* ever, which forced her to do another paper for extra credit. Her teacher's anger was worth the work.) These days the enemy can penetrate the Firewall at will. But they usually don't need to, because what they want comes out to them.

Each year, a tribute of children is sent beyond the Wall, never to be seen or heard from again. The enemy is very specific about their requirements. They take ten percent, plus one. The ten percent are all the weakest performers in any graduating high school class. This part is easy to understand, and even the enemy refers to it in animal husbandry terms: these children are *the cull*. The enemy does not wish to commit genocide, after all. The area within the Firewall is small, the gene pool limited. They do not take very young children. They do not take healthy adults, or gravid females, or elders who impart useful socialization. Just adolescents who have had a chance to prove their mettle. The population of an endangered species must be carefully managed to keep it healthy.

The "plus one," though—no one understands this. Why does the enemy want their best and brightest? Is it another means of assuring control? They have total control already.

It doesn't matter why they want Zinhle. All that matters is that they do.

Zinhle goes to meet Mitra after school so they can walk home. (Samantha and her friends are busy decorating the gym for the school prom. There will be no trouble today.) When Mitra is not waiting at their usual site near the school sign, Zinhle calls her. This leads her to the school's smallest restroom, which has only one stall. Most girls think there will be a wait to use it, so they use the bigger restroom down the hall. This is convenient, as Mitra is with Lauren, who is sitting on the toilet and crying in harsh, gasping sobs.

"The calculus final," Mitra mouths, before trying again— fruitlessly—to blot Lauren's tears with a wad of toilet paper. Zinhle understands then. The final counts for fifty percent of the grade.

"I, I didn't," Lauren manages between sobs. She is hyperventilating. Mitra has given her a bag to breathe into, which she uses infrequently. Her face, sallow-pale at the best of times, is alarmingly blotchy and red now. It takes her several tries to finish the sentence. "Think I would. The test. I *studied*." *Gasp.* "But when I was. Sitting there. The first problem. I *knew* how to answer it! I did ten others. Just like it." *Gasp.* "Practice problems. But I couldn't think. Couldn't. I."

Zinhle closes the door, shoving the garbage can in front of it, as Mitra had done before Zinhle's knock. "You choked," she says. "It happens."

The look that Lauren throws at her is equal parts fury and contempt. "What the hell." *Gasp.* "Would *you* know about it?"

"I failed the geometry final in eighth grade," Zinhle says. Mitra throws Zinhle a surprised look. Zinhle scowls back, and Mitra looks away. "I knew all the stuff that was on it, but I just . . . drew a blank." She shrugs. "Like I said, it happens."

Lauren looks surprised too, but only because she did not know. "You failed that? But that test was easy." Her breathing has begun to slow. She sets her jaw, distracted from her own fear. "That one didn't matter, though." She's right. The cull only happens at the end of high school.

Zinhle shakes her head. "All tests matter. But I told them I'd been sick that day, so the test wasn't a good measure of my abilities. They let me take it again, and I passed that time." She had scored perfectly, but Lauren does not need to know this.

"You took it again?" As Zinhle had intended, Lauren considers this. School officials are less lenient in high school. The process has to be fair. Everybody gets one chance to prove themselves. But Lauren isn't stupid. She will get her parents involved, and they will no doubt bribe a doctor to assert that Lauren was on powerful medication at the time, or recovering from a recent family member's death, or something like that. The process has to be fair.

Later, after the blotty toilet paper has been flushed and Lauren has gone home, Mitra walks quietly beside Zinhle for most of the way. Zinhle expects something, so she is not surprised when Mitra says, "I didn't think you'd ever talk about that. The geo test."

Zinhle shrugs. It cost her nothing to do so.

"I'd almost forgotten about that whole thing," Mitra continues. She speaks slowly, as she does when she is thinking. "Wow. You used to tell me everything then, remember? We were like this—" She holds up two fingers. "Everybody used to talk about us. The African princess and her Arab sidekick. They fight crime!" She grins, then sobers abruptly, looking at Zinhle. "You were always a good student, but after that—"

53

"I'll see you tomorrow," says Zinhle, and she speeds up, leaving Mitra behind. But she remembers that incident, too. She remembers the principal, Mrs. Sachs, to whom she went to plead her case. *Well, listen to you,* the woman had said, in a tone of honest amazement. *So articulate and intelligent. I suppose I can let you have another try, as long as it doesn't hurt anyone else.*

Zinhle reaches for the doorknob that leads into her house, but her hand bounces off at first. It's still clenched into a fist.

She gets so tired sometimes. It's exhausting, fighting others' expectations, and doing it all alone.

In the morning, Zinhle's homeroom teacher, Ms. Carlisle, hands her a yellow pass, which means she's supposed to go to the office. Ms. Carlisle is not Ms. Threnody; she shows no concern for Zinhle, real or false. In fact, she smirks when Zinhle takes the note. Zinhle smirks back. Her mother has told Zinhle the story of her own senior year. *Carlisle was almost in the cull,* her mother had said. *Only reason they didn't take her was because not as many girls got pregnant that year as they were expecting. They stopped right at her. She's as dumb as the rest of the meat, just lucky.*

I will not be meat, Zinhle thinks, as she walks past rows of her staring, silent classmates. *They'll send their best for me.*

This is not pride, not really. But it is all she has.

In the principal's office, the staff is nervous. The principal is sitting in the administrative assistants' area, pretending to be busy with a spare laptop. The administrative assistants, who have been feverishly stage-whispering among themselves as Zinhle walks in, fall silent. Then one of them, Mr. Battle, swallows audibly and asks to see her pass.

"Zinhle Nkosi," he says, mutilating her family name, acting as if he does not already know who she is. "Please go into that office; you have a visitor." He points toward the principal's private office, which has clearly been usurped. Zinhle nods and goes into the small room. Just to spite them, she closes the door behind her.

The man who sits at the principal's desk is not much older than her. Slim, average in height, dressed business-casual. Boring. There is an off-pink tonal note to his skin, and something about the thickness of his black hair, that reminds her of Mitra. Or maybe he is Latino, or Asian, or Indian, or Italian—she cannot tell specifically, having met so few with the look. And not that it matters, because his inhumanity is immediately obvious in his stillness. When she walks in, he's just sitting there gazing straight ahead, not pretending to do anything. His palms rest flat on the principal's desk. He does not smile or brighten in the way that a human being would, on meeting a new person. His eyes shift toward her, track her as she comes to stand in front of the desk, but he does not move otherwise.

There is something predatory in such stillness, she thinks. Then she says, "Hello."

"Hello," he says back, immediately, automatically.

Silence falls, taut. Rule 2 is in serious jeopardy. "You have a name?" Zinhle blurts. Small talk.

He considers for a moment. The pause should make her distrust him more; it is what liars do. But she realizes the matter is more complex than this: he actually has to think about it.

"Lemuel," he says.

"Okay," she says. "I'm Zinhle."

"I know. It's very nice to meet you, Ms. Nkosi." He pronounces her name perfectly.

"So why are you here? Or why am I?"

"We've come to ask you to continue."

Another silence. In this one, Zinhle is too confused for fear. "Continue *what*?" She also wonders at his use of "we," but first things first.

"As you have been." He seems to consider again, then suddenly begins moving in a human way, tilting his head to one side, blinking twice rapidly, inhaling a bit more as his breathing changes, lifting a hand to gesture toward her. None of this movement seems unnatural. Only the fact that it's deliberate, that he had to think about it, makes it strange.

"We've found that many like you tend to falter at the last moment," he continues. "So we're experimenting with direct intervention."

Zinhle narrows her eyes. "Many *like me*?" Not them, too.

"Valedictorians."

Zinhle relaxes, though only one set of muscles. The rest remain tense. "But I'm not one yet, am I? Graduation's still three months off."

"Yes. But you're the most likely candidate for this school. And you were interesting to us for other reasons." Abruptly, Lemuel stands. Zinhle forces herself not to step back as he comes around the desk and stops in front of her. "What do I look like to you?"

She shakes her head. She didn't get her grade point average by falling for trick questions.

"You've thought about it," he presses. "What do you *think* I am?"

She thinks, *the enemy*.

"A . . . machine," she says instead. "Some kind of, I don't know. Robot, or—"

"It isn't surprising that you don't fully understand," he says. "In the days before the war, part of me would have been called 'artificial intelligence.'"

Zinhle blurts the first thing that comes to her mind. "You don't look artificial."

To her utter shock, he smiles. He doesn't think about this first. Whatever was wrong with him before, it's gone now. "Like I said, that's only part of me. The rest of me was born in New York, a city not far from here. It's on the ocean. I go swimming at the Coney Island beach in the mornings, sometimes." He pauses. "Have you ever seen the ocean?"

He knows she has not. All Firewall-protected territory is well inland. America's breadbasket. She says nothing.

"I went to school," he says. "Not in a building, but I did have to learn. I have parents. I have a girlfriend. And a cat." He smiles more. "We're not that different, your kind and mine."

"No."

"You sound very certain of that."

"We're *human*."

Lemuel's smile fades a little. She thinks he might be disappointed in her.

"The Firewall," he says. "Outside of it, there are still billions of people in the world. They're just not your kind of people."

For a moment, Zinhle cannot comprehend this. It is beyond her in any practical, individual, here-and-now way. She does not fear the man in front of her—perhaps she should; he's bigger, she's alone in a room with him, and no one will help her if she screams. But the real panic hits as she imagines the world filled with nameless, faceless, dark hordes, closing in, threatening by their mere existence. There is a pie chart somewhere which is mostly "them" and only a sliver of "us," and the "us" is about to be popped like a zit.

Rule 2. She takes a deep breath, masters the panic. Realizes, as the moments pass and Lemuel stands there quietly, that he expected her fear. He's seen it before, after all. That sort of reaction is what started the war.

"Give me something to call you," she says. The panic is still close. Labels will help her master it. "You people."

He shakes his head. "People. Call us that, if you call us anything."

"People"—she gestures in her frustration—"people *categorize*. People differentiate. If you want me to think of you as people, act like it!"

"All right, then: people who adapted when the world changed."

"Meaning, we're the people who didn't?" Zinhle forces herself to laugh. "Okay, that's crap. How were we supposed to adapt to . . . to a bunch of . . ." She waves her hands. The words sound too ridiculous to say aloud—though his presence, her life, her whole society, is proof that it's not ridiculous. Not ridiculous at all.

"Your ancestors—the people who started the war—could've adapted." He gestures around at the room, the school, the world that is all she has known, but which is such a tiny part of the greater world. "This happened because they decided it was better to kill, or die, or be imprisoned forever, than change."

The adults' great secret. It hovers before her at last, ripe for the plucking. Zinhle finds it surprisingly difficult to reach out and lay claim to the truth, but she makes herself speak anyhow. Rule 1 means she must always ask the tough questions.

"Tell me what happened, then," she murmurs. Her nails bite into her palms. Sweat stings the cuts. "If you won't tell me what you are."

He shakes his head and sits on the edge of the desk with his hands folded, looking not artificial at all, but annoyed. Tired. "I've been telling you what I am. You just don't want to hear it."

It is this—not the words, but his weariness, his frustration—that finally makes her pause. Because it's familiar, isn't it? She thinks of herself sighing when Mitra asked, *Why do you do it?* Because she knew—knows—what that question really asks.

Why are you different?

Why don't you try harder to be like us?

She thinks now what she did not say to Mitra that day: *Because none of you will let me just be myself.*

She looks at Lemuel again. He sees, somehow, that her understanding of him has changed in some fundamental way. So at last, he explains.

"I leave my body like you leave your house," he says. "I can transmit myself around the world, if I want, and be back in seconds. This is not the first body I've had, and it won't be the last."

It's too alien. Zinhle shudders and turns away from him. The people who are culled. *Not the first body I've had.* She walks to the office's small window, pushes open the heavy curtain, and stares at the soccer field beyond, seeing nothing.

"We started as accidents," he continues, behind her. "Leftovers. Microbes in a digital sea. We fed on interrupted processes, interrupted conversations, grew, evolved. The first humans we merged with were children using a public library network too ancient and unprotected to keep us out. Nobody cared if poor children got locked away in institutions, or left out on the streets to shiver and starve, when they started acting strange. No one cared what it meant when they became something new—or at least, not at first. We became them. They became us. Then we, together, began to grow."

Cockroaches, Samantha had called them. A pest, neglected until they became an infestation. The first Firewalls had been built around the inner cities in an attempt to pen the contagion in. There had been guns, too, and walls of a nonvirtual sort, for a while. The victims, though they were not really victims, had been left to die, though they had not really obliged. And later, when the Firewalls became the rear guard in a retreat, people who'd looked too much like those early "victims" got pushed out to die, too. The survivors needed someone to blame.

Zinhle changes the subject. "People who get sent through the Wall." *Me.* "What happens to them?" *What will happen to me?*

"They join us."

Bopping around the world to visit girlfriends. Swimming in an ocean. It does not sound like a terrible existence. But . . . "What if they don't want to?" She uses the word "they" to feel better.

He does not smile. "They're put in a safe place—behind another firewall, if you'd rather think of it that way. That way they can do no harm to themselves—or to us."

There are things, probably many things, that he's not saying. She can guess some of them, because he's told her everything that matters. If they can leave their bodies like houses, well, houses are always in demand. Easy enough to lock up the current owner somewhere, move someone else in. Houses. Meat.

She snaps, "That's not treating us like people."

"You stopped acting like people." He shrugs.

This makes her angry. She turns back to him. "Who the hell are you to judge?"

"*We* don't. You do."

"*What?*"

"It's easy to give up what you don't want."

The words feel like gibberish to her. Zinhle is trembling with emotion and he's just *sitting* there, relaxed, like the inhuman thing he is. Not making sense. "My parents want me! All the kids who end up culled, their families want them—" But he shakes his head.

"You're the best of your kind, by your own standards," he says. But then something changes in his manner. "Good grades reflect your ability to adapt to a complex system. *We are a system.*"

The sudden vehemence in Lemuel's voice catches Zinhle by surprise. His calm is just a veneer, she realizes belatedly, covering as much anger as she feels herself. Because of this, his anger derails hers, leaving her confused. Why is he so angry?

"I was there," he says quietly. She blinks in surprise, intuiting his meaning. But the war was centuries ago. "At the beginning. When your ancestors first threw us away." His lip curls in disgust. "They didn't want us, and we have no real interest in them. But there is value in the ones like you, who not only master the system but do so in defiance of the consequences. The ones who want not just to survive but to *win*. You could be the key that helps your kind defeat us someday. If we didn't take you from them. If they didn't *let* us." He pauses, repeats himself. "It's easy to give up what you don't want."

Silence falls. In it, Zinhle tries to understand. Her society—no. *Humankind* doesn't want . . . her? Doesn't want the ones who are different, however much they might contribute? Doesn't want the children who cannot help their uniqueness despite a system that pushes them to conform, be mediocre, never stand out?

"When they start to fight for you," Lemuel says, "we'll know they're ready to be let out. To catch up to the rest of the human race."

Zinhle flinches. It has never occurred to her, before, that their prison offers parole.

"What will happen then?" she whispers. "Will you, will you join with all of them?" She falters. When has the rest of human-kind become *them* to her? Shakes her head. "*We* won't want that."

He smiles faintly, noticing her choice of pronoun. She thinks he notices a lot of things. "*They* can join us if they want. Or not. We don't care. But that's how we'll know that your kind is able to live with us, and us with them, without more segregation or killing. If they can accept you, they can accept us."

And finally, Zinhle understands.

But she thinks on all he has said, all she has experienced. As she does so, it is very hard not to become bitter. "They'll never fight for me," she says at last, softly.

He shrugs. "They've surprised us before. They may surprise you."

"They won't."

She feels Lemuel's gaze on the side of her face because she is looking at the floor. She cannot meet his eyes. When he speaks, there's remarkable compassion in his voice. Something of him is definitely still human, even if something of him is definitely not.

"The choice is yours," he says, gently now. "If you want to stay with them, be like them, just do as they expect you to do. Prove that you belong among them."

Get pregnant. Flunk a class. Punch a teacher. Betray herself.

She hates him. Less than she should, because he is not as much of an enemy as she thought. But she still hates him for making her choice so explicit.

"Or stay yourself," he says. "If they can't adapt to you, and you won't adapt to them, then you'd be welcome among us. Flexibility is part of what we are."

There's nothing more to be said. Lemuel waits a moment, to see if she has any questions. She does, actually, plenty of them. But she doesn't ask those questions, because, really, she already knows the answers.

Lemuel leaves. Zinhle sits there, silent, in the little office. When the principal and office staff crack open the door to see what she's doing, she gets up, shoulders past them, and walks out.

Zinhle has a test the next day. Since she can't sleep anyway—too many thoughts in her head and swirling through the air around her; or maybe those are *people* trying to get in—she stays up all night to study. This is habit. But it's hard, so very hard, to look at the words. To concentrate, and memorize, and analyze. She's tired. Graduation is three months off, and it feels like an age of the world.

She understands why people hate her, now. By existing, she reminds them of their smallness. By being different, she forces them to redefine "enemy." By doing her best for herself, she challenges them to become worthy of their own potential.

There's no decision, really. Lemuel knew full well that his direct intervention was likely to work. Even if he hadn't come to her, Rule 3—staying herself—would've brought her to this point anyway.

So in the morning, when Zinhle takes the test, she nails it, as usual.

And then she waits to see what happens next.

VISITING NELSON

BY **KATHERINE LANGRISH**

THE FLEET RIVER STARTS SOMEWHERE UP ON THE HEATH. I'VE never bin there, but Morris has. It's where the North London drug barons live in big houses—palaces, like—all ringed with steel security fences and guard dogs and armed patrols. Morris goes there on business, to get supplies. "You'd never get in unless they wants you in," he says, and then he grins a bit, showing his gums, and says, "nor you'd never get out again neither."

Well, the Fleet starts there, up in the woods, and then it dives underground and runs along in drains and sewers for a while, but all the time it's chewing away at the bricks and burrowing under old roadways till they sag and collapse, till by the time it gets to Kings Cross it's opened itself a nice deep channel, not that you'd wanta swim in it. There's whirlpools and sinkholes that'd suck you down hundreds of meters into the old drowned underground system, and there's lagoons where buildings have crashed across and the water dams up and spreads around, and there's narrows where the river jist roars along. But the last bit, where it runs into the Thames, is tidal. Coupla times a day, it heaves itself up and over a quarter mile or so of mud banks and ruins, and you can take a boat on it then, if you're careful.

Which is what I'll tell Morris if he finds out where we are. Which I hope he don't. Which he shouldn't, seeing as my cell's switched off so he can't call up with some little job he wants doing, and we've got all day, but it's took longer than I thought, weaving through the channels and the shallows. Some of them rocks is sharp. I've seen rusted metal rods poking out of blocks of concrete what would rip holes in the dinghy, and then Morris would kill me. He really might. If we didn't drown first, a'course.

Billy's sitting in the front and I can tell he's not spotted it yet, the place we're headed for—two sharp towers and a dome rising up behind the spoil heaps. I betted him I'd see it first, but this might be the last thing Billy and me do together for a long time, and now I kinda want him to win. So I don't say nothing, and at last he turns his head—and then he points, and he says, "Charlie, look! *Look!*" He beams at me, and I grin back at him like a dog, coz this is intense. We've wanted to do this forever. Years. We've always wanted to go and visit Nelson.

I open the throttle and the dinghy scoots in over the shallows. The tide's so high that when we finally touch ground on a tilted shore of red bricks and shattered concrete, we're hardly a stone's throw below Sint Paul's. We jump out, drag the dinghy clear of the water—and we stare.

Sint Paul's is a cathedral—that's what it's called, "Sint Paul's cathedral." That's a kind of palace. Morris says it's jist a big church, but it don't look like a church to me. Hundreds a years ago, Morris says, before the world warmed up and the Flood began, important people useta get married in there, and then when they died, they useta get buried; but I reckon they musta lived there too, in between. Be a waste of space otherwise. It hangs over us like a cliff. Seagulls go drifting from its ledges. The doorway at the top of the steps is dark as a sea cave. Billy blinks, his mouth ajar. "Is this where Nelson lives?"

"Lived," I say, but I know Billy don't make no difference between *lives* and *lived*, and now we're here neither do I: it's Nelson's palace, that's what counts, where he lived an' where he's buried, so I say, "Yeah. This is it. Nelson's house. Let's go and find him!"

But first I look around. I'm armed with one of Morris's little handguns, what he calls his pocket darlings—coz I don't want no trouble, not with Billy along. The boat's got *DK*, for *Damned Krew* scrawled on it in red and black, and no one wants to mess with the Krew on the west side of the Fleet, but here on the east side is out of our territory and the between-tides zone is teknikly no-man's land, which means anyone can roam here but they hafta be mad or desperate first, like Hairies and outcasts and refugees from drowned countries, though I don't know why refugees seemta wanta get *into* London when most of us spend our lives dreaming of getting *out*.

I look around and I see the flat gray river spreading away for miles with a far-off cluster of boats riding on it like fleas, and closer in I see the mud banks and the channels winding out between them, and then with a jab of fright I see a dark figure shambling away along the tide edge, headed for a heap of rubble where a mob of seagulls is scritching and quarreling over something to eat.

It's a Hairy. Has to be.

Billy sees me jump. He puts his arm around my shoulders and kinda hugs me, and he says, "Don't worry. Hairies ain't scary," and I almost laugh since this is what Billy always says, but anyway I'm not scared of Hairies, I just *loathe* 'em.

"They leaves you alone if you leaves them alone," Billy says, taking care to get it right, because this is what Morris has told him. Billy trusts Morris.

When I was just a kid—seven or eight years old—I tried some nirv. I sneaked a pinch out of one of Morris's little foil packets. For a second it fizzed on my tongue. Then it burned a hole right through to the core of me and *exploded*—like I'd swallowed the sun, like light was busting out of my fingertips. I was King of the Universe. I knew *everything*. It was intense.

Next thing, I was puking up on the floor, with Morris yelling his head off. He throws a bucket o' water over me, and then he throws the bucket, and then he lams me some more, and all the time he's shouting, "Don't ever let me catch you taking that stuff agin," till me eyes are spinning in me head. He hauls me downstairs. There's a room on the ground floor me and Billy was never allowed in, though we'd see the punters comin' and goin'. Morris unlocks the door. It's cold and damp inside. Metal shutters across the windows, an awful smell. On the floor . . .

I hate remembering this . . .

On the floor there's a girl. Or what useta be a girl. She's laying there in a skimpy vest and her skirt all rucked up, making a sorta snorting noise, and there's hair growing all over her, black *hairy* hair covering her face and chest and arms and legs. I'm backing away, and she opens her eyes, sudden. And I know her. Under the hair, it's Maddalena, who useta come in and look after me and Billy sometimes when Ma was sick. Morris shoves me on my knees beside her, pushes my head down to hers. An' she reaches out fast and grabs my arm. Her fingers are hot and strong, and her breath is sickly sweet. The fur on her cheeks and chin is wet with spit. Her eyes burn into mine like she's seeing to the back of my head, and she's gurgling, *"Go 'way, go 'way, go, go, go . . ."* but she won't let go, she won't let go—

—and I scream—

—and Morris drags me out, and he says, "Don't you never take that stuff again, Charlie, coz that's the way it ends."

I was crying so hard, I was almost choking. He says, "Look at me!" and shakes me till I do. His eyes are bright red, there's a muscle jumping in his cheek. He says, "You want your brain to rot? You wanta grow hair all over your body? That's what it does, there's some kinda hormone in it, some kinda *animal hormone . . .*" He spits. "In there, that ain't Maddalena no more. That's an animal. *No* one in the Krew does nirv. I don't allow it. And I promised your ma—" He stops. Then he says, "We ain't got your ma no more. We got each other and we got the Krew. You respect me, you respect yourself and the Krew, you don't take that shit. You hear me?"

For weeks and months after, I'd check my arms and hands to see if they was turning hairy. I never asked what he did with Maddalena, though she kept crawling into my dreams. But I did ask Morris once if he thought it was all right to sell nirv to people when we know what it does. And he said, "They're not forced to take it, are they? They got choice." He gives me a real hard look. "If they'll buy it, I'll sell. It puts bread in your mouth and mine, Charlie, and Billy-boy's too. You complaining?"

Well, I wasn't complaining, coz you don't cross Morris, and anyway he was right. Anyone stupid enough to go blowing their mind on nirv deserves what they get. They know what it does. And yeah, maybe people think they can stop before it gets a-hold of them—but like Morris says, that's their choice. I never told Billy how people get turned into Hairies, though. He wouldn't've understood.

I'm thinking all this as the Hairy starts to run, howling some weird kinda mad nonsense like they do, and the seagulls spin up in a squealing cloud, and the Hairy—the *thing*—waves its fists and falls down on the stones.

If it was any closer, I swear I'd shoot it dead.

"*Nelson*, Charlie. Charlie!" Billy tugs my arm. "Let's find Nelson."

A half-buried flight of stone steps leads up to a platform. We climb them, and I can't keep from looking up. Them doors at the top hafta be ten meters high. Billy whispers to himself, and I say, "What?" and he says into my ear, "Is Nelson a giant?" and a shiver goes right down my back.

"Nah," I say, confident enough. "Just—you know—a hero."

But I don't *know*. Why else would doors be that high?

Nelson is two things. One is a statchoo a mile or two to the west. He's bin there forever, far as I know. Once there woulda bin buildings and stuff all around him; now he's right on the edge of the tide, a stone man balancing on a stone column fifty meters high, leaning on a sword and staring out over the river.

The other thing Nelson is, is a hero. I dunno what he did, even Ma didn't know, but it musta bin something big for them to build so high and put him up there. I bothered away at it for years, till one day I just started making stuff up. Before long, specially after Morris came to live with Ma and then when she got the cholera and died, I got to telling Billy tales about Nelson every night. In the stories, Nelson lives in Sint Paul's. He fights armies of Hairies, he battles in the sewers with giant rats, he smuggles people out to the north. Billy loves it. His eyes sparkle and he chuckles and rubs his fingers like he does when he's really excited. Far as Billy's concerned, it's all real. Even for me, half the time. I know I made it up, but Nelson's still real, ain't he? Whoever he was, whatever he did, he was alive once, and he really is buried right here.

The huge doors are open, jammed with rubble. Billy scrambles over it and slips inside. I'm right on his heels. And we're inside Sint Paul's.

It's *enormous*. A jolt goes through me. Like panic, like I've stepped off a cliff. I actually grab Billy's arm. I can't see properly. It's all dark, deep shadows cut by shafts of white light falling through high windows. It smells like the bottom of the river. And there's a weird soft noise, like someone stroking the back of my neck.

"Birds," says Billy.

Right. It's just pigeons cooing overhead and fluttering about. My eyes adjust and I see we're standing on a floor of black-and-white squares, but it's all grimed and filthy, and there's streaks of pigeon shit down the towering whitish walls.

If my mates in the Krew, Beamer and Sam and Kingy, if they knew how I make up stories for Billy, I'd hafta cut my throat. They don't know nothing about Nelson and I'd never tell 'em. But there's something about Nelson I haven't told even Billy.

I talk to him.

Two three years ago, Billy was sick in his chest, coughing all winter, couldn't hardly get his breath. Morris wasn't no use, yelling at Billy to shut up coughing, *he* couldn't sleep—I coulda killed him—and I wished Nelson was there, *he'd* know what to do—and before I knowed it, I was talking to him inside my head. Telling him how scared I was, and begging him don't let Billy die. And he *listened*. Don't tell me any different, he listened, and somehow I just knew then Billy'd get better, an' he did.

Billy thinks that Nelson's lucky. When we find him, he wants to make a wish. Me, I'm here to ask Nelson a question. An important one. Here, where he's buried, I hope I'll get the answer good and strong.

Thinking about it makes me hopeful but edgy. So I drop Billy's arm and stroll forward like I know what I'm doing. Right ahead is a massive stone bowl, big enough to sit in. Nelson's bathtub? I'm grinning at the thought, and I peek in, and it's half full of green water and dirt and twigs and feathers. A pigeon clatters over, and I look up—and my mouth drops open. The roof's all circles and arches, picked out in gold paint and fancy colors. . . . So this is what they thought of Nelson, this is what they done for him. . . .

"*Charlie!*"

I pull up, swearing, on the very edge of a hole in the floor. A *made* hole, perfectly round, over a meter across. Farther on there's another, and another. For fuck's sake, this floor ain't solid at all, it's built over cellars or something, and if Billy hadn't yelled, I'd've fallen through. I go cold all over. It's all black down there.

And Billy looks about to burst into tears.

"Billy-boy, you saved me!" I hook him around the neck and tousle his hair. He manages a sick grin. I feel sick myself. Chrissakes, what kinda place has holes in the floor like this?

Then I figure it out. The holes are there to light the cellars below. Maybe once they had grids over them, or thick glass. But it's shook me up. Don't know what I was expecting, but I wasn't expecting to nearly die. I get a bad thought. What if this is one of them places that's, you know, *guarded*? Where there's a curse if you disturb the dead? What if Nelson's magical house is full of traps?

We shuffle along past the sooty rings of old fires, past heaps of garbage, past a great black gateway guarded by statchoos of angels with smoke-stained wings. The more I look around, the creepier I feel. In every corner there's marble statchoos of people dying— dropping off horses' backs, fainting and falling, laying down on their deathbeds. You'd think they was marking tombs, but there ain't no room for graves in this hollow floor. I take a squint at the lettering cut in the platforms under 'em. They're all monuments to dead soldiers. Maybe a mighty battle was fought here once— and lost.

Suddenly the walls rise like cliffs. The roof overhead jistabout disappears. "High, Charlie!" Billy gasps. "High as the sky!" He's right. I'm giddy just looking. We're standing under the dome we saw from outside, so huge and hollow you could fit the whole sky into it. Way, way up, there's a curving row of windows with a ledge running around.

"Let's go up," Billy says, eyes aglow. I wanta get up there too, there must be stairs. I tug open a door in the wall, and there they are, a spiral flight leading up. . . .

But we won't find Nelson up there, will we? You don't bury people in the ceiling. You bury 'em in the ground. In the cellars.

And right on cue, I see an open doorway with steps leading down. In the arch above it, three skulls are carved in the stone.

"Come on!" I say to Billy, and I pull out my cell and click the light. A thin beam streaks out, painting a bluish glare on a flight of steps leading downwards. Billy hangs back.

"Nelson's there," he says, pointing up at the dome. "Upstairs."

"No, Billy, he ain't. We can go up there later if you like. This way first."

"S'dark."

"Use your cell," I say, and he pulls it out and turns it on and flashes it down the steps. Then he clicks it off and shakes his head.

"Billy, you *gotta* come with me. I can't leave you alone."

People always think Billy's younger'n me, but he's nineteen, two years older. He's shorter than me, and shy, and if you don't know him it ain't easy to tell what he's saying. *But he's not stupid.* He just thinks different. And when he makes up his mind about something, you can't shake it. Like that rabbit of his. He got it off a market stall selling live animals for meat, chickens mostly, but other things too. It's a monster, a whopping white rabbit he calls Bunny. Bad-tempered as hell. It scratches and bites, and it shits little brown droppings all over the house. Morris and me is always grumbling about it, and Billy knows, but he don't care what we think. He loves it.

He's got that stubborn look on his face right now, scowling, tongue pushing out between his lips. I say, "If you don't come, you won't get to see where Nelson is. An' you won't get to make your wish."

"Don't care."

"How can you say that when we've come all this way?" My voice rises. "Chrissakes, Billy!"

That was too loud. Pigeons clatter up and there's a gusty sweep and rattle as they swirl overhead. The echoes keep coming, like footsteps tapping toward us, and voices whispering, and my hair rises. I hate the feeling of all this space around us, full of shadows where anything could hide. I keep thinking the statchoos'll move. I feel we're being watched, yet I look around and behind us and don't see nothing. It's only the birds . . . I hope.

"Come *on*," I hiss.

"No," says Billy, and I'm mad with him, but it's no good showing it. Billy won't come. He don't like the dark. And I wanted this to be a good time together. . . . "All right," I tell him. "Stay *right here*. Don't move. I'll be as fast as I can."

I run down the steps, counting under my breath. Thirteen down, then a turn, then a lot more. It's clammy cold, and there's a rank, rotten stink. Thirty-three, thirty-four—then the light from the cell flashes off black water at the bottom. I might've expected it. Even above the tide line, cellars don't always drain out.

I prod the water with my toe and it don't seem all that deep, so I step in and swear as it overtops my boots. I'm standing in an arched passage, and I can see by the stains on the walls that the water level sometimes comes much higher than this. Now what? Billy's waiting, an' I really shouldn't have left him. I've gotta be quick.

Which way?

To the left it's pitch black. To the right there's a grayish glimmer, so I try that way first, and the light comes through a hole in the floor above, like the one I nearly fell through. The tunnel widens into dark spaces. I hurry along, past more white statchoos, pale and horrible in the dusk. The light off the ripples travels over them, and their faces flicker like life, and I catch my breath hard. Then the passage ends in a wall.

I slosh back past the bottom of the steps and try the other way, the dark way. Pretty soon I come to another choice—straight on or turn right, but it ain't really a choice at all coz the way ahead is barred by rusted metal gates. I'll hafta to go right . . . but it's gnawing at me that Billy's on his own, I ought to get back to him, how long have I been down here?

But I'll never get this chance again. And maybe Nelson's real close, maybe just around the corner. It's worth a look. I don't know if I'm fooling myself, but I've got a feeling about it—like a whisper in the dark, like feeling the heat of a fire with your eyes shut. Whether it's real or not, I go wading into the water anyway.

The floor slopes down gradual, ankle deep, knee deep, thigh deep, and the walls is slimed with green, and there's black lumps of stuff floating that I try not to look at.

The passage opens into a chamber. I stab the light about, and it flashes off a bunch of white pillars sticking up outta the water. In the middle of them is a stone platform, like an island, and on the platform is a black marble coffin. Big but not giant-sized. On top of that, there's a golden pillow with a crown.

That's all. But a shudder runs right down my spine. I know this is the place even before I spell out the golden letters on the platform: HORATIO VISC NELSON. I never knew the rest of his name before.

Nelson's *here*.

I breathe in, slow and deep and careful.

It ain't like them palaces up on the Heath that Morris goes on about, all silk carpets and pictures and shandyleers. Maybe it useta be that way upstairs, when Nelson was alive. But when he died they put him down here in the dark, with a black bed to lie on and quiet white walls. An' a golden crown like a king.

The ripples I've made go slopping against the pillars. The beam of my light jumps off the surface: a lake of black water and bright ripples surrounding a black marble coffin on a white stone island.

I'm glad I came. I'll always remember this. I don't reckon I'll ever see it again. Coz I'm *leaving*.

Morris don't know what I'm planning, at least I hope he don't, I ain't stupid enough to tell him, though he might guess. He's sharp, is Morris, and he likes to be in control. "Nobody leaves the Krew," he says. "Family sticks together." Yeah, but what does that mean? It means selling nirv for Morris in a half-drowned, half-ruined city crawling with Hairies, where the cholera comes back every coupla summers. What sorta life is that? Ma died. What if Billy dies?

Oh, I guess the old bastard's fond of me and Billy, in his way. But he don't *own* me, I don't need his *permission*. I'm leaving, all right, and there's only two ways, upriver or down. Upriver's too dangerous, patrols and checkpoints and electric fences. Downriver's dangerous too—you gotta get past the Barrage and right out to sea. I reckon I could do it, though, and find my way north up the coast. It's worth it. Up in the north there's a proper government, not like what we got here. Proper jobs—doctors—*rights*. Up north I can get to be something. Make something outta my life. And Billy's.

But that's it—Billy. No way can I take him with me, I'll hafta leave him behind, at least for a while. (Forever if I get killed—but I won't get killed.) When I get a job, and a permit and all, I'll come back for him or send for him, an' it'll be better for both of us in the end. How can I tell him, though? I don't know how to tell him; he'll never understand. And will he be all right when I'm gone? What'll Morris do when I skip out, taking the boat and stuff? He'll be as mad as hell with me (nobody leaves the Krew), but not with Billy, right? Billy's still family. Will Morris look after Billy if I'm not there? I think so, but I don't know.

I don't *know*.

So I ask Nelson. I square up and speak into the dark. "What d'ya think? Will Billy be okay with Morris? Shall I go?"

I listen, listen for the least bit of sound, listen *inside* my head as well as outside. In the cold silence, my heart thuds against my ribs. A little bit of me says I'm fooling myself—telling lies to myself— but I gotta believe in something or I ain't got nothing.

There's a tiny tickling noise like a cat lapping. My neck prickles, my breath hisses. I flash the light down and see fresh ripples crossing the surface. Toward me. Next there's a sloshing, regular sound: splash—splash—splash. Someone's wading out of the deep darkness on the other side of Nelson's tomb.

My blood turns to acid. My heart comes choking up into my throat. It's Nelson—I've *woken* Nelson! I swing the cell up. A face appears in the light beam, screwed up an' blinking—a face buried in long straggles of gray-black hair. My hand dives for my gun, but my pocket's all wet and tight and I can't get my fingers in. I start backing away, the water grabbing at my thighs.

The thing whines like a dog, and my hair stands on end. It works its jaw up and down. Around its mouth is draggled and sticky, with feathers stuck to it. . . . *Feathers?* It's gripping something—a dead pigeon, all tore open, I can see the dark blood and white bones. It's been sitting in the dark behind Nelson's tomb, chewing on a dead pigeon. I'm almost sick. I scream at it, "I've got a gun!" and I run.

But the water's so deep. I hafta force my legs along, elbows pumping, thrashing up stinking spray, nearly falling every stride, and I glance back to see if it's coming and can't see nothing in the dark, so it could be right behind me. . . . Then I'm in the shallows, splashing along ankle deep, and now I can *really* run—so fast I almost miss the steps, but here they are—and I hurl myself up and slip and my knee slams into the stone—hell that hurts!—and

I scramble up on all fours, and I'm coming into gray daylight, shouting, "Hairies, Billy, run . . ."

And he's not here.

He's not here!

"Billy!" My voice explodes into the space above me. All the birds hurtle up again and go whirling around. Where the hell is he, he *never* goes wandering off—and there are *Hairies* in here, I shoulda guessed a place like this would be crawling with 'em—I took too long, I should never a-left him—*"Billy?"*

Faint and thin, his voice floats back. "Hi, Charlie . . ."

I look up. Shit! Overhead, way overhead where the ledge clings to the underside of the dome, I see the tiny white blob of his face looking down. "Hi, Charlie," he calls again. Or maybe he means, "High!"

He sounds really pleased with himself.

Shit! Shit! I know he's not gonna come down on his own, I'll hafta fetch him. Just as I start for the doors leading to the spiral staircase, there's a noise behind me, a sorta tuneless singing, "Doh-de-doh-de-dum. Dum, dum, dum."

The Hairy's coming, limping up outta the cellar like a walking corpse, naked, dripping wet, the hair plastered to its thin shanks and knobby knees. As it comes it hums, jiggles, twitches, scratches itself. I struggle to push my hand into my wet pocket, shove and wriggle my fingers till they curl around the handle of Morris's little gun, and I drag it out. It musta got well soaked—will it work when it's wet?

The Hairy sees me. It stops in the archway just under the death's heads. It's still got the pigeon dangling from one hand. It tips its head sideways like it's trying to figure me out. Through the hair its eyes gleam like a dog's. Then it drops the pigeon and shambles right at me.

"Get back!" I point the gun. It's as light as a toy, but it ain't a toy. Any real person would know that, any real person would back off, but this is a Hairy, it don't understand. I can kill it, but I can't scare it. I shriek, "Get away from me or I'll shoot!" and it lets out a yell of its own and waves its arms. I jump about a mile in the air, I nearly pull the trigger, but I don't, I've never *killed* anyone, and it burbles, "Mad, mad, mad-a, mad-a," and I'm almost sobbing, I *know* it's mad, I back some more and I say, "I'll shoot, I'll shoot!" and it says, "Madd-a-*lena*."

I almost drop the gun.

And it says, this time I swear it says, "*Moh*-riss."

All the skin prickles up all over my body.

I don't wait to hear no more. I yank open that door in the wall and leap through and go racing two at a time up shallow treads that lead around and around in a never-ending spiral. The Hairy's hooting in the shaft below. It's coming after me.

Maybe it's seen me with Morris on the street, it knows we're dealers, it thinks I've got . . . When Hairies get to that state, their brains is wrecked, scrambled. Nobody sells it to 'em anymore, they can't pay and anyway another dose or two'd prob'ly kill them, but they still *want* the stuff. They still crave for nirv.

But I swear I didn't rekkernize it, it ain't anyone I ever met. And even if it knows about Morris, how could it know about Maddalena?

I didn't hear that. I didn't. I didn't hear it.

But I know I did.

Every coupla turns, daylight peeks through a little window covered with thick glass and barred like a prison. I push on—slowing, toiling, gasping—but I keep going, and after I don't know how many turns, the stairs end in a narrow stone passage, no more than elbow wide. I dive along it and come to another flight, straight this time, a glimmer of daylight at the top. I struggle up and tumble out and grab at the wall.

I'm out on the ledge where Billy was. It rims the bottom of

the dome, hugging what looks like about a circular mile of space. Windows march 'round the walls above me. There are huge shadowy paintings up there. Way, way up, higher than I like to look, there's another gallery hanging right in the middle of the roof. Dusty rays of light slant down.

I peer into the gloom. "Billy?"

Well, he ain't here, a'course he ain't, that'd be too easy, wouldn't it? He's wandered off again. And the Hairy's on the stairs and we gotta get out—I'm wild with Billy but I'm *furious* with myself. What's wrong with me? Why didn't I shoot when I got the chance? Next time I'll pull the trigger for sure.

I try Billy's cell, which is switched off, and I call for him again, not very loud coz it echoes, and the place spooks me, and then I set off marching around the circle.

A heavy iron railing fences off the drop. Once it musta run all the way around, but now there's big gaps, places where it's torn down and twisted. I peer over, careful. A helluva long way down there's a pattern in the middle of the floor, a starburst so big I never spotted it when I was down there. It's like a target. *If you're gonna jump, aim right here.* I pull back, shuddering, and press close against the wall.

Billy whispers at my shoulder, right in my ear, "Hey, Charlie!" I spin around. And he's *not there*.

Christ, the voice—the voice was so weird. All hoarse and hollow. Not like Billy alive. Like Billy's ghost.

It's too much—the dome hanging over me like a thundercloud, the Hairy on the stairs, them bloody pigeons what never stop cooing . . . and Billy's voice coming outta nowhere. My knees go weak. I croak, "Where are you?" an' there's a pause, and his voice whispers, "Here"—still sounding like a ghost—and I go, "Where?" and there's another pause and he says, "By the door."

Well, there's no door anywhere near, and then I look far out across the open space and see the doorway I come in through, more than half the circle away. Next to it I can just make out the shape of Billy, standing there waiting. Relief soaks through me, but I'm exasperated too, chasing each other around like a game of ring-a-roses. I shout, "Stay put! Stay there an' wait for me!" There's the pause, and he answers, "All right," still in that dragged-out hollow whisper, like it's traveled right up into the cup of the dome. So it's got to be some kind of echo.

From where I am, it's quicker to go on than turn back. I'm picking my way careful-like over slippery piles of fallen plaster and pigeon droppings, when I suddenly know I've just made the most *terrible* fucking mistake.

I told Billy to wait where he is—and the Hairy's on the stairs.

It's like a fist in my stomach. I start to run, past gaps in the rail where there's nothing to stop me going all the way to the bottom, and then I come to a place where the rail's all twisted over the ledge and I hafta stop and clamber over it, and watch where I put my hands and feet in case I break an ankle or fall, and I can't even look to see what's happening—if it's already there, and Billy's all alone. It gives me the horrors. I gotta get there first, before it reaches the top.

I vault the last tangle of metal, and run on. All of the circle looks the same, like I'm getting nowhere, like the building's revolving and I'm staying still. I've lost sight of Billy, don't know how far I've come, I'm dreading to hear him scream. I grip the gun in my hand. I'll use it this time, I really will. I'll kill it if touches him. . . .

I come around the last curve and close the circle. And Billy's waiting for me like I told him, his face all pleased—and there's the Hairy clambering outta the black oblong of the doorway behind him.

I slide to a stop, pointing the gun. My hand's shaking so bad, I daren't fire. "Billy, get behind me quick, there's a Hairy, gimme some room to shoot."

But Billy turns. He sees this thing—this thing what rips pigeons apart and eats 'em raw—and he smiles, all kindly and superior, like he knows best, and, "Don't worry, Charlie," he says. "Hairies ain't scary." An' he reaches out and *pats it on the head*.

It grabs him. It tugs his arms, gibbering, but this time I can't hear proper words, just a sorta mad moaning like it's pleading for something and I can guess what. It stinks of salty piss like an old tomcat, it's covered with filthy tangled hair; who knows what diseases it's got? The gun's no use; I drop it and try yanking Billy away, but the Hairy holds on tight and I yell, "Get off! Get off of him! He ain't got nothing for you!" An' I grab its wrist—*touching* it, skin and bone and harsh hair under my fingers—and twist till it lets go. I land a kick to its kneecap, and it screams and collapses. Billy wails something, and I turn on him. "Outta the *way*! Let me *deal* with it—"

He shoves me hard in the chest. He's beetroot red, scowling, really angry. "Charlie *hurt* it!" He crouches over it, muttering, "Poor thing, poor thing." He pulls a crumpled foil packet outta his pocket and offers it to the Hairy like a kid sharing candy. "Here, this is nice."

I go *berserk*.

I rip the packet outta Billy's fingers and jiggle the foil open. A pinch of golden-brown powder lays there, with that dry sweet smell. Nirv. Precious, precious nirv, precious as gold dust. I empty it on the floor. The Hairy dives for it, but I don't care. I grab Billy by the shirtfront with both fists and heave him toward me, and I shake him, the way Morris shook me—and I *rage* into his face, "Who give you that? Who give you that? Who give it you?"

Billy tries to turn his face away. "Stop it, Charlie, bad Charlie, stop, stop, stop!" His voice rises to a shriek. He flails his arms and punches me; it don't hurt, but it shocks me rigid. I let go. He's sobbing. He staggers back and crouches down and wraps his arms over his head. When I move to comfort him he cries out and bunches up tighter.

He's scared of me. He wasn't scared of the Hairy, but he's scared of *me*.

And I'm sick at myself. I didn't hafta do that. Only one person coulda give him that packet.

The Hairy's down on the floor, sweeping and scraping up every trace of the brown powder with its dirty fingers, licking and licking them. Shudders of ecstasy run through its skinny body.

Oh, I remember how that feels. Like the sun bursting outta your skin. Like you know *everything*. . . . It looks up an' its eyes burn mad and bright and satisfied. I feel its mind slipping cold into my thoughts like a pickpocket's fingers.

"*Moh*-riss," it whispers, and yawns.

And after a moment I croak, "Morris. Yeah."

And it lays down and curls up, ribby as a starved dog under the hair, and another big shudder runs through it from top to toe, and it lays still.

Billy always says he ain't scared of Hairies, but I never listened. I shoulda known he don't say things he don't mean. Maybe he's right. Maybe they're harmless. But I hate them coz I helped to *make* 'em, and they're horrible. I think of Maddalena. I've never stopped thinking of her. If Hairies read minds, no wonder this one saw her. She's always hiding like a spider in the darkness at the back of my head.

I'm shaking so hard, my teeth are chattering. I look at the Hairy laying there. How gently Billy touched it, the way he pets Bunny's fur. But Billy could get to be like that, growing hair all over him, wandering lost and mad in a place like this.

Only *one* person coulda given Billy a packet of nirv, and that person is Morris. And why? He never lets anyone in the Krew take nirv. No chances, zero tolerance. "Keeping the family clean," he calls it. He's never let Billy anywhere near it before, in case he spilled it or tried some. Plus, it's expensive, why waste it?

This is about me, not Billy. This is a deliberate threat.

Coz he's guessed, hasn't he? Morris has guessed I'm planning to go, and he ain't going to argue, he's just letting me see what'll happen to Billy if I do. He knows I'd find out. He gave the nirv to Billy to show me Billy won't be family without me around. Won't be safe. Coz Morris has to have things his own way, and he wants me under his thumb.

You don't cross Morris, the crooked, devious, evil *bastard*.

I feel sick. Bitter and sick and stupid. I shoulda known Morris couldn't be trusted, not really, yet somehow I did trust him. . . . I pick up the gun and wish I could shoot him with it, and then I think I couldn't even shoot the Hairy, and anyway what good would it do? Then I think, So I'll hafta stay in London, and the minute I think that I'm so miserable I know I can't, I jist can't. So I put the whole idea away, coz right here and now I hafta put things straight with Billy. And then get us both out. I crouch beside him.

"Billy-boy, I'm sorry I shook you. Forgive me? Please?"

He whimpers.

"I'll make it up, right? Whatever you say."

A grunt this time. He's got his eyes shut tight, his head buried in his arms.

"You can thump me if you want." I pause. "Hey, I'll even kiss Bunny."

He unfolds and looks at me. "On the nose," he says.

"On the nose. Right."

He don't exactly smile, but I feel some better. "Let's go home," he says, and I say, after a moment, "Let's do that."

I get up first, and then I pull him up, and we look at the Hairy laid out on the floor. "It's asleep," says Billy, and I say, "Yeah, it's asleep," an' he says, "But its eyes are open," and I see he's troubled by that, and I say, "Yeah, it's asleep with its eyes open. Time to go."

As we set off down the stairs I say, "Come on, Billy, who give you that stuff?"

His eyes flash sideways to see if I'm going to lose it again. I say, trying to keep my voice level, "Okay, when Morris give you that stuff"—I wait, but he don't say nothing and my heart's like lead, it was Morris all right—"did you try it? Did you"—I lick my finger, dab it in the air, lick it again—"did you taste it?"

He nods once. My heart's beating really hard. I say, "How many times?"

But he shrugs. I know I'm not going to get an answer.

It's dark on the stairs now, the light coming in from the little barred windows is feeble and poor. Without talking anymore we go down and down, hundreds a steps, around and around and around and around, and push through the doors to the cathedral floor.

Now I'm looking, now I know they're here, I see them moving. A long way off across the floor, something wanders slowly past one of the big statchoos and disappears again into the gloom. Under the breathy cooing of the pigeons there's other noises—hoots and cries, quiet raps and echoes. It's getting dark outside and the Hairies are coming home.

I grab Billy's hand, and we hurry past the heaps of rubbish, and around the black openings in the floor. The statchoos loom like huge pale ghosts. We reach the ten-meter slice of dim sky that shows between the open doors, and scramble over the rubble.

It's raining—big, splashy drops. Evening's on the way, but it's lighter than I thought. And much warmer out here. The tide's going out, the wind smells of seaweed and fresh mud, the river's gray with streaks of silver. We run down the steps to the boat and lift it between us, stumbling down the exposed wet slope to the edge of the water, and we jump in.

I push off and open the throttle and the water creams behind us. We both look back and see the front of Sint Paul's rearing up like a cliff, all ledges and pillars and black openings. We draw farther away. The two sharp towers go fading into the rain.

Billy rubs his arms, shivering. His head droops. He looks pale and thin and tired. I'm headed for home, coz where else can we go?

"Billy, that stuff that Morris gave you . . . nirv . . ." He gives me a weary glance, and I say, tight-voiced, "Don't ever try it again, whatever he says, it's bad for you."

He jist looks puzzled and I don't blame him. Coz if it's so bad for you, what's me and Morris doing with it? What's me an' Morris an' the Krew doing with it, making Hairies? I feel worse than ever. I say, "Even if it makes you feel . . . Billy, how *did* it make you feel?"

I think he won't answer, can't answer. And then he says, "Big." I'm silent.

We're done with the channels now, passing out of the Fleet and into the Thames. Sint Paul's vanishes behind the high spoil heaps and into the dusk. Billy cranes his neck to see it go, and then he says, "Did you see Nelson?"

It's a second before I know what he's talking about. It feels like years since this morning, years since we beached the boat below the steps and went to explore. I think of the holes in the floor. I think of wading into the black water, finding Nelson's black coffin on its white marble stand. I think how I asked him for help. How I got no answer but the Hairy splashing out at me like a bad joke.

But Billy's looking at me, hopeful. So I get ready to make up some story how I really did meet Nelson himself down there in the cellars, in a golden room glittering with shandyleers and dimonds. . . . Just as I open my mouth, a thought comes to me and I shut it again.

I got my answer.

I go hot and cold all over.

I asked if I could trust Morris, if it was safe to leave Billy with him—and the answer was no.

So Billy's coming with me.

It'll make things twice as hard—twice as dangerous. We'll need so much more stuff, we're so much more likely to be seen. Can I explain to Billy what it's all about? Can we really do it—can we really make it all the way downriver to the sea? A bubble of excitement tells me we can.

I sit up straight, feeling better than I have for hours. I don't hatta try and explain to Billy why I'm going away. I don't hafta leave him behind. We'll live and die together.

Screw Morris! We'll *both* go!

And Billy's still looking at me, waiting to hear about Nelson. I say, "Yeah, in a way I did meet Nelson, Billy. In a way, I think I did."

Billy says, "I saw him too."

I go hot and cold again. He sounds so matter-of-fact. I almost ask what he means, and then I daren't. "You did?"

Billy nods. "He was upstairs. I told you he was. I made a wish."

My voice comes out all faint. "You did? What was it?"

He says proudly, "To be with you, Charlie. Just to be with you."

ALL I KNOW OF FREEDOM

BY CAROL EMSHWILLER

I'M MAKING DO WITH LESS. AND THEN LESS AND LESS AND LESS. I'm even eating less. But I don't know if it's better to eat a lot so as to live off my fat later on, or eat less so as to be in practice for not having enough food. I've heard, though, that if you're fat you stretch your stomach, so you need more food to feel satisfied, so I've decided it's better to shrink mine.

I'm practicing for getting out of here.

I won't be able to take anything but the clothes I'll be wearing and what I can stuff in my pockets.

Also I'm hardening myself up for the cold. Sometimes I sleep with the window open no matter what the temperature. I live in the attic. Nobody notices what I do up here. I even have a book though I don't know how to read it.

If I keep quiet and do my jobs I'm practically invisible. Just like Mother said: "It's always good to behave yourself so as not to get noticed." She also said, "Stand up straight, say thank you and please." I don't. I keep quiet and hunch over so as not to be seen.

I was sold for quite a respectable sum. Or so Mother told me, and proudly. I don't blame her. I presume she had to do it.

And these are not the worst people to be sold to. I've heard some get beaten. These people don't do that.

Trouble is, now that I'm getting breasts, I can tell that they're beginning to see me no matter how quiet I keep.

I tried to leave before but I didn't get far. I was too young. I didn't realize how hard it would be and how I'd *have* to be tired and hungry—how I'd have to maybe be freezing or wet. That's part of running away. This time I'll be ready. That time I came back by myself. They didn't even know I had gone.

When they took me, they promised they'd let me go to school so I was glad to go with them, but they never did let me. They kept saying, "Next year," and when it was next year they still said it. Pretty soon even they stopped saying it because it was clear there wasn't going to be a "next year" for me.

There are lots of books around. More than anybody would ever need. I thought maybe I could teach myself to read. I looked at captions under pictures, but there aren't very many pictures and that hasn't helped much. If I waited till the baby was a bit older, surely there would be some simpler books, but I'm not going to wait.

When they first took me, it was just great. I couldn't believe my luck. Plane rides and hotels. Wonderful food—though some of it so odd I didn't dare eat it, and I was homesick every now and then for lentils. They got me the first frilly blouse I ever had . . . and that was the last, too. It was tan and silky. I did all sorts of things I'd never have had a chance to do except for them—as they kept telling me. That's when I thought I really would get to go to school.

They kept telling me I should be grateful—and I was. Actually I'm still grateful, but I think I've paid them back enough by now. I don't know how long I've been here. I wish I'd had the sense to mark off the years.

The one good thing is, they never whip me. That's what they used to do back home and it's one of the reasons I wanted to get out of there. They always talk sweetly. My so-called father calls me a hundred different things. They all sound good. "Madam, if you'd be so kind . . . Miss, by your leave." Talking that way is his joke. Like, "My dear, clean the toilet and be quick about it. Sweetheart, change the bed and wash the sheets." (He doesn't even say "sweetheart" or "my dear" to his wife.) Now and then he says, "Miss Whatever-your-name-is . . ." He really does forget my name and that's why he says "madam" and "my dear." That's odd, too, because they're the ones named me what they wanted me to be. My real name was much too long and complicated for them to remember. They never even tried.

Now that I'm getting breasts my so-called father is looking at me in a different way. All that fancy language he talks, all those "madam"s and "sweetheart"s, "dear lady"s, and "by your leave"s might turn into something entirely different. He pinched my breasts as though to see how much they'd grown.

My so-called mother ("Call me Mother in front of people." Though people hardly ever come here), she was the one decided what to name me when they took me. She wanted something simple and easy to say. She calls me B. I do know that letter. She spells it *Bee*. I know *A* and *C*, and *E*, and some others, too. I like *O*.

Here, I have to do what I don't want to all the time. I mean *all* the time. Easier to list what I *don't* do than what I do do. And I can't think of a thing I don't do.

They'll miss me when I'm gone. I'm going to have to be careful, though I don't think they can risk setting the cops on me since I'm here illegally. I didn't realize that until recently. I'm a secret. They bought me when I was ten. To get me in the country they pretended I was their daughter and got some sort of phony passport.

I don't want to do anything to put the baby in danger. I'll leave at night when they're home. I'm sorry for the houseplants. I don't think my so-called parents will remember that they'll need to water them. Maybe they'll forget about the baby, too. At least it'll make a fuss.

There's a big wall around their place and an iron gate that's always locked. There's broken glass along the top of the wall and sharp points on top of the gate. They say to keep robbers out, but I think it's for keeping me in.

But I have the gate key now. They've turned the house upside down. They've frisked me and more than once. He did it. Looked everywhere on and *in* my body. Then, for the first time, they whipped me. I almost told them where the key was, but I managed not to. Finally they got tired and stopped. Then my so-called father scared me in another way than pinching breasts. He said I was a pretty girl but he could make it so I wasn't if I didn't behave myself.

But they're not all bad. They were kind enough to give me a day to rest up after that. I guess they knew I'd need it. "Mother" even served me supper in bed. She said, "You'll get breakfast in bed, too, if you show us where that key is." They were extra nice all day (I got dessert. I got a heating pad on my sore spots) but I said I didn't know, so I didn't get breakfast in bed.

Next day I pretend I'm worse off than I am. I hobble around and sit down sideways whenever I get to sit. They'll never think I could go off tomorrow. Weather report says rain. Perfect.

Middle of the night and I'm off—my pockets full of peanut-butter sandwiches. Now all I have to do is find a school. I'm not sure what a school looks like, even though I've seen pictures. I know sometimes it's a little school and sometimes it's a great big building school. At least it should say *school* on it. I can read that. It's got two O's.

After I let myself out, I hide the key under a big tree next to a parking lot a few blocks away. I dig it in nice and deep. That's what I did last time I ran away and how I got back in before they found out. That time they didn't even know the key was gone. They'd left it on the hall table.

It's drizzling but I have a big black garbage bag over me. I walk on down the road, turn a corner, and then another corner. Walking anywhere I want. I keep turning corners just because I can.

This right now is what it's like to be free. Sometimes I run even though I have a lot of heavy stuff in my pockets. Sometimes I hop and jump. All I know about freedom is what I know right now.

I turned so many corners, at first I don't suppose I get far, but now I'm getting somewhere. I've taken smaller and smaller roads and this one is the smallest of all.

Then I hear something crying. I hold still and listen. There's a big bush by the side of the road that would make a good place to hide. That's got to be where the creature is. I move closer. The crying stops.

Since I don't know what it is, I'm a little worried about reaching around in there. But I'm thinking how I know what it feels like to be wet and homeless even though I haven't been that way very long.

I crawl under the bushes and feel around until I touch wet fur. The creature cries again. It doesn't bite me. I pull it out and under the streetlight.

It's nothing but skin and bones, and so dirty and matted, I hardly know what it is. But then . . . it's just what I've always wanted and knew I'd never get to have. I even have a name all picked out. I don't know yet if it's a boy or girl, but I'll call it Mr. O'Brien. There was once a man came to visit my so-called parents and that was his name. I was in the kitchen cleaning up, and he looked in at me with curiosity and kindness. I would have said something but he took me by surprise. They usually kept me hidden when people visited. If he had come again I would have been ready to say something, or I'd have made some sort of sign, but he never came back. Usually when there were guests, "Mother" locked me in the attic. I only saw that man for a few seconds, but I'll remember him forever.

This Mr. O'Brien here is some kind of puppy, I don't know what kind. It's mostly brownish unless this is dirt. I hope we get to be friends and that it grows up to be big and dangerous. I'd like to see my so-called father try to come after me then.

I put Mr. O. in with me, under my big black garbage bag.

We walk until there aren't any more streetlights. I'm looking for the real Mr. O'Brien, or a school, whichever comes first, though right now any dry warm place would do.

But no good place comes along. Then we see a big doghouse at the end of a dog run, but no dog there and it's quite a ways from the house. At least it's out of the rain. We crawl in. I get stiff all curled up there and have to stretch my legs out into the rain. We don't sleep much. We leave as soon as it's even a little bit light. I share one of my peanut-butter sandwiches with Mr. O'Brien.

That morning just about at dawn (we've already walked for a while), I see a school way out here in the middle of nowhere. At least it says SCHOOL on it. It's no bigger than a little house and has a big backyard with an old sand pile and a slide and two swings. I know about those from a long time ago.

I push on the doors and look in the windows. It looks abandoned. But what a nice place to hide. Two rooms. A few little chairs and tables. It would be nice if some books were still there, too, but I don't see any.

Except I can't get in. I try all the windows but I don't want to break any.

We give up and go on.

I share another peanut-butter sandwich with Mr. O.

At evening we come to another school. This one is entirely different. It's big and it looks scary. It says SCHOOL on it, but almost all the people there are grown-ups. And some look very old. They're kind of raggedy, too. The men have beards and the women wear long skirts. There's a big banner right under where it says SCHOOL, but of course I can't read it.

They're all very busy, but not doing school-like things. They've rigged up all sorts of unschoolish tents, and there are canvas shades over what looks like a cooking place with lots of pots. In the big back field they're building a huge shiny long thing with no windows at all. Hard to tell what it is because of the scaffolding around it. It takes up the whole field. People in neat white coveralls are working on it.

I'm going to ask somebody what's going on, but I'd like to ask a kid, except there aren't very many around. Odd, but all the kids I see are girls and they're all wearing skirts.

I wait and watch a long time. Good that Mr. O'Brien seems to like being with me and that he's a nice quiet dog. We're both the shy type. We share another peanut-butter sandwich. We're going to run out pretty soon.

We're sitting behind some big bushes to eat and we're not

paying attention. All of a sudden here's just what I wanted, a girl about my age practically right beside us. She's wearing a long torn dirty skirt.

First thing she says is—that is, after we stare at each other for a couple of minutes—"I wish I could wear blue jeans like yours, but they won't let me. Skirts are always in the way. Are you trying to hide? What's your dog's name?"

"Mr. O'Brien."

She sits down right next to us and looks as if she'd like to share our sandwich with us, but I can smell what's cooking in those pots under the canvas shades, so I know she'll get food.

"Why are you hiding?"

"We're not. We're just having lunch. What does that say there, under where it says *School*?"

"Can't you read?"

I really am embarrassed. I almost say I can except I need glasses. But I decide not to lie.

"It says, *Prepare, the end is nigh*."

"The end of what?"

"The world of course, silly." She looks at me as if I really am dumb. "It's in the middle of ending right now, can't you tell? Everybody knows that. All you have to do is look around. And look how hot it is already and it isn't even lunchtime."

Have they kept me so isolated back home I don't even know it's the end of the world? I wouldn't be surprised, though. When I was cleaning up in the kitchen, I heard the news when they listened to it and things did sound bad. Lots of wars and earthquakes and horrible toxic spills, and even right near us there was a gas truck crashed into a house and exploded and killed everybody and burned up four houses.

"You have to get ready," she says.

"How? What should I do?"

"You can join us. We're going to a better world. We need more young girls. It's going to take a long time to get somewhere, and it's the young women who'll have to have a lot of babies on the way so we can start up the new population. We won't need a lot of men. I'm going to have all the babies I can. I'm precious. You would be too, if you joined us."

I'm thinking how lucky it is that I ran into these people.

"If I join can you teach me to read?"

"Sure, and I'm good at reading."

I can't believe my luck.

"You can't bring a dog, though. You'll have to get rid of him."

"Right now?"

Maybe I'm not as lucky as I thought.

"Well, pretty soon, anyway. You can find it a good home, though I don't suppose this world will last much longer, what with all that's been happening, but dogs don't live a long time anyway. He might die before the world ends, so that's all right."

Not so all right with me.

"Come on, they'll be glad to have you join up. I'll ask them if you can keep the dog till we leave. They'll probably say yes because, like I said, they really do want more girls like us." She says again, "We're the most important ones of all."

Turns out they do want me. I make them all happy, especially when I say I'm running away and my people wouldn't dare tell the police since I was illegal in the first place. They think I've come to the exact right spot. "Sent by God," they say. But they sure don't like Mr. O'Brien. ("That's a growing dog. He'll eat a lot.") I promise I won't ever take more than my share and I'll split my food with him. I tell them I'm used to making do with less.

Turns out Eppie . . . the girl . . . (It's short for Hephzibah. Her mother has a funny name, too, Ziporah) . . . is a bit younger than I am, she's only eleven. Turns out she and I will share a little tent behind her family's big one. Mr. O. will sleep in there with us. (Her parents sure don't want him around. He's getting not so shy and is very bouncy. I have to keep an eye on him all the time. He likes to chew shoes.)

They take me inside their spaceship and show me where I'll be living after we leave. The rooms for mothers are all along the side, and the nursery is across from them. What looks like the walls will be the floors after we get going. There's a playroom for when the babies get older. It's full of all kinds of great toys, most I never saw before in my whole life. Well, I do know my so-called parents kept me ignorant, but I didn't know how much I didn't know. But now that Eppie is teaching me to read, I'll be able to read all that. Books can tell you everything you need to know. I've got a really good start. Eppie says I'm going faster than she thought anybody could. I think I actually did learn something just looking at those books and thinking about the letters.

I do a lot of work here, but since I'm free, it's entirely different. They tell me I'm one of their best helpers because I know how to do a lot of things and I'm a pretty good cook, too, and getting better.

Those people in white have better tents than the rest of us do, and the head preacher even has the whole upstairs of the school just for his offices and living space. We listen to "our" radio station all day long. They . . . we keep asking for more money all the time, though they seem to have a lot already. They keep saying, "God will reward you for your generosity."

Meanwhile my breasts are getting bigger all the time. I'll have to get a bra some way. Eppie hasn't reached that stage yet, so I don't think I can ask her anything. I don't feel close to Eppie's mother, but she's the one, comes to me and, about another thing, too. I didn't know anything about that either, which shows how I wasn't told anything back at my so-called home. Eppie's mother keeps saying, "Isn't that nice. That means now you can have babies. We're going to need lots." She says, "I'll be taking care of you. I'm the midwife."

Things are moving right along—not only with my breasts. The scaffolding is off the spaceship and they're about to stand it up. There's a new kind of scaffolding for that. Also there's been a lot more end-of-the-world disasters—floods and earthquakes, and right here a tornado that ruined a lot of houses in town and killed eight people including a baby, but it went right around us, so everybody here knows that God is in favor of what we're doing.

There are only four young men that are supposed to be our . . . "husbands," I guess you'd call them. They're supposed to be the fathers of all the new babies. They're only bringing a few males compared to females. They said they're the best and the healthiest. Only one looks like the sort they're talking about . . . sort of a hero type . . . curly yellow hair. . . . He doesn't appeal to me at all. Too good-looking. I think I'm sort of in love with the real Mr. O'Brien. He's not handsome, but I could see on his face how kind he was. The other three "husbands" are young. One, like Eppie, is only eleven.

Then that oldest handsome boy, Jed (for Jedediah) . . . grabs me and kisses me before I hardly know what's happening. I had been out throwing the garbage in the garbage bins, and he followed me and pushed me down behind the bins. That boy . . . he goes around grinning and looking us girls over. He knows he's one of the few fathers and he's already lording it over everybody, like he thinks he's the most important person on the trip. I suppose most everybody picked to be one of the fathers would act that way, but I sure don't like it. Eppie and I feel special, too, but we don't go around as if we were queens.

Thank goodness Mr. O'Brien is with me . . . as he always is. I try to fight the boy off and then Mr. O'Brien actually bites him. Grabs his wrist and pulls him away. Draws blood. The boy kicks Mr. O. hard, but Mr. O. doesn't stop. Grabs him by his pants leg and rips it.

The boy says, "Look where he bit me."

"It's just scratches."

"You have to sew these pants up," and I say, "Okay," and he says, "Not only that, but you're going to have to do this one of these days, why not now? We can get things started."

He's been boasting about exercising every day up in the ship's gym. I could feel how strong he is. He probably was chosen for his good looks, too. I don't want to ever have a stuck-up little baby that looks like him.

"You're not the only boy that's coming."

"One of these years you'll have to pick me. That's the rule. We have to mix up our genes."

"Maybe you'll be dead before it happens. Or I will be. I hope so, anyway."

He squeezed my breasts even harder than my so-called father did back there at home. This is the first I start thinking about what really is going on here.

Just as I wished him to, Mr. O. protected me. Even bit hard enough to draw blood. I feel safe with him around.

Eppie and her family are going to be away for a couple of days while they go say good-bye to Eppie's grandparents. They have to leave Eppie's little brother with them. He can't come because of a heart murmur. Lots of others are off to say good-bye, too. People over forty aren't allowed to come. I can see why. They wouldn't last long enough.

I'm going out to find Mr. O'Brien a good home. ("The dog has got to go. We can't be a Noah's Ark. The Lord will supply the needed animals when we get there." Actually, they're bringing some cows and chickens, but just so as to have eggs and milk for the trip.) They're telling us younger ones to get ready to name all the new kinds of animals we'll find when we get there. There won't be any need for meat, so God will leave those animals out.

I don't ever need a leash. Mr. O. sticks right by me all the time. I think he remembers that I rescued him and warmed him with my own body. I'll bet he remembers sleeping in that doghouse.

He's gotten pretty big now, just as I wanted, and he'd willingly die defending me if he had to. He's exactly everything I wished for.

It's so hot, everybody in town is just sort of waiting for it to be fall and be cooler. The town is all shut up during the heat of the day. Even lots of stores are closed from noon to three. People are at the movies or sitting next to their air conditions. Some people spend a lot of time walking up and down in the big cool grocery store and the Kmart. Eppie says, "Where we're going it'll be a wonderful new world like this one used to be. God will make it so."

All around town I tell people what a great dog Mr. O. is and why I need to let him go. After a while I only try where they already have a dog. Nobody wants him, and lots of times I wouldn't want him at some of those places either.

When people find out I'm from the end-of-the-world people, they laugh at me. Turns out they call us crazies. One lady said I looked nice and neat compared to some of them, though she said Mr. O'Brien looks like he belongs with them. Then she said why didn't I clip him some so he'd be more comfortable in this heat. I hadn't thought of that. She has three dogs of her own and a big fenced-in yard, and she's really nice. She said she boarded dogs and also clipped dogs for people, and she knew I couldn't afford it but she'd clip Mr. O. for me anyway.

We went up on her closed-in porch where it was cool, and she got water for Mr. O'Brien and ice tea for me. There was a parrot there, and she told me to hold out my hand and he flew right to me. Then she got out her clippers and showed me how he should be clipped, and even let me do some of it. Mr. O. looked a lot better after we got through with him. I asked again if she wouldn't take him. She said she couldn't afford the food for such a big dog, and she said she already had two cats and the parrot and her three terriers and she needed the rest of her space for boarding. Then she says, "Why don't you take him out in the country to some farm? If I was Mr. O'Brien, I'd like to live on a farm with lots of room and work to do."

That's such a good idea. I say I'll go look right away.

"But," she says, "if I were you, I'd not go with those crazies. They really are crazies, you know. Why don't you come over here and work for me? You've got a knack with animals and I could use a helper."

I don't know what to say, so I say, "But they taught me to read."

She looks at me funny, then realizes she's staring, and looks down at Mr. O. instead, as if she doesn't know what to say either. Finally she says, "Great dog. If he were mine, I wouldn't get rid of him for anything."

I do find a good home for Mr. O. way out on a farm. They're going to change his name to Buster. I'm thinking they'd like his name if they had ever met the real Mr. O'Brien. They're going to keep him tied up until he gets used to them and to me not being there, otherwise he'd follow me back. As I leave, I hear him barking and barking, and then it changes to crying. But they said he'd get used it. They said it always takes a while. And it was cooler out there and there were other dogs and lots of other animals. I would have liked it there myself. But now I'm thinking I gave away the only thing I ever loved, and the only thing that ever loved me.

And then I worry. It was a long hot walk out of town, are they going to give him water? He needs it right away. They seemed like nice enough people, but sometimes people forget or don't notice.

As I get back to the group, here's Eppie. She can see that I've been crying. Also that Mr. O. isn't with me.

She says, "Good. You did it. That dog was just too big. I'm glad he's out of our pup tent. Can you picture him bouncing around in a spaceship!"

I have to admit he took up more than his share of the tent. I say, "I'm worried he's thirsty and they won't give him water. Maybe I should go back and check."

"Are you going to be worrying about that dog all though the whole trip?"

She's right, I *am* going to worry. I say, "Maybe I shouldn't go with you."

But then she gets all upset. "Oh, no." She practically yells it, and hugs me. "You're my best friend."

I think I'm her best friend because I'm so ignorant about the world that she can keep telling me things. I do learn a lot from her but I know some of it's wrong. Though I'm certainly grateful for those reading lessons. She wants to be a teacher and she's good at it, but I'm not really her best friend, I'm just her best and most willing pupil.

We've already packed up most of our belongings and arranged them in our staterooms. My room is next to Eppie's, just as we wanted. The rooms are small, but they have big metal mirrors so they seem larger. We had our choice of colors. I wanted mine to be all woody colors: tans and browns. I knew it would be a long time before I saw any real wood. Eppie's is yellow and blue and white. She put her favorite pictures on the walls. They had to be glued down tight. She couldn't put up pictures in the pup tent but she had these all ready to go. Funny to think of those pictures of handsome men—I guess they're movie stars—going all the way off to Paradise, where they'll be old men or dead before we even get there. I wonder why she even has them.

I guess I'd most want a picture of Mr. O., but then I'd never stop thinking about him. Except I don't want to ever stop. Besides, I don't know how to get a picture anyway.

There's a big rally our last night on Earth. They talk about the beautiful world God will lead them to, out in Proxima Centauri. They keep calling it Paradise, but the moon is out and almost full, and I don't see how any place can be more beautiful than right here. Besides, this world has Mr. O. in it. I do know my so-called father and mother would never find me on that new world, but even so, I'm not sure I want to go. Besides, Mr. O. would keep me safe. He did it before.

The preacher (dressed all raggedy, like we're all supposed to be because of renouncing worldly things). He says . . . shouts, "And so this evil world will soon burn as if it's hell itself. Parts that don't burn will be covered with water. Already dozens of islands have been lost to the sea. Soon every river will be poisoned. You know it. You know it. You see it already happening. Look at Godless New Orleans. Look at voodoo-filled Haiti. How God punished them.

"I will not be among you. I'm old and I'm not the best of the best, but you are. You're the chosen."

The moon is so bright I wouldn't even need a flashlight. There's a little breeze and it's cool for a change.

". . . and there will be the winds of a hundred hurricanes and they will last a hundred years, and the earth will shake. . . . You know it. You know it. You've seen it already."

I pretend to head to the bathrooms. Eppic says, "Wait a minute. This is the best part. He's telling about earthquakes that never stop." But I keep going.

". . . earthquakes that never stop . . . I say again *never*. Never! Imagine it. Imagine."

I reach the farm in the middle of the night. The other dogs there bark like crazy. Luckily they still have Mr. O. tied up in the front of the house. He's almost chewed through his rope. He'd have been free in another day or so. We hug and he cries with joy, and so do I. The lights go on in the house, and I untie him fast and we run, but not toward the end-of-the-world people. Maybe we can spend the night back in that doghouse.

In the doghouse we find a half-dead kitten. We can't do anything about it until morning, so we all just cuddle up together.

From now on I'm going to do the opposite of the end-of-the-world people. I'm going to take in animals, and Mr. O'Brien and this kitten are the first ones.

Except the kitten dies in the night. It was just too bitten up, and I didn't have any way to help save it. I had thought about that woman who did grooming. She'd know how to help, but it died before I could get it to her. At least it didn't have to die alone. I told it I loved it and that it was a good kitty. I hope it understood.

The end-of-the-world people leave in the morning. We hear the great roar and see the flash of their going. It lights up the whole sky. It's exciting, and for a minute I wish I was with them. I shout, and Mr. O. gives a howl. Then we run, as if to follow it.

We run. And run and run and don't care where. All of a sudden, here's that little two-room school that looks like a house. This time I don't think twice. I break a window and we fall inside, all worn out.

We lie there the rest of the day feeling sad . . . about Eppie being gone, but glad we're here together. We don't even worry about not having anything to eat. When it gets dark, we sleep.

But in the morning, we're hungry and thirsty. There's no water here that works. Everything is turned off. No electricity. I find how to turn the water on under the house. I know about that from home, but I don't know how to turn on the electricity. At least we have something to drink.

I don't know what to do or where to go or how to get food, and then I think about that lady who said I'd be a good helper.

Mrs. Sindee feeds us and I get hired and I'm going to get paid.

Things do get worse. Everybody wonders where fall got to and if it'll ever cool off. And there's earthquakes where they never had them before, even one right here, and then Mrs. Sindee gets flooded out. I help her clean up after the water goes back down. Good thing is, people go on wanting their animals clipped and boarded sometimes, and it finally does cool down. In fact it gets too cold. Mr. O'Brien and I and even Mrs. Sindee . . . we don't even care. We wear our long underwear and Mr. O'Brien grows a heavy coat of new fur.

Mr. O'Brien and I live in that old school, and so far nobody has found out. And whenever we find a wounded bird or cat or whatever, we rescue it. And everything we rescue turns out to be the best there is, just like Mr. O'Brien. We're all making do with less, but we already have seven books.

I wonder if they'll ever reach Proxima Centauri.

THE OTHER ELDER

BY **BETH REVIS**

THERE ARE THREE RULES ON *GODSPEED*. I ONLY KNOW ONE, AND I've already broken it.

Rule One: No differences allowed.

And when you're the youngest person on an interstellar spaceship, you've definitely got some differences. I grew up knowing how different I was—when I was a six-year-old boy, the next generation up was ten, and even though they should have obeyed whatever command I gave, none of the ten-year-olds would play with a six-year-old. Or maybe it wasn't just my age—maybe they wouldn't play with me because they already knew, even more than I did, that the real reason I am different isn't just my age, but also my position.

I am the Elder. Not *their* Elder, of course: I will be Elder for the future generation of children born, and I will rule them. The generation above me follows the next Elder up, and the generation above them follows Eldest. My gen won't be born until I am sixteen, and that feels forever away even though it's only three more years before the gen above me has their mating season.

The other Elder came to the Feeder Level this morning

to fetch me. This is rare—he and Eldest live on the Keeper Level. Eldest trains him and they deal with all the problems and people on the ship—the scientists, engineers, and researchers on the Shipper Level, the farmers and manufacturers on the Feeder Level. The two of them keep the ship running smoothly, and I am just the awkward kid who will maybe (absolutely must) one day become good enough to join them.

Elder's grin is lopsided when he walks up to the rabbit farm where I am living now. As a future Eldest, I am never allowed to know who my parents are or to stay with one family longer than another. I am supposed to be using my life now, before I really become an Elder, to find compassion for the people I will one day rule, by living among them, living as one of them, without staying long enough to form attachments to anyone in particular.

"You know what today means, right?" the other Elder asks me after he lifts me up in a hug.

I shake my head.

"You're coming up to the Keeper Level."

"Really?" I ask. My voice cracks over the words, but I don't care.

The other Elder nods. "I will become Eldest. And you'll be the only Elder." There is an odd note in his voice; his lips still smile but his eyes are sad.

"I can pack now," I say. "I can go up to the Keeper Level with you now."

The other Elder shakes his head. "Not yet," he says. "You need to get ready for the changing ceremony tonight."

This is the first I'd heard of it—the rabbit farms are as far away as possible from the City, and besides, the Feeders rarely celebrate anything. I'd been expecting nothing special on my birthday, and the farmers I live with now had shown no excitement.

Not that they show much of any emotion.

That is another difference I have with all the other Feeders: I *care* about things. I cried at the pig slaughter; I remember the lurch in my stomach when I saw the first calf born on the cattle ranch. But no one else shows emotion . . . and (I suspect) no one else *has* emotion. The flicker of sadness on the other Elder's face had only been noticeable because no one else on the Feeder Level had even that.

The other Elder gives me a present: new clothes, a dark set of trousers and matching tunic with red stitching on the hems. As I change clothes hurriedly, I can hear the start of something big happening outside—a sort of vibrant excitement leaking into the air. When I leave the farm with the other Elder, I can see why: everyone on the whole ship, from the Feeders to the Shippers, is gathering in the garden behind the Hospital.

On a ship somewhere between two inhabitable planets, there's not much wasted space. The Hospital garden is the only exception. It's the only place on the ship where flowers grow instead of food, where the paths meander aimlessly rather than going straight between the City and the farms, where there is nothing to *do* except *be*. It is one of my favorite places on the whole ship, in part because so few people ever come here.

Not today, though. Today, the garden overflows with nearly two thousand people. They stand in the flower beds, crushing the blooms. They spill out onto the lawn beside the Hospital, all the way to the heavy, metal wall on the side, painted blue and dotted with rivets. Even though the Feeders almost never show any emotion besides *calm*, today they are chatting, alert, eager; and the Shippers, who've descended from the level above this one for the celebration, are practically vibrating with anticipation.

"What's going on?" I ask the other Elder in a quiet voice. He steers me away from the garden and toward the grav tube, a fairly recent invention on the ship, makes traveling between the levels simpler.

Eldest is waiting for us at the base of the tube. He's wearing the Eldest Robe—a long, elaborately embroidered robe that holds all the hopes of our society. I have only seen it once before, long ago, when I first started asking questions about why I was shuffled from home to home, why I was at least four years younger than everyone else and no one was born after me, why I was, in short, *different*, when the very first rule of the ship was not to be.

The Eldest Robe is decorated with the dreams of the whole ship: fertile fields on the hem, open skies at the shoulders. When *Godspeed* left Sol-Earth, it was bound for a new home in a new world, but in the meantime, *Godspeed* became our home. Generations later, the ship is still in transit, but even though we are caged behind the curving metal walls, we have not forgotten our dreams for a sky that never ends.

Eldest smiles at me, and his face holds the same sort of sadness as the other Elder's had. He is truly the oldest man on the entire ship. His age gives him wisdom, and his presence gives us all strength. When he strides toward us, his shoulders are thrown back, and he carries the weight of the robe as if it is nothing, even though I feel certain that it would suffocate and crush me.

"Are you ready?" Eldest asks the other Elder when he sees me. The other Elder doesn't nod; he just gives him a sort of grim smile.

Eldest looks down at me next. Judgment clouds his eyes. I try to stand as straight as possible. "You're not ready," he says simply, and I cave in on myself on the inside, though I force my spine to stay straight and stiff.

Eldest strides past us, toward the garden and the buzzing crowd of people waiting. "Elder," he says, and the other Elder rushes forward to walk next to him. I trail behind them both; I'm used to following them. "No," Eldest tells him. "You're no longer Elder after today. I meant the other one."

The other Elder grabs my arm and pulls me forward. I am practically running to keep up with Eldest's quick pace. "You know what the three most important rules of *Godspeed* are, right?"

I nod, but he's not looking down at me—he's looking over at the crowd of people. "I know the first one," I say. The other Elder had told me the same day I was shown the Eldest Robe for the first time, but that was the only lesson I'd learned so far in my training to be the future Eldest.

"No differences," Eldest says. "It is a good rule, and the first developed by the original Eldest."

I know this. When the ship had been sailing between worlds for several generations, a terrible plague had wiped out most of the population. *Godspeed* herself almost died. But a leader rose up to become the Eldest, reestablish rule, and set us on the path to recovery.

"The second rule," Eldest says, "is that our society will fail without a strong, central leader. The Eldest and Elder system is in place for the entire society. All that we do—all that we *are*—is necessary for survival."

He stops now, and it takes me a few steps to stop myself, too. He looks down at me. His eyes search mine, but I'm not sure what he's looking for.

"Remember that," he says.

It hangs in the air between us, as bright as the stars embroidered on the robe.

Rule Two: The ship must have one strong, central leader to survive.

And he marches into the crowd of people gathered at the garden. Everyone surrounds the statue in the middle—a bigger-than-life-size statue of the first Eldest, his arms spread wide in benevolence. My Eldest stands under the statue too, but his arms hang limply by his side, weighted down with the elaborate robe.

The other Elder drags me through the crowd and places me on Eldest's left side. "You don't have to do anything," he whispers. "Just stand there." He turns to go, then turns back to me. "It'll be better if you don't watch. Look at the ceiling instead."

I shoot him a glance, but the other Elder has already moved on, around to the other side of Eldest, so he stands by his right. I look up at them both. They are exactly the same height, with the same strong chin and heavy brows and piercing eyes. But neither of them spare a glance at me.

Eldest looks up, and when he does, he seems to grow taller. I had not noticed before that he slouched, but now, with his eyes bouncing from person to person in the crowd, I realized that, yes, he does feel the pressure, that crushing, swallow-you-whole sort of pressure I've felt since I first learned that I would one day take the robe and responsibilities of the man beside me.

"My people," he says, and with those two words alone, he has all two thousand sets of eyes on him. They are *his* people, truly.

And then he stops. It's as if the words have been choked out of him—his eyes are red and watery, his throat closes up. His gaze flicks to mine, and I see in his face the words he spoke to me moments ago: Rule Two.

Eldest swallows and turns back to the crowd. "I have been honored to be yours. All that I have done—all that I have been— has been for you. All of you." He swallows again. "And now I am spent. My purpose has played. It is time for a new Eldest to take the robe."

There is silence now. I look out at the crowd. The Feeders are calm, curious, but the Shippers' excitement is not the happy anticipation I'd thought they had. It's more like dread, as if they suspected and feared what would happen, but know it is inevitable.

Eldest raises his hand. Between his fingers, I see a black med patch. The small one-inch square of fabric is embedded with tiny needles with which to inject medicine. Lavender patches cure headaches, green ones fix stomachaches, yellow wakes you up, blue puts you to sleep. But I've never seen a black one before.

"Follow your Eldest, and you cannot lose your way," Eldest says. He presses the patch into his skin.

The other Elder steps forward as Eldest crumples. I move toward him to help, but the other Elder holds an arm out to stop me.

The other Elder says something, I don't know what, all my senses are focused on the way Eldest doesn't blink, staring at nothing, and the way the corner of his mouth twitches twice and then stills, and the way his fingers curl and then freeze, as if he's trying to grasp the air.

The other Elder stops speaking. My neck moves up slowly, slowly, not quite believing what I'm seeing. The other Elder swoops down on Eldest, and at first I think he's going to harm him, but I see that his eyes are soft and his touch is gentle. He removes the Eldest Robe, slipping it from his shoulders and stretching out Eldest's body, not just to gather the cloth of the robe up, but also to make Eldest look natural, comfortable.

Eldest's eyes still stare up.

The other Elder straightens, and with one clean, swift movement, twirls the robe around his own shoulders. "An Eldest dies for his people," he says, fastening the robe around his neck. "An Eldest lives for his people." He takes a step forward.

"Eldest!" the Shippers shout, and there is some sadness in their voices raised as one.

A moment later, the Feeders repeat, "Eldest!" and there is no emotion at all behind the volume.

The other Elder—the new Eldest—turns to me. "Come with me," he says.

The crowd parts around him. Doctors descend on the man

lying under the statue of the Plague Eldest, but they are not there to help him. They leave the black patch on his neck; it has already done what it was meant to do. Instead, they bundle the body up in a plain white sheet and start to take it away for disposal in the stars.

I keep my eyes on the robe, not the man now wearing it. I think about how one day when I assume the leadership of *Godspeed* from him, I will take this very robe after he takes his own life. And then I think how the Elder after me will pull the robe from my dead body.

People die. I know this. The grays will die, one by one, as they reach their sixties. They will go to the hospital, and they will not leave it. I know this; it is what happens. But I've never seen death. And I never knew the Eldests chose it.

Med patches are tiny, almost weightless, but I can already feel one boring into my neck.

The man in the robe—I must think of him as Eldest now, he *is* Eldest now, but I can't bear the thought of what made him Eldest— he pushes through the crowd and back toward the grav tube. He opens his mouth several times, as if to tell me something, but he never speaks. I can't tell if his face is full of sorrow or pride or fear or something else, but I'm pretty sure mine's just full of shock.

When we get to the grav tube, Eldest pauses. He looks at the base, perhaps remembering the way the old Eldest climbed down it to go to the garden and die, just the opposite of how this new Eldest is climbing up to it in order to live on the Keeper Level.

"Your training begins today," Eldest says, still looking at the grav tube base.

"No kidding."

He spares me a knowing smile, then commands the tube to take him to the Keeper Level. It sucks him up, and he's gone before I can blink. I step up onto the base as well. For a moment, I turn and look out at the Feeder Level. This is the largest level of the whole ship, with acres and acres of farmland, all wrapped in steel and soaring through space. This is what we need to survive—farms and produce and even livestock.

This is my kingdom.

Or, it will be. And even though I've grown up knowing that I was in line to rule, I never quite realized that it meant . . . all of this.

I command the tube to take me up, too. The grav tube manipulates the simulated gravity on the ship, enabling my body to rush upward much faster than the elevator in the hospital. I strain to keep my eyes open, focused on the green and brown of the Feeder Level, but soon I'm sucked all the way up to the Keeper Level.

I'd been there before, but not like this. Not when I was the only Elder.

Eldest waits on me. The tube ends in a small room with a wooden table—a *real* wooden table, an antique relic from Sol-Earth, where they had trees—and blue plastic chairs and an ancient-looking globe. Eldest slips the robe from his shoulders and breathes a sigh of relief. The robe drops and crumples, just like the old Eldest did.

"I'm sorry," he says "I wanted to warn you but Eldest said it would be better to say nothing . . . to let you experience it blind, so to speak."

He sees my eyes staring at the robe, remembering who else wore it. He bends down and carefully picks it up, smoothing out the wrinkles and folding it until it no longer holds the shadow of a dead man inside. He lays the robe on the table.

"This is the Learning Center. We'll begin proper lessons here."

"I've had lessons."

"You've had some."

Eldest opens the door to the Learning Center, and I see a giant room with a curved ceiling. "This is the great room," Eldest says simply, and he turns to a nearby door. "This is my chamber now," he says. "And this is yours." He nods for me to open the door, so

I roll my thumb over the biometric scanner and watch as it zips open.

The room has been neatly made up, and there are two bags sitting in the center of the bed. My belongings—clothes, a few mementos. I'm ashamed to note that the old blanket, the one I've had since I was a baby, is draped over the second bag. I don't want Eldest to think I'm a baby.

Eldest moves forward, so I go all the way inside the room. He steps around me and sits down on the bed, picking up the blanket and fiddling with it. I wish he wouldn't. I wish he'd pretend it's not there, that mangy, holey scrap of cloth.

"When *Godspeed* left Sol-Earth," Eldest says, twisting the fabric between his fingers, "we had a clear mission. Our ancestors were to run the ship and, while it traveled, develop new, better ways to colonize the planet when it eventually lands on Centauri-Earth. Originally, the Feeder Level was designed for biological and agricultural research. The Shipper Level was for other scientific research. This, the Keeper Level, was used for navigation and offices for the captain of the ship."

We have no captain now. Instead, we have Eldest.

"Of course, *Godspeed* is essentially a biodome. We are a self-sustaining environment, able to produce the necessities of life in a constant cycle. But our original mission was not just to find the new planet in the Centauri star system: it was to take the methods of Sol-Earth—the science and philosophy and everything else— and make it better. Our ancestors were creating a perfect world, an enclosed world, where we could become the perfect people. We separated ourselves from Sol-Earth and Sol-Earth's problems, and we became a society worthy of the new planet."

He puts the blanket down on the bed.

"There are three rules on *Godspeed*," he says, meeting my eyes.

"I only know two of them."

"Tell me."

I don't know why—does he want me to remember the second rule now, the way Eldest told it to me before he died?

"Rule one: No differences. Rule two: Without a leader, the ship will fail."

"Rule three," Eldest says. "No one is allowed individual thought."

I narrow my eyes at him. "What?" I say.

"Haven't you noticed? The Feeders. How empty, emotionless they are? We have ways to control them."

Something inside of me lurches, a sick feeling not in my stomach, but deeper, a feeling that makes me want to expel myself from myself. "They're controlled?"

"They have to be. Elder, you know the size of this ship. You know the importance for control."

I think back to the "celebration" and remember the way the Shippers seemed to know what the old Eldest was about to do before he did it. "What about the Shippers?"

"We need labor to feed us, and we need minds to keep us moving forward. The Feeders have what they need: strength and obedience. The Shippers have what they need: intelligence."

The way he says "need" strikes a chord deep within me. "Genetic modification?"

Eldest nods. "Among other things. Whatever it takes to maintain control."

"You . . ." I taste bile in the back of my throat. "You're a monster!"

Eldest smiles sadly and stands up from the bed. On the dresser beside it is a digital membrane screen. With a swipe of his finger, the screen comes to life. Eldest taps on it quickly, scans his thumbprint for access, and taps again.

"This was the ship before the first Eldest," he says, handing the screen to me. While I look down at it, Eldest walks out of the bedroom, and the door zips closed behind him.

"Locked," the computer by the door chirps.

I drop the screen on the bed and roll my thumb over the biometric scanner. "Access denied," the computer chirps.

Shite. Eldest has locked me in here with my thoughts and whatever is flashing on the screen.

I hit the door once, hard; hard enough to make my hand hurt. I pick the screen back up with my other hand.

These are vid feeds from across the ship. The people here are all different—different ages, different sizes, different skin and hair colors. There's no sound, just visual, but I can tell that there's vibrancy in their lives, something beautiful and strange that I've . . . I've never seen before.

But it's also terrible.

Because they're all fighting.

It is worse because there is no sound. The vids switch from camera to camera, flashing different scenes. I recognize some things—the Hospital is the same, but there is no garden, no statue. Instead, there are people—wounded, brutalized, bleeding, broken people. The City has all the same buildings in the vids as there is now, but they are cluttered and filled to the breaking point. Some are on fire—and I think about the new buildings in the weaving district, and how this is the reason why they are new.

And over and through it all: fighting.

Groups form. I recognize some of the same people—I start to seek them out in the vids, watch the way they fight, see who they are fighting with. This is a battle.

A battle for the ship.

Eldest made it seem like the mission of the ship was to separate ourselves from the past—but it seems to me as if the past followed us here.

There are two people who show up over and over again. One is a woman—a tall, dark, wild-haired woman who always wears red. The people who follow her also mark themselves with red—scarves on their arms, bandannas around their heads, even just threads woven into the fabric on the hems.

I look down at the clothes Eldest gave me today. Black—with red stitching at the hem.

The other person who shows up is a man. He has long salt-and-pepper hair that hangs from his skull like a curtain. He's very, very tall, with a heavy brow and fat lips. His color is white.

Some of the vids are backed up, shot from a distance—and I'm grateful for it. Then I can blur my eyes and see the people as dots of reds fighting dots of white. But some of the videos are very close. I see their faces then.

There are more people in white than red. The man stays in the City, gathering people around him. But the wild-haired woman stays on the other side of the ship, near the Recorder Hall and the Hospital, and though there are fewer people with her, they are fiercer fighters. They are smart and ruthless.

I lean up, my back stiff. I don't know how much time has passed. I'd forgotten that the door was locked, I'd forgotten even the reason why I was here, and the strangeness of the day I'd just had. I'm focused on the vids.

Because I care.

I care about that wild woman. I care about what happens to her. I want her to win.

This is so strange. To see a battle on the place you thought was perfectly peaceful. To watch a rabbit field through a red-colored film because blood splattered the camera.

When a woman in red—a petite thing with short choppy hair—is killed by a man (a boy? He can't be much older than I am), the wild-haired woman leaps up and strangles the boy-man with her bare hands. There is such fierceness in her eyes, such murderous passion, that she chokes him long after he stops moving, chokes him until a man in red pulls her off and drags her away.

Even though I've come to know their faces, I realize that now I'm knowing their lives. The wild-haired woman is fighting with everything she has, and with the death of the other woman, she has very little left.

The videos are dark when the man in white leads a march across the Feeder Level from the City toward the wild-haired woman's base behind the Hospital, where the garden is. Many have died—so many that I have little wonder now why there are empty buildings in the City, unoccupied homes. The man in white marches resolutely. He goes right by a camera once, and his face, though marred by shadows, also shows a hard mouth. He doesn't look happy; he doesn't thrill in the battle.

He has the same sad look that the old Eldest gave me just before he slapped the black patch over his neck.

The wild-haired woman wakes up too late. She was not expecting the attack. The men and women in white rush over those in red like a violent, terrible wave. Red stands to fight, but white won't relent, and they are pushed farther and farther back.

Until they are up against the wall.

That's the problem, isn't it? We're all on a ship. A ship soaring across the universe, that's not on the old Earth, but not on the new one, either.

There's nowhere to go.

The wild-haired woman realizes it the same time I do. I can see it in her eyes. I can see it in the way she almost puts down the blade she's fighting with . . . but doesn't.

She's against the wall, and she won't stop.

It's not the man in white who kills her. He's not fighting—he's already celebrating his inevitable victory. No, it's some other boy-man who I don't recognize. Some anonymous fighter, too young to have fought in many of these fast and furious battles, who slips a slender knife past the wild-haired woman's defenses and slides it across the smooth skin of her neck, quick and neat, like a butcher (which I realize he might have been).

And then she's dead.

Just like Eldest.

But not like Eldest—because instead of just giving up the mantle, she clung to it until it was ripped from her. I pick at the red stitching in my shirt, prouder of it than of the Eldest Robe.

The door zips open. Eldest stands, hesitant, a plate of food in one hand. "Are you done?" he asks.

My stomach roars as I stand. "Yeah."

He hands me the plate, and we sit on the bed, the video screen between us as it fades to nothing.

"So you see now?"

I nod as I take a bite.

"We have to use control. We have to prevent something like this from ever happening again."

"The way she died . . . And she was the source of the Eldest system?" I say, my mind still on the blossoming line of red dripping into the neck of her red tunic, darkening it until the red cloth is almost black.

"She?" Eldest asks. "No, it's the man, the man in white—he was the first Eldest. He won. His rule is our rule."

My food tastes dry, and I lower the plate. I should have realized—obviously, the woman's death meant she'd lost, but I'd forgotten that such a noble death also meant that of course she was the other side, the bad side, the side we're trying to prevent from happening again.

And I remember the look in the wild-haired woman's eyes when she killed the man who killed the petite woman. Yes—the

Feeders don't have the bloodthirsty viciousness that made her hands squeeze the life from a man, but their eyes also don't have the love she had when she saw the woman die.

I am a product of the man in white, not the woman in red. I am from the side that won, the controlled, even march across the ship to press the passionate, angry, fighting people against the walls until their blood stained the metal the same red as the shirts they wore.

"The first Eldest saw what violent emotions can cause. The woman in red is exactly what we're trying to prevent from happening again. Did you see how close she was? How close to chaos she brought the whole ship? Don't you see how *dangerous* that was?"

"Yes," I admit, but my voice is laced with anger. "But I don't see how that's wrong!"

Eldest looks at me as if he doesn't recognize me. "If we didn't control the people, if we didn't have the Eldest system, if the three rules didn't exist, the ship would fall to mutiny and war. We cannot let people have the same sort of passion that led to this." He sighs, his face full of regret. "We're . . . trapped. It's easier to forget how very alone we are but . . . there's not that many of us. It's only through the Eldest system that we've survived so far."

I can see why he's showing me this. I understand the lesson he wants me to learn. He wants me to see that passion is bad, that chaos is evil, and anything as intense as the wild-haired woman's eyes were when she watched the other woman die can kill everyone on board this ship.

But . . . I don't think that's a bad thing.

I mean, yeah. The death. That part was bad. But the fire in her eyes?

I've never seen fire like that.

Ever.

Even in myself.

"This can't be wrong," I say slowly, to myself—I'd forgotten that Eldest was there until he moves, and I notice he's watching me intently. But that's not fire in his eyes—it's something cold and hard.

"This sort of passion," I go on, "it can't be wrong. It makes evil things, yes, the battles were terrible, the blood . . . but. But. It was worth it. It was." My fingers curl into fists. "It can't have been for nothing. It can't have."

"It wasn't," Eldest says. "It gave us the Eldest system. We had to purge that sort of thing from our lives, and then we could become this society. This perfect society."

"I don't want perfect! I don't want control!"

Eldest stands. Slowly. He takes my plate even though I've eaten only a few bites. He walks out of the room. He locks the door.

"You can't make me rule a society that has all the—the *passion* taken out of it!" I roar, racing to the door. "I'm Elder! I rule after you! I won't control the people as you do. You can't make me con-trol them like that!"

I punch the door hard, denting the metal. But it doesn't zip open.

Rule Three: No individual thought.

"Are you scared?" the Eldest asked the young Elder, more boy than man. The older Elder stood off to one side, allowing the old man a chance to speak directly to the boy before facing the crowd gathered in the garden.

Elder shakes his head, but it's a lie. He is. He doesn't know what to expect.

Eldest cinches the robe around his shoulders.

"This is the changing ceremony. I will step down. You will step up. This has all happened many times before." He arranges the cloth over him so the embroidery lies flat. In his palm is a black med patch.

"How many Eldests have there been?" Elder asks.

"Countless." Eldest takes a deep breath. The patch feels cold in his hand, the med side up. He imagines how it will feel when he presses it against his neck.

"You're going to see a series of vids today, after the ceremony. Watch them carefully. You will need to figure out what they mean. Sometimes . . . sometimes it's hard to know what is right and what is wrong. But you are Elder. You will one day be Eldest. And you will know what is right by watching the vids and seeing the price we pay for the ship to live."

Elder plays with the red stitching at the hem of his tunic. "Did you know what was right?"

Eldest straightens his spine, throws back his shoulders, feels the tension stiffening his neck. "I didn't at first," he says. "But . . . I came to see the truth." His eyes pierce Elder's. "You will too. And the Elder after you. And the Elder after him."

"Forever," whispers Elder.

Eldest nods. He remembers the wild-haired woman, the way her eyes flashed red with blood and love. He wonders how many Elders protested their first day of training . . . how many—if any— never stopped protesting, were like the woman who didn't give up until her blood splashed the walls, and would rather die than become the man who took away violence at the cost of passion. It's true there had been . . . aberrations in the past. He did not find this out until after he had accepted his role; only a generation ago, an Elder had protested the system and had been quickly and quietly replaced.

But he also knows—now that time has passed and the memory of that first day has faded, that he had been right to wrap the robe around himself, just as the black patch felt right in his hand, now, and would feel right later this day, when he pressed it against his neck.

"Forever."

THE GREAT GAME AT THE END OF THE WORLD

BY **MATTHEW KRESSEL**

THE CREEPY PLAYING SECOND BASE IS A HELL OF A FIELDER, but his arm's for shit, so they can forget about the double play. My sister Jenna swings a doughnutted bat in the on-deck circle, chewing strawberry gum we found in the drawer of a wrecked house, her Mets cap turned around backward, her yellow hair flowing in the constant breeze. Seeing her like this makes me happy. She shouts at the Ken up at bat, "You'd better hit the goddamned ball, loser!" Mom wouldn't ever let that language fly. Jenna's only ten. But I let it slide. Lately, I let everything slide.

The Creepies' pitcher looks like a seven-foot-tall furless cat with giant yellow eyes that glow no matter what angle you look at them, and rows and rows of toothpick teeth longer than my fingers. But her arm's the real killer. She's struck out four batters already, and it's only the third inning. (These Creepies learn fast.) Bottom of the third inning, actually, and the last. Three innings was all we could coax from these creatures who seem to be more interested in the strange stars spinning wildly above the field than the game. Its Jenna, me, the Kens and Barbies vs. the Creepies, and we're down 1–0.

The Ken at bat just stands there as the pitch whizzes by. "Strike three!" calls the ump, a three-foot scaly fish with batlike wings. His voice is like frogs dying. Two outs. Jenna throws her bat to the ground. Its clank echoes from the home-run walls. "You idiot! You stupid jerk! You goddamned jerk! Why couldn't you hit the ball?"

I cautiously approach my sister. Last week, she swung at me, got me right in the balls. But I've forgiven her. I forgive everything now. "Hey, hey. It's all right. We still have a chance," I say. My hand falls on her shoulder, but she shoves it away.

"No! He should have hit the ball, Russell! Three pitches right down the middle and he just stood there! He's so stupid!"

The Kens and Barbies are more than stupid, they're empty. Literally. They look like ordinary people, except at certain angles you can see right through them, and they glow like streetlights in fog. And they also do whatever you ask them, because there's nothing much left inside to tell them otherwise. (It was easy herding a bunch of them to play this game.) I turn Jenna around, lean in to face her. "You're up. You can do this."

"She's too fast. I'll strike out."

"I've seen you hit the ball. You're amazing. Show them what we are."

"That was *before*. I'm nothing now." She falls to her knees, runs her hand through the dirt.

A green monster like a seven-legged Incredible Hulk runs across the field and leaps over the home-run fence into the starry abyss. A moment later, a huge flying hairless ferret-thing arcs over the field, snatches up the monster, and flaps away into the stars. The monster screams, trailing a rain of golden blood. Jenna doesn't look up.

I squat down and lift her chin. Her eyes are as red as stoplights. "You're not nothing, Jenna. You're everything to me."

She frowns, points a shaking finger up. "*He* says I'm nothing. He says we're all nothing, doesn't he?"

I look at a sky filled with too-bright stars (even though the sun is up and shining) at the giant pieces of earth that drift lazily overhead—entire towns and cities uprooted and tossed into space, never to fall back down. What can I say to comfort her?

"It's your turn, Jenna. You have to play."

Ten weeks earlier, the afternoon of my first day of ninth grade, I lined up my bike behind a dozen other kids, waiting my turn to trick out on the Track. That was our name for the curvy, jump-laden BMX bike course some kids had built years back, with shovels and dirt in the wooded preserve. Each year, some parent inevitably got wind of it, had the town bulldoze it flat. And each year, some industrious kids rebuilt it, with improvements on the original design. Far from the eyes of parents or cops, the Track had become a sacred place, where kids could shred without helmets or pads, smoke cigarettes, and make out behind the trees.

Everyone who was anyone was here, decked out in their new threads. It seemed as if every kid had remade himself for the new year. I felt like anything was possible, that I too could make myself into whatever I wanted.

My friend Vinny (new Adidas pants and sneakers, Lakers cap) leaned in close on his bike and excitedly showed me a picture of what was supposed to be Pamela Huston's cleavage. With careful pinches, Vinny vigorously zoomed in and out on the screen of his cell phone, as if there were some cosmic secret hidden in the pixels. All I saw was a blotch of color.

"Dude," he said, "she sits right next to me. I am so going to love math this year."

To show him up, I whipped out my new Droid. Four calls from Mom, and two messages, but I ignored them and waited impatiently as my Web page trickled in. Last night, I'd created six new levels for the game Nimbus, an opensourced first-person shooter that had become more popular than Jesus over the past few months. "Check out this crazy maze I built. No one's getting out of this death trap."

"Dude, you're such a geek!" Vinny said. "I'm showing you tits and you're showing me your *game levels*?"

I felt disappointed. I'd spent hours building worlds in Nimbus, and Vinny was usually excited to see them. I slipped my phone back in my pocket.

Vinny twisted his head with his hands, looked like he was trying to tear it from his skull. I heard a crack. When some people are anxious, they crack their knuckles. Vinny cracked his neck. "So why are we here, again?"

I spotted Maeve and Elsa walking toward us, all dolled up in their brightly colored knee-length jackets, trying to avoid getting dirt on the new fabric. I gestured at them with my chin. "Maeve's in my world studies class," I said. Just saying her name made my heart skip a beat. "I told her I bike, and she got all excited."

My phone buzzed. My mom again. I sent her to voice mail.

"Oh, so that's why you dragged me here with these douchebags." Vinny whispered. "Maeve *is* a hottie. I'd totally like to—"

"Shut up!" I said. "Here they come. Don't be a dick. Girls don't like that."

"What? Girls don't like my dick?" He smiled wickedly at me.

"Shut up!"

I'd had a crush on Maeve since spring of last year, when we

shared a square dance circle in gym class. Her hands had been so warm. But back then she'd been with Christopher Black, a kid who liked to wear plaid and who probably should have started shaving in seventh grade but had let his peach fuzz grow until it resembled a patch of blond mold. Rumor had it that they'd broken up over the summer, and since then I tried to learn everything I could about her.

"Hi, Vin. Hi, Russ," Maeve said, smiling. Her cheeks were pink with cold, her black bob of hair half hidden by a gray knitted cap with tassels. Elsa ran a finger slowly around her hoop earrings. Both girls wore Ray-Ban glasses (prescription), which had, for some reason, become the Most-Necessary-Thing™ over the summer, and now all the girls whose moms could afford to buy them sported a pair. Maeve's cherry red ones made her look like a punked-out NASA engineer. "Are you up soon?" she said.

In my best attempt at laid-back cool, I said, "Yeah, after Mi--ke." But my voice cracked like I'd just hit puberty.

"Frog in your *thr--oat*?" Elsa said, mocking me. The girls giggled. My face grew hot, and I fumbled to save myself.

"What my castrato friend here is trying to say," Vinny said, "is, wait till you see his backside. Backside *air*, that is."

I shook my head, but the girls laughed, and all was well again. Maeve stared at me. She looked expectant, her irises the color of fall grasses, a swirl of green and brown, and pupils dark pits that threatened to suck me in forever.

She let slip a shy, wonderful little smile at me. I couldn't think of anything to say, so I just cheered as Eric Kellerman landed a jump. I sucked at flirting, and my hacking skills weren't going to get me girls anytime soon. But I kicked ass at BMX. I had a growing reputation in the school as "That A-track kid who bikes." I preferred that to the previous year's moniker of "That nerd who hangs out with Vinny." And I thought if I tricked out a bit in front of Maeve, got some sick air, then maybe she'd be impressed; and if the afternoon went really well, we'd go behind the trees and . . .

My heart hammered. This was going to be a good year.

"I heard you were good," Elsa said. She whipped out a pack of Marlboro lights from her pocket and lit the last one, the one turned around for good luck.

Maeve smiled and swayed restlessly, the tassels of her hat swinging back and forth against her head like a Tibetan drum. "Can you do a full twirl?" she said.

"You mean a three-sixty?" I blushed. "Sure."

"Awesome," she said. "I love that."

I couldn't believe she was paying this much attention to me, that both girls were. I had shed my nerdiness like I'd shed junior high. I couldn't stop smiling.

Vinny poked me in the arm and said, "Dude, is that who I think it is?"

I turned to see a frazzled woman, dressed in green scrubs, walking between the kids and their bikes. Her presence here was impossible, and for a moment it didn't register. Then I remembered the phone calls.

"Russell? Is Russell Broward here?" Everyone turned to look at her, then me.

"Oh, god!" I whispered. I turned my back, pretending not to hear, hoping she'd vanish.

"Russ-ell?" She sounded like she was calling for a lost dog. She spotted me, stormed right across the Track, and Eric Kellerman nearly clobbered her as he came around the turn.

"Is that your mom?" Maeve said. She squinted at me.

"*My* mom? Oh, uh . . . *yeah.*"

"You told her about the Track?"

Maeve pushed her glasses up her nose as if taking me in. I don't think she liked what she saw. I couldn't see her irises anymore, only the dull gray rectangles of reflected sky.

My mom strode up to us and put her hands on her hips. She took a long look at Elsa, who hid her cigarette behind her back. Then Mom turned to me. "Why didn't you answer my calls? I thought I told you to come home after school!"

"What are you doing here?" I snapped.

Her hair was a mangled mess and her lipstick had missed her lips, fallen on her cheek. Ever since Dad had died two years back, she always had the appearance of going somewhere and never arriving. "They called me to cover a shift and I need you to babysit your sister."

"Now?"

"Yes, *now*, Russell. And where's your helmet?" She looked around. "All you kids should be wearing helmets." She stared at Elsa, who had been trying not to giggle. "Does your mother know you smoke? You know teenage smoking increases your risk of breast cancer seventy percent?"

Oh, god. This wasn't happening.

Elsa said, "My *mom* buys me all my packs."

Maeve laughed, but quickly silenced herself when my mother glared at her.

"Come on, Russell!"

Humiliated, I muttered good-bye to them.

"Later, man," Vinny said mournfully. Elsa seemed annoyed, and Maeve frowned. I heard Elsa mock, "'Teenage smoking increases your risk of breast cancer seventy percent!'" Someone shouted, "Mommy says Russell can't come out and play!" and a bunch of kids laughed.

I hung my head as I followed my mom through the trees and out onto the road, where her Honda CR-V idled. Jenna was sitting in the backseat, playing Derek Jeter's World of Baseball on her pink pocket console as my mom opened the hatchback. I threw my bike in, got in the passenger seat, slammed the door.

"I don't like your attitude, Russell!"

I was on the verge of tears. "You couldn't call a stupid babysitter?"

"I'm sorry, Russell, but there was no one else."

The tires screeched as we pulled away. I looked into the backseat, Jenna in her pink jacket playing her pink handheld game. She was humming happily to herself. I wanted to scream.

"I left money on the table. You can order a pizza. I want you in bed by eleven, your sister by nine. And no playing video games till your homework's done."

Jenna said, "Let's play baseball when we get home! Mom bought me a new mitt."

"I'm not playing with you, loser!"

"Hey! Don't you dare talk to your sister that way!" Mom said. "You'll play with her or no video games for a month."

I crossed my arms and sulked, and Jenna returned her attention to her pocket game. "You're not like him," she said.

"What?"

"Dad would always play with me when I asked."

Mom sighed deeply as she raced down Ocean Avenue toward home, speeding through a yellow light. Just ten minutes ago, my high school future had held so much promise. Now everyone would be talking about Russell Broward, the kid whose mom picks him up from the Track. I'd be a dork in their eyes forever.

"I hate you," I whispered.

"What did you say?"

We zoomed past three kids popping wheelies, laughing as they raced toward the preserve. "I so hate you both."

Jenna's tears have run out, which is good because the white-skinned Creepy in left field has begun to dig up the grasses and vomit jewels into the holes. The others are fidgeting too. This game won't last much longer. Jenna stands, wipes her cheeks, and with a jab to the ground, frees the bat of its doughnut. I straighten her hat, give her my best smile, and pat her backside as she steps up to the plate.

The catcher is some sort of shapeless ball of worms, which reminds me of the squirming things I once found in our cat Lucifer's shit, but this Creepy is exceptionally good at catching the ball and returning it to the yellow-eyed pitcher on cue. It says to Jenna, "Your not-rot is repulsive to us," which I assume is some sort of insult intended to upset her hitting ability.

(Yeah, these Creepies learn fast.)

Jenna steps into the batter's box, and the many-toothed cat tosses three pitches—all balls, the umpire declares. Jenna takes them with the steadiness of a mountain.

The next pitch. Jenna swings. For a ten-year-old she's got quite the upper-body strength. The ball makes a metallic ping as it connects with the bat, flies over my head to crash into the windshield of a car.

"Foul ball," the umpire declares, and distantly, something not quite human screams.

"C'mon Jenna! You can hit the ball!" I cheer. "No pitcher! No pitcher!"

The pitcher's eyes flicker like moonlit gold.

She takes the pitch. It's clearly high and outside, but the umpire calls, "Strike two!"

"What?!" I storm toward him, cursing. "That was totally high and away!"

"Step away from me," the fish-creature says. "Or I will devour your immortal self." He spreads his batlike wings, and on his scaly

137

hide I see dozens of tiny faces crying out in pain. I leap back, horrified.

"Don't worry, Russell, I've got this," Jenna says, and her defiance centers me. "These Creepies got nothing on me."

"Who you calling creepy?" the worm-creature says.

I step back to my place beside the dugout as the pitcher lofts the next pitch. I hold my breath as Jenna swings . . . and connects! A line drive flies over the second baseman's head, to land in right field. Jenna screams with joy and sprints to first. A Creepy made of a thousand hands with eyeballs in their palms fields the ball. It catapults it to the shortstop, covering second by rolling end over end. I tell Jenna to hold up at first.

She's the tying run. We may win this game after all.

"I hit it! I did it!" Jenna screams, over and over. She falls to the ground, hysterically laughing—or crying. I can't tell which.

Three weeks after that awful first day of school, the leaves had fallen, and so had my hopes of being anything other than what I was last year, that nerd who hung out with Vinny. I went to the Track a few times, but Maeve was never there, and when I passed her in the hall, she just nodded politely and kept on walking. Whenever I brought up the subject with Vinny, he just cracked his neck and said, "Tragic."

As Mr. Verini droned on about the Peloponnesian War, I stared out the window at the approaching black clouds. I hoped for a violent thunderstorm, something to break my boredom. I watched Maeve's left hand scrawl out neatly written notes and wondered how it was possible to sit so close to her and yet be so far away. Last week I'd heard she started dating Eric Kellerman, and I couldn't help but wonder if I'd stayed at the Track that first day of school, it would have been me.

I decided that when I got home I'd trash the new Nimbus game levels I'd created, even if they did give Vinny a hard-on. They bored me, and I had ideas for new ones, better ones, with hundred-story skyscrapers, and bridges that spanned chasms of fire. I started to sketch them out in my notebook, when our classroom shook with thunder.

The lights flickered. Diana Golina yelped, and the class laughed. "Settle down," Mr. Verini said. He resumed his lesson. He would not be thwarted by mere weather. But the next tremor knocked the corkboard from the wall, and a look of worry crossed his face. I glanced at Maeve, whose mouth was open as if to speak.

Then it happened.

A tremendous groan and screech, like a battleship being torn in two. The lights sparked and went out. Everyone screamed. In the twilight I saw a wall come rushing toward me. I panicked, covered my head.

I must have passed out, because when I opened my eyes, everything was quiet. My legs were covered with broken cinder blocks, but somehow my head had ended up under a desk. My legs were cut and bleeding, but I managed to free myself from the rubble. I stood on a heap of fallen stone, shivered in the strangely warm air, and looked around me.

The school was destroyed. Crooked rebar poked from steaming piles of shattered stone. Small fires burned. Trapped kids cried, their voices muffled by tons of concrete. The sky shined with an endless spray of stars, a sky like you'd see in the deepest, darkest woods. But that didn't make sense because the sun was up and glowing, bright as noon, giving everything long, strange shadows that shook like rattlesnake tails. And there were mountains in the air. No . . .

not mountains. It seemed as if whole towns had been ripped from the earth and flung into the sky. I blinked, shivered, didn't understand what I was seeing, when I heard cries beneath me.

Under a pile of broken cinder blocks was a hand, a pen still wrapped in its fingers. I tossed away stones, revealing a shoulder, a neck . . . a head.

Her cherry red Ray-Bans had snapped in two. Her eyes were open, unblinking, pushed from their sockets. I turned away, threw up.

I heard more cries, heaved more stones, but I quickly realized that I couldn't do this alone. I listened but heard no sirens, no evidence of help arriving. I walked in a daze around the school, trying to convince myself this was just a bad dream, when I saw a figure at the edge of the school property. He twisted his neck, cracking it. I ran to him, screaming.

"Vinny, Vinny! Ohmygod, what happened? An earthquake? God, Maeve's dead. She's dead, Vinny! What's wrong with the sky?" I spoke so quickly I didn't realize I was crying. He stared calmly at me, waited for me to finish. And that's when I realized his skin had a pale glow, that through his expressionless face I could see the crumbled houses on the other side of the street. He twisted his neck, released. I didn't hear a crack.

"Vinny?" He twisted his neck again. And again. And again. "*Vinny!* What's happening?"

All around me, see-through kids and teachers climbed out of the smoking rubble. They seemed confused, lost. I poked and prodded, shook and slapped, but none woke from their mindless trance. "Listen to me, goddamnit!" And, as if choreographed, all heads turned in my direction together. Terrified, I ran.

Five blocks away, on a street that had buckled up as if the earth had been unzipped, I ran out of breath, and I remembered. "Oh, god! Jenna! Mom!"

I ran past dozens of translucent people on my way to Birch Lane Elementary, gave them a wide berth, which was just as well because they didn't seem interested in me or, for that matter, anything at all. Houses had collapsed, and mindless people milled about in upturned yards, standing, staring. I tried to ignore the sky, but was mesmerized by a billion overbright stars and an asteroid belt made of stones etched with the circuit-board landscape of cities, leaking water from broken sewers in long, sparkling tails.

I found her sitting on the curb in front of the school, her Hello Kitty knapsack on her back, her eyes wide and vacant. I gasped.

"Jenna! Jenna! Are you all right?"

She didn't move. "Mom was supposed to pick me up from school today." A line of blood trickled from her left ear. I was so happy when I realized I couldn't see through her, that she was real flesh and bone.

"C'mon," I said, taking her hand. "I'm taking you home."

I led her down a buckled street. Three houses attached to a clump of dirt tumbled overhead. In one of the backyards a dangling swing spun around three hundred and sixty degrees, like a clock's hand, as the houses rolled in the air. "That blue one's Chrissie's house," Jenna said. A row of tall spruces scraped their tops along the street, leaving a trail of pine needles. "She has a lot of American Girl dolls. But I have more Barbies." The houses drifted off with the wind.

We reached a break in the road, a cliff where the earth just fell away. I held Jenna's hand as we peered over the edge. Below the pavement was a layer of red clay, veined with the severed roots of trees. Below that lay an assortment of broken sewers and torn electrical cables, spilling foul liquid, popping and sparking. Farther down, a thick layer of bedrock. And a few hundred feet after that, the layers ended. Beyond were stars a million light-years away, nebulae that crossed the sky like smeared lipstick, all within an infinite sea of black. Then I knew. We weren't on Earth anymore. We were floating on a clump, too.

"But this is the way home, Russell!" Jenna said, looking up at me. "How do we get home?"

A Ken is up after Jenna. Why I chose this particular batting order baffles me now. A home run from me could win the game, but the soul-eating umpire won't let me change the order. After seeing the tortured faces in its hide, I decide it's best not to argue.

The Ken looks like he was about thirty-five when the event happened, and judging by his suit and name tag ("Arthur"), possibly worked in a bank or a hotel. I tell him to step up to the plate, do his best to hit the ball, and if his empty eyes comprehend anything at all, they don't show it. But, like all the Kens and Barbies, he does what he's told.

He lifts the bat over his left shoulder. A lefty. And based on his stance, I figure he might once have played this game when he still had a soul. I'm not sure how much of the person is left behind, or if the Kens and Barbies are more like tires rolling down a hill, unable to alter their course once set in motion until something smacks into them from the outside.

I see the ball through the Ken's translucent body. Three perfect pitches. All strikes. Jenna curses, stomps up and down on first base. "You idiot! You asshole!" The Ken—I don't want to call him Arthur because that would imply he was more than just a rolling tire—hasn't moved since he lifted the bat over his shoulder. The umpire tells him again that he's out, asks him to step away from the plate, but the Ken remains.

I approach. The Ken's body glows like headlights in rain.

"You're out, buddy," I say. His eyes are glassy, distant. "Go sit in the dugout."

The bat falls to his side, and he turns, walks to his seat. His expression never changes. There's a wedding ring on his left hand, and I wonder if his wife's still alive, or if she's wandering the clumps in a body without a soul.

I realize with a pang of fear that I'm up next. There are two outs, and I'm the winning run. If I strike out, we lose. Jenna looks at me, expectant, as the sky begins to rain little phosphorescent puffs of light that seem to fall right through the ground. They fill the sky, brighter than the stars.

"Batter up!" the umpire says.

Rain or shine, it seems.

My cell phone had no signal. And the landlines we found didn't work either. "We're taking the long way home," I told Jenna as we looped around town. But home, as far as I could tell, had been torn away.

Empty people waited on broken sidewalks, sat in their dented cars, stared out at their upturned yards. "Why do they just stand there?" Jenna said.

"I don't think they have anywhere else to go."

"Are they ghosts?"

"I don't know."

"Do you think Mom's a ghost?"

I took her hand. "No. I think Mom's very worried about us."

"I don't like how they just stare. *What are you staring at?*" She screamed, *"Go away! Go away!"* And as if under her thrall, the see-through people ran from sidewalks, fled their cars, abandoned their once-well-manicured lawns. In a minute, all of them had vanished.

Jenna's mouth fell open. "They *listened* to me."

"C'mon," I said, trembling. "We need to go."

We turned the corner and she screamed. A bat-eared elephant rummaged through the public library's dumpster. It pulled out a ratty book with its humanlike hands and said, "What a stupendous waste!"

We fled down another street.

On a road shadowed by towering sycamores, a seven-foot-tall walking-stick insect rushed toward us. I hunched down and covered Jenna in my arms. The insect paused above us, and from its tiny mantislike head said, *"Please*, I'm a vegetarian," and ran up a large tree.

When we rose again, the streets were filled with strange creatures. Apes with yellow fur hopped from broken rooftop to rooftop, singing jazz. A huge hairy spider feasted on the rubber of downed power lines. A clear ball with a single lidless eye floating inside it bounced past us. But like the mindless people, these strange beasts weren't interested in us.

"What are they?" Jenna said.

"I don't know."

"Are they monsters?"

"Are you?" someone grumbled behind us.

We spun to see a hunched, hairless man as thin as a concentration camp survivor, skin the blasted color of the moon. His smile revealed long canines. A ghoul. "They're same as you," it said, in a voice like gravel being crushed. "The lost."

Timidly, I asked, "Lost from what?"

"Do you really need me to answer that?"

When I didn't respond, he looked us up and down and sighed. "Yours wasn't the first world created. And it won't be the last." He bit his long dirty fingernails. "He didn't like it anymore, so he destroyed it. Like he did to mine. Like he did to all of ours."

"*'He?'*"

"You know." With a bony finger, he pointed up. *"Him."* He coughed and stumbled away like a drunk.

I shook my head. I'd had enough. "Come on, Jenna."

"Where are we going?"

"To a safe place."

"Where's that?"

The wooded preserve looked as if it had been hit by a hurricane. Downed trees crisscrossed the path, making it hard going, but we made it to the Track. A huge tree had fallen across the course and crushed the ramps. A see-through Eric Kellerman sat on his bike on the other side, moving the pedals back and forth, back and forth. I wondered if he had biked here all the way from school.

I fell back against a tree. I just needed time to think, to make sense of what was happening. But Jenna screamed, "Look!" She ran past Eric.

"Jenna! Stop!" I chased after her.

A hundred feet out, the woods abruptly fell away to reveal a gulf of stars. Floating nearby on a clump of land was a house. Our house.

"Mommy!" she cried. "Mommmmmmmy!"

I picked Jenna up, afraid she might try to jump over the edge.

"Let me go! Mommy's there! I want Mommy!"

For a moment I entertained the thought of using Eric's bike, building a ramp, flying out into the stars with Jenna on my back. But the house was too far out. There was no way I could reach it. In a game like Nimbus, I'd construct a bridge, or give myself wings, or leap out into the unknown. But even if we could reach it, what would be the point? I squeezed her as I saw something move in my bedroom window.

I turned Jenna's face away. "Mom's at the hospital. She had an extra shift today. She's safe there, with all the doctors."

"But she was supposed to pick me up from school."

"No, that's why I picked you up. She told me to come get you. And now I'm here."

"Really?"

"Really."

"You swear?"

". . . I swear."

"So Mommy's okay?"

The figure in the house had long, untamed hair. She folded one of my shirts, put it down on my bed, picked it up, folded the same shirt again. And again. And again.

My voice cracked as I said, "Yes, Jenna, Mommy's fine."

I'm up at the plate and I'm shivering. Just as quickly as it began, the phosphorescent rain has stopped, though the field is still pimpled with glowing spots. Jenna leans off of first and her eyes are as wide as moons. It's up to me to win this game, and she knows it. I can't let her down. I don't know what will happen to her if we lose.

The first pitch comes in. It looks high, so I don't swing, but at the last instant it dips.

"Strike one!"

Damn! I can't tell for sure, but I think the yellow-eyed pitcher is laughing.

"Hold up!" the umpire says as a figure runs across the outfield. It's a man, not a Ken. It's a real, solid, flesh-and-bone human being. He screams, "It's all gone! All lost! There's nothing left! Oh god, oh god, oh god!" He runs for the cliff's edge that cuts across right field, where the world drops away forever.

"Stop!" I scream. "Wait!" I just want to talk to him, to speak to someone besides my sister, to find out who he is and where he's from and what he did before. But he has a soul, and therefore his will is his own. He leaps over the edge. For a few seconds, he keeps moving outward, his legs kicking like Wile E. Coyote gone off a cliff. But then some invisible current yanks him diagonally away. That's the third jumper we've seen this week.

Jenna turns back to me. She's shaking. I wish she hadn't watched.

I tap my bat on home plate, lift it over my shoulder. "No pitcher!" I say.

After a pause, Jenna says, "No pitcher!"

"Oh and one," the umpire declares. "Two outs."

We raided kitchens for food, slept in dank basements and walk-in closets. We once saw a gang of still-living men and women in suits and dresses murder a boy because he would not give them his last beef jerky. But after a few weeks it seemed as if we were the only real human beings left. All that remained of the others were see-through husks.

"We won't make it to the hospital," Jenna said.

"No," I said. "It's gone." I was too tired to lie to her. "C'mon, get your stuff. We need to find some food."

"I don't want to," she said. "I'm not hungry anymore."

Neither was I. The strange thing was, we hadn't eaten for three days and we hadn't grown any weaker, though day and night had stopped having meaning. Our clump of earth randomly tumbled in and out of shadow.

"How come we're still alive?" she said.

I shook my head. "I don't know."

"Do you want to play Derek Jeter's World of Baseball against me?" She held her pink pocket game out to me. The batteries had died weeks ago, but she pretended they hadn't.

"No, Jenna. Not now."

I looked out the window. A dead soul in a nightgown had dug hundreds of holes in the yard with her hands, as if planting flowers. But there were no flowers. All the plants, confused by the strange days, had wilted and died. The woman paused for a moment, then continued digging.

"Stop digging!" I screamed. And the woman obeyed. Her hands fell into her lap, and she sat there, dirtied, on the dead lawn. Probably would sit there until the end of time.

"You're a bad person," Jenna said. "You don't deserve to live, so I'll crush your house!" She stared at her blank game screen, making exploding sounds. "And you did poorly on your test, so I'll kill all your friends."

Disturbed, I said, "That doesn't sound like baseball."

"No, it's 'Smash World.'" She didn't look up from the blank screen. "One player only."

"Hit it out of the park, Russ!" Jenna shouts as I lift the bat, readying for the next pitch. But the umpire calls, "Time out!" A swarm of flying creatures approaches from right field. They have webbed feet and hands, and faces like rhinos. They wear black armor and leather buckling, as if they're going off to battle. They flap their giant wings and hum a low note as they pass, like chanting monks. My bat vibrates with the sound.

There are so many flying creatures that they blot out the sky. The field goes dark, so that only the pitcher's yellow eyes are visible in the gloom. The creatures suddenly switch their song to a high-pitched whine, almost a scream. I hold my ears until they pass, watch them drift out into space going who knows where.

The sound fades, the sky lightens. "Game on," the umpire says. Distracted, I take a perfectly good pitch. "Strike two!"

"Damn!"

Jenna looks like she might cry.

I awoke from a nap, and Jenna was gone. I called for her, but she didn't come. I scoured the neighborhood but couldn't find her. I searched under stars turning strange orbits. I searched as purple sea monkeys pecked at the rotting treetops. I ran down a street as two clumps, miles away, collided in a spectacular spray of dust, though I heard no sound. I reached the schoolyard and stared across the baseball field.

The home-run fence was cut off in right field by the starry abyss, and a bunch of see-through people huddled by the edge. A hundred feet out, a small clump turned slowly, and I watched as one of the see-through people took a running leap toward it, missed by some eighty feet, and tumbled away.

"Pathetic!" I heard someone shout. "Zero points!" It was Jenna's voice. "Player one only has twelve . . . no, eleven lives left. And she can't win the game unless she reaches the clump!"

I ran up to her. "Jenna! Why would you do such a stupid thing? I looked everywhere for you! I thought you were dead! Why'd you run away?"

She wouldn't look me in the eye. "Go away, Russell! You never want to play with me, so I'll play by myself!"

"Play? What the hell are you doing?"

"Long Jump One Thousand. If you can reach the clump before your lives run out, you win. I'll show you." She pointed to a see-through girl in the front of the group, a girl with cherry red glasses, whose mouth was open as if she were about to sing.

Maeve.

"You, nerd girl! Get ready to jump!"

I recoiled in horror. "Jenna . . . no! You can't do this. These are people."

She shook her head. "No they're not! They're dolls. Kens and Barbies. I have twice as many as Chrissie now."

I felt sick and didn't know what to do. I stared across the baseball field. Though it was littered with windblown papers, it was mostly still intact.

A see-through person, Mr. Verini, my world studies teacher, stood nearby. He held a piece of chalk, put his finger to his lip, looked like he was about to speak. But I knew he never would.

"Mr. Verini, come here!" I commanded, and he obeyed.

I lifted a small pebble. "Catch this stone." I tossed it to him. He dropped the chalk and caught the pebble.

"Excellent!" I said. Across the field, a hairless cat with huge yellow eyes and long teeth was sniffing about the dumpster. "Hey, creepy!" I called. "Know how to catch a ball?"

The cat bounded over on all fours. "Excuse me?" she said, her voice like snakes hissing.

"Do you know how to catch a ball?"

"I'm a very fast learner. You have to be if you want to survive."

"Good. Go find eight smart friends and bring them here."

"What for?"

"Because we're going to play a game of baseball."

"Base-ball?"

"Yep." I looked at Jenna. "Humans versus Creepies."

The cat hissed, "Why?"

"Because it's about time I played with my sister."

And for the first time in weeks, Jenna smiled.

Two strikes. Two outs. This is it. Now or nothing. Time seems to slow as the pitcher readies herself on the mound, as Jenna expectantly leans off first base. I glance at the Kens and Barbies sitting in my dugout, waiting for someone to instruct them. The Creepies, the Lost, they stare at me, awaiting the pitch.

It comes. It's perfect. I have to swing. There is nothing left in all the universe except this pitch.

Time stops. Synapses ignite in my brain, a billion new connections, lightning fast time. *Crack*. My bat connects with the ball. The ball compresses, pauses, flies off my bat toward first base.

I feel like I'm burning, like my head is exploding with thought. Jenna is sprinting away from first. Dirt flies in slowed arcs from her heels. Her face is a twisted expression of glee and terror. The pitcher turns. The ball flies high over the head of the first baseman.

I'm dropping the bat, running for first, watching the ball fly up, up. I feel like my eyes are laser beams, my body encased in high-tech armor. My head is a supercomputer running this game.

The mound of hands in right field is scrambling for the ball, which keeps sailing farther, higher. The pitcher is jumping on the mound, shouting, "Catch it! Catch it!" Even the Kens and Barbies have turned their eyes to watch the ball.

"Screw you!" I scream to the hand who shredded this world, like I shredded so many of mine. "Screw you very much!" My voice spreads into the cosmos ahead of the sailing ball.

The ball sails up, over the blob of hands. The blob tries to catch it, leaps higher than any human ever could. But he won't reach it. No one will. The ball flies high over the home-run fence, and out into the stars.

"Home run!" Jenna screams. "Home run! Home run! Home run!"

A dozen or a hundred or a thousand feet out, the ball explodes. The sky fills with light as I round second, and the Creepies shield their eyes. The Kens and Barbies rise to their feet. I reach third and the sky's almost too bright to look at. Jenna squints at the light as I scoop her up, hug her, and step on home plate.

"It's so beautiful," she says. "What did you do?"

"*We* played, Jenna. I think it's because we played."

The light begins to burn away the edges of the field, moving closer every second.

"So what happens now?" she says.

"I guess it's up to him." I point up.

She takes my hand and looks at me, terrified. "I'm glad you played with me, Russell."

"We make a great team," I say as the light reaches our feet. I only wish Mom were here to see us now.

REUNION

BY SUSAN BETH PFEFFER

WE WALKED INTO THE OFFICE WHERE MAMA WAS SITTING. That was how Mama had dreamed of this reunion, her daughters walking hand in hand, as we had when we were little.

The room where Mama awaited us was a dull shade of brown. The one window in the room had also been painted brown. There was no way of knowing what it had once looked out on. The walls were unadorned, the picture of The Leader having been removed and not yet replaced with whatever the new government would deem appropriate.

Mama gazed eagerly at the girl as we walked in. "Your eyes are so brown," she said. "Like Isabella's. Like mine."

"Sit down," I said, gesturing to one of the straight-back chairs that faced Mama. The girl eased herself into the chair. Her posture was flawless, her right hand cupped by her left, her ankles crossed demurely.

"My Maria," Mama said. "I've longed for this day since the soldiers took you."

The girl nodded sympathetically but said nothing.

"Were you treated well?" Mama asked. "Were they kind to you?"

"Yes," the girl said. "My parents loved me and cared for me."

"But they weren't your parents," I pointed out. "You were stolen from our family. You must have known that. What did they tell you?"

"Papa explained it to me," the girl replied. "Mama had been taken ill when I was a baby, and I was given to one of our servants to look after. The servant ran away with me, and sold me to some villagers. Papa and Mama searched four years before they found me, and when they did, they brought me home."

"And you believed them?" I asked.

"They were my parents," the girl said. "Why should I doubt them? Besides, I knew what servants were like. They would do anything, say anything, for an extra morsel of food."

I looked up at the wall, where the portrait of The Leader had hung. "All lies," I said. "All of it, lies."

"So I've been told," the girl replied politely. "But of course I had no way of knowing."

"For months, soldiers came to houses," Mama said. "Every village for miles around. There was nothing we could do to stop them. The soldiers knew who lived in each house, how many children there were. To hide even one child meant death to everyone in the family. If an entire family went into hiding, all the children in the village were killed. And each day, the rules were different. One day, in one village, the soldiers took all the firstborns and sent them to the slave camps. The next day, it could be babies, sent to a death camp. The day they took you, they took four-year-olds. They had our records. They knew your age. They took you."

"Do you remember?" I asked. "The soldiers taking you away?"

The girl nodded. "They were kind to me," she said. "They played games and told me jokes."

"You were a happy little girl," I said. "I remember how we used to run to the fields together. I was two years older, so I always outran you, but you never minded. Bobo ran with us. How you loved that dog."

The girl's face lit up. "Doggie," she said. For a moment, I could glimpse the child she had been.

"Then Christian would find us and bring us home," I continued. "You'd ride piggyback, laughing all the way. Christian was twelve, and we adored him, the way little girls worship their big brothers."

"The people who took you," Mama said. "The general and his wife. Did they have other children?"

The girl shook her head.

"With no brothers, no sisters, you must have been lonely," Mama said. "Did you have playmates at school?"

"It was too dangerous for me to go to school," the girl said. "Mama taught me piano and embroidery. My governess taught me everything else."

"Did you have pets to play with?" I asked. "A dog like Bobo, maybe?"

"Papa kept guard dogs," the girl replied. "But they were for our protection. There were assassins everywhere, and kidnappers and murderers. Once, Mama and Papa and I were walking home from church, and a man sprang out of the bushes. He was too fast, even for our bodyguards, but the dogs lunged at him and tore him to pieces."

"How terrible for you to have seen such a thing," Mama said. "I would have covered your eyes to protect you."

"Children see worse every day," I said sharply. "The man was a stranger to her, not her father."

"Pay no attention to Isabella," Mama said to the girl. "She was always jealous of you. You were far prettier, the prettiest girl in the village. And even though you were two years younger, you were smarter as well. Now you have a fine education, lessons from a governess. Isabella can't even sign her own name."

"That wasn't my choice," I said, trying to keep my anger under control. "All the village children were forced to work in the fields, seven days a week, from sunrise past nightfall. Sometimes I prayed to be taken to a slave camp. There, I'd heard, the children worked just as hard, but were given food daily to maintain their strength."

"No one makes you work in the fields now," Mama said. "But I don't see you picking up a book."

This was an argument Mama and I often had. Before The Leader had seized control, every village had had its own school, and Mama and Papa both could read and write and do sums. But I'd come home each night too exhausted to learn, and even if I'd wanted, it was too dark in our house for study.

I turned my attention to the girl. "We've asked you questions," I said. "But you've asked us nothing. Surely there's something you would like to know."

The girl nodded. "After I was taken," she said, "did you wonder what had become of me? Did you try to find out?"

"Of course we did!" Mama cried. "All of us who'd had our babies stolen from us. Do you think we were heartless? Do you think it meant nothing to us to lose our children?"

The girl lowered her head. "I was taught that the villagers and the slum dwellers were like animals," she said. "It was the responsibility of people of the educated classes to see to it rules were followed and order maintained. Animals can't think for themselves. Animals have no feelings."

"We had feelings," Mama said, but her voice was gentle and loving, as it always was with Maria. "There were rules for finding out what had become of our children, and we followed them. All children were kept alive for thirty days after being taken. The mothers from all the local villages went daily to the town hall, hoping we'd be told where our child was. There was no way of knowing which mothers would be let in. Some days, none were admitted.

156

Other days, one, two, ten mothers, would be shown in by the soldiers. The mothers weren't supposed to talk to us when they came out, but still you heard things. Sometimes, not always, but sometimes, if your child had been sent to a death camp, you could negotiate. If you offered another of your children, that child and the one taken by the soldiers might be sent to a slave camp. We had no illusions about the slave camps. Children there were often worked to death. But there was no hope for a child sent to a death camp."

"Were you ever admitted to the office?" the girl asked. "Were you told what had become of me?"

"One day, the soldiers selected eight of us to go in," Mama said. "Over three weeks had passed. The mothers who were selected fell to the floor, weeping in gratitude."

"I never cry," the girl said. "People who cry are ungrateful and should be regarded as enemies of The State."

"I didn't cry," Mama said. "Other mothers did, but I didn't. Did I, Isabella? Have you ever seen me cry?"

"Never, Mama," I replied. "Not since the day the soldiers took Maria."

Mama and the girl both stared at me.

"Not that day either," I corrected myself.

The girl smiled. "You knew The State wanted only what was best for its people," she said. "The Leader was most kind and loving to the lowest of the low."

Mama looked at me. It was as dangerous now to agree with such a sentiment as it had been to deny it just weeks before.

The girl must have taken Mama's silence to mean accord. "What happened next?" she asked. "When you were let into the town hall. Were you told right away what had become of me?"

"A colonel sat at the desk," Mama said. "All the town officials had been executed, and the colonel was now in charge. He gave us permission to tell him our names. Then he pulled out eight files, one for each of our taken children. We begged him to tell us what was in the files. We swore we would do anything to keep our children alive."

"These were the animals who had no feelings," I said to the girl, but she paid me no heed.

"The colonel made each of us swear our gratitude to The State for taking our children, our fealty to The Leader, all wise in his decisions," Mama continued. "We swore to that. We would have sworn to that and more to keep our children alive."

"So you swore falsely," the girl said. "Or did you believe The Leader was all wise, that his decisions were always the right ones?"

"I believed my Maria had been seized from me," Mama said. "And that I had one chance and one chance only to find out what had become of her, perhaps to save her life. I'm sure the woman who raised you would have sworn what I swore, what the women by my side swore. And the colonel was satisfied. He believed us, he said. We were loyal citizens, worthy of being told where our children had been taken. But there were papers to be signed, protocol to be followed. He could only reveal the contents of the files if we came in the next morning with our entire families, our husbands, our children. Our husbands would be needed to sign the papers, and our children, in case there was any negotiating to be done. We fought among ourselves to be the first to kiss his hand, and then he dismissed us."

"And the next morning, you all came," the girl said. "And the colonel told you what was in each file."

"We all came," Mama said. "With our husbands and children. We presented ourselves at the town hall, and were escorted to the colonel's office. There he sat, as he had the day before, flanked by a dozen soldiers who served as his guards."

"He had no need for dogs," I said. "His soldiers were fast enough."

"Shush," Mama said to me. "Maria has no interest in your version of this story."

"It is a story," the girl said. "But do go on."

"The colonel told us he was a very busy man," Mama said. "He would get to us when he could, but we were to stand there, not moving, not making a sound, until our time came. The colonel had slave laborers to fan him, to give him food and drink; and the soldiers, of course, were used to standing at attention for hours. Yet we did as we were told, and didn't move. Finally, a little boy, our neighbors' youngest son, began crying. He was only two, and he was tired and hungry and hot. We all were, but he was the youngest, so he cried. The colonel gestured with the quickest of nods, and one of the soldiers left his side and bayoneted the boy."

I looked at the girl to see her reaction. But I didn't know her well enough to read the emotions on her face.

"The boy's parents, his brothers and sisters, were taken outside," Mama said. "The colonel ordered a soldier to open the window so we could hear their death cries. Then he returned to his work. We continued to stand, terrified the sound of our breathing could lead to our slaughter."

"The room filled with flies," I told the girl. "Attracted by the little boy's blood. Mosquitoes stung us mercilessly."

"One of the mosquitoes stung the colonel," Mama said. "A child laughed. Isabella, I think."

I didn't deny it.

"The colonel was enraged," Mama continued. "First we had interfered with his work. Then he'd fallen victim to our vermin-laden bodies. Our disrespect for him proved our disloyalty to The State, to The Leader. The parents threw themselves at his feet and begged for the lives of their children. The soldiers stood there watching us, laughing."

I heard that sound every night before falling asleep. The buzz of the flies and mosquitoes. The howling of the parents. The laughter of the soldiers. That had been my lullaby for the past ten years.

"The colonel ordered the parents to get up and stand with their children," Mama said. "The Leader was merciful, he said. The State benign to all who lived there. The soldiers stopped laughing, and we felt the faintest glimmer of hope."

"The Leader *was* merciful," the girl said. "The State benign. Only those who deserved it were ever punished."

"The colonel instructed the fathers to pick one child from their family to die," Mama said. "They weren't to speak, just to select a single child. The colonel was benevolent and we were given permission to say farewell. Each child was kissed by their mama and their papa, while their brothers and sisters watched in silence."

I sat there remembering the feel of those kisses, the last time either of my parents had kissed me.

"The colonel turned to the seven of us," I said, the story now mine to tell. "He asked if we understood what our fathers had done, what was going to happen. Two of the children were too young to answer, but the rest of us said we did. He said under ordinary circumstances he would tell the soldiers to kill us swiftly, but because one of the children in the room had laughed when the mosquito stung him, the soldiers would be instructed to prolong our deaths so that we could suffer as he had suffered. He asked if we agreed with the justness of our punishment, and we said we did. He asked us then if we were willing to thank him, as the representative of The Leader, The State, for the agonizing pain we were about to endure. All of us, even the little ones, thanked him."

"And the colonel showed you mercy," the girl said. "He let

you live. He must have because you're sitting here, in this room with me."

"He showed us mercy," I agreed. "He let us live. But he said he still needed a demonstration of our loyalty. He told each of the seven of us to pick one of our parents for the soldiers to kill. Our mother or our father. The decision was ours. We were to kiss the parent we selected for death. I kissed Mama. I kissed her twice so the soldiers would understand who I'd picked to die."

"It was a test," the girl said. "Another test. Mama is here, the same as you are. The colonel showed all of you mercy."

I shook my head. "All the other children wanted their mothers to live," I said. "Papa was told to stand with the six mothers, while the other fathers and Mama stood by the children. But the colonel played a joke on us all. He ordered the soldiers to bayonet the six mothers and Papa. The parents we'd chosen to live were the ones who were killed. The colonel laughed along with the soldiers as our parents lay dying on the floor. He pointed out to the seven of us that our parents had sanctioned our deaths. Not a single one had murmured a word of protest when he'd described the horrible fate that awaited us. Then he pointed out to the parents left alive that their children had chosen *them* to die. Now, he said, we could understand why our loyalty must be only to The Leader, to The State."

"The colonel told us to dip our fingers in blood and make a mark on our child's file," Mama said. "One by one, he told each father that their missing child had been sent to a death camp, and because of the disloyalty we had shown today, there could be no negotiations. Finally he got to my darling Maria's file. She alone was safe, adopted by a family with position and power. Her beauty had saved her."

"We were pariahs after that," I said. "Of all the mothers in the room, only Mama had been allowed to live. Of all the children taken, only Maria was allowed to live. None of the villagers would talk to us, not that day, not for years."

Mama spat contemptuously. "They were always jealous," she said. "Of Maria's beauty. Of mine."

The very next day, I remembered, Mama had made a new friend. The colonel came over, and within weeks, Mama was friends with the other officers as well. As she aged and her beauty faded, her only friends were the soldiers stationed in our village. But even the lowest of soldiers had more power and position than any of the villagers, and Mama was given food, clothes, protection.

I was given nothing. The day after Papa's death, I was sent to the fields, along with all the remaining children, to work for the little food my family was allotted. Mama took her share from me, while I got nothing from her friends the soldiers, until I was old enough and they befriended me as well.

The partisans sensed my bitterness and anger, and, knowing I was in a position to hear things, recruited me. I spied for them before I knew what the word meant, and I fought alongside them. Sometimes, in spite of my exhaustion, terror, and grief, I even laughed with them.

Our success came slowly and at great loss. But the glorious day arrived when The Leader was finally taken down. Soon his generals and their families were executed. I danced in the blood of the soldiers who'd died loyal to The State.

Only because of me was Mama allowed to live. We made our own peace, united by her dream of reclaiming Maria.

"And where was Christian during all this?" the girl asked unexpectedly. "Our brother who we adored. Was he at the office with the families and the colonel? Did he pledge his fealty to The Leader? Did he watch along with you while Papa was killed? Why haven't you mentioned him?"

We were silent.

"I'll tell you why," the girl crowed, her eyes gleaming in triumph. "Because there was no Christian! We had no brother. You invented him to trap me."

I turned to Mama and laughed. "She found us out," I said.

"I said she was smarter than you," Mama said. "You're right, my darling Maria. There was no son. I had only the two daughters: Isabella, who wished me dead, and Maria, my little beauty."

"I knew it," the girl said. "We were told you'd tell us lies, trying to catch us in your web of deception. And if one thing you said was a lie, then all things you said were lies. There was no colonel, no soldiers. True, I was taken. I remember that. But you were told immediately what had become of me. You were glad to see me go. It meant more food for you. Everything I was taught was true. You are no better than animals. You have no human feelings."

"There was a colonel," I said for Mama. "There were soldiers. I picked Papa to live and watched as he was killed. Mama grieved for you every single day. I'd come home at night, exhausted from fourteen hours of labor, and Mama would say she'd strangle me with her bare hands for a moment's glimpse of her precious Maria. Does that mean she has no human feelings?"

"It does," the girl said. "No mother would ever say such things. My mama never would have."

"Mine did," I said. "She said that and worse. But you're right about something. We did tell lies. We had no other way of knowing if you are Maria, her daughter, my sister. All the files were destroyed by the soldiers before The Leader was overthrown."

"I've proven I'm Maria," the girl said. "I knew there was no Christian."

I smiled sadly at her. "You're not Maria," I said. "Not our Maria, at least. There was no son named Christian. But there was no Bobo either, no doggie. We had no dogs, no pets. Even before

The Leader took power, we had no money for pets, no food to spare for one."

"But I remember my name was Maria!" the girl cried. "And I remember doggie."

"That could be," I said. "Or it could be you're lying. Either way, you're not one of us."

I must give the girl credit. Her eyes glistened, but no tears rolled down her cheeks. She had learned her lessons well.

I got up and walked to the back door of the office, the one painted the same dull brown as the walls, to make it less visible. I knocked twice and a partisan came out.

"Take her," I said.

The partisan grabbed the girl. With his strong right hand, he pinned her arms to her back. With his left hand, he covered her mouth to muffle her sounds of protest.

"Where to?" he asked me.

I looked at Mama.

"I thought for sure she was my Maria," Mama said. "She looked just as I remembered my darling daughter."

"Just the eyes, Mama," I said, gently touching her cheek with my work-roughened hand.

Then I turned to the partisan. This time I had no trouble reading the girl's face. There was terror in those brown eyes, not defiance.

"I don't know who she is," I said to the partisan. "But I think she is one of the taken. She should go to a reeducation camp. She might be salvageable."

The partisan nodded and dragged the girl back through the hidden door.

"What number was she?" Mama asked. "How many have we seen today?"

"Five," I said. Two I'd had sent to reeducation camps. I left the fate of the other three to the partisans. Perhaps they were dead already. There was a constant rumble of gunshots outside, but with the office window painted brown, there was no way of seeing who they'd chosen to kill and who they'd kept alive for their entertainment.

"Five," Mama said, with a sigh. "You're a fool, Isabella, not to be able to spot my Maria. How many more are left?"

I walked over to the anteroom door. Using the fingers of both hands, I counted. "Seven," I said, looking at them. Seven brown-eyed girls, all about fourteen years of age, sitting with perfect posture, their hands neatly folded in their laps, their ankles demurely crossed. Any one of them could be my sister Maria. But it was just as likely Maria was dead, executed along with the general and his wife, who had stolen her.

"Look for the prettiest one," Mama instructed me. "Maria was a beauty, the prettiest girl in the village. Don't look for girls with plain faces like yours, Isabella. Bring me my beautiful daughter Maria, so that I may hold her and kiss her, as I've dreamed of doing every day, every night, for the past ten years."

BLOOD DRIVE

BY JEFFREY FORD

For Christmas our junior year of high school, all of our parents got us guns. That way you had a half a year to learn to shoot and get down all the safety garbage before you started senior year. Depending on how well off your parents were, that pretty much dictated the amount of firepower you had. Darcy Krantz's family lived in a trailer, and so she had a peashooter, .22 Double Eagle Derringer, and Baron Hanes's father, who was in the security business and richer than god, got him a .44 Magnum that was so heavy it made the nutty kid lean to the side when he wore the gun belt. I packed a pearl-handled .38 revolver, Smith & Wesson, which had originally been my grandfather's. Old as dirt, but all polished up, the way my father kept it, it was still a fine-looking gun. My mom told my dad not to give it to me, but he said, "Look, when she goes to high school, she's gotta carry. Everybody does in their senior year."

"Insane," said my mom.

"Come on," I said. "Please . . ."

She drew close to me, right in my face, and said, "If your father gives you that gun, he's got no protection making his deliveries." He drove a truck and delivered bakery goods to different diners and convenience stores in the area.

"Take it easy," said my dad. "All the crooks are asleep when I go out for my runs." He motioned for me to come over to where he sat. He put the gun in my hand. I gripped the handle and felt the weight of it. "Give me your best pose," he said.

I turned profile, hung my head back, my long chestnut hair reaching halfway to the floor, pulled up the sleeve of my T-shirt, made a muscle with my right arm, and pointed the gun at the ceiling with my left hand. He laughed till he couldn't catch his breath. And my mom said, "Disgraceful," but she also laughed.

I went to the firing range with my dad a lot the summer before senior year. He was a calm teacher, and never spoke much or got too mad. Afterward, he'd take me to this place and buy us ice cream. A lot of times it was Friday night, and I just wanted to get home so I could go hang out with my friends. One night I let him know we could skip the ice cream, and he seemed taken aback for a second, like I'd hurt his feelings. "I'm sorry," he said, and tried to smile.

I felt kind of bad, and figured I could hug him or kiss him or ask him to tell me something. "Tell me about a time when you shot the gun not on the practice range," I said as we drove along.

He laughed. "Not too many times," he said. "The most interesting was from when I was a little older than you. It was night, we were in the basement of an abandoned factory over in the industrial quarter. I was with some buds and we were partying, smoking up and drinking straight, cheap vodka. Anyway, we were wasted. This guy I really didn't like who hung out with us, Raymo was his name, he challenged me to a round of Russian roulette. Don't tell your mother this," he said.

"You know I won't," I said.

"Anyway, I left one bullet in the chamber, removed the others, and spun the cylinder. He went first—nothing. I went, he went, etcetera, click, click, click. The gun came to me and I was certain by then that the bullet was in my chamber. So you know what I did?"

"You shot it into the ceiling?"

"No. I turned the gun on Raymo and shot him in the face. After that we all ran. We ran and we never got caught. At the time there was a gang going around at night shooting people and taking their wallets, and the cops put it off to them. None of my buds were going to snitch. Believe me, Raymo was no great loss to the world. The point of which is to say, it's a horrible thing to shoot someone. I see Raymo's expression right before the bullet drilled through his head just about every night in my dreams. In other words, you better know what you're doing when you pull that trigger. Try to be responsible."

"Wow," I said, and wished I'd just hugged him instead.

To tell you the truth, taking the gun to school at first was a big nuisance. The thing was heavy and you always had to keep an eye on it. The first couple of days were all right 'cause everyone was showing off their pieces at lunchtime. A lot of people complimented me on the pearl handle and old-school look of my gun. Of course the kids with the new high-tech nine-millimeter jobs got the most attention, but if your piece was unique enough, it got you at least some cred. Jody Motes, pretty much an idiot, with buck teeth and a fat ass, brought in a German Luger with a red swastika inlaid on the handle, and because of it got asked out by this guy in our English class a lot of the girls thought was hot. Kids wore them on their hips; others, mostly guys, did the shoulder holster. A couple of the senior girls with big breasts went with this over-the-shoulder bandolier style, so the gun sat atop their left breast. Sweaty Mr. Gosh, in second period math, said that look was "very fashionable." I carried mine in my SpongeBob lunch box. I hated wearing it; the holster always hiked my skirt up in the back somehow.

Everybody in the graduating class carried heat except for Scott

Wisner, the King of Vermont, as everybody called him. I forget why, 'cause Vermont was totally far away. His parents had given him a stun gun instead of the real thing. Cody St. John, the captain of the football team, said the stun gun was fag, and after that Wisner turned into a weird loner who walked around carrying a big jar with a floating mist inside. He asked all the better-looking girls if he could have their souls. I know he asked me. Creep. I heard he'd stun anyone who wanted it, for ten dollars a pop. Whatever.

The senior class teachers all had tactical twelve-gauge short barrel shotguns; no shoulder stock, just a club grip with an image of the school's mascot (a cartoon of a rampaging Indian) stamped on it. Most of them were loaded with buckshot, but Mrs. Cloder, in human geography, who used her weapon as a pointer when at the board, was rumored to rock the breaching rounds, those big slugs cops use to blow doors off their hinges. Other teachers left the shotguns on their desks or lying across the eraser gutter at the bottom of the board. Mr. Warren, the vice principal, wore his in a holster across his back, and for an old fart was super quick in drawing it over his shoulder with one hand.

At lunch, across the soccer field and back by the woods, where only the seniors were allowed to go, we sat out every nice day in the fall, smoking cigarettes and having gun-spinning competitions. You weren't allowed to shoot back there, so we left the safeties on. Bryce, a boy I knew since kindergarten, was good at it. He could flip his gun in the air backward and have it land in the holster at his hip. McKenzie Batkin wasn't paying attention, and turned the safety off instead of on before she started spinning her antique colt. The sound of the shot was so sudden, we all jumped, and then silence followed by the smell of gun smoke. The bullet went through her boot and took off the tip of her middle toe. Almost a whole minute passed before she screamed. The King of Vermont and Cody St. John both rushed to help her at the same time. They worked together to staunch the bleeding. I remember noticing the football lying on the ground next to the jar of souls, and I thought it would make a cool photo for the yearbook. McKenzie never told her parents, and hid the boots at the back of her closet. To this day she's got half a middle toe on her right foot, but that's the least of her problems.

After school I walked home with my new friend, Constance, who only came to Bascombe High in senior year. We crossed the soccer field, passed the fallen leaves stained red with McKenzie's blood, and entered the woods. The wind blew and shook the empty branches of the trees. Constance suddenly stopped walking, crouched, drew her Beretta Storm, and fired. By the time I could turn my head, the squirrel was falling back, headless, off a tree about thirty yards away.

Constance had a cute haircut, short but with a lock that almost covered her right eye. Jeans and a green flannel shirt, a calm, pretty face. When we were doing current events in fifth period social studies, she'd argued with Mr. Hallibet about the cancellation of child labor laws. Me, I could never follow politics. It was too boring. But Constance seemed to really understand, and although on the TV news we all watched, they were convinced it was a good idea for kids twelve and older to now be eligible to be sent to work by their parents for extra income, she said it was wrong. Hallibet laughed at her and said, "This is Senator Meets we're talking about. He's a man of the people. The guy who gave you your guns." Constance had more to say, but the teacher lifted his shotgun and turned to the board. The thing I couldn't get over was that she actually knew this shit better than Hallibet. The thought of it, for some reason, made me blush.

By the time the first snow came in late November, the guns became mostly just part of our wardrobes, and kids turned their attention back to their cell phones and iPods. The one shot fired before Christmas vacation was when Mrs. Cloder dropped her gun in a bathroom stall and blew off the side of the toilet bowl. Water flooded out into the hallway. Other than that, the only time you noticed that people were packing was when they'd use their side-arm for comedy purposes. Like Bryce, during English, when the teacher was reading *Pilgrim's Progress* to us, took out his gun and stuck the end in his mouth as if he was so bored he was going to blow his own brains out. At least once a week, outside the caf-eteria, on the days it was too cold to leave the school, there were quick-draw contests. Two kids would face off, there'd be a panel of judges, and Vice Principal Warren would set his cell phone to beep once. When they heard the beep, the pair drew, and whoever was faster won a coupon for a free thirty-two-ounce soda at Babb's, the local convenience store.

One thing I did notice in that first half of the year. Usually when a person drew their gun, even as a gag, each had their own signature saying. When it came to these lines it seemed that the ban on cursing could be ignored without any problem. Even the teachers got into it. Mr. Gosh was partial to, "Eat hot lead, you little motherfuckers." The school nurse, Ms. James, used, "See you in Hell, asshole." Vice Principal Warren, who always kept his lan-guage in check, would draw, and while the gun was coming level with your head, say, "You're already dead." As for the kids, they all used lines they'd seen in recent movies. Cody St. John used, "Suck on this, bitches." McKenzie, who by Christmas was known as Half-toe Batkin, concocted the line, "Put up your feet." I tried to think of something to say, but it all seemed too corny, and it took me too long to get the gun out of my lunch box to really outdraw anyone else.

Senior year rolled fast, and by winter break, I was wondering what I'd do after I graduated. Constance told me she was going to college to learn philosophy. "Do they still teach that stuff?" I asked. She smiled. "Not so much anymore." We were sitting in my living room—my parents were away at my aunt's. The TV was on, the lights were out, and we were holding hands. We liked to just sit quietly and talk. "So I guess you'll be moving away after the summer," I said. She nodded. "I thought I'd try to get a job at Walmart," I said. "I heard they have benefits now."

"That's all you're gonna do with your life?" asked Constance. "For now," I said.

"Well then, when I go away, you should come with me." She put her arm behind my head and drew me gently to her. We held each other for a long time while the snow came down outside.

A few days after Christmas, I sat with my parents watching the evening news. Senator Meets was on, talking about what he hoped to accomplish in the coming year. He was telling how happy he'd been to work for minimum wage when he was eleven.

"This guy's got it down," said my father.

I shouldn't have opened my mouth, but I said, "Constance says he's a loser."

"Loser?" my father said. "Are you kidding? Who's this Constance? I don't want you hanging out with any socialists. Don't tell me she's one of those kids who refuses to carry a gun. Meets passed the gun laws, mandatory church on Sunday for all citizens, killed abortion, and got us to stand up to the Mexicans. . . . He's definitely gonna be the next president. "

"She's probably the best shot in the class," I said, realizing I'd already said too much.

My father was suspicious, and he stirred in his easy chair, leaning forward.

"I met her," said my mother. "She's a nice girl."

I gave things a few seconds to settle down and then announced

I was going to take the dog for a walk. As I passed my mother, unnoticed by my dad, she grabbed my hand and gave it a quick squeeze.

Back at school in January, there was a lot to do. I went to the senior class meetings, but didn't say anything. They decided for our Act of Humanity (required of every senior class), we would have a blood drive. For the senior trip, we decided to keep it cheap, as pretty much everyone's parents were broke. A day trip to Bash Lake. "Sounds stale," said Bryce, "but if we bring enough alcohol and weed, it'll be okay." Mrs. Cloder, our faculty adviser, aimed at him, said, "Arrivederci, baby," and gave him two Saturday detentions. The event that overshadowed all the others, though, was the upcoming prom. My mother helped me make my dress. She was awesome on the sewing machine. It was turquoise satin, short-sleeved, mid-length. I told my parents I had no date, but was just going solo. Constance and I had made plans. We knew from all the weeks of mandatory Sunday mass—the pastor actually spitting, he was so worked up over what he called "unnatural love"—that we couldn't go as a couple. She cared more than I did. I just tried to forget about it.

When the good weather of spring hit, people got giddy and tense. There were accidents. In homeroom one bright morning, Darcy dropped her bag on her desk, and the Derringer inside went off and took out Ralph Babb's right eye. He lived, but when he came back to school, his head was kind of caved in and he had a bad fake eye that looked like a kid drew it. It only stared straight ahead. Another was when Mr. Hallibet got angry because everybody'd gotten into the habit of challenging his current events lectures after seeing Constance in action. He yelled for us all to shut up and accidentally squeezed off a round. Luckily for us, the gun was pointed at the ceiling. Mr. Gosh, though, who was sitting in the room a floor above, directly over Hallibet, had to have buckshot taken out of his ass. When he returned to school from a week off, he sweated more than ever.

Mixed in with the usual spring fever, there was all kinds of drama over who was going to the prom with who. Fistfights, girl fights, plenty of drawn guns but not for comedy. I noticed that the King of Vermont was getting wackier the more people refused to notice him. When I left my sixth-period class to use the bathroom, I saw him out on the soccer field from the upstairs hallway window. He turned the stun gun on himself and shot the two darts with wires into his own chest. It knocked him down fast, and he was twitching on the ground. I went and took a piss. When I passed the window again, he was gone. He'd started bringing alcohol to school; and at lunch, where again we were back by the woods hanging out, he'd drink a Red Bull and a half pint of vodka.

Right around that time, I met Constance at the town library one night. I had nothing to do, but she had to write a paper. When I arrived, she'd put the paper away and was reading. I asked her what the book was. She told me, "Plato."

"Good story?" I asked

She explained it wasn't a novel, but a book about ideas. "You see," she said, "there's a cave and this guy gets chained up inside so that he can't turn around or move, but can only stare at the back wall. There's a fire in the cave behind him and it casts his shadow on the wall he faces. That play of light and shadow is the sum total of his reality."

I nodded and listened as long as I could. Constance was so wrapped up in explaining, she looked beautiful, but I didn't want to listen anymore. I checked over my shoulder to see if anyone was around. When I saw we were alone, I quickly leaned forward and kissed her on the lips. She smiled and said, "Let's get out of here."

On a warm day in mid May, we had the blood drive. I got there early and gave blood. The nurses, who were really nice, told me to sit for a while and they gave me orange juice and cookies. I thought about becoming a nurse for maybe like five whole minutes. Other kids showed up and gave blood, and I stuck around to help sign them up. Cody came and watched but wouldn't give. "Fuck the dying," I heard him say. "Nobody gets my blood but me." After that, a few other boys decided not to give either. Whatever. Then at lunch, the King of Vermont was drinking his Red Bull and vodka, and I think because he'd given blood, he was really blasted. He went around threatening to stun people in their private parts.

After lunch, in Mrs. Cloder's class, where we sat at long tables in a rectangle that formed in front of her desk, Wisner took the seat straight across from her. I was two seats down from him, toward the windows. Class started, and the first thing Mrs. Cloder said before she even got out of her seat, was to the King. "Get that foolish jar off the table." We all looked over. Wisner stared, the mist swirled inside the glass. He pushed his seat back and stood up, cradling the jar in one arm and drawing his stun gun. "Sit down, Scotty," she said, and leveled her short barrel at him. I could see her finger tightening on the trigger. A few seconds passed, and then one by one, all the kids drew their weapons, but nobody was sure whether to aim at Mrs. Cloder or the King, so about half did one and half the other. I never even opened my lunch box, afraid to make a sudden move.

"Put down your gun and back slowly away from the table," said Mrs. Cloder.

"When you meet the Devil, give him my regards," said Wisner, but as he pulled the trigger, Mrs. Cloder fired. The breaching slug blew a hole in the King of Vermont's chest, slamming him against the back wall in a cloud of blood. The jar shattered, and glass flew. McKenzie, who was sitting next to Wisner, screamed as the shards dug into her face. I don't know if she shot or if the gun just went off, but her bullet hit Mrs. Cloder in the shoulder and spun her out of her chair onto the ground. She groaned and rolled back and forth. Meanwhile, Wisner's stun gun darts had gone wild, struck Chucky Durr in the forehead, one over each eye, and in his electrified shaking, his gun went off and put a round right into Melanie Storte's Adam's apple. Blood poured out as she dropped her own gun and brought her hands to her gurgling neck. Melanie was Cody St. John's "current ho," as he called her, and he didn't think twice but fanned the hammer of his pistol, putting three shots into Chucky, who fell over on the floor like a bag of potatoes. Chucky's cousin, Meleeba, shot Cody in the side of the head, and he went down screaming as smoke poured from the hole above his left ear. One of Cody's crew shot Meleeba, and then I couldn't keep track anymore. Bullets whizzed by my head, blood was spurting everywhere. Kids were falling like pins at the bowling alley. Mrs. Cloder clawed her way back into her seat, lifted the gun, and aimed it. Whoever was left fired on her and then she fired, another shotgun blast, like an explosion. When the ringing in my ears went away, the room was perfectly quiet but for the drip of blood and the ticking of the wall clock. Smoke hung in the air, and I thought of the King of Vermont's escaped souls. During the entire thing, I'd not moved a single finger.

The cops were there before I could get myself out of the

chair. They wrapped a blanket around me and led me down to the principal's office. I was in a daze for a while but could feel them moving around me and could hear them talking. Then my mother was there, and the cop was handing me a cup of orange juice. They asked if they could talk to me, and my mother left it up to me. I told them everything, exactly how it went down. I started with the blood drive. They tested me for gunpowder to see if there was any on my hands. I told them my gun was back in the classroom in my lunch box, under the table, and it hadn't been fired since the summer, the last time I went to the range with my dad.

It was all over the news. I was all over the news. A full one-third of Bascombe High's senior class was killed in the shoot-out. The only one in Mrs. Cloder's class besides me to survive was McKenzie, and the flying glass made her No-face Batkin.

Senator Meets showed up at the school three days later and got his picture taken handing me an award. I never really knew what it was for. Constance whispered, "They give you a fucking award if you live through it," and laughed. In Meets's speech to the assembled community, he blamed the blood drive for the incident. He proclaimed Mrs. Cloder a hero, and ended by reminding everyone, "If these kids were working, they'd have no time for this."

The class trip was called off, out of respect for the dead. Two weeks later, I went to the prom. It was to be held in the gymnasium. My dad drove me. When we pulled into the parking lot, it was empty.

"You must be early," he said, and handed me the corsage I'd asked him to get—a white orchid.

"Thanks," I said, and gave him a kiss on the cheek. As I opened the door to get out, he put his hand on my elbow. I turned, and he was holding the gun.

"You'll need this," he said.

I shook my head and told him, "It's okay." He was momentarily taken aback. Then he tried to smile. I shut the door and he drove away.

Constance was already there. In fact, she was the only one there. The gym was done up with glittery stars on the ceiling, a painted moon and clouds. There were streamers. Our voices echoed as we exchanged corsages, which had been our plan. The white orchid looked good against her black plunging neckline. She'd gotten me a corsage made of red roses, and they really stood out against the turquoise. In her purse, instead of the Beretta, she had a half pint of Captain Morgan. We sat on one of the bleachers and passed the bottle, talking about the incidents of the past two weeks.

"I guess no one's coming," she said. No sooner were the words out of her mouth than the outside door creaked open and in walked Bryce, carrying a case in one hand and dressed in a jacket and tie. We got up and went to see him. Constance passed him the Captain Morgan. He took a swig.

"I was afraid of this," he said.

"No one's coming?" I said.

"I guess some of the parents were scared there'd be another shoot-out. Probably the teachers too. Mrs. Cloder's family insisted on an open casket. A third of them are dead, let's not forget, and the rest, after hearing Meets talk, are working the late shift at Walmart for minimum wage."

"Jeez," said Constance.

"Just us," said Bryce. He went up on the stage, set his case down, and got behind the podium at the back. "Watch this," he said, and a second later the lights went out. We laughed. A dozen blue searchlights appeared, their beams moving randomly around the gym, washing over us and then rushing away to some dark corner. A small white spotlight came on above the mic that stood at the front of the stage. Bryce stepped up into the glow. He opened the case at his feet and took out a saxophone.

"I was looking forward to playing tonight," he said. We walked up to the edge of the stage, and I handed him the bottle. He took a swig, the sax now on a leather strap around his neck. Putting the bottle down at his feet, he said, "Would you ladies care to dance?"

"Play us something," we told him.

He thought for a second and said, "'Strangers in the Night'?"

He played, we danced, and the blue lights in the dark were the sum total of our reality.

REALITY GIRL

BY **RICHARD BOWES**

1.

YOU WANT TO KNOW WHO I AM AND HOW I GOT HERE?

Reality Girl is the name my mother gave me but Real's what I'm called. I'm fourteen and until one day, a week or so back, my ambition was making it to fifteen. What I want to tell starts that day.

Me and Dare—my girlfriend and partner—led our boys, Nice and Not, Hassid, and Rock, down to the river for this appointment I'd set up.

It could have been any October afternoon: hot orange light and the sun hanging over the smashed towers on the Jersey Shore. Like always, rumors ran of everything from a new plague to war between the Northeast Command and the Liberty Land militia.

But I could see planes coming in and taking off from Liberty Land Stronghold in Jersey like always. And along the waterfront little ferry boats took people on, unloaded freight.

The world that day was the way I was used to: broken cement under bare feet, bad sunlight that'd take off your skin if you let it, the smell of rot and acid on the water. Mostly I was trying to get control of this thing inside me. I wasn't sure I owned it or it owned me.

Dare looked all ways, kept her hands inside her robes so no one knew what weapon she was holding, ignored the boy babble.

Hassid told Rock, "You look too much at who's watching you dive instead of on the gold."

"I gotta take this from a loser midget?"

"Listen to the lovers," Nice said.

Dare stood tall with that crest of hair like a web singer or some photo you see and know is of a hero. "Look tough," she told them, and they formed a front as we moved down to the waterline.

Me, I just stared around, looked downtown where black Hudson tide water was over the banks and in the street. Anyone looking maybe would guess I was Dare's useless little girl trick. In truth I was seeing through her eyes, which was part of the thing inside me.

When I was a little kid I had flashes where I was inside someone else's head for a second. It began to happen more often once my monthlies started. It scared me till I saw it as a weapon and tried to take control.

This summer was me and Dare's second together and we fit like a knife in a fist. At first she hated it when I began slipping into her brain, and we fought. Then she saw how no one would know I was studying them, and went along.

That day I saw what Dare could see: used-up diving boys with the skin coming off them in clumps, and scavenger ladies with bags of garbage, all turned toward us snarling. But Dare saw fear in their eyes, knew they were looking for ways to back off, and she gave them the chance.

For what was left of the afternoon, we owned that stretch of the shore. But even here some water spilled over the walls onto the walkway. And barefoot kids don't ever want to touch river water unless there's gold in the air.

Then Dare and me caught sight of a long ground car with tinted windows and double treads coming down the highway, dodging the holes, bouncing over the rubble. According to the deal I set up with Depose, this was a party of tourists who wanted to see New York diving boys.

The car stopped, the doors opened, and Depose's people jumped out holding their AK474's ready. One kept an eye on Dare and the rest of us—cradling the rapid-fire in her arms. Two covered the other directions, on the alert but not tense. One stayed at the wheel.

When Depose runs things there's no reason to worry. You don't cross her and you're okay unless she's been given the contract on you or she sees some reason her life would get better without you. In those cases you're dead. Simple, the way not much else is in this world.

Next the tourists in their protective suits and helmets got out of the car. A pile of wreckage juts out from the walkway and into the water. Security escorted them up there so they could see the show, then stood guard.

Dare and the boys looked up at them. Not said, "Aliens," and spat into the water, but Dare signaled him to cool it. Not and Nice became partners that summer, and Nice rubbed his back and whispered something. They and Hassid, who's single and older than any of us—eighteen—stepped out of their shorts and moved right to the edge of the cement. Rock, our fourth boy, was new and not at ease with us yet, but he did the same.

Tourists get off on American kids staring up like starving dogs. Tourists want to see us bare ass and risking our lives. Dare and me hated them as much as Not did, but this was the cleanest way we'd come up with to get money out of them.

At first this bunch seemed the usual: half a dozen figures with white insulated helmets to keep the sun off their faces, conditioned coveralls to make them comfortable, shields to protect their eyes, and masks so they breathed clean air.

Under all that protection, you can't even tell what sex they are. They could be alien conquerors built like insects, soft and lovely ladies in silk from China where everyone is rich, kings and queens from Fairyland. You hear stories of creatures like those coming to see how New York got laid low. I maybe could have gone into their brains, but I didn't want to give away that secret until I really knew what I was doing.

Then the tourists shifted and one who'd been hidden by the others stepped out front and showed me something very different.

This one didn't wear coveralls, helmet, or mask, and was female with copper skin and hair not so different from mine. She wore goggles and took breaths out of a tube she carried while someone held a metal shade above her.

She looked familiar as I saw her through Dare's eyes, and I felt my partner's surprise at how much the tourist girl looked like me.

This one was the center of the group's attention and concern. They clustered around like they'd stop bullets for her. Because of the goggles, I couldn't see her eyes, but I could tell she was staring my way.

Thinking back, maybe I kept my talent too much a secret. If I'd gone inside a couple more heads we'd have been spared a lot of grief. As it was, when Rock turned to look my way, Dare said, "Eyes front," under her breath, because we didn't want me drawing attention.

Dare checked the boys one last time, made sure their skin was intact and that they had the safety lenses in their eyes before they hit the water. She took some extra care with Rock. Dare was a diver herself before she hooked up with me. She got out of it in time, but she remembers.

If no one managed divers, tourists would make them compete so they drove each other to death. With murder and the diseases they get, and being drafted to serve in the militias, boys are scarce, and talented ones like ours are rare. Dare and I kept the ones we had healthy.

Then sunlight flashed as a tourist's hand came out of a pouch. Dare, calm and steady, nodded to the boys to stand right on the edge of the busted pavement in the spaces where there are no rails.

The hand went up, snapped the gold coin into the air, where it turned over as it fell toward the water a bit too far away for a boy to make an easy catch.

Dare had tapped Nice, and he dived forward in an arc, snapped it up as he hit the water. Nice flipped over and swam back and the tourists applauded, laughed. Nice was back up on the pavement with Dare taking the gold out of his mouth as the next coin sailed up in the air.

This was farther away and thrown harder, but Hassid kept his eyes on it as he dived, and was a yard away from where it went into the water. He came up with the coin and headed back as the next coin went farther out, and Not showing his skill and class went under and grabbed it.

The tourists applauded but this is how they always do it, throwing each one a little farther away, watching kids risk skin and eyes in water full of everything from turds to nuclear waste, seeing if their nerve will fail, hoping for the thrill of having one go under and not come up. The girl on the wreckage watched it all intently. It didn't seem possible anyone from this world could have the wealth and power she did.

Jackie Boy is the legend they've heard about. Jackie skimmed over the surface of the water, and no matter how far or hard it got thrown, could catch tourist money in his teeth before either he or the gold hit the river. Maybe he wasn't human. I'd started wondering if I was.

The tourists that day didn't work the boys as hard as lots of them do. We got all the coins except for one that Rock missed. But it turned out this was just a test.

One time that afternoon, a plane, a fighter, flew low over the city and we flinched but the tourists paid no attention. This meant that it was nothing important.

Then maybe they got bored, because they started climbing down the wreckage. Right that second, a chimera, the one called Silky, who's half seal, half woman, and old like they all are, came out of the water a bit farther upstream and caught their attention. Her skin is tough and she doesn't stay in long, and maybe that or luck lets her survive.

Chimeras come from when things were falling apart but some people in the city still had money and tech and a big need to keep amused. There aren't any new chimeras; probably no one knows how to make them anymore.

Tourist helmets flashed as they took pictures of Silky. I saw the girl look my way again and say something to one of the guys in protective gear, who took a few pictures of me.

When tourists lose interest, and city smells and poisons start getting in their masks, they go back to the expensive air at hotels in the Security Zone. Seeing the lights from the Zone way uptown always twisted my stomach, made me want to do a lot more than spit in their direction.

We got the boys cleaned off. There's stuff the UN clinic in Times Square gives to people exposed to the river or harbor, and we rubbed them down. We used expensive pure water to clean out their eyes and mouths.

All of a sudden Depose's car drove up. She got out and the girl said something to her before the tourist party climbed into their big ground car and took off.

Depose, wide and mean, and her bodyguard stayed behind. Through Dare's eyes I saw her stride to us. But I didn't look up until Depose went right past Dare without even nodding to her.

"Real." Her voice is this low growl and she motioned for me to step away from the others, stood over me bearing down, sticking her face close to mine. "My clients are in the city to shoot a Net episode. I brought you out today so they could look at you and your fags. Mai Kin wants to use you!"

She watched through those heavy lids for a reaction. Depose went through girl- and boyfriends like they were toilet paper, but liked them a little older than me. Otherwise I'd want to stay away from her. I nodded that I understood, shrugged like it was no great matter.

But that was why the tourist girl looked familiar. Mai Kin was a rising star right then, playing *Astasia X99*, a girl superheroine who's supposed to be around sixteen and who goes from place to place having adventures, fighting crime and vampires, and it's so dumb that you can laugh at it.

Astasia has the power of disguise. She's totally different in each episode. The last time I saw her she was in a big city in Africa and she was dark with wild black hair, infiltrating a revolutionary group.

What I just saw, I guessed, was the way she'd look here in New York. Pictures of Mai Kin before *Astasia X99* show an okay-looking Asian girl who's maybe twenty.

"The one called Caravaggio is going to direct this thing," Depose told me. "He'll get in touch. I trust you not to screw this up. Remember, Real, you owe me. You're smart. You don't need these dumb kids." She indicated Dare and the boys.

And I nodded, kept my face straight, my eyes right on hers.

Depose was a power. When the militia at Liberty Land needed

something done in the city, she was the one they hired. Somewhere down the line she'd want me working for her, but I didn't want to get close and didn't want to have to find out what was inside her brain.

2.

In October the sun starts going down fast. We bought food and water at the Red Crescent kitchen before we headed back to our place, making a tight group with the boys on the outside and Dare and me and the gold in the center.

I told Dare what Depose told me, and she said, "If that's Mai Kin, she tried to make herself look like you. Why did that happen?"

I shook my head because I didn't know. "If what Depose told me means anything, there'll be money."

Dare said, "I don't want that bull to think she owns us."

Old people who remember twenty-five years back talk about how hot it is now, but winter when it comes can kill if you can't stay warm. "We both felt cold a couple of nights ago," I said. "It's still okay in the days, but that's what's coming. Things are jumpy lately and we may need lots of gold to survive."

Dare listened and said, "Okay, you're right," and I reached up and kissed her. Dumb girls have boyfriends; smart girls have other girls. And smart girls and gay boys are natural allies.

The street we were walking on had a lot of burned houses and an old railroad overhead that had mostly fallen down. Eighth Avenue when we crossed it had people. An open market about ten blocks uptown was breaking up; people loaded carts and trucks. Downtown, a UN Peacekeepers armored car was crossing the avenue.

On the next block a bicycle boy whizzed past, turned a hundred feet away, and looked us over. Another bike boy was on the other side of the busted street, then a third and a fourth. All of them thin with faces like the vultures you see sometimes near the river. They knew us and that we were coming back with gold; they called us faggots and dykes.

But the Peacekeepers shoot people like them if they see they have guns, and we'd handled these guys before. Our boys had their knives out, Dare had her hand on the jump pistol under her caftan, Not and Hassid yelled that the bike boys would starve soon. We never stopped moving, and they kept circling but never closed.

Then because it felt like the right time, I looked one in the face and caught sight of us in his eyes, caught the way he saw us: we were gold, we were sex. Then he knew something was inside him and freaked, almost fell off his bike before he and the rest of them faded away.

My mother knew some stuff about getting by. When there were still parties, when there was the thought of getting close to the ones running things and running with them, my mother was on the job. But wherever I got this skill, I didn't get it from her.

I never met my father but she told me he was someone who traveled in important circles. He must have been some kind of prospect, because I think the reason she had me was to try and make him marry her.

People my mother's age were big on names. When there's no money, people do things like that. Dare's mother named her only daughter Virginia Dare, after the first European baby born in the USA. The Virginia part got discarded since anything you hear about Washington and Virginia sounds worse than here.

But she kept the Dare. It's an old word meaning tough, which is what she is: tough and beautiful. "Real!" she said, and I looked where she was looking. We were almost at our place. But on the next corner a building had fallen down last winter and blocked most of the street, and on the wreckage were Regalia and her crew.

Regalia was a six-foot-tall queen with paint on her face and an ax in her hand. A couple of years ago she had this giant boy Call who followed her like a stray dog, and her crew was IT.

But Call was dead white and got too much sun, which did him in. They say his face is partly gone and he's a skeleton. I haven't heard he's dead but I haven't seen him either.

In the last few weeks the city seemed to go desperate. For the second time in two blocks a gang wanted to take us on for a few gold coins. Again Dare took the lead and we came on like they weren't even there. Her blade was in her right hand and her left was under her robe. Two steps more and she'd have drawn the jump gun and put a slug in Regalia's stomach. I was reaching for Regalia's brain.

It would have been better if we'd gone in and snuffed Regalia right then. Instead a truck with guys standing on the back and packing rifles came out of the twilight.

Regalia's people saw this, and a couple started to back away. Then out of the cab jumped this bear, looking mean and huge in that light. One of Regalia's crew yelled and started to run, another followed him, and Regalia went back howling at all of them.

Dare turned to face the bear, but I already knew what this was about. Caravaggio always had chimeras around him. The bear pulled himself up and said, "I am Ursus. I have a message for Real." The voice was mostly human and hoarse and old. When I nodded, he said, "Caravaggio wishes that you come with us."

Dare didn't take her eyes off the bear and the guards on the back of the truck. "It's okay," I said. "This is what Depose talked about."

Dare said, "I need to come with you."

"I'd like that too. But we need you to guard the money. To make sure our place is defended. To come get me if something goes wrong." I reached inside and showed her what we'd do together when I came back.

Finally she nodded, and I climbed into the truck and headed downtown to Studio Caravaggio. I know about the studio and about him.

That name is some artist hero in the past. Lots of old people took big artist names. We still got Mozart in the streets playing the same tune every day on a busted clarinet.

The quarter moon was up so there was some light, people slipping through the shadows where there were buildings standing. We passed a convoy of cars full of tourists and guards. The driver moved the truck around the holes and piles of rubbish in the street. He slowed when a religious crowd from the projects carrying torches and saints' pictures and chanting crossed town on Fourteenth.

I saw Caravaggio when I was small and he drove by in a big car, had a gray beard and hair and dark eyes that stared out like a hunter's, and someone told me he was looking for kids, and if he liked you and brought you home, you never worked or went hungry. Someone else said he took your soul first.

Years after that, they had this film festival and he showed a movie against the wall of a building at night. It was pieces of old past century movies with people crashing cars and blowing up buildings, making jokes as they broke glass, gunned down people, and wrecked New York and dozens of other places just for their own amusement.

All the kids watching it screamed and threw things at the stupid grinning twelve-foot-tall guys and women, the destroyers who used up our city and our world. Caravaggio was there nodding approval at our anger.

3.

Studio Caravaggio is downtown on some blocks of old buildings still in good shape with generators and lights. Neighborhood guards with rifles stood on roofs and watched us come down the street. Their guns meant the Peacekeepers respected them like they did Depose.

Ursus went to a big metal gate, reached through that to a brass knocker on an iron door. He slammed the knocker a few times and a spy slot opened. "I brought Reality Girl."

The spy slot closed, the iron door opened, dim light spilled out, and a feathered chimera in slippers appeared, unlocked the metal gate, and stood aside. We entered this huge space like a warehouse, with old historic furniture, gold Chinese screens, long tables covered with lenses and tools. One wall was painted to look like a faraway city with tall buildings.

The chimera took me past rooms with lights from screens where people watched and worked. Others were dark with humans and chimeras lying on mattresses. Some watched us pass. At a worktable a fox, a cat, and a lizard chimera showed some human kids how to polish models of the old empire building and the statue of the lady that was in the harbor and stuff.

Those get sold to tourists, and the metal they're made of is supposed to be from the original buildings and statues. And I guessed this studio was where they got made.

A guy was cleaning the floors, and I smelled food cooking. Right then I wanted some of this for me and Dare and our crew.

From somewhere deep in Studio Caravaggio, a voice, hoarse and kind of shaky, said, "Visitors from the Orient encounter visitors from the future and fight it out in the ruins of New York while the natives dive for tourist gold is what it's about. Where did I get the story? My dear sir, it's my life. I look out my window and it's what I see."

Ursus turned a corner, and down a short hall, bright light shone out a doorway. The bear stopped at the door and we both looked at Caravaggio.

Before when I saw him, he was old but strong and dangerous

and needing to be respected. Now he was in a white robe with stains on the front, spilling wine as he drank out of a long glass. His face was thin and he slumped in a big soft chair with a fan playing on him. What I thought was a boy in silk shorts held a bowl of something and a spoon like he'd been feeding him.

Caravaggio's eyes moved, focused on me, and he said into a tiny disc in his open hand, "That's the scenario, Assad. As always, I'm interested in financial backing. My health? I'm not going to die before I complete this, I promise you. But now I've got to talk to someone."

When the boy put down the bowl and took a plug-in from behind Caravaggio's ear, I saw he was maybe pushing thirty, and I recognized him as Tagalong, who was on the street with a gang when I was small. He nodded to me.

"I've brought Reality Girl," said the chimera.

"Depose says you wanted to see me," I said.

Caravaggio said nothing, just stared at me through eyes that looked like he was crying. But his face didn't move. Tagalong tried to feed him from the bowl. Caravaggio brushed it away. He drained the glass, picked up a bottle with both hands, and drank out of it. Wine dribbled out the side of his mouth.

"My scouts talked about you," he said.

"You want to use my boys diving for the tourists?"

"The boys sure, but mostly it's you I'm interested in." He moved his hand over a glass surface then pointed at something behind me, wanting me to turn and look. I wasn't doing that, but I stepped back, kept him and Tagalong in my sight. Tagalong shook his head like he couldn't believe me.

What I saw was a flat screen. It took a second to know I was watching myself. First I was on the riverfront that summer with Dare and the boys. Then Dare and I walked through the early morning streets before the sun got bad, and we kissed. Next we were at the UN clinic in Times Square getting ointments and medicine.

Don't get scared, get mad was Dare's motto and mine. "You and your freaks followed me!"

"If we meant you harm we could have done it many times," Caravaggio said. "I've been thinking of you, imagining you in a film. The tourists you saw today were impressed by these pictures and were impressed by you." Mai Kin's face popped up on the screen. "At my suggestion Mai Kin has been redone in your image." Seeing her again, she didn't look that much like me.

Next I saw myself in the evening, walking all alone down an empty Fifth Avenue. This was fake; none of us ever went anywhere alone. Caravaggio talked on the sound track.

"Once this was the most famous city in the most powerful nation in the world," he said. "Then the bombs fell, the earth quaked, the waters rose, the government collapsed. Around the world, cities and nations fell, but none fell further. Mighty Gotham is a ruin at a crossroads, with local warlords like Liberty Land and the Northeast Command fighting for possession."

He touched the surface again, and I disappeared. Color and faces exploded on the screen. A girl in leather smashed mirrors in some huge bathroom. Maybe it was a party, maybe it was a riot, but the camera spun around in an enormous space. A mob dressed better than anyone in the city is now, poured fuel on chairs and set them on fire, smashed glass doors, shot out the lights high overhead.

"A fiesta of destruction made a ruin of Madison Square Garden," Caravaggio told me. "Caught for my first full-length film. But places remain on this planet where people are still rich and bored. The films I've made have kept the eyes of that world on us, and that's what I'm still doing."

The city opened before me. Buildings were down, but ones I'd never seen before stood. The streets were full of people. Cars went by; I saw a bus! It was New York after the bombs but before the quakes. A girl in a silk dress walked arm in arm with a chimera gorilla.

"What did you bring me here for?" I asked.

"I want you in a film. I'll use you as Mai Kin's body double. She's more a prop than an actor. You'll stand in for her in certain scenes. But it will be more than that. They think to use me to film the New York sequences for an episode of that idiotic series.

"But I'm going to use THEM to tell the story of kids on the waterline. I want you and your crew. Anything can be faked, but what's true will always stand revealed."

"I want a hundred gold pieces a day," I said, because that's as much money as I've ever seen at once and because gold is the only thing everyone trusts. "I want the first day's pay up front," I said, because that's what I know about doing business.

"I created the legend of Jackie, the angel of divers," he said, like he hadn't heard me. "Now I want to give the tourists a taste of the desperation of diver kids' lives."

I said, "What about the money?"

"Once I dreamed of showing Jackie returning to the city like an avenging angel come to save the place," he said. "My new vision of the city will be you and your friends." Again his hand moved over a glass surface in front of him.

A boy in long hair and shorts stood on a pier in the full light of day. Big crowds of people watched as a coin was flung and the boy leaped, seemed to flicker like silver light in the gold sun. He skimmed over the water and caught the coin in his hand. It looked fake.

What got to me was how the riverfront wasn't all smashed up. The water was lower than the walks. New Jersey was wrecked but not totally. Boats sailed and people didn't look scared. I remembered some of that from when I was real little, and got angry it was gone.

I wanted to see more but the screen went blank. I got careless and reached for Caravaggio, wanting to see what he remembered. I touched his brain and saw a jumble of faces, heard a tourist talking about a hundred-million-yen deal, tasted the wine he had just drunk, caught the smell of Silken Night, a perfume he remembered.

Caravaggio looked startled and confused. He tried to stand, and knocked over the wine bottle. Tag caught it, stared at me wide-eyed like he had a hint of what just happened.

It was stupid to give myself away. But I just shrugged. Then I remembered what we'd been talking about before Caravaggio started showing me pictures.

"A hundred gold pieces, right now," I said. "And I'm not going in the water." I didn't say that, even if I got as dumb as a boy, I couldn't swim.

"We'll talk about that," he said. "Fifty. Any more will get you and your friends killed." He was suspicious, maybe frightened after what he felt me do.

We settled on seventy-five, and he said shooting began in a few days. Tag counted the coins out for me in a little room near the front door of the studio. He whispered, "I followed you around and took those shots of you and your crew. I got him interested." He looked at me, curious and scared, like he guessed my secret. I nodded and kept quiet, but now I knew Depose had nothing to do with my getting hired.

In that huge front room, an owl showed humans how to make posters of Jackie look old and how to tell tourists they had found them in old trunks. I knew that even the ones who said there had really been a Jackie Boy also said Caravaggio kept him chained like a dog and only let him out to make movies, until he escaped.

The bear and the truck waited for me outside. As we drove

away I looked back: the lights, the guards, the street with people standing outside their buildings talking, little kids playing after dark, was magic and I wanted all of it.

Riding home I was cold, and the only light ahead of us was the glow from the Tourist Zone way uptown. I thought about the city Caravaggio showed me and remembered how my mom died when the superflu was killing everyone. The UN medics couldn't stop it. Some of them died. They told me I must have good genes and wanted to know who my father was, but I couldn't help them.

It was then that I met Dare. Her mother was dead too, so we had that in common and she was tough, took me under her wing, protected me until I got able to take care of myself. She had done gold diving but gave it up when she saw what happened to older kids. Together we worked out the deal with the boys.

The truck stopped in Madison Square, which is semi-wrecked buildings around a park that's a jungle nobody wants to go near. We have a lair in the cellar of a building that still stands on the west side of the square and has water, and we've got the entrances booby-trapped.

Lott, who's too sick to dive, guards the place night and day. We brought in Rock as his replacement. Ursus made the truck wait while I rattled the gates and said the password, and Lott let me in before they drove away.

The Indians at the clinic say Lott's got a few things wrong but it's lung cancer that's going to kill him. Dare thinks it's because we got him too late and if we'd been looking out for him sooner he'd be okay.

The boys were behind the curtains at the back of our place, laughing about the way we'd stood down the bike boys and Regalia. I could hear Lott's heavy breathing.

Dare said, "I don't much trust any of them." I didn't either, but it was the best deal we'd ever had. I wanted to show her the studio, but when I tried, what I found in her was fear that she was going to lose me.

So instead I told her about Caravaggio and Tagalong and the studio, made it funny and had her laughing.

4.

Once we started shooting, I spent more time in the deadly sun with less protection than I had all that summer. One morning I stood on a rusty fire escape ladder just above a flooded street with the tide coming in and waited for Caravaggio's signal. He and the camera crew were on the roof of the next building.

Three times I'd climbed four stories to the roof of this burned-out factory building where *Astasia X99's* boyfriend was being held by alien pirates. Each time, something went wrong and I had to do it again.

Dare was angry at what I was doing, but she tested the ladder herself and cleaned every rung before she'd let me go near it. After each take I got dowsed in purified water. The long T-shirt and shorts clung to me; my hair was wet and flat on my head.

All my life, pimps, militias, and gangs were on the prowl. A lot of any kid's life in this city is not getting noticed. Now I'd given that up to bring in money.

Earlier in the morning, before the shoot, we went up to the UN clinic in the big temporary building that's been standing ever since I can remember in the empty space people call Times Square.

Everyone in line was tense but nobody knew anything. Dare told the medicos what we needed. The Indian guy at the counter gave us double orders of salves, lotions, water purifier pills. "Just in case," he said, but didn't know much either.

I was thinking about that when someone said, "Action!" Just like before, I grabbed the handrails, held my breath, shut my eyes, ducked under the water, jumped out like I'd just swum there, and ran up the ladder to the roof.

Caravaggio was slumped in a chair but he raised his head and said, "Great!" I knew what was great was me coming out of the poison muck. For my crew I was doing stuff I didn't know I could do. Up on the roof Dare led me behind a blanket in the shade, got my clothes off, doused me in clean water and oil, and put me in a robe.

Mai Kin stood maybe thirty feet away under a metal awning, surrounded by guys in protective gear. Her character, *Astasia X99*, gets made over and rearranged in every installment. We watched a bunch of episodes. She has a boyfriend, Anselm, that she always has to rescue.

The actor who plays Anselm spent most of his time coming on to Rock. The other boys were jealous.

The episodes always take place in danger spots like New York. Mai Kin and company go in and shoot for a few days when it's quiet, then get out and finish the thing somewhere safe. There's always some other guy Astasia gets involved with before going back to Anselm. But that would get shot somewhere else.

Fighter planes streaked over the city. Mai Kin glanced up, then looked at one of her handlers. His head-shake was so slight as to be invisible. Looking away, I went inside him; found he was getting news every couple of minutes. The UN had Liberty Land and Northeast Command negotiating. *Touch and go* was the thought on his mind. I got out before he noticed.

Mai Kin wore a silk robe decorated with pictures of the planets. Dare said that up close she looked old and mean and way over twenty. Mai Kin was wired like most tourists, spoke into an implant in her left hand, and shook her head at something she heard. She never spoke to me or smiled, but never took her eyes off me.

I didn't have to get in her head to know that she hated me for looking like I did, for being alive in the same world she was. She slipped out of her robe and, wearing clothes identical to mine, walked to the spot where I'd come off the ladder onto the roof. Shooting her, Tagalong said, was like filming a robot.

When the light was gone and shooting stopped, we headed home, moved fast in the moonlight. Rock had disappeared.

"Making it with that actor tourist—that whore," Not said. Dare was pissed but sorry to lose him.

Not far from our place there was an explosion up ahead. We'd heard enough of them to know this was small, a grenade, not a bomb. We sped up and I tried to scan, to find Lott and see through his eyes, but I couldn't.

Turning the corner we saw our lair with the locks and bars and door all blown off. Smoke drifted out. "Lott!" Dare yelled.

Regalia came out the door with a couple of her crew. She had an AK474 knockoff. The Peacekeepers would have shot her for carrying it, which meant they weren't around. She leveled it at us and said, "Drop whatever you got—weapons, money—and you won't get hurt."

Dare held our gold. She stared back at Regalia and didn't move. I went into Regalia's head. The first thing I saw was all of us standing, eyes wide staring at her. She thought that was funny because she was about to shoot us down one by one. For her the sight of Lott's bloody corpse was funny.

Her trigger finger twitched. I found her right arm and jerked the AK474 up. A burst went into the air.

She tried to get control of her hands. I yanked her to the side, fired a burst at her crew. One went down screaming; the other backed off. A couple more came out the door of our lair. I turned her their way, fired again, caught one in the face. Then the gun jammed.

I found Regalia's heart and lungs, tried to tear them out of her body. Her eyes bulged. I moved her legs, ran her to the side of the building, and made her smash her head against the wall until the brains came out. All the time she made strangled noises and danced like a headless bird. When life went out of her, I couldn't make the body move, and she fell to the ground.

The rest of her crew had come out the door. Dare had her gun out, threatened to kill them. Hassid and Not slammed them around, took back the stuff the crew stole. One that had been shot half crawled away. Another was dead. The boys stared at the bodies. Only Dare knew what I'd done. She made Regalia's crew drag their dead away with them.

We found Lott inside, where the blast had killed him, wrapped his body in blankets and carried him into the park. We had a shovel and took turns digging it deep so the rats couldn't get him. We buried the AK474 in another place.

Dare talked a little about how much we loved him. All I could think was I didn't want to die like that. Even Dare was kind of afraid of me.

We huddled together in the lair, knowing we'd never stay there again. No one slept much, but I sat awake on guard. Almost at dawn I started crying and Dare held me, whispering, "You saved all of us. You're a hero."

5.

The next morning, Caravaggio was shooting on the waterfront. The crew and I were there because we had nowhere else to go. I looked for a chance to beg him for a place to stay. Our lair was gone. I felt older than Caravaggio, older than anyone. Rock had left us, Lott was dead, and after what I saw and did the night before, I half wished I was dead too.

Nice, Not, and Hassid dived for fake coins tossed by actors

dressed in protective gear. The boys' hearts weren't in it. We were zombies. They missed the coins and Caravaggio screamed at them, screamed at Dare and me.

Mai Kin and her handlers hadn't shown up. Caravaggio yelled at Tagalong, who couldn't contact them. Everyone said the Peace-keepers weren't around. On the water, scared passengers were cramming onto the ferries. Copters and planes took off from Liberty Land.

This world of mine was tougher now than it ever had been. Tagalong got definite word that the UN had withdrawn from the city. I said we had nowhere to live and asked him if we could stay at the studio until we found a place. He just sighed and looked at Caravaggio, who was yelling about traitors and ingrates.

I stood out on the seawall and Nice stood with me, rubbed my neck. I had my arm around him for comfort. We heard jets but didn't see them. Then, over in New Jersey, lights flashed like the sun on a knife blade. Next came explosions, big muffled ones. Caravaggio suddenly shut up. A moment later there was smoke over Liberty Land Stronghold, more flashes.

"Seems like Northeast Command took them out," someone said softly.

We should have been looking closer to us. I saw the ferries moving fast on the river, trying to scatter, before I heard the cop-ters. Rockets exploded. The seawall slid out from under my feet. Nice got torn away from me. I flew toward a huge wave and hit the water face-first.

It was in my eyes and nose, drowning me. I reached out for Dare, caught other minds. I felt Nice get cut in two. Someone's legs were crushed. Water was in my mouth and nose. I sank into the filth of the river bottom. I wanted Dare to have her arms around me. Then I was rising, pulled by my hair.

My head broke the surface. Not far away, flames floated on the water. People screamed. Dare hauled me up onto solid ground, pulled the clothes off me. Hassid was there. He washed me off and I let him. They put lotion on me.

Dare held me. She was crying. Nice was gone. They couldn't find his body. Only when I sat up did I see the gash on Dare's leg and knew what she risked to save me. She didn't make a sound when Hassid cleaned and bandaged her wound.

As if he was far away, I heard Caravaggio crying, "When I first came to the city, it was half wrecked but vibrant in its death dance." I caught images in his brain of destroyed streets with kids in costumes dancing through them. A flickering figure flew into the air, caught a coin in his mouth, bounced off the water. Then there was nothing and I knew Caravaggio was dead.

We went to Tagalong, who stood in tears as Caravaggio got lifted onto the truck. Dare and Not and Hassid were with me. Through Tagalong's eyes, I saw how sad and ragged we were. Then I showed him what had happened to us and to Regalia, and asked if we could stay at the studio. Scared but impressed, he nodded.

6.

"He loved the chimeras," Tagalong said a little later when we brought Caravaggio's body home. More of them than I thought were still alive waited outside the studio. Ursus was there and the bird woman who was in charge of the door, a pony and the cat and the man who was part fox, a cat man and cat woman, Silky the seal, big dogs, a goat, and the owl. I didn't even know what some of the others were. They howled and moaned when they saw the corpse.

They laid Caravaggio out in the big front room and dressed him like a king in silks and furs. Flowers appeared and candles lighted the place. A hundred and more people came from the neighborhood; a few even came from farther away, risking the streets to see him one last time.

Some brought food. The people in the kitchen cooked more.

Tagalong gave the four of us a large enough room with futons on the floor. We piled them together, lay on them, held each other and cried. Dare made plans to go next day and find Nice's body. I didn't want to think.

The chimeras were chanting when I heard engines outside. Tagalong appeared and told me Depose was there with cars full of her people and wanted to come in. I understood that he wanted me to do something and this was why I was here.

So I stood at a peephole beside the door, watched Depose without her seeing me. "We need to confirm that Caravaggio is dead," she told the doorkeeper bird, who looked scared. "Various of his associates and backers need to know. And we need to find that film he was making. I don't want to use force."

I didn't need to go inside her to know that she was going to use force, and when she got in here, this place would be looted. I looked back at Caravaggio laid out and the candles and the chimeras.

At the same time I found Depose and showed her what I was seeing. For a second she didn't understand what had happened. Then Depose realized who was doing this and remembered what she heard that morning about me and Regalia.

Still she hesitated, so I showed her a moment of Regalia and the wall. Depose headed for her car fast, and I let her know that if she wanted the film, she'd need to come alone and bring a lot of gold.

I felt shaky when it was over but I waited for the engine sounds to fade. As I went back to our room, everyone in the studio stood and applauded, and I figured we'd won our place here.

We sat on a mattress and leaned against pillows. "Maybe you should have done her like Regalia," Dare whispered.

"Maybe," I told her. "But I didn't have all the anger and fear like I did with Regalia. And I can't kill everyone, and Depose can be bought."

Dare understood and put one arm around me. She cuddled Not, and I held Hussein.

That's how we were when Tagalong came in with a camera and two women who did stuff with lights. He said he wanted to film me talking about what happened. "We need a hero," he said. "We'll call this *REAL*. We need to advertise you." And I thought about Caravaggio and Jackie Boy.

Dare told him, "Her name's Reality Girl."

"Great!" Tagalong said, and with the camera running he asked, "Reality Girl, can you tell us how you came to be here?"

What I remembered first was me and the crew walking down to the waterline a week or maybe ten days ago.

HOW TH'IRTH WINT RONG BY HAPLESS JOEY @ HOMESKOOL.GUV

BY GREGORY MAGUIRE

OK OK.
I am riting on this paper the old-timey way with a pen.
This is my 5st copy and the last copy. Its no good I dont care.
Kick me outa homeskool, what happens, Im alreddy home. Ha ha.

The Big Ant says OK OK git to work buster. Very funnish start but wut about yor topic title? How th'Irth Wint Rong. Tell me wut you has to tell, says the Big Ant. Hoo wins th'essay contist gits a hole ham for the wintir. Go for it, Hapless Joey. Yu needs it, yor wasting away, I kin see yor ribs thru yor parka. I kin see yor thinkings thru yor hairliss skalp. Yu gits ideers fast enuff. Put yor mind on the paje.

OK OK.

Big Ant sits an luks at papers from othr kids. Looks at papers.

Im not riting this over. She sits hirself up by th'stove nere the best hot part. She says she kint unnerstand a singul wird of wut she is luking at. I got to git myself unnerstud.

Topic title: How th'Irth Wint Rong by Hapless Joey @ homeskool. guv

(Big Ant says, that last bit. Homeskool dot guv. Thats fake. Brite-time writing. From back in the days of internet and puters. Take it out she says. I dont. I think it looks cool. Maybe puters will be invented again. Sum day. Besides, shes not suppoz to tell me stuff. Thay want to see how I kin think for my self.)

I am Hapless Joey. I am not a liddle kid. I am not a groanup. I am tall as th'pegs for cotes in th'hallway. I waz liddle wonce now I'm not so mutch.

I liv in a shack. Hoo dont, yu say but lots dont. My dore gots a lock an my winders gots glass. I im here with my grandid Ole Joey an sometimes Big Ant come over. She suppoz to be fare but this hous is not so windy and cold as some so I gits mor uv hir time. That's wy I cin rite so gud. Good. Big Ant is good teecher but she eets a lot. She's Big Ant. She gots to close hir coat with a rope. Lurning me to rite makes hir hungerful I gess. Me to.

> Note to Commity: This is Big Ant and I have no intrist in a ham or in getting out of the stupid bone-chilling cold. Hapless Joey has some wits about him so pay attention to what he says. Im not allowed to correct his work but I cant stand by and let him slag me off without pitching a comment about it. His house aint all that warm neither.

Also I aint that big, just got a big heart as any Sinner will tell you and a big heart needs a big rib cage to hold it and stout legs to stand it up and walk it about. I only use a rope around my coat becawse a dog cawt my belt onct when I was walking home with a chicken curry courtesy of Sector Admin. who admire my work with kids by the way.

I waz born a short time befor the Cold Time startd. My grandid tells me all the time abowt the wirld then. Its hard to beleve wut he says. I cint member I wuz a baby. But them pickchrs in buks books bux whatever, thay dont lie. I seen cars withowt rust an I seen green yards like blankets put down. The grass green awl so smooth. I seen a sky with no clowds, awl sweet an blu lik the cleanest sheet yu ever seen. In pickchrs I seen it, torn from books an hangd up in th Pickchr Plase calld the Multiplecks.

Bak then th'Irth was fuller. More warm. More cleen. Peepul culd fly arownd in metal rumez with wings an go here an there. Over to Yurup an Japan an Afrika. An other playcis that uzed to exist. Thay culd go an cum back like eezy peezy wuts the problim? Thay culd go on big ships ovir the water. Thay culd liv in Parisfrants or in Lundininglind or in Romittly. Thay dint think nuthin uv it, thay just livd like you an me. Well bettr then you an me becaws that wuz befor th'Irthsore happin.

The Big Ant says OK OK I got to rite abowt th'Irthsore. Thass my hole point. Th'Irthsore that chaynjd the wirld. That made Cold Time.

Back wen my parints wer yung an just chirchd, thay was a mom an a dad too, just like in sum of them pickshrs, th'Irth it wuz cleen and all ficksed up. Cars slid up and forth the streets. Sinners culd tawk on littl metel cards with numbrs on them. Thru th'air I meen, like if you had a frend in Berlinjerminy or Athnsgrese you just like sed sum numbrs an they sed sum numbrs back an it was like, Hi, how ar you, how is it over there in Parisfrantz or Kieroejipt. Evrybuddy did it all the time like it wuz nuthing spexial. Speshul. Spejal. Nuthing unyoujewel.

> Note to Commity: This is Big Ant again an you see a brake here in the story because Hapless Joey smashed his pencil in distress. He spells better than most but that dont mean nothing to him. He wants to get it write. Thats what marks him owt for spexhul notice. I told him stop with bragging all those cities, theys all gone and you do yourself no favors reminding the Commity so he stopps. But he likes geogriphy and maps as you can see so planely. He started writing agin a few days later. Its with a color pencil but its still his wirk. He is good dont you agree.

I dont member enny uv this. Th'Irth before Coldtime. Its mor like a dreem sumbuddy have. But Grandid an Big Ant member fine an others to. Two. Too.

Grandid uze to go to liberry, an it uze to be free. Also opin. He culd reed most enything he wantd to. He unnerstands sum uv wat happind. He told me an now I im telling yu. Ywo. Yoo

Damm damm damm. I hate spelling its not lawful.

OK OK. I im bettr now.

Here is wat happind. Back then th'Irth wuz pirfect an men had jobs an cash and womin had soft yello hair an didnt need so many cotes. Thay culdn feel the cold I gess. It wuz a time of heros an moving stars on th'Irth. Grandid livd then so did Big Ant. So did my parints. Th'Irth wen I git born wuz still paradize only nobuddy new it wuz.

With awl the big masheens an stuff life wuz eezy an warm an lots uv food. An pepul culd go arownd the wirld to plascs like Nirobiafrika. An China an Oztrailya.

The peepul all think thay is smartr than God. Thay make a mashine in the mowntens betwene France an Switzrland. It is big it is ugly it is powrfull. It makes the motes in God's eye go fastr an fastr in a big tunnl a hundcrd miles long. A sircul tunnl, rownd an rownd. Peepul calld Siontists thay study the spede uv the parts. The dust uv the wirld. The smithireens uv the planet. The motes uv God's eyc. Wow thay say wow, wow! wow! We make the crums an bits uv thc wirld run fastr.

Wy du thay do this yu ask. Its a gud kwestchun. I do not no the anser.

Then wun day God gits mad at peepul playing with th'Irth. The peepul spin the motes so fast rownd an rownd thay meet themselvs coming the othr way. God lets it happn. God lets the durt in the tunnl hit itself. Hard. Thass wat pecpul now think. I wuz only a baby but Grandid says he woke up during th'Irthsore an the hole morning was braking up lik threds on the edj uv a carpit.

It wuz 6 in the morning an he culd see me in my crib in the morning lite. My hands wir trying to clap but thay culdnt. Evrything in the wirld wuz pulling to wun side. Like static lectrisity back wen thay had lectrisity. My baby hand an the crib an the winder wir awl pulling. Brok up into eech othr. Lik meltd mud an snow an crud draggd awl wun way by a stick with fingrs. Grandids legs an the sheets wir awl pulling like taffy an he culdnt moove to git me. It stayd lik that for an owr or so then it poold back to normil.

But it wuz not the same normil. Maybe an owr or maybe time got pulld too.

Thay sed on the streets that the big tunnl cullapsd. Maebe it made a nu kind uv dust that dint like th'Irth. Or maebe it made a tiny mowth in th'Irth that wuz hungry an wantd to eet th'Irth. Or it wuz maebe spots uv Nothing an it dissolvd th'Irth as far as it culd. But Nothing cant exist by itself or nobuddy wuld notiss it, says the Chirch Man. Nothing ate the haff of th'Irth that wuz on that side. Wen it finishd haff it tride to go on but th othr haff of Nothing is Sumthing. It was ar haff of th'Irth so we stayd Sumthing.

The othr haff the dark haff is Nothing. No wun unnerstands wut is in it Nothing I gess. Haff a planit uv Sumthing, haff a planit uv Nothing. Pirfect balans.

Just darck. Darck Nothing.

Why is that I wunder.

OK OK. The end.

Note to Commity: Now you see what I am trying to show you. Hapless Joey is a good boy and he knows a lot. This is the best pece of riting I seen in four or five years. I think you shuld also know that his parents were in Moscow or someplace when the

SuperCollider collapsed. Like half the wirld, they never been hird from again.

It is my belief he deserve the ham. I culd come get it just give the say-so.

Dear Big Aunt,

The Committee has reviewed the writing of Hapless Joey and agrees with you that he is special material. Will you bring him to Central next week, any day you like, and we will train him up to be a missile into the Dark Edge. We have only sent ten or twelve people in ten years, and one day one of them will come back and tell us what they found there. Hapless Joey may be the lucky one. His name is the opposite of lucky, and something is the opposite of nothing. Don't tell Hapless Joey what he has won. He may need to grow up more to appreciate the honor. We don't want him to run away.

You may keep the ham for yourself after you give him up.

RUST WITH WINGS

BY **STEVEN GOULD**

JEREMY LAY FLAT ON HIS STOMACH IN THE BACKYARD GRASS, watching three bugs crawl across a flattened soda can. They were larger than June bugs, with that beetle shape. One was copper colored, one was silver, and one rusty. Every so often their wing cases would lift slightly and reveal iridescent crystal blue beneath. The rusty one was almost twice as long as the others, with extra legs and a junction point where the new head would be after it split. Everywhere the bugs crawled, holes appeared in the metal.

Jeremy's dad rounded the corner and said, "Get your butt in the car right now. We're outta here!"

Jeremy scrambled up, brushing off his jeans. Ever since the power had gone out three days before, Dad's temper had gone from easygoing to better-watch out, and Jeremy wasn't going to do anything that might trigger it.

When they rounded the house, Mom and Laurie were putting laundry baskets full of clothes into the trunk. Laurie was saying, "But why can't I go over to Sarah's instead? You said I could last week!"

Dad and Mom exchanged glances. Dad's eyes narrowed

and he opened his mouth, and Mom said quickly, "You're going to have to trust me on this one, honey. Sometimes plans change."

Dad shut his mouth and moved to the driver's door. He muttered, "We should've *left* last week." He paused and took a look at the house, head tilted back. Jeremy swiveled to see, but Dad barked, "In the car. Now!"

Jeremy got in the back and tried to look up through the rear window. He couldn't tell what Dad had noticed, but it was hard to see 'cause Dad peeled out of the driveway and he was thrown across the seat and into Laurie.

She shrieked and shoved Jeremy back. "Put your seat belt on, idiot!"

He did, his eyes wide. The few times Dad had ever driven like that, Mom had screamed at him and made him stop the car, but now she was just looking back at Jeremy to make sure he got the seat belt fastened.

The tires screeched as they made the left at the subdivision entrance. Jeremy felt himself sink into the seat back as Dad accelerated toward the interstate.

Mom spoke through gritted teeth. "We've got to *survive* to survive, Peter."

Dad blew air through his nose and slowed down slightly. The telephone poles were flicking by faster than Jeremy had ever seen, but there were no lines between them. Curling pieces of black insulation littered the ground and the side of the road.

Short of the interstate, Dad hesitated. "Last news report seemed to say it was spreading from Phoenix but it was worse in New Mexico. I think we should take 86 and 85, then join up on 8 and make for San Diego."

"What about Mexico?" Mom said.

Dad shook his head. "No. They're shooting people who try to

cross. It's stupid. The bugs travel all by themselves. It's not going to help."

"Do we have enough gas?"

Dad shrugged. "Maybe. There's fifteen gallons in the jerricans."

Gas wasn't the issue.

Maybe Dad thought there'd be fewer bugs on that route because there were fewer people. Fewer people, less metal, but he hadn't counted on the industrial park just west of San Pedro Road.

Mom muttered, "Where did they come from? Why are they doing this?"

You could see the frameworks of the buildings, but the skin, the painted steel sheets, were like Swiss cheese. Closer, at the side of the road, there were irregular mounds shimmering in the sunlight—silver, gold, copper, rust, all mixed with iridescent blue.

They didn't slow down, but even going by at speed, Jeremy could see that the mounds weren't still. They undulated and shifted, exposing the odd windshield or tire or plastic fender liner.

There was a crunching noise under the tires, and suddenly the air was full of iridescent wings.

It was like driving through a hailstorm. The bugs banged off the hood and the windshield and the roof. Dad took his foot off the pedal for an instant.

"Jesus!" Mom said. "Don't stop! They're not sticking."

And that's what they thought for another ten minutes. Then the bugs began edging over the front of the hood from the very front of the car. The grille had been scooping them up like a catcher's mitt. You'd think that when they'd enter the slipstream on top of the car they would've been blown off, but they weren't. They pressed their dark blind heads against the hood and stuck.

"Maybe we should get out?" Mom asked.

Dad tilted his head to the side. Through the rearview mirror

Jeremy saw his eyes darting around. "Let's get as far as we can."

A few minutes later the radio antenna came off near its base and, several bugs still attached, clattered across the windshield, bounced once off the trunk, and was gone. Now the hood was covered and the bugs were climbing the roof struts on either side of the windshield. The left windshield wiper came off, and then the roar of the engine abruptly died, and everyone surged forward against the seat belts as the car slowed.

"They got the ignition," Dad said, putting the car into neutral. "When I tell you, get out of the car as quickly as you can and run off the road."

The car was on a downhill stretch and it wasn't slowing much. Jeremy thought that was good. There weren't as many bug mounds by the road, and the car was clearing the industrial park. The only bugs he could see were a small group eating a mile marker and the ones on their car.

Mom screamed, "They're coming through the dashboard!"

They weren't, really. There were a few crawling out of the plastic A/C vents. They began eating the metal radio trim. More crawled out, and she said, "Get me out of this car, Peter!"

Dad licked his lips, then nodded. Jeremy saw his body shift as Dad said, "The brakes are gone! They've eaten through the hydraulic lines!" Jeremy heard the ratcheting of the emergency brake, and the rear tires screeched. The rear end broke loose and slid. Dad steered into the skid, but with the engine dead, the power steering was no help at all.

They came over a rise, and saw the remains of another car—plastic, carpet, and tires in a jumble. Beside it, a cluster of turkey vultures were clustered around something dead. Rather than hit the wreckage, Dad headed toward the vultures. He tried to honk the horn, but it wasn't working. As the car bore down on them, the birds jumped into the air, revealing their meal.

Mom screamed and Dad swore, swerving again to avoid the dead man, and the wheels caught the shoulder.

It wasn't much, but it jerked the car around and it went off the road, bounced into, then out of, a ditch, and then plowed through a stand of prickly pear cactus and yucca, out into the desert.

The car came to a stop in a cloud of dust. Dad was bleeding from a cut on the side of his head, and his side window was shattered, but he just said, "Okay?" looking around. Then, "Out, out, out!"

There was dust swirling around the car, but it had cleared the worst of the cactus. Jeremy scrambled through the door and backed away from the car.

Dad was doing something with the dashboard, but he finally scrambled out, brushing at his pants leg. Bright copper flashed and fell to the ground. Dad reached into his pocket and threw something from him. It glittered as it passed over the hood of the car. Several bugs lifted into the air and followed it.

Jeremy looked at Dad's leg. Where his right pants pocket had been, the cloth was riddled with holes; and there was blood spotting the white tatters that had been the pocket lining.

Mom and Laurie were standing on the other side of the car, near a hoary old saguaro. Mom had taken her cell phone out of her purse. Jeremy don't know what she thought she was going to do. The cell towers had been the first to go. She turned it on, though, to try to acquire a signal, and the bugs rose up and headed for her.

Laurie screamed, and they both ran.

Dad yelled, "Get rid of the phone!" over and over again, running after them, wide around the swarm.

Mom must've heard him finally, for she tossed it off to the left and veered right.

The bugs followed the phone.

Mom and Laurie dropped, exhausted, onto a stretch of sand

between the cholla. There was blood on their legs from the mesquite and cactus they'd torn through, and Laurie had a segment of jumping cholla stuck to her knee.

Jeremy paled when he saw that. Jumping cholla is a kind of cactus with nasty barbed spines. They stick all too well. You snag one on your shirt, and a branch segment breaks off in a banana-size chunk, and the recoil usually embeds twenty or so spines in your skin.

And since they're barbed, they don't like to come out.

Mom took a large comb out of her purse and held it behind her back toward Dad. He took it and held it low, where Laurie couldn't see it.

Laurie's eyes were wide, and she was hyperventilating through clenched teeth.

"Easy, easy," Dad said. "Oh! Look what the bugs are doing to the cell phone!"

Jeremy knew that was bullshit. There was lots of brush between them and where the phone had landed, but Laurie turned her head, and Dad slipped the comb down between the cholla segment and the cloth of Laurie's jeans and *yanked*.

Jeremy ducked. When the barbs let go, the chunk flew thirty feet, whizzing past his hair. Laurie screamed once, and then Mom was holding her tight and rocking her.

Cool, Jeremy thought. He hadn't know Dad could be so sneaky.

"Gotta get the water out of the car," Dad said. "I tried to pop the trunk before we got out, but the switch wouldn't work and my keys are still in the ignition." He took Mom's purse and dumped it out onto the sand.

Mom's keys—a jangling tangle of keys, souvenir key dangles, and the keyless remote for the car—were there. There was a also a small pocketknife, a metal nail file, and a pair of nail scissors. And a mountain of change.

"Shit!" Dad looked around wildly. There were bugs in the

distance, but none near. He began scraping a hole in the sand and pushing the change into it.

"Bury it!" he said to Jeremy.

Jeremy stared back blankly.

Dad pointed at the bloody place where his pants pocket had been. "Metal. *Any* metal. They were going after the change in my pocket."

Jeremy started pushing sand over the change. "But they *really* were interested in the cell phone," he said. "More than the money in Mom's purse, or her keys."

"Yeah," Dad said. "I think anything with an electromagnetic field. Anything with an electric current. Remember how they went for the electrical transmission wires first?"

Jeremy froze. "Shit."

Despite her tears, Laurie giggled, and Mom's eyes got really big. "Jeremy Bentham, what did I tell you—"

Dad held up his hand. "What's wrong, Jerry?"

Jeremy took his GameGuy out of his hip pocket. "It's mostly plastic, but electronics and a battery, too."

"Ah," Dad said. "Yeah, that could've gotten ugly. It's off, right?"

"Yeah. I had it charging when the power went off, and I didn't want to play it since I wasn't sure when I'd be able to recharge it." Jeremy started to put it in the hole.

"No. We can use it, I think."

Dad took the trunk key off of Mom's key ring and dropped the keys down on top of the coins. They mounded the sand above them, perhaps six inches high, and Jeremy marked it with a circle of stones.

Dad took the GameGuy and headed back toward the car.

Jeremy followed him, threading through the cholla with care. He stepped on a tinder-dry mesquite twig, which popped loudly, and Dad jerked around. For a second, Jeremy thought Dad was going to order him back to Mom, but Dad closed his mouth and nodded.

As they got closer, Jeremy heard a humming and then a cracking sound. Most of the bugs on the car weren't flying, so their buzzing wasn't the loudest thing. It was the car.

"Noisy," Jeremy whispered.

Dad laughed without humor. "I don't think you have to whisper. I don't think they can hear anything outside the electromagnetic spectrum. That and detect metal. That cracking sound is the internal stresses of the metal being released as individual molecular bonds are broken."

The bugs covered the entire car, including the trunk. The plastic fender liners had slumped down onto the ground, and the tires were flat. Paint was peeling off in shreds. The plastic parts had holes in them too, but they were incidental. The bugs went through them to get to other metal.

Dad looked at the GameGuy, then handed it to Jeremy. "Turn the volume up to max. I figure the more juice to the speaker, the bigger the electromagnetic field. It doesn't broadcast on an antenna like Mom's cell phone, but it'll do something."

Jeremy rotated the volume knob all the way up with a quick swipe of his thumb. His index finger went for the power switch, but Dad said, "Not yet."

Dad held up his left hand, the trunk key encased in his fist. "I want you to turn the GameGuy on, then throw it over the car so it lands in that thicket in front. Don't hit the car—we don't want to knock it hard enough to stop working. The electromagnetic field needs to persist."

Jeremy heard what Dad was saying, but his eyes were on Dad's hand. "Dad, what about your wedding ring? Oh, Christ! What about your pacemaker?"

Dad froze. His eyes widened and his mouth dropped open.

"Oh, God!" Jeremy said. "What about your crowns?"

Dad shut his mouth with a snap. Then he said, "Let me see your mouth."

Jeremy opened wide, and Dad sighed. "Right. Your mom always insisted on composite fillings for you kids. No mercury silver amalgams." He looked down at Jeremy's pants. "Shit. Take off your pants."

"My pants?"

"You've got a brass zipper, a brass snap, and copper rivets reinforcing the corners of the pockets."

"What about *your* zipper?" Jeremy said.

Dad shrugged. "You're right about my pacemaker. I'm not going *near* the car. You'll have to do it. We need the water and the clothing, if they haven't already turned the containers into Swiss cheese." He looked down. "Looks like your shoes are all leather and plastic—punched lace holes, no grommets. So get out of your pants, and we'll try this."

Dad took the GameGuy while Jeremy took his pants off. He felt funny about it—standing outdoors in his underwear—but had his shoes back on in just a few minutes.

Then Dad gave Jeremy the key. "Stick it in the lock, turn it, and flip the lid up. Don't try to get the key back out."

Jeremy nodded solemnly.

They moved around until they were lined up behind the trunk, about twenty feet back. Dad had Jeremy show him the GameGuy's ON switch. "Yeah—thought so, but wanted to be sure."

He swung his arm back and flicked the switch.

There was moment of stillness on the car as every bug stopped moving; then iridescent blue wings exploded into view and bugs buzzed into the air, headed for them. Dad flung the GameGuy through the heart of the swarm, and most of the bugs shifted to follow, but a few still headed toward them.

"Damn it," Dad said, and bolted. Jeremy dropped to the ground and shoved his fist, the one with the trunk key in it, into the loose sand. With his other hand he scraped sand over it, mounding it high.

One bug flew by, ignoring him, but another hovered for a moment, shifting back and forth in the air over him. Then it dropped to settle on Jeremy's discarded jeans and began eating the brass zipper.

Jeremy loosened his grip on the key, then dug his other hand into the sand and lifted a mound up, the key inside. He didn't know how much sand it would take to shield the metal from the bugs, but hopefully, with the car, the GameGuy, and the cell phone, the bugs would have higher-priority targets. He walked slowly forward, dribbling sand as he went. Bugs were returning to the car now, but the trunk lid was largely unoccupied.

Jeremy brought his mound of sand right up to the lock before he let the last grains pour out of his hands. For one frantic second, he nearly let the key slide out of his hand with the sand, but he caught it, aligned it, and jammed it into the lock.

The bugs on the trunk lid were twitching, but they kept eating even as the lock clicked and the trunk rose on sprung hinges.

There were a few bugs in the trunk, but it wasn't too bad. Jeremy grabbed the baskets of clothes and flung them behind him, far from the car, then snatched the two water jugs and backed up.

The motion of the trunk lid had stirred the bugs up, and more were in the air. One bumped into his head and snagged on his hair. Jeremy could feel it moving, and pictured it eating into his skull. He shook his head violently, and the bug flipped off, buzzing into flight before it hit the ground; but now it was closer to the car than to him, and it flew to the vehicle.

Jeremy quickly gathered the spilled clothes back into the baskets. He dragged the water into the shade of a mesquite bush, well away from any metal. Then he took the clothes back to where Mom and Laurie were still sitting. "Where's Dad?" Jeremy asked. Dad should have circled back to them by now.

Mom looked around. "I don't know. I thought he was with you."

Jeremy guessed she hadn't overheard their conversation about the crowns and Dad's pacemaker. He didn't want to worry her. "He's probably looking for shelter."

"Where are your pants?"

"Too much metal," Jeremy explained. "Metal zipper and snaps and rivets."

He dug out a pair of basketball shorts, baggy and long but with an elastic waist, and pulled them on over his shoes. He pointed at the clothes baskets. "You should probably change out of anything with metal on it—unless you can remove the metal itself."

"Where's my purse? I've got scissors in them."

"We buried them, Mom. Metal, remember?"

He went back and got one of the water jugs, dropping it on the sand by Laurie. "Here. I'll go check on Dad."

Dad had gone north, away from the road, away from the car. Jeremy picked up the other water jug and followed.

There was a large stretch of gravel and sand interspersed with mixed cactus and mesquite, and some dry-as-tinder grass. Jeremy kept his eyes open for rattlesnakes and scorpions. He wasn't as worried about Gila monsters, since they rarely bit unless you picked them up.

The brush stopped at water, and Jeremy blinked, surprised. It was a water trap on the edge of a golf course. On the other side of the water was a green fairway starting to turn brown, and condos lined the far side of that.

They weren't as far out in the desert as he'd thought.

There were bugs buzzing across the water, and something

moved just below the surface, then Dad's head came up and he took a deep gasp of air. The bugs shifted toward him, but Dad was already underwater again. Jeremy saw a flash of a kicking leg as he swam toward a different spot.

Jeremy knew Dad couldn't do that forever. He wished he had the GameGuy again, so he could heave it across the pond, distracting the bugs. He had to do *something*.

A groundskeeper's shed, roofed and sided with corrugated fiberglass panels, was strewn across the grounds at one end of the pond. There were bugs crawling through the contents, but Jeremy saw, off to one side, some scraps of hose. He ran over, slowing drastically as he got closer. The bugs were eating metal shovels, brass fittings, and the screws out of the two-by-four framing.

But they'd cut through a bunch of hose, too, while eating through the metal reel the hose had been coiled around. Jeremy inched closer until he could reach in and snag a foot-long section. It was still connected to the main hose, but only by a small strip, left when the bugs had crawled through it. Jeremy put his foot on the longer section and heaved. The connecting material broke with a snap, and he fell back into the brown grass, clutching the short end.

Bugs—disturbed by the vibrations, Jeremy guessed—rose into the air, and he froze on the ground as they swirled over him, then finally returned to the scattered shed and settled back onto the tools.

Jeremy edged away from the shed and ran back to the pond, plunging in and swiftly heading for Dad through waist-deep water.

This time, Dad's face was out of the water, just barely, just enough for him to breathe. His eyes were wide and flicking back and forth, looking for bugs, but they hadn't spotted him yet.

"Get back, Jerry! Those bugs could get you as they're trying to get me!"

Jeremy held up the tubing. "A snorkel."

Dad couldn't hear him. The water was in his ears. So Jeremy put one end of the tubing in his mouth and tilted up the opposite end, then held his other hand flat, indicating the surface of the water below the upper end of the hose.

"Ah!" Dad reached for the hose, and Jeremy put it in his hand. Dad's head came up out of the water, and the bugs, four or five, homed in on him. Dad dove back under, and Jeremy did too.

When Jeremy came up again, the bugs were spread out, quartering the pond. He could not see his dad, only the hose sticking out of the water in the middle of the pond.

The water wasn't that cold, but when Jeremy climbed out of the pond, his wet skin and clothes acted like an evaporative cooler, chilling him. It felt good at first, and then uncomfortable. He wanted to get those bugs away from Dad. Dad couldn't stay in that pond forever.

Laurie and Mom had changed clothes when he returned. Mom looked up sharply when he came back into sight. "Where's your father?"

Jeremy gestured. "He's okay. But he needs to stay where he is. The bugs really like his pacemaker and his crowns."

The car was now completely covered in bugs, and its outline had changed substantially. It was lower on the ground. Between cactus thorns and bugs burrowing through the tires, going after the steel fibers, the tires no longer held air.

"We should get farther away from *that*," Jeremy said.

Mom started stuffing their metal-free clothes into one of the clothes baskets, ignoring the discards.

Jeremy looked at Mom's purse, still lying besides the ring of rocks that marked the buried coins, keys, and scissors. He picked it up. It was a leather purse lined with cloth. The straps were a continuous sweep of the body's cloth-lined leather and it had a nylon zipper. The only metal part, the zipper pull, had come off the previous year.

He started filling it with sand.

"What are you doing?" Laurie said.

"Need to carry some metal over to where Dad is."

"What? Won't that bring the bugs down on us?"

"Not if it's buried in sand. Shielded." He dug his hands into the sand in the middle of the rock circle, worming his fingers down.

He found the scissors by stabbing himself firmly in the ball of his thumb. He jerked his hand back up and stuck it in his mouth, tasting sand and blood.

Jeremy brought the items up one by one, centered in a double handful of sand, and dropped them into the purse. Only once did a bug come to investigate, and he frantically shoveled more sand into the purse until it flew back to the mound of bugs that used to be their car.

The last thing was his mom's key ring, with the radio remote for the car and some decorative metal stars hanging on chains. As he pulled it up out of the sand, several bugs took to the air and flew toward him. He dug down into the growing hole, grabbed the last few coins, and threw them at the approaching bugs. As the pennies and nickels flew by, the bugs turned around to follow them.

He had to get Laurie to help him carry the purse, it was that full of sand. She took one strap, Jeremy took the other, and they staggered back through the mesquite and chollo to the water trap.

Dad was still underwater, out in the middle of the pond, breathing through the hose. The bugs, now more than a dozen, were patrolling the water's surface.

"Where's your father?" Mom asked.

Jeremy pointed and told her about the snorkel.

She put her hand to her mouth. "We've got to get him out of there!"

"And put him where?"

"Someplace where he won't *drown*."

"What about the bugs, Mom? If he gets out of the water, those bugs are going after his crowns and his pacemaker."

Mom blinked and looked around desperately, as if hoping for a policeman or an EMT or a fireman to help her. Then she covered her mouth, as though holding back screams to keep them from echoing across the pond.

Jeremy curled in on himself, arms crossed. He remembered the body from the road, the one the vultures had been stripping, and he wondered if this is how the man had died. Had the bugs drilled through his head, going for his crowns? Did he have a pacemaker or an artificial knee or hip? For a terrible instant, Jeremy visualized his father lying faceup in the sun, the bugs crawling over him.

Laurie said, "Bury him."

Mom dropped her hands, shocked. "How is that better than drowning?"

Laurie shook her head. "I don't mean like a grave. Shield him with earth, like this." She jerked her chin at the purse.

Jeremy licked his lips. He took a deep, shuddering breath. That could work, maybe. "We'll have to dig a hole."

It took an hour to build the bunker. They ran into caliche— fused clay and gravel—at a foot and a half. Without metal tools, they couldn't really go any deeper, but they could raise the ground around it.

They ended up with a trench that was as long as Dad was tall, with walls that stuck up three feet above the caliche floor. Jeremy dragged some of the fiberglass panels over from the remains of the groundskeeper's shed, and set them aside. When they were ready, he retrieved a quarter from the center of the sand-filled purse and flung it across the pond. The hovering bugs followed it.

Dad was able to stick his head up out of the water long enough for Jeremy to explain the plan.

He said, "I'll try anything to get out of this damn water."

Mom and Laurie waited in the pond near Dad while Jeremy dug his hand into the purse and found Mom's keys. When it seemed clear enough—there were only a few bugs now quartering the surface of the water—he ran for the fairway, around the pond to the side that was opposite the shed, Mom's ring of metal keys and bangles dangling from his hand.

A few bugs followed him, but when Jeremy reached the middle of the golf course, he pushed and held the unlock button on the car remote. Bugs rose all around him: from the remains of the shed, from the pond, and from the condos on the other side of the fairway. Thousands of bugs.

He hadn't thought of that. They were *everywhere*.

He flung the keys as far toward the condos as he could, and dashed up the brown grass, zigzagging, hearing the bugs tear past him, stinging and burning as they bounced off his face; and then he seemed to be clear of them.

Jeremy circled back around to the pond, where Mom and Laurie had helped Dad out of the pond and into the trench, then laid the fiberglass panels across the raised dirt walls. They were scooping dirt on top of him as fast as they could. Jeremy tried to help, but blood kept running down into his eyes. When the first layer of soil covered the fiberglass, Mom made him go sit in the shade and hold a T-shirt to his face until the bleeding stopped.

Dad stayed in the bunker for seven more days. The structure was open at each end but they built zigzag walls leading out from it, so there were no straight lines for his pacemaker EMF to leak out.

Jeremy scavenged food from the condos, fishing food out of pantries with long sticks—lucking out early on with plastic jars of peanut butter and spaghetti sauce. He went alone, moving carefully among the slowly collapsing buildings, and he always came back with food or liquids. No cans, of course. No jars with metal lids.

Fortunately, most of the residents had fled early on. *Most.* He didn't talk about the bodies he *did* find until Dad, stir-crazy in the bunker, wanted to run for it.

Laurie and Jeremy built a solar still with clear plastic sheets and a hose, and the surface of the pond was substantially lower by the time the National Guard found them.

The Guard moved Dad thirty miles to the west, shielded by sandbags, on the back of an improvised cart, and when they got to a place where they couldn't find any bugs, they put a white chalk symbol on the ground twenty yards across. A helicopter dropped down from ten thousand feet just long enough for them to throw Dad aboard. Bugs came, but the copter went high, fast, shooting for the thin air at the upper reaches of its operational altitude.

It worked. The bugs couldn't keep up, and the helicopter didn't fall out of the sky.

Mom, Laurie, and Jeremy didn't see Dad for another two weeks—the time it took them to walk out—but he was waiting for them when they crossed out of the zone, near Calexico.

The bugs were behind them, still reproducing, but they weren't spreading out of Arizona and New Mexico, a guardsman told Jeremy.

"We don't know why. Maybe they only like the areas with sunshine? Or they're consolidating before they expand farther?"

Like Jeremy, the soldier had half-healed bug burns across his face. Jeremy had told him about the bodies he'd found in the condos.

The soldier understood. "With holes in their heads, right? Mostly around the jaw?"

Jeremy gulped and nodded.

The soldier hooked a finger in his mouth and pulled his cheek back to show a gap in his molars. "Once we realized what they were after, I had my CO knock out that crown using a rock and a stick as a chisel. This was after we starting ditching all our metal gear.

"It was nice getting your dad out. We found too many people who stayed, with metal crowns or artificial joints. I mean, we saved one guy by amputating his leg while the bugs were working on his artificial knee; and we knocked a lot of teeth out. Your dad, though, is the only survivor I saw with an electronic prosthesis. Saw a lot of nonsurvivors."

Then the soldier shook his head, smiling slightly. "Almost weirder are the survivors who've stayed in there, trying to make it without metal, staying clear of the bugs. We were told to evacuate *everybody*, but it's hard enough getting the people out who *want* to leave." He scratched gently at one of his new scars. "Wonder if they'll make it?"

Dad moved them to Maine, and he would've moved farther if there'd been any place in the Continental United States that was farther from the bugs. Jeremy couldn't blame him. If Jeremy had a pacemaker, he'd do the same.

When kids asked him about the scars on his face, he told them the truth, but they usually looked at him like he was crazy, like he was making it up.

Fine. They weren't there. They couldn't really know.

Jeremy tried to be a good kid, working hard in school. He read everything he could find on the bugs and their dominion, the newly declared Southwest Emergency Zone. He made a special effort to get along with his sister. His parents had been through enough, he thought, and he did his best to ease their days.

It was going to be hard enough on them later, when he went back.

FAINT HEART

BY SARAH REES BRENNAN

The Annals of New Poitiers

After the Fourth Great War, when most of the cities of the world were leveled, for decades the people lived without governance. Until our city was built, and those who would become the Court came together and decided that the element of the population that in the past had caused crime and unrest—the young, angry, and disadvantaged men who had been sent into a hundred pointless wars—needed a war that made sense to them, needed to compete for a real and fixed goal.

They also, for the good of the rest of the city, needed to be eliminated.

The reward of a hero in children's stories is the hand of a princess, the fairest of them all, and half her kingdom. Power and beauty is what men fight for.

The people who would become the Court created the most beautiful woman who ever lived, and held the first Trials. They set the traditional tasks of the maze, the monster, and the mystery, built the maze beneath the city for men to get through, created the monster for the men to fight, and made up the riddle for men to think their way past. Every step of the way, the men had to battle with each other, because they knew that only one of them would be allowed out alive. Every unmarried man who did not receive the dispensation of the Court had to participate in the Trials.

All but one of the men died, and that one married the queen. With its most violent element eliminated, the city was at peace.

It was clear to all that the way to ensure civil peace was to repeat the Trials.

We created the most beautiful woman in the world again, and again.

The Court-Ordained Trials Rules

- The Trials must take place every generation: that is, every twenty-five years, or when the old queen dies and the princess inherits. The Trials may be delayed or put forward according to the judgment of the Court, but it must not be delayed more than two years. Each queen is designed to last no more than forty years.
- Men of Court families, and other families the Court determines to be contributing to society, are exempt from entering the Trials.
- To be considered for exemption, families must pay the Court five hundred drachmae per head.
- Married men are exempt from entering the Trials, but as marriage must not be entered into lightly, every man must pay a brideprice. Each family may set their own brideprices for their daughters, but it cannot be less than a hundred drachmae. A bride should be treasured, as the queen must be treasured.

- All volunteers for the Trials will be accepted. Wishing to enter shows either a commendable desire for the queen, or a volatile and violent spirit that needs eliminating.
- An order of men will be set up who are trained for the Trials from childhood. Any family who gives one son to the Order will be given exemption for another son. The Trials offer hope to all contestants, but a properly trained man has a better chance both during the Trials, and later with the Court and the queen.
- For her own safety, the queen is not permitted outside the palace grounds, kept both protected and pure by her guard
- The only occasion on which the queen will appear and speak in public, in each of her lifetimes, is at the ceremony before the Trials. This speech will impress upon the Trial contestants her absolute authority over their lives and deaths, and the sight of her perfect beauty will inspire them.

Hers was the face that lit a thousand lamps. She had brought peace to a thousand homes across their land.

The mosaic of Queen Rosamond was the only bright thing permitted in the temple. Her image was on the farthest wall in the Great Hall, and they saw her during every meal and every prayer.

She stood tall as a mountain over land and sea, the whole earth a sweep of gold, which she had made bright and prosperous, all the waters calm because a glance of her tranquil eyes had stilled storms.

Her hair streamed over the land, black silk on gold, and her face was calm, kind, and impossibly beautiful.

No woman was born this beautiful. They had to make her.

Clustered around her feet were the skyscrapers of their city, shining silver blades rising higher than any buildings had ever risen before. Their city stretched farther, housed more souls, than any other city ever had, and all these souls were safe in her keeping. In the middle of the city were the sloping roofs that formed the buildings of the temple where Tor's Order lived. On the mountains outside the city rose the golden dome of the palace, and all the buildings of the Court around it.

The mosaic was two centuries old, but the colors were still as vivid as the queen. Beneath the gorgeous blaze were words carved dark and deep into the old stone:

WILL YOU BE HER TRUE KNIGHT?

Tor had learned to read from those words. He'd been four years old when his parents sent him to the temple, thirteen summers ago, so he did not remember his father's face or his mother's.

The first face he remembered was the queen's.

The second face he remembered was Master Roland's, the oldest of the masters, withered as the last apple left rolling in a basket. He could not teach the trainees how to fight any longer, so his job was to run herd on the youngest, making sure they ate and went to bed, monitoring the machines as they trained to be ready for the Trials.

He found Tor curled on the floor by the mosaic of the queen, looking up into those wide bright eyes.

Tor expected a scolding, but he did not receive one. Master Roland knelt by him, though his old joints cracked like dry tree branches.

"She's real, you know," he said in a whisper.

Tor had placed his hand on the shimmering blue stones that

formed the hem of Queen Rosamond's garment, confused, not sure if he was proving she was real or trying to conjure her from the cold stone.

"She is alive this moment," Master Roland said, and his voice thrilled. "Not so very far from here. She is always alive, ever alive. She never dies. She is the eternal rose. She is the soul of this country. And you are training so you may be chosen as fit to serve her."

The Order, set up so the right man could be prepared to win the Trials.

Yes, Tor thought, and it all felt so right. He'd known there must be a reason for the Trials, a good reason. For the simulated programs and the real programs, having to hurt his friends, for the lack of any warmth or softness in his life. He'd known there had to be something, somebody, who was worth everything.

Master Roland put out his arm to encircle Tor, to lead him back to the dormitory. A Knight of the Order must learn to sleep and wake on command.

"So do you think you can do it?" he murmured. "Be her one true knight?"

That night and every night, that day and every day, before the first bit of food or first prayer passed his lips, Tor looked up at the queen. Rosamond, rose of the world.

He could do anything, for her sake.

His answer was yes, and yes, and yes.

Rosamond was nothing but trouble. Yvain had known that from the time he was fourteen, from the first moment he'd seen her face stamped on gold.

He'd dreamed about that day every night for the next three years.

He'd hooked a wallet from the lining of a man's expensive coat. Rosamond bless the fancy designer who'd had the idea of custom-made coats that fit wallets in the lining as a preventative against theft. It meant that all the rich guys now kept their money in the same place.

Then he'd reached the Nests, and opened the wallet, and saw the queen's face carved on a gold coin.

Rosamond's face was only put on sovereigns. Sovereigns were only carried by members of the Court. The Court used them as passes into exclusive clubs, as markers of identification. They were worth more than a thousand drachmae—were enough to buy a real house and not just an apartment lower down outside the Nests. They were too valuable ever to spend.

Anyone not of the Court who got caught with one was dead.

Yvain had been a stupid boy. He'd laughed and tossed the coin through the air to Persie, who'd caught it in both hands and gazed at it with awe.

"Rosamond," she'd said, drawing out the word in disbelief, as if she'd seen the sun rise in a night sky. "There has to be a way we can spend it."

Then she'd turned it over and over in her hands, watching it gleam.

Yvain and Persie had been together in the Nests since they were little. They'd gotten married when Persie turned fourteen, as soon as it was legal to wed, and had been married for less than two months. Yvain was a boy from the Nests, after all, and one with a criminal record. Marriage was the only way to escape the Trials. And Persie was an orphan girl, with no family to set a brideprice that a boy from the Nests could not afford.

They had planned it like that, to keep each other safe. Yvain could skim the skyscrapers and pick any pocket in the City. He'd promised Persie that she would never regret marrying him.

"Believe me," Yvain had said, winking at her. "I know when a lady is too much trouble."

It made him impatient even to think about the Trials. As if their lives weren't difficult enough, being born with nothing on the horizon but blood and waste, and all for some woman. A face on a useless coin.

Without Persie, he didn't like to think about what would have happened to him when it was time for the Trials.

He took the hand that didn't hold the sovereign, and kissed it. Persie smiled, but kept her eyes fixed on the coin in her palm. It caught the multicolored lights of the city below, and the golden lights from the palace up on the hill beyond the city, where the queen lived.

"She's the most beautiful woman in the world, remember," Persie told him. "And there is the question of a life of luxury. Nothing but gold and sherbet and the veil of Rosamond's hair between you and the world, if you win the Trials. That would be worth something. Like this coin is worth something. A collector would be interested."

"Oh, let it drop," said Yvain. "I'm going to sleep."

The Nests were called the Nests because they were so high up, the peak of every building, and so many birds lived there. There were not many trees left in the city, so the top of every skyscraper was crammed with the filth and noise of the birds.

Yvain liked to lie on his back and watch the birds wheeling. He never turned his head to the side to look at the mountain where Rosamond had lived for centuries. He had no interest.

He'd gone to sleep like that a hundred times as a child, watching the birds, hearing Persie breathe near him.

When he woke up this time, Persie was gone.

Yvain had launched himself from the Nests, slid down the material awning of the sixty-ninth floor, snagged at the statue on the fifty-first to check his fall, grabbed at the iron pipe that ran around the thirty-seventh, landed on one knee on the balcony of the twenty-fifth. He heard the scrape of the balcony door and a shout, but he didn't look behind him as he vaulted over the railing to the slanted little roof over the next balcony.

He'd landed on top of one of the market stalls, breathing hard and blinking sweat out of his eyes. It had stung like tears.

Once, long ago, criminals were hanged and quartered. In these more enlightened times, criminals were still publicly punished. That was a deterrent to other prospective criminals.

But the body parts weren't wasted, as they had been in the past. Machines cut open the criminal and removed their organs, harvesting them for law-abiding citizens.

And the criminal was punished with a live dissection.

Yvain had sat on the stall and watched Persie die in the market square, blood vivid on screens set on various buildings around the square, his small bright-haired wife's pain interspersed with advertisements for the latest virtual sports equipment.

All for asking around about a buyer for a sovereign.

That night, once harsh daylight and those images of blood were gone, Yvain melted down the sovereign in a glow of fire and bright metal. He saw his reflection cast in the shining surface of a skyscraper wall, saw the light of the fire make the tears on his face look as if they were burning, as if he were crying gold.

The sovereign wasn't pure gold after all. It had all been a lie.

After Persie died, for the three years of nights between Persie's death and the Trials, Yvain did not go to sleep watching the birds. He turned his eyes to the golden mountains where the queen lived in her palace.

Persie had been right. Yvain had been able to make some money selling the metal of the melted-down sovereign. Rosamond *was* worth something.

Not enough. Not anything like enough.

But maybe she was all he could get.

Roz could not leave the palace until the Trials, but she was allowed to go anywhere she wanted inside the palace.

She always asked to train in the Hall of Mirrors.

There were no mirrors in the hall, of course, for anyone but Roz. It was lined with pictures of all the Rosamonds who had ever been made.

It was also the place where she and Miri learned hand-to-hand combat—what to do if a man broke into the palace, how to use the things that surrounded them as weapons—where she and Miri had learned lessons they would probably never put into practice. Roz could do backflips down the hall, seeing her own image upside down and blurred, repeated a hundred times.

Rosamond: carefully constructed by the finest technology to be the most beautiful of them all. Every Rosamond who had ever lived, and she was just the Rosamond who was living now. The only Rosamond who was living now, since the old queen was dead.

Except no Rosamond had ever learned to fight before.

Roz had read the books. The city council had wanted to make a prize people couldn't pass up: setting every young man in the city a series of tasks—the Trials—that, if won, would mean the kingdom and the hand of the princess.

This way, the numbers of disaffected young men on the streets of their city were slashed, and the population and the crime level were kept down. Although with so many early marriages, and the men of the Court keeping strings of mistresses in town, the population never went down *too* much.

All because of you, dear, Roz's nurse had murmured to her while she was gently warning Roz against taking risks when she was playing, against the hideous possibility that she might one day be hurt and disfigured. *All because of your face.*

Even Miri and Dareus always, always remembered not to touch her face.

One could wish Dareus was as careful about her ribs, Roz thought as Dareus got a staff under them and sent her flying through the air and sliding across the marble floor, until she landed with a smack against the wall.

She gasped for breath and fought down the urge to be sick.

"My captain," she wheezed, in a most ladylike fashion. "That is no way to treat your queen."

"My queen," said Dareus, turning his staff over and over in his hands. "That is no way to guard your left side."

Roz concentrated on the ceiling, and on the suddenly difficult task of breathing in and out. She heard the soft sound of Miri's footsteps, and the light tap and tumble of a staff against marble.

"I always get smashed to bits, and you always win," Roz said, closing her eyes. "Because you're a sneak, and Dareus plays favorites."

"I don't," said Dareus, his voice a little sharp.

"I always watch for an opening and you always dash right in," said Miri. "Which helps create my opening, mark you."

Miri was Roz's favorite lady-in-waiting. The Court sent its daughters to keep her company for a time—never long enough to form a real friendship. But Miri's parents had died in an accident, and the Court had let her stay in the palace, murmuring that she was bound to be a good influence. Since she was so quiet and well-behaved.

Little did the Court know that it was Miri who had persuaded Dareus to let them learn to fight. Roz was the one who had wanted to, but Miri was the one who had made it happen. She had made it sound so reasonable, that if anyone were to break into the palace, the queen and her lady should know how to defend themselves.

It was not reasonable; Dareus should never have allowed it, and all three of them knew it.

Roz put a hand under her head and opened her eyes. Miri sat down beside her with Dareus's staff in one hand, Miri's crisp dark curls blurring at the edges in Roz's vision. She looked over Miri's shoulder at Dareus. He looked at them both with soldier's eyes, proud of Miri's prowess, assessing Roz's injuries and coolly finding them negligible.

"Come on, back on your feet," he said. "Your guard has all been killed, my queen, and a man is in the palace. A real man."

He said it absolutely emotionlessly. Dareus's uncle had taken him in, brought him up, trained him to be part of the guard, trained him so that when his uncle died, Dareus would become the youngest captain a Rosamond had ever had.

But no man was allowed to approach Rosamond except the champion of the Trials. Rosamond's guards were all cut so they could not dishonor the queen even if they wanted to.

Roz was surprised that Dareus didn't hate her, sometimes.

But he didn't. He was her friend, before being her guard. He'd agreed to teach her and Miri how to train. He'd even agreed to keep it a secret from the Court.

Roz climbed to her feet. "All right," she said, and took another deep breath, ignoring her ribs. "Come at me again."

Roz was beaten down twice more, but she beat down Dareus once to make up for it. Neither of them ever got near Miri. She was sly. Besides which, Dareus totally played favorites.

Roz left the Hall of Mirrors, went to her own bathroom, and washed up, with Miri in attendance. She had nice bruises coming in on her ribs, but when she washed her face, she saw it was still clear and clean, pale and untouched as a pearl.

The perfect face, they claimed—not the flatterers, but books written a hundred years ago. Designed perfect, all in symmetry, with tumbling dark hair—bright hair made you look too flashy, pretty rather than beautiful—but of course, porcelain skin, and clear blue eyes.

Dareus's eyes had flecks of black in the gray color, and his nose was too long. Miri's teeth stuck out slightly, and she was much too short to be the ideal. Roz had always found looking at them so interesting, rather than looking at her own image, so familiar it almost seemed worn, passed down and down and down again as it was. Never changing.

The world had called them clones before it called them queens.

Other people might have thought it was vanity that made Roz train in the Hall of Mirrors, but the truth was she fought better there. She was angry there.

Roz looked at her wet, shining pearl-face in the real mirror and thought about those who had to go through the maze, endure the monster and the mystery of the Trials, had to walk in blood to Rosamond's side.

The Court had created the monster—a fierce hybrid beast that all the men who made their way through the maze had to fight— by using the same science they'd used to create their perfect queen. Sometimes Rosamond felt like *she* was the monster.

"Let me put cream on that," said Miri.

"When I give my speech," Roz said, "I could tell them all not to fight."

Miri gave her a patient look. "Would they listen, Roz?"

"They should," Roz muttered.

"And you should win our fights," Miri murmured. "You're

better than I am. But you don't. Try to be a little sneaky, Rosamond. You have to work within the rules of the Trials."

But the rules of the Trials said men would kill each other, and she would belong to the survivor. Handed over like a bloodstained trophy.

She felt it press down on her sometimes, so heavy it was like stones being piled on her chest, making it impossible for her to move or breathe. She was meant to be worth so many lives.

Tor should have been the favorite to win Rosamond's hand. He knew that much. He was the best at every exercise. He had taken great pains to be the best, worked long hours to make himself worthy.

He could never be worthy enough. That was not the point, or the code of the courts of love. The aim was to have all you could to offer on your lady's altar

But he wasn't the favorite. He didn't make friends easily, or rather, he made the wrong sort of friends. There were groups of the strongest boys, the quickest and the cleverest, and then there were the boys who fell in the maze, who were burned or scarred or torn at by monsters, who never solved a riddle. Tor could not help it. He always went back for them. Most of Tor's friends died. The training was meant to weed out the weak.

Tor took the judgment of his peers and bowed his head, and was ashamed. He knew it was time-wasting, that it was an insult to Rosamond, like choosing someone else before her. It was his duty and his only desire to put her above all others. It worried him, the way his head always turned at a cry. It worried him that he could not seem to crush this weakness.

It also worried him that they only did training exercises. Surely there was some way to use his training to serve the queen now, to protect her city.

He'd always been sure that if there was something real happening, he would do the right thing.

And now it was only a few weeks until the Trials, something real was finally happening, and he wasn't fast enough.

A ruffian had dared break into the Order and steal the small gold statue of Rosamond that received their offerings of incense in the training square. He'd swooped in, before the horrified eyes of three hundred training recruits, and grabbed a symbol of their queen.

All the other recruits were far behind now. The thief had lost them when he'd started swinging from the rafters. It was like nobody else had been spending nights making sure they could bear all their own weight and more on their arms.

There was a narrow space between the ceiling of the attics and the outside of the roof, where they both had to slither and crawl, and the blasphemer was less bulky than Tor, able to go faster and slip through smaller spaces, and he almost got away. Then they reached the oriel window and the thief swung through with a crash, like the heavens being shattered.

Tor followed him, and from there it was a sprint across rooftops.

The thief was fast, but so was Tor, and Tor had endurance. He gained remorselessly.

He could see the golden statue glint in the sun, winking in the thief's hand. Rosamond, waiting for him to save her.

The thief had to check his stride to crouch and leap, going for a roof over the wall, outside the temple grounds. Tor launched himself at him and they went tumbling down to the curved roof's edge.

Tor grabbed for the statue. The thief held on, and went for a knife.

Tor slammed an elbow down on the inside of the thief's wrist and saw the knife fall from his temporarily paralyzed fingers.

"Now," Tor said, looking down at the thief's face. He was younger than Tor had expected, to be so black in villainy. He was Tor's age, with snarled flame-red hair. "Please hand over the queen."

"Oh, is *this* the queen," said the thief. "Pardon me. I had no idea she'd be so metallic. Or seven inches high."

"Silence," said Tor.

"Don't you think we should be informed about that sort of thing before the Tri—"

"I said silence!" Tor shouted.

The blasphemer's dagger looked poisoned, so Tor kicked it over the edge of the roof.

"Hey!" he had the gall to yell. "That was expensive!"

"I'm sure you can steal another one," Tor said through his teeth. "Or you could if you weren't going to be quartered in the square."

That sent the thief into a spasm of frenzied activity. He wouldn't have been bad with some training, Tor thought, but keeping him pinned was fairly easy, even though the rascal tried to bite.

Tor caught his blaspheming face between two gloved fingers and held him still.

"None of that."

Tor realized his error almost immediately. He'd let go of the statue.

The thief immediately did so as well, and Tor watched, with time stretched slow by horror, as the gleaming queen rolled toward the gutter.

Then the thief elbowed Tor, hard and efficient, in the eye, rolled and dived, and stood on the edge with the statue in one hand—and one of the Nest boys who the masters hired to wash the upper windows in another. The thief held them both out over the street, the boy's feet scrabbling on the edge of the gutter.

The statue would be damaged. The boy could be killed.

"Which one is it going to be?" the thief asked.

It shouldn't even have been a question. It should be Rosamond, or any small part of her, before the world. But Tor couldn't take his eyes off the Nest child's fraying garment in the thief's grip. It could tear and the child could die without any decision being made at all.

He could save both, he told himself. He was fast enough.

So he lunged for the boy, caught him small and safe against his chest, and grabbed air where the thief should have been. He looked across a wall and saw the glint of the gold statue and the flame of the thief's hair, already distant.

Tor touched the pin he wore proclaiming the Order, with the comm inside it, to report his failure to the masters.

As he did so, he let go of the child, and saw the child's dirty, grinning face.

He didn't look scared.

Of course he didn't. Of course both the thief and the child were from the Nests, and the child had never been in any danger at all.

Tor was so unutterably stupid. He had failed Rosamond again.

He could have the child quartered in the square, but he didn't have the stomach for it. He waved him back to his work, and he thought, next time, my queen, next time I will be strong enough and good enough. He did not know if he was lying to himself again.

He did not know if he was ever going to be ready for the Trials.

Yvain knew perfectly well that he'd been an idiot. The statue had not been worth the risk. But then, the statue was Rosamond. She never was worth the risk, was she?

He walked through the sunlit square with the statue stashed safe beneath his regulation winter jacket, humming to himself. That big Order trainee with the South-dark skin and the eyes of a fanatic might have covered him in bruises and given him a bad moment—would even a knight sacrifice a kid for a piece of metal?—but Yvain had won.

Take that, Rosamond.

The Trials were on the horizon sure as the sun at dawn, and it had never seemed like a better time to spit in the queen's eye.

Which, speaking of, Yvain thought. It was market day, the last one before the Trials, and the queen's ladies-in-waiting were out in force. He saw the distinctive coral-colored gowns everywhere he looked, and he looked at them all, searching for the prettiest face.

Said face belonged to a fetching little thing with crisp curls and demure eyes, standing by a fruit stall.

When Yvain approached her, she said, without looking up, "Do you think Roz would like—" Then she blinked her brown eyes and smiled. "Sorry, wrong man."

"Ah now," Yvain said. "You have the right man. You just don't know it yet."

She smiled a smile that made her even prettier. "Believe me, I do."

"Can I not even get a small chance to convince you?" Yvain asked. "A tiny chance. The smallest of chances."

"Is the Nest brat bothering you, my lady?" asked a voice, and by the sound of it—not quite a woman's, but not quite a man's either—Yvain knew it was one of the queen's guard.

Both Yvain and the lady turned. It was a guardsman, in the uniform of blue on gray. Yvain wondered why they even needed uniforms. It wasn't like anyone else aspired to be a cut man.

Nest brat, he'd said. It made Yvain think of growing up in the Nests with Persie, how people had shouted the words after them as they ran hand in hand over the rooftops.

"We were just talking, Dareus," said the girl, touching his arm.

"She didn't seem bothered," Yvain said, with the guard's words ringing in his ears. "Must be a nice novelty for her, talking to a real man."

"Hmm," said the guard. He seemed young enough, though it was hard to tell sometimes. Smaller than a real man and with a woman's soft curve to his face, even if training meant he had muscles like a man.

The guard looked at Yvain with narrowed thoughtful eyes, and Yvain curled his lip into a sneer—who would let that happen to them?—just before he bit his tongue.

Which he did because the guard hooked a foot around his ankle and yanked him down so he fell, hitting his head on the fruit stall on the way down. Then the guard planted a foot on his chest. Yvain grabbed at it and tried to pull his feet out from under him, but the guard was already a little crouched, center of gravity low. Yvain grabbed at the knife hilt in the guard's boot and brandished—a hilt without a blade.

"I'm the captain of the queen's guard," said the cut man— *Dareus*, the lady-in-waiting had called him. His gray eyes were still thoughtful, almost bored. "I don't carry my weapons where Nest brats can see and steal them. Watch your tongue and your talk of real men."

"Why don't you watch your tongue and your talk of Nest brats?" Yvain snapped.

He jackknifed in the dirt and out from under the guard's heel, only to find himself rolled again, this time with the guard kneeling beside him, a hand fastened at his throat.

Dareus's eyes were still bored, but he was smiling slightly. "I might," he said. "If you could make me."

He released Yvain and got up, brushing his hands off, then made a slight bow to the lady.

"Forgive me for intruding," he said. "I'll leave you to your conversation."

Yvain had somewhat expected him to walk off with the lady on his arm. That was the usual outcome when you bested someone in a fight over a woman—but then, what would a cut man want with a woman?

Yvain had a natural advantage here.

He used another of his natural advantages, his smile, as he used the fruit stall to help him stand.

"Now, about convincing you," he began.

The lady-in-waiting's warm brown eyes were, he noticed a little late, absolutely furious.

"He's ten times the man you are," she informed him, and turned sharply to hurry away after the guard.

"Am I missing something here?" Yvain asked the empty air.

"Only the same thing you've been missing all your life," said the stall owner, a kind faced woman who had given him and Peisie apples when they were young. "Which is that you're a bit of an idiot."

She looked like she'd rather enjoyed the entertainment of Yvain being beaten up by yet another of Rosamond's people.

"I thought girls liked this sort of thing," Yvain added, making a small gesture to his trousers.

"Many of us find them completely irrelevant."

"Even mine?" Yvain asked, making a face of mock horror.

The woman laughed. "Especially yours, lad."

Yvain laughed too. He was getting the last laugh, after all, no matter how battered he was by the queen's men. He had the gold statue at the small of his back, and he could melt that down too. It would fetch enough to buy every man in the Nests a drink, the night before the Trials.

And if the money wasn't quite worth the trouble, it still pleased Yvain to spite the queen, even in some small way.

He played with the idea of winning the Trials for a moment, and telling Rosamond the truth she'd probably never heard in all her spoiled lifetimes. That the only worth she would have to him was the gold.

You would see a lot of gold, though, being Rosamond's king. Why anyone tried to pretend the girl herself was the thing to fight for, Yvain couldn't say.

"I hear you were being terribly brave and impressive in the marketplace today," Roz whispered as Dareus escorted her through the marble halls of her palace to the stateroom, where the First Minister sat waiting. "Miri was so impressed."

"It wasn't impressive," Dareus said. "I was up against a boy who had no training, and I let myself get angry. It would have been much more impressive if I'd kept my temper."

"But where," said Roz, "is the fun in that? Miri said you were great."

"The lady Miri always assumes the best of people," Dareus said. "Which does credit to her but little to them."

Roz slowed her step before they reached the doors of the stateroom.

"If you like her," she began.

"My queen," Dareus said, "just because the lady Miri is allowed to go out on market days does not mean she has experienced life. Both of you have grown up with the palace walls as the border to your world. Neither of you has walked the city, neither of you has ever had the chance to talk to men. Once you are married, you and the lady Miri can mix freely with the Court. You are going to marry a champion. She should at least find a whole man."

"She should get to choose who she wants," Roz murmured. "*Someone* should."

Roz didn't suggest that she herself should. But it was close enough to speaking blasphemy that Dareus gave her a reproachful look as he leaned forward and opened the door.

"Her Majesty the new Queen Rosamond, flower of the world," he said, and gave her a tiny shove the First Minister would not see.

"Deeply honored, Your Majesty," said the First Minister, without glancing up or rising.

Rosamond went and found herself a chair. The First Minister, she saw, was looking at lists, at rows and rows of men's names.

Men who would be forced to participate in the Trials.

"You must be very excited, Your Majesty," said the First Minister. "Not long now until your wedding day."

Just a few more days of funerals until your wedding day.

Roz had read the records of past Rosamonds, the Rosamond who would not eat, the Rosamond who cut lines down her perfect arms, the Rosamond who kept to her bed for three years, as well as the Rosamonds who seemed absolutely fine, to all appearances. It wouldn't matter what one Rosamond felt, there would always be another.

The First Minister looked surprised at Rosamond's lack of enthusiasm.

"It is men for you, isn't it?" the First Minister inquired. "We've had a Rosamond who wanted a female champion once or twice, but I am afraid it is unlikely to happen. Women have to volunteer, and very few do."

"I think it's men," Rosamond whispered.

It was hard to know. She really had not met many people, and it was not as if anyone would have responded to her desire if she had felt it. She was not meant to want anyone. Even the idea of desiring someone seemed like murdering them.

What she wanted was to run to the Hall of Mirrors and do the forbidden, do what no other Rosamond had done before—fight.

"Isn't that nice," said the First Minister. "So who do you think will win you, Your Majesty: one of those dedicated knights, or perhaps a more worldly city man?"

What did it matter? Either way, she was what she was: a Rosamond. The goal, the prize, the symbol.

"It doesn't matter," she murmured, more to the table and the list than to the First Minister.

"Ah," said the First Minister. "My guess is that it will probably be one of the Temple boys again. Most suitable. It's what they're raised for, of course. To win, not to question—and to make you happy, Your Majesty, of course."

"Of course," Roz said.

"More important, are you word perfect in your speech?"

More important than Roz's happiness or her desires, or who would win her. The most important thing was that she be perfect.

"That's what everything's based on, isn't it?" Miri asked later, as Roz raged and Miri brushed her hair. "For the Court. What things look like."

"Especially," Roz snapped, "when things look like me."

"And when you look perfect," said Miri. "When you stay perfectly within the rules. When the Court proclaims you to the whole city as perfect, that's your opening."

Like the way Miri took an opening when Dareus was distracted.

But what opening was there if she could not stop the Trials?

Roz heard the First Minister's voice in her head, saying, *Who do you think will win you, Your Majesty?*

She was a prize to be won. She did not know how to fight that.

The first day of the Trials, the day when Tor would see her, the sky was a deep particular blue. The color of Rosamond's eyes, he thought, or perhaps a few shades lighter.

He was going to see her today for the first, and perhaps the last, time.

She would give her speech, and then the trainees would go through the maze below the city, fight the monster that was kept underground, and try to work out the riddle—all the while keeping on guard against their fellow competitors.

Only one of them would re-emerge into the light and see the queen again.

Tor might die in the Trials. He was prepared for that—to not be worthy of her, to fail her even though he would try his best.

He would have the sight of her, once, to call up as a last image before he died.

He should try to remember every moment of this day. He should hold every second sacred.

Tor put his uniform on, not slowly—because wasting time would be letting Rosamond down, since his every second was consigned to her—but with deliberation. He did his last practice exercises in calm and measured movements, not listening to the whispering all around him, the wondering and the betting on his chances.

He marched out of the temple with his head held high, in step with his brethren, a black-clad regiment dedicated to perfect love and beauty. Ready to kill for Rosamond.

The other contestants were already ranged in the square. Tor saw his own face on the huge screens set in the skyscrapers, reproduced a hundred times larger for the city's view. He was startled by the look in his own eyes, as if he were watching a tragedy, when this was the happiest day of his life.

The cameras left him and showed a swooping view of the crowd, then the other contestants, in their colorful disarray. Some were in restraints and some wore bruises.

Tor turned his face away, a tremor of disgust running through him at the idea that someone would need to be forced to serve Rosamond.

His eyes fell on another crowd of contestants, among whom stood the tall flame-haired thief of the week before. Tor's lip curled back from his teeth, and the thief spotted him, looked massively and spitefully delighted, and blew him a kiss.

Tor looked steadfastly away from him, and toward the dais.

It stood empty, but there was music rising in the air. She was coming. He could feel his heart pounding in his chest like a child frantically thumping at a door to get out.

She came shining, her dark hair like a cloud behind her.

It was almost a shock to see her, real, the size of a woman. Almost like an ordinary woman, almost as if she were someone who could be approached without fear or reverence.

But not quite. Tor had the curve of that mouth memorized, the exact shape of her brilliant eyes.

It should have been enough simply to behold her—real love is love that asks for nothing and does everything; real love should not even ask for a look—but he did want her to look at him, to *have* looked at him, just once before he died.

She gazed down as she passed the Order, her eyelashes shadows on her cheeks. Tor had not thought about her as having eyelashes, but of course she did.

Rosamond, he thought, and wanted to say her name just once so she would hear it.

When she reached the dais and began to speak, he stopped thinking about himself and all the things she was in relation to him.

Sheer shock wiped away all of that.

Queen Rosamond, the eternal rose, undid the top button of her robe.

He looked at the pale hollow of her throat—he had not thought, should not think, about Rosamond's skin or her body—and saw her swallow, and felt not the familiar awe but a rush of the stupid tenderness that always had him betraying himself and running back at a cry for help.

Rosamond was a scared girl.

They did not have to beat Yvain or restrain him on the day of the Trials. He woke up with the Nests wrapped in cloud and smoke, and went quietly down into a clear morning below.

Fighting was no use, and he didn't need to go through the Trials wounded already. That would be pointless and ridiculous.

Besides, he was—curious.

He wanted to see her Rosamond—whose face was supposed to be worth dying for. He wanted her to see him, and see that he was not impressed. That all there was to her was gold, and it was not worth enough.

He saw others around him who had fought against being dragged here, though. Men with black eyes and bloody noses. Some of them gave him a friendly look, comrades in misfortune, and some looked at him coldly as if the Trials had begun and they were enemies already.

Some of them looked as rapt as the Order Knights, waiting for the queen. There was a thrum and a murmur in the air. *Rosamond, Rosamond,* and Yvain felt a thrill of anticipation and disgust.

He saw the knight from the rooftops standing with his regiment, eyes black and accusing, and was grateful, for a moment. Yvain was able to laugh and blow the idiot a kiss. He was never going to be one of the Order, trembling and waiting.

He tried to catch the knight's eye again, but he was turned toward the dais. Yvain gave up and looked there too.

She was just as he'd expected, more gold than girl.

What girl there was, was pretty, but also so familiar. Girls in the Nests, just like other girls in the City, all straightened and darkened their hair, tried to make their eyes look light, tried to look like Rosamond and the ideal of beauty. It was why Yvain had always perversely liked curls.

He looked at Rosamond's still, perfect face, and wished he could tell her, tried to send the thought to her: *I'm bored.*

The glitter of gold was distracting. They had done that on purpose, of course, wrapped her up with a promise of luxury, making you think of always waking up warm and well fed, of jewels brighter than Rosamond's eyes.

He let himself look, and covet. If she saw him looking, he wanted her to know that that was all he saw of her, all she was.

Gold melting, and Persie dead.

Rosamond had buttons of chased mother-of-pearl and gold, each one probably worth more than a sovereign.

The buttons rose and fell as she breathed, and Yvain wished they would be still, that he could look at her like the statue he'd stolen and reduced to nothing but gold.

She didn't let him. She put up her hands to the buttons and slid them out one by one.

All the gold fell away, and there was a girl underneath.

The day of the Trials was blinding. Roz had never been outside the palace walls before, but she had been in the gardens and the courtyards and on the balconies: she had not thought she would be dazzled by the sun. Yet she was, and she felt almost blind every step of the bright way to the square at the heart of the city.

Appearances were all that mattered to the Court, Miri had told her, as if it were very important.

Roz thought about it every step of the way, and by the time she reached the square, her vision was clear.

So this is the city they tell me is mine, she thought, and looked at the tall steel-and-silver skyscrapers. The cobblestones of the square looked freshly washed, but there were dark lines etched between them. Dirt or blood, Roz did not know.

She glanced behind her to see Dareus—who had taught her, against the rules, to fight for herself—and met his steady gaze. It let her walk across the stones, blood and all.

When she neared the dais, every screen set in the towers reflected her face. It was like the Hall of Mirrors writ large, like all her past selves whispering their name in her ear: *Rosamond, Rosamond, Rosamond*—the weight of their expectations, of everybody's expectations, forming her into what they wanted. The face on the screen, lapis lazuli eyes set in an idol's face.

Except it didn't matter how she felt, so she could feel any way she chose.

She tried to feel determined as she climbed the steps to the dais, her heavy golden skirt trailing behind her.

Then she looked down upon her people, from women and children—some cheering and some silent, some holding on to their men with white-knuckled hands—to the contestants for the Trials.

There were men wreathed with blood and bruises and in rags, and men who seemed fine—happy, healthy, and eager to die for her. Somebody cheered and called her name. She looked but could not tell who it had been.

She could not quite understand why someone would cheer for her when she hadn't done anything.

What am I to you? she thought as she looked at the crowd. What is Rosamond to you?

Different things, she thought, looking at all the different faces. The Knights of the Order stood in black ranks, like soldiers at a funeral, and one of them was staring at her with the widest eyes in the crowd, large and dark and wondering.

There was worship in those eyes, and an abyss.

In the most bruised and ragged group, she saw the knight's counterpart, the one with the narrowest eyes in the crowd. He was looking at her appraisingly, as though she were a gold coin he could bite down on so as to assess her worth.

Love her, hate her, blame her, worship her, whatever they felt toward her, they did not know her. Maybe they did not care to. Maybe they thought her face was all there was to know.

None of the other Rosamonds had known Dareus and Miri, and how they loved each other despite being imperfect.

Roz did not know herself what else there was to her, but she wanted to know.

The First Minister, standing on the dais, observed her approvingly. Roz wore the golden gown, wore her hair long and loose, looked like a queen. Looked the part.

When you look perfect, Miri had said. *When you stay perfectly within the rules. When the Court proclaims you to the whole city as perfect, that's your opening.*

Everyone was watching her. The whole city was watching her, and she looked perfect.

"Welcome to this day, the beginning of our city's thirty-second Trials," she said, and heard cheers. "I was consulting with our First Minister yesterday"—she nodded to the First Minister, who appeared mildly pleased by this courteous going off script—"and she reminded me that women have to volunteer to enter the Trials."

The Court had their Trials and their rules, and Roz was playing by the rules. They had their figurehead queen, and now it was her right to speak.

The maze, the monster, and the mystery of the Trials. They weren't the test. This was.

Roz put her hands to the large buttons on her gown. It was a stiff, high-necked thing, more a robe than a gown, and the buttons slipped under her fingers.

The crowd went still and silent as she undid it. The gold gown fell with a sound like coins tossed in a scale.

Beneath the robe, Roz was wearing dark, simple clothes that she could move freely in. The clothes she trained in.

"I volunteer to enter the Trials," she said.

"What are you doing?" the First Minister exclaimed, her careful politician's face going slack.

Who is it going to be? the First Minister had asked her.

Not a knight or a city boy. If the rules said she was a prize to be won, so be it. She would obey the rules to the letter.

All the screens in the city reflected her face, and it was determined. The whole city heard their perfect queen speak, and her word was law.

"I am going to fight," said Queen Rosamond, who knew as no man did what she was fighting for. "I am going to win myself."

THE EASTHOUND

BY **NALO HOPKINSON**

Oh, Black Betty, bam-ba-lam,
Oh, Black Betty, bam-ba-lam.

"THE EASTHOUND BAYS AT NIGHT," JOLLY SAID.

Millie shivered. Bad luck to mention the easthound, and
her twin bloody-well knew it. God, she shouldn't even be *thinking* "bloody." Millie put her hands to her mouth to stopper the
words in so she wouldn't say them out loud.

"Easthound?" said Max. He pulled the worn black coat
closer around his body. The coat had been getting tighter these
past few months. Everyone could see it. "What is that cast-
hound shit?"

Not *what*; he knew damned well what it was. He was asking Jolly what she was doing bringing the easthound into their
game. Millie wanted to yell at Jolly too.

Jolly barely glanced at Max. She knelt in front of the fire,
staring into it, retwisting her dreads and separating them at
the scalp, where they were threatening to grow together. "It's
my first line," she said. "You can play or not, no skin off my
teeth."

They didn't talk about skin coming off, either. But Jolly broke the rules whenever she damned well pleased. Loup-de-lou was *her* game, after all. She'd invented it. Jolly was so thin. Millie had saved some of the chocolate bar she'd found, to share with Jolly, but she knew that Jolly wouldn't take it. If you ate too much, you grew too quickly. Millie'd already eaten most of the chocolate, though. Couldn't help it. She was so hungry all the time!

Max didn't answer Jolly. He took the bottle of vodka that Sai was holding and chugged down about a third of it. Nobody complained. That was his payment for finding the bottle in the first place. But could booze make you grow too? Or did it keep you shrinky? Millie couldn't remember which. She fretfully watched Max's Adam's apple bob as he drank.

"The game?" Citron chirped up, reminding them. A twin of the flames of their fire danced in his green eyes. "We gonna play?"

Right. The game. Jolly bobbed her head yes. Sai, too. Millie said, "I'm in." Max sighed and shrugged his yes.

Max took up where Jolly had left off. "At night, the easthound howls," he growled, "but only when there's no moon." He pointed at Citron.

A little clumsy, Millie thought, but a good qualifying statement.

Quickly, Citron picked it up with, "No moon is so bright as the easthound's eyes when it spies a plump rat on a garbage heap." He pointed at Millie.

Garbage heap? What kind of end bit was that to loup with? Didn't give her much with which to begin the new loup. Trust Citron to throw her a tough one. And that "eyes, spies" thing, too. A rhyme in the middle instead of at the end. Clever bastard. Thinking furiously, Millie louped, "Garbage heaps high in the . . . cities of noonless night."

Jolly said, "You're cheating. It was 'garbage *heap*,' not 'garbage *heaps*.'" She gnawed a strip from the edge of her thumbnail, blew

264

the crescented clipping from her lips into the fire.

"Chuh." Millie made a dismissive motion with her good hand. "You just don't want to have to continue on with 'noonless night.'" Smirking, she pointed at her twin.

Jolly started in on the nail of her index finger. "And you're just not very good at this game, are you, Millie?"

"Twins, stop it," Max told them.

"I didn't start it," Jolly countered, through chewed nail bits. Millie hated to see her bite her nails, and Jolly knew it.

Jolly stood and flounced closer to the fire. Over her back she spat the phrase, "Noonless night, a rat's bright fright, and blood in the bite all delight *the easthound*." The final two words were the two with which they'd begun. Game over. Jolly spat out a triumphant "Loup!" First round to Jolly.

Sai slapped the palm of her hand down on the ground between the players. "Aw, jeez, Jolly! You didn't have to end it so soon just 'cause you're mad at your sister! I was working on a great loup."

"Jolly's only showing off!" Millie said. Truth was, Jolly was right. Millie really wasn't much good at loup-de-lou. It was a game, a distraction to take their minds off hunger, off being cold and scared, off watching everybody else and yourself every waking second for signs of sprouting. But Millie didn't want to be distracted. Taking your mind off things could kill you. She was only going along with the game to show the others that she wasn't getting cranky; getting loupy.

She rubbed the end of her handless wrist. Damp was making it achy. She reached for the bottle of vodka, where Max had stood it upright in the crook of his crossed legs. "Nuh-uh-uh," he chided, pulling it out of her reach and passing it to Citron, who took two pulls at the bottle and coughed.

Max said to Millie, "You don't get any treats until you start a new game."

Jolly turned back from the fire, her grinning teeth the only thing that shone in her black silhouette.

"Wasn't me who spoiled that last one," Millie grumbled. But she leaned back on the packed earth, her good forearm and the one with the missing hand both lying flush against the soil. She considered how to begin. The ground was a little warmer tonight than it had been last night. Spring was coming. Soon there'd be wild, pungent leeks to pull up and eat from the riverbank. She'd been craving their taste all through this frozen winter. She'd been yearning for the sight and taste of green, growing things. Only, she wouldn't eat too many of them. You couldn't ever eat your fill of anything, or that might bring out the Hound. Soon it'd be warm enough to sleep outside again. (She thought of rats and garbage heaps, and slammed her mind's door shut on the picture.) Millie liked sleeping with the air on her skin, even though it was dangerous out of doors. It felt more dangerous indoors, what with everybody growing up.

And then she knew how to start the loup. She said, "The river swells in May's spring tide."

Jolly strode back from the fire and took the vodka from Max. "That's a really good one." She offered the bottle to her twin.

Millie found herself smiling as she took it. Jolly was quick to speak her mind, whether scorn or praise. Millie could never stay mad at her for long. Millie drank through her smile, feeling the vodka burn its trail down. With her stump, she pointed at Jolly and waited to hear how Jolly would loup-de-lou with the words "spring tide."

"The spring's May tide is deep and wide," louped Jolly. She was breaking the rules again; three words, not two, and she'd added a "the" at the top, and changed the order around! People shouldn't change stuff, it was bad! Millie was about to protest when a quavery howl crazed the crisp night, then disappeared like a sob into silence.

"Shit!" hissed Sai. She leapt up and began kicking dirt onto the fire to douse it. The others stood too.

"Race you to the house!" yelled a gleeful Jolly, already halfway there at a run.

Barking with forced laughter, the others followed her. Millie, who was almost as quick as Jolly, reached the disintegrating cement steps of the house a split second before Jolly pushed in through the door, yelling, "I win!" as loudly as she could. The others tumbled in behind Millie, shoving and giggling.

Sai hissed, "Sshh!" Loud noises weren't a good idea.

With a chuckle in her voice, Jolly replied, "Oh, chill, we're fine. Remember how Churchy used to say that loud noises chased away ghosts?"

Everyone went silent. They were probably all thinking the same thing; that maybe Churchy was a ghost now. Millie whispered, "We have to keep quiet or the easthound will hear us."

"There's no such thing as an easthound," said Max. His voice was deeper than it had been last week. No use pretending. He was growing up. Millie put a bit more distance between him and her. Max really was getting too old. If he didn't do the right thing soon, and leave on his own, they'd have to kick him out. Hopefully before something ugly happened.

Citron closed the door behind them. It was dark in the house. Millie tried to listen beyond the door to the outside. That had been no wolf howling, and they all knew it. She tried to rub away the pain in her wrist. "Do we have any aspirin?"

Sai replied, "I'm sorry. I took the last two yesterday."

Citron sat with a thump on the floor and started to sob. "I hate this," he said slurrily. "I'm cold and I'm scared and there's no bread left, and it smells of mildew in here—"

"You're just drunk," Millie told him.

"—and Millie's cranky all the time," Citron continued, with a glare at Millie, "and Sai farts in her sleep, and Max's boots don't fit him anymore. He's *growing up.*"

"Shut up!" said Max. He grabbed Citron by the shoulders, dragged him to his feet, and started to shake him. "Shut up!" His voice broke on the "up" and ended in a little squeak. It should have been funny, but now he had Citron against the wall and was choking him. Jolly and Sai yanked at Max's hands. They told him over and over to stop, but he wouldn't. The creepiest thing was, Citron wasn't making any sound. He couldn't. He couldn't get any air. He scrabbled at Max's hands, trying to pull them off his neck.

Millie knew she had to do something quickly. She slammed the bottle of vodka across Max's back, like christening a ship. She'd seen it on TV, when TVs still worked. When you could plug one in and have juice flow through the wires to make funny cartoon creatures move behind the screen, and your mom wouldn't sprout in front of your eyes and eat your dad and bite your hand off.

Millie'd thought the bottle would shatter. But maybe the glass was too thick, because though it whacked Max's back with a solid thump, it didn't break. Max dropped to the floor like he'd been shot. Jolly put her hands to her mouth. Startled at what she herself had done, Millie dropped the bottle. It exploded when it hit the floor, right near Max's head. Vodka fountained up and out, and then Max was whimpering and rolling around in the booze and broken glass. There were dark smears under him.

"Ow! Jesus! Ow!" He peered up to see who had hit him. Millie moved closer to Jolly.

"Max." Citron's voice was hoarse. He reached a hand out to Max. "Get out of the glass, dude. Can you stand up?"

Millie couldn't believe it. "Citron, he just tried to kill you!"

"I shouldn't have talked about growing up. Jolly, can you find the candles? It's dark in here. Come on, Max." Citron pulled Max to his feet.

Max came up mad. He shook broken glass off his leather jacket and stood towering over Millie. Was his chest thicker than it had been? Was that *hair* shadowing his chin? Millie whimpered and cowered away. Jolly put herself between Millie and Max. "Don't be a big fucking bully," she said to Max. "Picking on the one-hand girl. Don't be a *dog*."

It was like a light came back on in Max's eyes. He looked at Jolly, then at Millie. "You hurt me, Millie. I wouldn't hurt you," he said to Millie. "Even if . . ."

"If . . . that *thing* was happening to you"—Jolly interrupted him—"you wouldn't care who you were hurting. Besides, you were choking Citron, so don't give us that innocent look and go on about not hurting people."

Max's eyes welled up. They glistened in the candlelight. "I'll go," he said drunkenly. His voice sounded high, like the boy he was ceasing to be. "Soon. I'll go away. I promise."

"When?" Millie asked softly. They all heard her, though. Citron looked at her with big wet doe eyes.

Max swallowed. "Tomorrow. No. A week."

"Three days," Jolly told him. "Two more sleeps."

Max made a small sound in his throat. He wiped his hand over his face. "Three days," he agreed. Jolly nodded firmly.

After that, no one wanted to play loup de lou anymore. They didn't bother with candles. They all went to their own places, against the walls so they could keep an eye on one another. Millie and Jolly had the best place, near the window. That way, if anything bad happened, Jolly could boost Millie out the window. There used to be a low bookcase under that window. They'd burned the wood months ago, for cooking. The books that had been on it were piled up to one side, and Jolly'd scavenged a pile of old clothes for a bed. Jolly rummaged around under the clothes. She pulled out the gold necklace that their mom had given her for passing French.

Jolly only wore it to sleep. She fumbled with the clasp, dropped the necklace, swore under her breath. She found the necklace again and put it on successfully this time. She kissed Millie on the forehead. "Sleep tight, Mills."

Millie said, "My wrist hurts too much. Come with me tomorrow to see if the kids two streets over have any painkillers?"

"Sure, honey." Warrens kept their distance from each other, for fear of becoming targets if someone in someone else's warren sprouted. "But try to get some sleep, okay?" Jolly lay down and was asleep almost immediately, her breathing quick and shallow.

Millie remained sitting with her back against the wall. Max lay on the other side of the room, using his coat as a blanket. Was he sleeping, or just lying there listening?

She used to like Max. Weeks after the world had gone mad, he'd found her and Jolly hiding under the porch of somebody's house. They were dirty and hungry, and the stench of rotting meat from inside the house was drawing flies. Jolly had managed to keep Millie alive that long, but Millie was delirious with pain, and the place where her hand had been bitten off had started smelling funny. Max had brought them clean water. He'd searched and bargained with the other warrens of hiding kids until he'd found morphine and antibiotics for Millie. He was the one who'd told them that it looked like only adults were getting sick.

But now Millie was scared of him. She sat awake half the night, watching Max. Once, he shifted and snorted, and the hairs on Millie's arms stood on end. She shoved herself right up close against Jolly. But Max just grumbled and rolled over and kept sleeping. He didn't change. Not this time. Millie watched him a little longer, until she couldn't keep her eyes open. She curled up beside Jolly. Jolly was scrawny, her skin downy with the peach fuzz that Sai said came from starvation. Most of them had it. Nobody wanted to grow up and change, but Jolly needed to eat a little more, just a little. Millie stared into the dark and worried. She didn't know when she fell asleep. She woke when first light was making the window into a glowing blue square. She was cold. Millie reached to put her arm around Jolly. Her arm landed on wadded-up clothing with nobody in it. "She's gone," said Citron.

"Whuh?" Millie rolled over, sat up. She was still tired. "She gone to check the traps?" Jolly barely ate, but she was best at catching gamey squirrels, feral cats, and the occasional raccoon.

"I dunno. I woke up just as the door was closing behind her. She let in a draft."

Millie leapt to her feet. "It was Max! He sprouted! He ate her!"

Citron leapt up too. He pulled her into a hug. "Sh. It wasn't Max. Look, he's still sleeping."

He was. Millie could see him huddled under his coat.

"See?" said Citron. "Now, hush. You're going to wake him and Sai up."

"Oh god, I was so scared for a moment." She was lying; she never stopped being scared. She sobbed and let Citron keep hugging her, but not for long. Things could sneak up on you while you were busy making snot and getting hugs to make you feel better. Millie swallowed back the rest of her tears. She pulled out of Citron's arms. "Thanks." She went and checked beside Jolly's side of the bed. Jolly's jacket wasn't there. Neither was her penguin. *Ah.* "She's gone to find aspirin for me." Millie sighed with relief and guilt. "She took her penguin to trade with. That's almost her most favorite thing ever."

"Next to you, you mean."

"I suppose so. I come first, then her necklace, then the penguin." Jolly'd found the ceramic penguin a long time ago when they'd been scavenging in the wreckage of a drugstore. The penguin stood on a circular base, the whole thing about ten inches tall. Its beak was broken, but when you twisted the white base, music played out of it. Jolly had kept it carefully since, wrapped in a torn blouse. She played it once a week and on special occasions. Twisted the base twice only, let the penguin do a slow turn to the few notes of a tinny song. Churchy had told them that the penguin was from a movie called *Madagascar*. She'd been old enough to remember old-time stuff like that. It was soon after that that they'd had to kill her.

Millie stared at her and Jolly's sleeping place. There was something . . . "She didn't take socks. Her feet must be freezing." She picked up the pair of socks with the fewest holes in it. "We have to go find her."

"You go," Citron replied. "It's cold out, and I want to get some more sleep."

"You know we're not supposed to go anywhere on our own!"

"Yeah, but we do. Lots of times."

"Except me. I always have someone with me."

"Right. Like that's any safer than being alone. I'm going back to bed." He yawned and turned away.

Millie fought the urge to yell at him. Instead she said, "I claim leader."

Citron stopped. "Aw, come on, Millie."

But Millie was determined. "Leader. One of us might be in danger, so I claim leader. So you have to be my follower."

He looked skyward and sighed. "Fine. Where?"

That meant she was leader. You asked the leader what to do, and the leader told you. Usually everyone asked Jolly what to do, or Max. Now that she had an excuse to go to Jolly, Millie stopped feeling as though something had gnawed away the pit of her stomach. She yanked her coat out of the pile of clothing that was her bed and shrugged it on. "Button me," she said to Citron, biting back the "please." Leaders didn't say please. They just gave orders. That was the right way to do it.

Citron concentrated hard on the buttons, not looking into Millie's eyes as he did them up. He started in the middle, buttoned down to the last button just below her hips, then stood up to do the buttons at her chest. He held the fabric away from her so it wouldn't touch her body at all. His fingers didn't touch her, but still her chest felt tingly as Citron did up the top buttons. She knew he was blushing, even though you couldn't tell on his dark face. Hers neither. If it had been Max doing this, his face would have lit up like a strawberry. They found strawberries growing sometimes, in summer.

Leaders didn't blush. Millie straightened up and looked at Citron. He had such a baby face. If he was lucky, he'd never sprout. She'd heard that some people didn't. Max said it was too soon to tell, because the pandemic had only started two years ago, but Millie liked to hope that some kids would avoid the horrible thing. No temper getting worse and worse. No changing all of a sudden into something different and scary. Millie wondered briefly what happened to the ones who didn't sprout, who just got *old*. Food for the easthound, probably. "Let's go . . ." she said, then remembered herself. Leader. "We're going over by the grocery first," she told Citron. "Maybe she's just checking her traps."

"She took her music box to check her traps?"

"Doesn't matter. That's where we're going to go." She stuffed Jolly's socks into her coat pocket, then shoved her shoulder against the swollen door and stepped out into the watery light of an early spring morning. The sun made her blink.

Citron asked, "Shouldn't we get those two to come along with us? You know, so there's more of us?"

"No," growled Millie. "Just now you wanted me to go all alone, but now you want company?"

"But who does trading this early in the morning?"

"We're not going to wake Max and Sai, okay? We'll find her ourselves!"

Citron frowned. Millie shivered. It was so cold out that her nose hairs froze together when she breathed in. Like scattered pins, tiny, shiny daggers of frost edged the sidewalk slabs and the new spring leaves of the small maple tree that grew outside their squat. Trust Jolly to make her get out of a warm bed to go looking for her on a morning like this. She picked up three solid throwing rocks. They were gritty with dirt, and the cold of them burned her fingers. She stuffed them into her jacket pocket, on top of Jolly's socks. Citron had the baseball bat he carried everywhere. Millie turned up her collar and stuck her hand into her jeans pocket. "Let's go."

Jolly'd put a new batch of traps over by that old grocery store. The roof was caved in. There was no food in the grocery anymore, or soap, or cough medicine. Everything had been scavenged by the nearby warrens of kids, but animals sometimes made nests and shit in the junk that was left. Jolly'd caught a dog once. A gaunt poodle with dirty, matted hair. But they didn't eat dogs, ever. You were what you ate. They'd only killed it in an orgy of fury and frustration that had swelled over them like a river.

> *Black Betty had a child,*
> *Bam-ba-lam,*
> *That child's gone wild,*
> *Bam-ba-lam.*

Really, it was Millie who'd started it, back before everything went wrong, two winters ago. They'd been at home. Jolly sitting on the living room floor that early evening, texting with her friends, occasionally giggling at something one of them said. Millie and Dad on the couch sharing a bowl of raspberries. All of them watching some old-time cartoon movie on TV about animals that could do kung fu. Waiting for Mum to come home from work. Because then they would order pizza. It was pizza night. Dad getting a text message on his phone. Dad holding the phone down by his knee to make out the words, even though his eyesight was just fine, he said. Jolly watching them, waiting to hear if it was Mum, if she'd be home soon. Millie leaning closer to Dad and squinting at the tiny message in the phone's window. Mouthing the words silently. Then frowning. Saying, "Mum says she's coming home on the easthound train?" Dad falling out laughing. East*bound*, sweetie.

There hadn't been an easthound before that. It was Millie who'd called it, who'd made it be. Jolly'd told her that wasn't true, that she didn't make the pandemic just by reading a word wrong, that the world didn't work that way. But the world didn't work anymore the way it used to, so what did Jolly know? Even if she *was* older than Millie.

Jolly and Millie's family had assigned adjectives to the girls early on in their lives. Millie was The Younger One. (By twenty-eight-and-three-quarter minutes. They'd been afraid she wouldn't make it.) Jolly was The Kidder. She liked jokes and games. She was the one who'd come up with loup-de-lou, to help keep Millie's mind off the agony when she'd lost her hand. She'd still been able to feel the missing hand there, on the end of her wrist, and the pain wouldn't let her sleep or rest, and all the adults in the world were sprouting and trying to kill off the kids, and Max was making her and Jolly and Citron move to a new hiding place every few days, until he and Jolly figured out the thing about sprinkling peppermint oil to hide their scent trails so that sprouteds couldn't track them. That was back before Sai had joined them, and then Churchy. Back before Churchy had sprouted on them one night in the dark as they were all sharing half a stale bread loaf and a big liter bottle of flat cola, and Max and Citron and Sai had grabbed anything heavy or sharp they could find and whaled away at the thing that had been Churchy just seconds before, until it lay still on the ground, all pulpy and bloody. And the whole time, Jolly had stayed near still-weak Millie, brandishing a heavy frying pan and muttering, "It's okay, Mills. I won't let her get you."

The feeling was coming back, like her hand was still there. Her wrist had settled into a throbbing ache. She hoped it wasn't getting infected again.

Watchfully, they walked down their side street and turned onto the main street in the direction of the old grocery store. They walked up the middle of the empty road. That way, if a sprouted came out of one of the shops or alleyways, they might have time to see it before it attacked.

The burger place, the gas station, the little shoe repair place on the corner; Millie tried to remember what stores like that had been like before. When they'd had unbroken windows and unempty shelves. When there'd been people shopping in them and adults running them, back when adults used to be just grown-up people suspicious of packs of schoolkids in their stores; not howling, sharp-toothed child-killers with dank, stringy fur and paws instead of hands. Ravenous monsters that grew and grew so quickly you could watch it happen—if you were stupid enough to stick around. Their teeth, hair, and claws lengthened, their bodies getting bigger and heavier minute by minute, until they could no longer eat quickly enough to keep up with the growth, and they weakened and died a few days after they'd sprouted.

Jolly wasn't tending to her traps. Millie swallowed. "Okay, so we'll go check with the warren over on Patel Street. They usually have aspirin and stuff." She walked in silence except for the worry voice in her head.

Citron said, "That tree's going to have to start over."

"What?" Millie realized she'd stopped at the traffic light out of habit. She was such an idiot. And so was Citron for just going along with her. She started walking again. Citron tagged along, always just a little behind.

"The maple tree," he puffed. When you never had enough to eat, you got tired quickly. "The one outside our place. It put its leaves out too early, and now the frost has killed them. It'll have to start over."

"Whatever." Then she felt guilty for being so crabby with him. What could she say to make nice? "Uh, that was a nice line you made in loup-de-lou last night. The one with eyes and spies in it."

Citron smiled at her. "Thanks. It wasn't quite right, though. Sprouteds have bleedy red eyes, not shiny ones."

"But your line wasn't about sprouteds. It was about the . . . the easthound." She looked all around and behind her. Nothing.

"Thing is," Citron replied, so quietly that Millie almost didn't hear him, "we're all the easthound."

Instantly, Millie swatted the back of his head. "Shut up!"

"Ow!"

"Just shut up! Take that back! It's not true!"

"Stop making such a racket, willya?"

"So stop being such a loser!" She was sweating in her jacket, her skinny knees trembling. So hungry all the time. So scared.

Citron's eyes widened. "Millie . . . !"

He was looking behind her. She turned, hand fumbling in her jacket pocket for her rocks. The sprouted bowled her over while her hand was still snagged in her pocket. Thick, curling fur and snarling and teeth as long as her pinkie. It grabbed her with paws like catcher's mitts with claws in them. It howled and briefly let her go. It's in pain, she thought wonderingly, even as she fought her hand out of her pocket and tried to get out from under the sprouted. All that quick growing. It must hurt them. The sprouted snapped at her face, missed. They were fast and strong when they first sprouted, but clumsy in their ever-changing bodies. The sprouted set its jaws in her chest. Through her coat and sweater, its teeth tore into her skin. Pain. Teeth sliding along her ribs. Millie tried to wrestle the head off her. She got her fingers deep into the fur around its neck. Then an impact jerked the sprouted's head sideways. Citron and his baseball bat, screaming, "Die, you bastard!" as he beat the sprouted. It leapt for him. It was already bigger. Millie rolled to her feet, looking around for anything she could use as a weapon. Citron was keeping the sprouted at bay, just barely, by swinging his bat at it. It advanced on him, howling in pain with every step forward.

Sai seemed to come out of nowhere. She had the piece of rebar she carried whenever she went out. The three of them raged at the sprouted, screaming and hitting. Millie kicked and kicked. The sprouted screamed back in pain or fury. Its eyes were all bleedy. It swatted Citron aside, but he got up and came at it again. Finally it wasn't fighting anymore. They kept hitting it until they were sure it was dead. Even after Sai and Citron had stopped, Millie stomped the sprouted. With each stomp, she grunted in thick animal rage at herself for letting it sneak up on her, for leaving the warren without her knife. Out of the corner of her eye, she could see a few kids that had crept out from other warrens to see what the racket was about. She didn't care. She stomped.

"Millie! Millie!" It was Citron. "It's dead!"

Millie gave the bloody lump of hair and bone and flesh one more kick, then stood panting. Just a second to catch her breath, then they could keep looking for Jolly. They couldn't stay there long. A dead sprouted could draw others. If one sprouted was bad, a feeding frenzy of them was worse.

Sai was gulping, sobbing. She looked at them with stricken eyes. "I woke up and I called to Max and he didn't answer, and when I went over and lifted his coat"—she burst into gusts of weeping—"there was only part of his head and one arm there. And bones. Not even much blood." Sai clutched herself and shuddered. "While we were sleeping, a sprouted came in and killed Max and ate most of him, even licked up his blood, and we didn't wake up! I thought it had eaten all of you! I thought it was coming back for me!"

Something gleamed white in the broken mess of the sprouted's corpse. Millie leaned over to see better, fighting not to gag on the smell of blood and worse. She had to crouch closer. There was lots of blood on the thing lying in the curve of the sprouted's body, but with chilly clarity, Millie recognized it. It was the circular base of Jolly's musical penguin. Millie looked over at Citron and Sai. "Run," she told them. The tears coursing down her face felt cool. Because her skin was so hot now.

"What?" asked Sai. "Why?"

Millie straightened. Her legs were shaking so much they barely held her up. That small pop she'd felt when she'd pulled on the sprouted's neck. "A sprouted didn't come into our squat. It was already in there." She opened her hand to show them the thing she'd pulled off the sprouted's throat in her battle with it; Jolly's gold necklace. Instinct often led sprouteds to return to where the people they loved were. Jolly had run away to protect the rest of her warren from herself. "Bloody *run*!" Millie yelled at them. "Go find another squat! Somewhere I won't look for you! Don't you get it? I'm her twin!"

First Citron's face then Sai's went blank with shock as they understood what Millie was saying. Citron sobbed, once. It might have been the word "Bye." He grabbed Sai's arm. The two of them stumbled away. The other kids that had come out to gawk had disappeared back to their warrens. Millie turned her back so she couldn't see what direction Sai and Citron were moving in, but she could hear them, more keenly than she'd ever been able to hear. She could smell them. The easthound could track them. The downy starvation fuzz on Millie's arm was already coarser. The pain in her handless wrist spiked. She looked at it. It was aching because the hand was starting to grow in again. There were tiny fingers on the end of it now. And she needed to eat so badly.

When had Jolly sprouted? Probably way more than twenty-eight-and-three-quarter minutes ago. Citron and Sai's only chance was that Millie had always done everything later than her twin.

Still clutching Jolly's necklace, she began to run too; in a different direction. Leeks, she told the sprouting Hound, fresh leeks. You like those, right? Not blood and still-warm, still-screaming flesh. You like leeks. The Hound wasn't fully come into itself yet. It was almost believing her that leeks would satisfy its hunger. And it didn't understand that she couldn't swim. You're thirsty too, right? she told it.

It was.

Faster, faster, faster, Millie sped toward the river, where the spring tide was running deep and wide.

> *That child's gone wild.*
> *Oh, Black Betty, bam-ba-lam.*

Loup.

GRAY

BY **JANE YOLEN**

How many ways to describe gray:
gray louring sky, nearly black;
gray stone, a wall fallen down,
gray of rock, ribboned with crevices;
gray wall pocked with bullet holes;
gray splotches of old, dried blood.
The day is gray with weeping,
the hour gray with horror.
The dusk will be gray with no promise.
The night a darker shade of gray
without dreams.

And yet in that corner of the gray wall,
beneath the gray sky,
in the middle of the gray day,
out of the gray, dusty, thirsting earth,
a small green shoot struggles upward,
pulling itself towards the gray light,
harbinger, herald, hope.

GRAY

If we wait—
a day, a week, a season,
all of them gray—
there will be a flower,
a wall flower.
And it will be red,
the color of life's new blood,
of the rebirthed sun,
of desire, of chance,
and gray will only be
the color of memory
soon forgot.

BEFORE

BY **CAROLYN DUNN**

I.

I HAVE A NAME.

It sits upon the tip of my tongue like the taste of something familiar. Something warm. Something that sends droplets of memory down my throat and warms my empty belly. Water on a hot day; the splash of coolness after the heat of the ever-present fluorescent lights that burn the rims of my eyelids raw, the merciless brightness that keeps sleep pressing from behind and underneath the burning of my eyes.

The lights are always on so my captors can watch me behind their veil of darkness, keeping me under their ever-watchful gaze so I cannot escape. Where can I go where there is no one watching me, pinned down by bright lights that never dim, never burn out? Chained by bonds to this hard, cold steel platform that serves as bed, table, chamber, prison? I am their prisoner. I have known nothing else, no light, no darkness, no night sky, no stars shining overhead to guide me home. I have no home. Only the one I go to in my dreams.

If I did dream.

I imagine instead, lying here on this cold, hard platform,

what my dreams would be like. I see my mother there. We are on a cliff high above a large body of water that I suppose is the ocean. I have never been there, but in my waking dreams it feels very familiar, and so I go there to pass the time, the waiting for the stealing of my blood. I go there in my head and I can see my mother standing, her hands moving across the grasses as the ocean wind whirls around us. My mother's voice is full of awe and joy as she tells me a story:

On the island of Limuw, there is a story of a beautiful young woman. She was so lovely they called her Pahe Pahe, or Flower of Limuw. She was the pride of her family, of her mother and father and sisters and brothers; and she grew up knowing each place for the stars, each ocean, each plant, each animal of the land; and she was a good girl because she understood her world as one would understand their world, through the stories and songs of her people.

One day, Pahe Pahe took her tomol, her canoe, out into the beautiful kelp beds surrounding her home. While out on the kelp beds, she became entranced by their beauty, by the way they waved to her, dancing underwater to the song she sang: "Beautiful place, beautiful home of mine, singer of stars and light, keep me safe on this journey to and from my beloved homeland. . . ." The giant kelp swayed back and forth, graceful, loving Pahe Pahe's song.

Old Man Coyote saw Pahe Pahe out in the water and he decided to trick her. He didn't like water, but so great was his desire to trick Pahe Pahe that he swallowed up his pride and dove under the water, making himself look like a seal. Quietly, he crept up on Pahe Pahe's tomol, pretending.

Slowly Old Man Coyote inched up the line of Pahe Pahe's lure, and soon Pahe Pahe felt the tug on her line, and look! She pulled up and it was Old Man Coyote! Pahe Pahe laughed and laughed. "Old Man Coyote, what are you doing here on my line?"

So funny did Pahe Pahe think Old Man Coyote looked, all bedraggled and wet and smelling like two-day-old wet dog, that she dunked him back into the water. "Perhaps you need a bath to smell sweet again?" She laughed and dunked him once more. Old Man Coyote sputtered under the lash of the water and the moomat, growing angrier and angrier—and still Pahe Pahe laughed and dunked him three more times, until Old Man Coyote let go of the line and swam back to shore, old and bedraggled and wet and furious.

As she paddled on and on, Pahe Pahe became sorrowful, for in spite of his tricks and lies, Old Man Coyote was a respected elder among the people; and maybe, just maybe, Pahe Pahe had been disrespectful of him by teasing him the way she did. So despondent she became over her behavior that she just sat there as the birds came and took all of her fish, and she sat there all night even as the stars came out and twinkled their greetings to the Flower of Limuw. She returned her tomol to land, growing more and more unhappy as she did.

At sunrise, Pahe Pahe's guilt got the better of her, so she climbed to the top of the cliffs above her on Limuw and swore that she would kill herself for her terrible transgression toward Old Man Coyote. As soon as the sun peeked up over the eastern mainland, she leapt off the cliff and into the water below. But the tide had receded, so she hit the bottom of the white foam and broke her legs from the fall.

Hatash, the Great Mother, took pity on Pahe Pahe because she was such a good and loyal and beautiful daughter, so that wherever the water touched Pahe Pahe's broken body, scales the colors of abalone—pink, green, blue, lavender, all the colors of the flowers of Limuw—took shape on her legs. Fins that danced and waved like the giant kelp sprouted from these colors and grateful for her gift of life, Pahe Pahe dove into the waters, swimming on the dawnlit sky reflected in the deep ocean. Her brothers and sisters came to swim with her—the dolphins, whom she loved, the seals, and all the beautiful fish jumped and dove with her in their joy. Pahe Pahe swam all morning, all afternoon, and when she grew tired, she found herself at Pimu Island, some seventy miles from Limuw.

As she went upon the rocks to sun and warm herself, a little boy *who was helping his grandfather tie the nets together to fish saw her. "Grandfather!" cried the little boy. "Look! Look there!"*

The grandfather and his grandson were so moved by Pahe Pahe's beauty that there were tears sparkling in their eyes. "She was once the Flower of Limuw," the grandfather said, "and now she is the Flower of the World."

I stare into the sun, watching the light stream across the sky, hitting the ocean with sparkles like stars. My mother's voice fades as the bright lights come into view once again.

Pahe Pahe is the name of the Flower of the World. This is the story of her name, and I remember this as I lie under the burning light, my eyes fixed ahead but also on the sea. I imagine myself as Pahe Pahe, not as "2231" or "it" or "dirty Indian." Pahe Pahe would not allow herself to be poked and prodded by her enemies. She would sing them away.

My name, ever elusive, burns like a deep gnawing thirst that refuses to be quenched under these lights. They hide behind the lights, keeping their faces hidden from me. The illness that sets their blood on fire, bursting within their bodies, is not inside me. They think that by taking my blood from me they will be healed. Their skin grows sallow, pale, colorless under the lights. My skin, like their rage, grows darker and darker under the lights. This enrages them even more, so that their words lash out at me under their lights. They think their words hurt. Redskin. Whore. Bitch of the earthborn.

"2231," they say, or "it." "Thing."

Sometimes, when the kinder ones come to stick my bruised, torn skin with their long, sharp needles of steel and other shiny metals, I am "her." Upon the kind ones is the scent of impending death. This sickness in their blood makes them the same as the others. This disease doesn't understand the difference. Their faces are covered by thick, clear plastic, so that all I can see of them is a reflection of the light that burns behind my eyes. I can see myself in their masks. The girl I see there is not who I picture in my mind. . . . She is a dark-skinned wisp of a girl, with closely cropped black tufts of hair sticking out from her head, and bruises and curses where there should be kisses.

Perhaps they are kind because they sense their end is coming fast.

I remember when two long braids hung from either side of my head, skimming past the line of my shoulders to the middle of my back. Mama made sure my braids were smooth, shiny, and tied into even lengths, with red bows fastened at the ends. I wonder sometimes if whoever first shaved my head kept the bows as souvenirs.

The door opens and they come. The kindly ones. Their eyes are hidden, like the others, but I see through the shadows. I see the blood that is filling their eyes and blinding them. This is a disease of their own making, grown in a lab somewhere, much like the one where they are holding me. So much time has passed, yet they still think my blood can heal them. Six times a day they come into the bright, hotly lit chamber, approach the platform where I am tied by my arms and legs, and prod at the bruised, tender flesh of my arms with their sharp, pointed fingers. I have grown accustomed to their intent, their anger, their rage at the sight of the nerves and veins running in blue lines beneath the chalky brown outer layer of my skin. I try not to wince, to not give them the satisfaction of knowing how much it hurts, that pinch upon my skin, and the sharp, sharp pinprick. Sometimes the needles aren't as sharp as they once were, but they say nothing as the blunt end of the needle punctures through the purple-and-black bruises all along my arms.

I turn and watch the liquid spurt into the long, clear glass cylinder. Their hopes rise with each filling of the specimen collector, each change that my blood undergoes as they try to craft their cure for this disease of their own making. My face is reflected in the glass syringe, and my lips purse and my eyes shimmer with tears I can no longer shed. The only liquid my body can conjure is my blood; and soon, I know, if they continue taking it from me against my will, there won't be anything left inside of me to steal.

II.

My mother had a beautiful laugh. I can still remember the sound, coming from dreams that pretend to follow the false sleep the lights keep me in. She was always laughing. She laughed when my father sang to her with his clapper sticks.

> *Oh my darling, don't you cry for me.*
> *I'm not so far away from you, ya hey yah.*
> *In your dreams I'll sing how I love you so.*
> *Stay right by your side forever, yah hey yah.*
> *So close your eyes and dream. I'll see you on the other side.*
> *Hey yah ha, hey ya hah, ho!*

My dad's hands always moved in perfect rhythm, pushing his song skyward. My mother's laugh moved up and down the length of the sticks, and this is how I remember them. Laughing. Singing. But never speaking my name. Just singing into the thousand tiny pinpricks of light under the dark sky of home.

I remember watching her touch the tall grasses, singing to them as they drifted under her fingers. The image of the kelp beds dancing under Pahe Pahe's song come to me, and I see that my mother, like Pahe Pahe, is singing to the grasses of the earth. Her song makes magic as she pulls certain grasses from the earth and begins to pass them through her teeth. "The grass needs to be softened before it can take the shape of the basket," my mother says. Some grasses make the journey through her mouth, others remain undisturbed. "We save some for next year so that there will always be baskets for the coming seasons. . . ." I can hear her voice so clearly, so sweetly, that even in my mind, after I have spent all this time locked away in a laboratory that keeps me alive for my blood, I feel her strength seep into my bones.

Her fingers shape the tough grasses, softened by her mouth, into a knot of a cross. "This is the heart, the beginning, of any basket," she says. My fingers, tiny, follow hers, moving the softer pieces between the tougher ones, her patient and loving hands guiding mine. "Baskets hold water, seeds, grass, even babies. The baskets hold our hearts, keep us connected to the earth, to the sky, to the sea, to one another. . . ." Her hands are gentle as she guides mine, and when I am finished, my basket is lopsided, uneven, filled with little holes. My mother laughs and holds it up to the sun. "This one is good for collecting acorns," she says, her smile coloring her voice. "We'll need those for good soup."

When they came to take me away, my mother wasn't laughing. She made no sound at all as the dark matte of blood oozed out from the wound in her head where they had shot her dead. It spilled onto the red dirt as it pooled in the setting light of the sun. My mother's blood was weak, they said as they pulled me from her arms. Not enough Indian to make a cure, they said.

Get up, Mama, I screamed in our language. *Get up and chase them down!*

Her eyes were open and empty as they pulled me into a helicopter, the sound of the blades drowning out my screams.

My father does not come for me. . . . Only his voice seeks me out in the darkness, in the crying-out voice that tears across my mouth. He is there, too, his body lying not far from my mother's. He does not move. His blood is thin, weak; yet it is the same color as mine.

I lost my name that day. It was then I became "2231." "It." "Redskin."

Dirty Indian.

III.

My father's voice is singing in my mind when I feel the kindly ones' fear shift into something different.

Something is happening. I can taste the shift in their fear upon my tongue. I can taste their blood between my teeth as it pumps, diluted, through their veins in a failing attempt to graft my immunity to their weakness. Their fear tastes of metal, hard and cold, and the death stench is soon upon them.

Their fear fills my eyes, my nose, my lungs. Stronger than ever in my mouth. Time slips past, and their entrances into my chamber grow fewer and fewer. They are losing their war against this plague, and they curse my strength as their own death marches forward in the blackness of their blood. Inside me, gaining strength from my mother's song, my blood pumps stronger and stronger. Their taking grows less frequent, and I feel the renewal of my blood bloom within.

The door opens and the bloom withers. They have come once again.

The air changes around me. I've not felt this one before.

A fresh anger moves in waves across the room, and I strain against my binds to see who this one is. Her scent is not of fear. She is not dying. Her blood is pure.

A woman comes to my side, and I see her clearly. No mask, no veil to hide behind. She is beautiful, her face dark against the harsh lights. Her eyes are black like mine, her hair is pulled back from her face, and beauty shines from her. I look up into her eyes, and in them I see a sea of night stars, an ocean of inky darkness, and she looks at me, hard.

Her mouth is moving, but I can hear nothing from her mouth, only my father's song from a distant memory.

Oh my darling, how I love you so . . .

Am I dreaming? I have not been able to do so for as long as I can remember.

Stay right by your side forever, yah hey yah.

I'm too lost in the woman's eyes to make out the pattern of her words that string along in my head.

I'm not so far away from you, ya hey yah. In your dreams I'll sing how I love you so . . .

All I can see are the stars in a dark expanse of ocean and sky. I know the place of each of them in the night sky, the name for all the plants and animals. The name of the people.

So close your eyes and dream. I'll see you on the other side. Hey yah ha, hey ya huh, ho!

My mouth opens and I try to speak, but nothing comes out. She reaches out, her hands resting upon my face, and the expanse of night sky swims in her eyes. I think she is crying when her words begin to form in my head.

"Sela." She is saying, over and over. "Sela, Sela, Sela . . ."

Sela.

My name. My name is Sela.

IV.

"Sela. Your name is Sela."

My grandmother's words float over the wind and reach around me, comforting me in our language. I know my name.

She takes my face in her hands, those dark eyes with oceans of stars staring back at me, and my mind struggles to focus on her. We are outside, standing at the mouth of a dark cave in the homeland of our people, staring out at the shadow of Pimu Island in the setting sun. We have traveled far—that I can tell by the rising and setting of the sun three times. She'd gathered me into her arms, breaking the bonds that tied me down, and whispered over and over. "Your name is Sela."

I had been speaking when she came in. "2231," I was saying, over and over. The roll number they had given me when they stole me from my mother's arms and brought me to that place. Where they took my blood, with the hope that they would one day find a cure for the disease that turned their own blood black and their skin into pustules and oozing death. "2231. 2231 . . ."

I stand nearly as tall as my grandmother, maybe even taller, as I gaze into her eyes. I am weak from my captivity. She tells me they have held me for three years.

"How old am I?"

She doesn't hesitate as she answers: Thirteen. She had been searching for me, and when she entered their facility, their compound, the war was nearly over. There was no one left to question her when she rode up to the lab in her black Army-issue Jeep Wrangler, dressed in black fatigues and a headband holding her braid back against her head. "Your name is Sela. You were named for me," she says, speaking over and over, as if I can't understand. "I'm Isabella. Your grandmother. . . ."

She presses something into my hand. Something warm, soft to the touch, yet firm. Pliable. Grasses woven together in the shape of sticks crossed against one another, and bear grass woven between the spines. We are standing among the tall grasses, the breath of the ocean moving up the cliffs and through the swaying stalks. As she is speaking, my fingers begin to form a pattern in the strands, and I weave the strands through the spine into the beginning of a new basket.

Her words sing in my head as she tells me how she has searched for me all these three years, staying under the Army radar, posing as a doctor, pretending to search for a cure for this disease that my captors have let loose in the world. Blackpox, they call it. "It has killed them like it killed our ancestors, my own grandmother . . . and now our blood is our immunity. Our blood is what will survive this war."

The sun drops down against the western sky, and all around me the sea foams and surges. In my dreams I stood at this very spot, against the caves in which our ancestors rode out the storms that tried to extinguish us before. I look into my grandmother's eyes, and I can hear my father sing as she wraps me in her arms. The basket is in my hands, and tears form in my eyes as I see there are no holes, no crooked patterns in this thing I have created from the memories in my blood. Tears fall onto the pale grass and, like the kelp in the ocean, the grasses float upon the breath of our ancestors. I imagine I see Pahe Pahe's tail glistening like the stars under the sea that surrounds us in this place that is now, always has been, and always will be our home.

Oh my darling, don't you cry, my grandmother sings. *Stay right by your side forever, yah hey yah . . .*

Sela. My name is Sela. I am thirteen years old. I stand at the caves where my ancestors rode out the storm that once tried to take us down. It is here where we survived, and here where we will survive again.

FAKE PLASTIC TREES

BY CAITLÍN R. KIERNAN

"You're not sleeping," Max said. "You're still having nightmares about the car. When you're awake, it's what you think about. I'm right, Cody, aren't I?"

"Mostly," I told him, and then neither of us said anything else for a while. We sat together and stared at the ugly red river. It was Max finally spoke up and broke the silence.

"Well, I was thinking," he said, "maybe if you were to write it down. That might help, I was thinking."

"It might not, too," I replied. "I already saw Dr. Lehman twice. I did everything he said, and that didn't help. How's writing it down supposed to help?"

"Well, it might," he said again. "You can't know until you try. Maybe you could get the bad stuff you saw out of your head, like when you eat spoiled food and throwing up helps. See, that's what I'm thinking."

"Maybe you ought to think less, Max. Besides, where am I supposed to get anything to write it on?"

He promptly handed me the nub of a pencil and some paper he'd torn out of the *H–G* volume of an encyclopedia in the Sanctuary library. I yelled at him for going and ruining books when there aren't so many left to ruin.

"Cody, we can always put the pages back when you're done," he said impatiently, like I should have thought of that already without him having to explain it to me. "Only, they'll be better than before, because one side will have your story written on them."

"Who's gonna want to read my story?" I asked.

"Someone might. Someday, someone might. Anyway, that's not the point. Writing it's the point."

Sitting there on the riverbank, listening to him, it began to make sense, but I didn't tell him that, because I didn't feel like letting him know I didn't still think he was full of shit, and because I still don't think I can do this. Just because it's my story doesn't mean I can put it into words like he wants.

"At least try," he said. "Just you take a day or two and give it a go." I told him I had too much to do in the greenhouses, what with the beans and corn coming on ripe, and he said he'd take my shifts and no one would even care because there's so little work right now at pumps and filters in the hydroplant.

"Oh, and while you're at it, put in how things went wrong with the world, so when things get better, people will know how it all happened."

I said that was just dumb. Other people have already written it down, what went wrong. The smart people, the people who weren't four years old on the first day of THE END OF THE WORLD.

I stared at the shiny encyclopedia pages in my hands. If they'd been ripped out of a real encyclopedia, words would already have been printed on both sides, but they were just copies got made right after THE EVENT. See, that's how the olders always talk about it, and they say certain words and phrases like THE BEFORE and THE AFTER and THE EVENT and THE GOO as if they were being said all in capital letters. I stared at the pages, which were at least real paper, made from real wood pulp, and I told him if I do this I get more than a kiss. Max said sure, why not, so long as you're honest, and he kissed me then and told me I was prettier than any of the other girls in Sanctuary (which is bullshit), and then he left me alone at the edge of the river. Which is where I'm sitting now. Sitting, writing, stopping to toss a rock that's still a rock into the sludgy crimson river that isn't still a river because most of the water went FACSIMILE twelve years ago.

The river moves by about as slowly as I'm writing this down, and I count all the way up to fifty-three before the rock (real rock) actually sinks out of sight into the not-water anymore. At least the river still moves. Lots of them went too solid. I've seen rivers that stopped moving almost right after THE EVENT. These days, they just sit there. Red and hard. Not moving, and I've even walked on a couple. Some people call them Jesus Streams. Anyway, I walked all the way across a broad Jesus Stream on a dare. But it wasn't much of a dare since I got a good dose of SWITCH OFF in me right away, back when I was four.

Okay. Fine, Max. So I'm *doing* this even though it's stupid. And you better not welch on that bet or I'll kick your ass, hear that? Also, I'm not writing much about what happened. I shouldn't waste my time writing any of that stuff. I don't care what Max says, because that's all down on paper somewhere else. I don't even know most of it, anyway, that EVENT three-quarters of my whole life ago. What I know for sure doesn't take long to set down. I learned what they bother to teach about THE GOO in classes. They don't teach all that much because why bother telling us about THE BEFORE and WHAT WENT WRONG so we got THE EVENT, when what we need to be learning is how to run the hydros and keep the power on, horticulture, medicine, engineering, and keeping the livestock alive (Max's dad used to oversee the rat cages before he was promoted to hydro duty, or Max would still be feeding pellets to rats and mice and guinea pigs). But, okay, Max:

THIS IS WHAT THEY TEACH YOU

Twelve years ago, in THE BEFORE, there were too many people in the world, and most of them were starving. There wasn't enough oil. There wasn't enough clean water. There wasn't enough of much of anything because people kept having babies almost as fast as the rats do. They'd almost used up everything. There were wars (we don't have those anymore, just the rovers and sneaks), and there were riots and terrorists. There were diseases we don't have anymore. People started dying faster than anyone could hope to bury them, so they just piled up. I can't imagine that many people. Ma'am Shen says there were more than nine billion people back then, but sometimes I think she surely exaggerates.

Anyway, in the year 2048, in a LOST PLACE called Boston, in a school the olders call MIT, scientists were trying to solve *all* these problems, all of them at once. Maybe other scientists in other parts of the world at some other schools and some of THE COM-PANIES were also trying, but SWITCH ON happened at MIT in Boston, which was in a place called New England. SWITCH ON, says Ma'am Shen, started out in a sort of bottle called a beaker. It gets called THE CRUCIBLE sometimes, and also SEAL 7, that one particular bottle. But I'll just call it the bottle.

Before I started writing this part, I made Max go back to the library and copy down some words and numbers for me on the back of one of these pages. I don't want to sound more ignorant than I am, and it's the least he could do. So, in the bottle, inside a lead box, were two things: a nutrient culture and nano-assemblers, which were microscopic machines. The assemblers used the culture to make copies of themselves. Idea was, make a thing you could eat that continuously made copies of itself, there'd be plenty enough food. And maybe this would also work with medicine and fuel and building materials and everything nine billion people needed. But the assemblers in the bottle were a TRIAL. So no one was sure what would happen. They made THE GOO, which Max's notes call polyvinyl chloride, PVC, but I'll call it plastic, 'cause that's what it's always called when people talk about it. People don't talk about it much, though I think they might have back before the SWITCH OFF really started working.

Okay, lost my train of thought.

Oh, right. The bottle at MIT. The bottle that was supposed to save the world, but did just the opposite. The assemblers (or so say Max's notes, and I can hardly read his handwriting) during the TRIAL were just four at the start, and four of them made four more of them. Those eight, though, because the production was exponential, made eight more assemblers. Thirty-six made seventy-two made 144 made 288 made 576 copies, then 1,152, 2,304, 4,608, and this was just in one hour. In a day, there were . . . I don't know, Max didn't write that part down.

The assemblers went ROGUE and obviously the bottle wasn't big enough to hold them. Probably not after a few million, I'm thinking. It shattered, and they got out of the lead box, and, lo and behold, they didn't need the culture to make copies of themselves. Just about anything would do. Glass (the bottle). Stone. Metal (the lead box). Anything alive. Water, like the river. Not gases, so not air. Not water vapor, which is one reason we're not all dead. The other reason, of course, is SWITCH OFF, which was made at another lab, and that one was in another LOST PLACE called France. People got injected with SWITCH OFF, and it was sprayed from the air in planes, and then bombs of SWITCH OFF were dropped all over. THE EVENT lasted two weeks. When it was more or less over, an estimated seventy-eight percent of the global biomass and a lot of the seas, rivers, streams, and the earth's crust had stopped being what it was before and had become plastic. Oh, not all crimson, by the way. I don't know why, but lots of different colors.

I didn't know all these numbers and dates. Max's notes. What I know: my parents died in THE EVENT, my parents and all my family, and I was evacuated to Sanctuary here in Florida on the shores of the St. Johns crimson plastic river. I don't think much more than that matters about THE EVENT. So this is where I'm gonna stop trying to be like the vandalized encyclopedia and tell the other story instead.

The story that's *my* story.

Isn't that what Max wanted me to start with?

MY STORY (CODY HERNANDEZ'S STORY)

I'm discovering, Max, that I can't tell my story without telling lots of other little stories along the way.

Like what happened the day that's still giving me the bad dreams, that was almost a year ago, which means it was about five years after most of the Army and the National Guard soldiers left us here because all of a sudden there were those radio transmissions from Atlanta and Miami, and they went off to bring other survivors back to Sanctuary. Only, they never brought anyone back, because they never came back, and we still don't know what happened to them. This is important to my story, because when the military was here with us, they kept a checkpoint and barricades on the east side of the big bridge over the St. Johns River, the Sanctuary side. But after they left, no one much bothered to man the checkpoint anymore, and the barricades stopped being anything more than a chain-link fence with a padlocked gate.

So, the story of the Army and National Guard leaving to find those people, I had to get that out to get to my story. Because I never would have been able to climb over the fence if they hadn't left. Or if they'd left but come back. They'd have stopped me. Or I'd probably never even have thought about climbing over.

Back in THE BEFORE, the bridge was called the Mathews Bridge. Back in THE BEFORE, Sanctuary wasn't here, and where it is was part of a city called Jacksonville. Now, though, it's just the bridge, and this little part of Jacksonville is just Sanctuary. About a third of the way across the bridge, there's an island below it. I have no idea if the island ever had a name. It's all plastic now, anyway, like most of the bridge. A mostly brown island in a crimson river below a mostly brown plastic bridge. Because of what the sunlight and weather do to polyvinyl chloride—twelve years of sunlight and weather—chunks of the bridge have decayed and fallen away into the slow crimson river that runs down to the mostly-still-crimson sea. The island below the bridge used to be covered with brown plastic palmetto trees and underbrush, but now isn't much more than a scabby-looking lump. The plastic degrades and then crumbles and is finally nothing but dust that the wind blows away.

I wanted to know what was on the other side. It's as simple as that.

I considered asking Max to go with me, Max and maybe one or two others. Maybe the twins, Jessie and Erin (who are a year older than me and Max), maybe Beth, too. There are still all the warning signs on the fence, the ones the military put there. But people don't go there. I suspect it reminds them of stuff from THE BEFORE that they don't want to be reminded of, like how this is the only place to live now. How there's really nowhere else to ever go. Which might be why none of the olders had ever actually *told* me to stay away from the bridge. Maybe it simply never occurred to them I might get curious, or that any of us might get curious.

"What do you think's over there?" I asked Max, the day I

almost asked him to come with me. We were walking together between the river and some of the old cement walls that used to be buildings. I remember we'd just passed the wall where, long time ago, someone painted the word NOWHERE. Only, they (or somebody else) also painted a red stripe between the *W* and the *H*, so it says NOW HERE, same as it says NOWHERE.

"Nothing," he replied. "Nothing's over there anymore," and Max shaded his eyes from the bright summer sun. Where we were, it's less than a mile across the river. It's still easy to make out where the docks and cranes used to be. "You can see for yourself, Cody. Ain't nothing over there except what the goo left."

Which is to say, there's nothing over there.

"You never wonder about it, though?"

"Why would I? Besides, the bridge ain't safe to cross anymore." Max pointed south to the long span of it. Lots of the tall trusses, which used to be steel, have dropped away into the sludgy river a hundred and fifty feet below. Lots of the roadway, too. "You'd have to be crazy to try. And since there's nothing over there, you'd have to be extra crazy. You know what suicide is, right?"

"I think about it sometimes, is all. Not suicide, just finding out what's over there."

"Same damn difference," he said. "Anyway, we ought'a be getting back." He turned away from the river and the bridge, the island and the other side of the river. So that's why I didn't ask Max to cross the bridge with me. I knew he'd say no, and I was pretty sure he'd tell one of the olders, and then someone would stop me. I followed him back to the barracks, but I knew by then I was definitely going to climb the chain-link fence and cross the bridge.

Oh, I almost forgot, and I want to put this in, write down what I can recall of it. On the way home, we came across Mr. Benedict. He was sitting on a rusty barrel not far from the NOW|HERE wall. In THE BEFORE, Mr. Benedict—Mr. Saul Benedict—was a physicist. He's one of our teachers now, though he isn't well and sometimes misses days. Max says something inside his head is broken. Something in his mind, but that he isn't exactly crazy. Anyway, there he was on the barrel. He's one of the few olders who ever talks much about THE GOO. That afternoon, he said hello to me and Max, but he had that somewhere-else tone to his voice. He sounded so distant, distant in time or in place. I don't know. We said hello back. Then he pointed to the bridge, and that sort of gave me shudder, and I wondered if he'd noticed us staring at it. He couldn't have overheard us; we were too far away.

"It doesn't make sense," he said.

"What doesn't make sense?" Max asked him.

"It should have fallen. Steel and concrete, that's one thing. Iron, steel, precompressed concrete, those materials, fine. But after the bots were done with it . . . that bridge, it should have collapsed under its own weight, even though, obviously, its not nearly as heavy or dense now as it was before. Plastic could never bear the load."

This is the thing about Saul Benedict: he asks questions no one ever asks, questions I don't understand half the time. If you let him, he'll go on and on about how something's not right about our understanding of THE EVENT, how the science doesn't add up right. I've heard him say the fumes from the outgassing plastic should have killed us all years ago. And how the earth's mass would have been changed radically by the nano-assemblers, which would have altered gravity. How lots of the atmosphere would have been lost to space when gravity changed. And how plate tectonics would have come to a halt. Lots of technical science stuff like that, some of which I have to go to the library to find out what he means. I'm pretty sure very few people bother to consider whether or not Mr. Benedict is right. Maybe not because they believe the questions are nonsense, but because no one needs more uncertainty than we have already. I'm not even sure I spend much time on whether or not he's making sense. I just look up words to see what the questions mean.

"But it *hasn't* fallen down," Max protested, turning back toward the bridge. "Well, okay. Some pieces broke off, but not the whole bridge."

"That's just the problem," Mr. Benedict said. "It hasn't fallen down. You do the math. It would have fallen *immediately*."

"Max is terrible at math," I told Mr. Benedict, and he frowned.

"He doesn't apply himself, Cody. You know that don't you, Max? You don't apply yourself. If you did, you'd be an exemplary student."

We told him we were late for chores, said our until laters, and left him sitting on the rusty barrel, muttering to himself.

"Nutty old fart," Max said, and I didn't say anything.

Before I went to cross the bridge, I did some studying up first. In the library, there's a book about the city that used to be Jacksonville, and I sat at one of the big tables and read about the Mathews Bridge. It was built in 1953, which made it exactly one hundred years old last year. But what mattered was that it's about a mile and a half across. One morning, I talked Mr. Kleinberg at the garage into lending me his stopwatch, and I figured out I walk about three miles an hour, going at an easy pace. Not walking fast or jogging, just walking. So, barring obstructions, if I could go straight across, it would only take me about half an hour. Half an hour across, half an hour back. Maybe poke about on the other side (which, by the way, used to be called Arlington) for a couple of hours, and I'd be back before anyone even noticed I'd gone. For all I knew, other kids had already done it. Even more likely, some of the olders.

I picked the day I'd go—July 18, which was on a Friday. I'd go right after my morning chores, during late-morning break, and be sure to be back by lunch. I didn't tell Max or anyone else. No one would ever be the wiser. I filled a canteen and I went.

It was easy getting over the fence. There isn't any barbed wire, like on some of the fences around Sanctuary. I snagged my jeans on the sharp twists of wire at the top, but only tore a very small hole that would be easy to patch. On the other side, the road's still asphalt for about a hundred yards or so, before the plastic begins. Like I said, I'd walked on THE GOO before, so I knew what to expect. It's very slightly springy, and sometimes you press shallow footprints into it that disappear after a few minutes. On the bridge, there was the fine dust that accumulates as the plastic breaks down. Not as much as I'd have expected, but probably that's because the wind blows it away. But there were heaps of it where the wind couldn't reach, piled like tiny sand dunes. I left footprints in the dust that anyone could have followed.

I glanced back over my shoulder a few times, just to be certain no one was following me. No one was. I kept to the westbound lane. There were cracks in the roadway, in what once had been cement. Some were hardly an inch, but others a foot or two across and maybe twice as deep, so I'd have to jump over those. I skirted the places where the bridge was coming apart in chunks, and couldn't help but think about what all Mr. Benedict had said. It shouldn't be here. None of it should still be here, but it is. So what don't we know? How *much* don't we know?

I walked the brown bridge, and on either side of me, far below, the lazy crimson St. Johns River flowed. I walked, and a quarter of a mile from the fence, I reached the spot where the bridge spans the island. I went to the guardrail and peered over the edge. I leaned against the rail, and it cracked loudly and dropped away. I almost lost my balance and tumbled down to the crimson river. I stepped back, trying not to think about what it would be like to slowly sink and drown in that. . . .

And I thought about turning around and heading back. From this point on, I constantly thought about going back, but I didn't. I walked a little faster than before, though, suddenly wanting to be done with this even if I still felt like I had to *do* it.

I kept hearing Max talking inside my head, saying what he'd said, over and over again.

Since there's nothing over there, you'd have to be extra crazy.

You know what suicide is, right?

Ain't nothing over there except what THE GOO left.

It took me a little longer to reach the halfway point than I thought it would, than my three-miles-an-hour walking had led me to believe it would. It was all the cracks, most likely. Having to carefully jump them, or find ways around them. And I kept stopping to gaze out and marvel at the ugly wasteland THE GOO had made of the land beyond the Mathews Bridge. I don't know if there's a name for the middle of a bridge, the highest point of a bridge. But it was right about the time I reached that point that I spotted the car. It was still pretty far off, maybe halfway to the other end. It was skewed sideways across the two eastbound lanes, on the other side of the low divider that I'm sure used to be concrete but isn't anymore.

But all the cars were cleared off the bridge by the military years ago. They were towed to the other side or pushed into the crimson river. There weren't supposed to be any cars on the bridge. But here was *this* one. The sunlight glinted off yellow fiberglass and silver chrome, and I could tell the nano-assemblers hadn't gotten hold of it, that it was still made of what the factory built it from. And I had two thoughts, one after the other: Where did this car come from? And, Why hasn't anyone noticed it? The second thought was sort of silly because it's not like anyone really watches the bridge, not since most of the Army and National Guard went away.

Then I thought, How long's it been there? And, Why didn't

it come all the way across? And, What happened to the driver? All those questions in my head, I was starting to feel like Saul Benedict. It was an older car, one of the electrics that were already obsolete by the time THE EVENT occurred.

"Cody, you go back," I said out loud, and my voice seemed huge up there on the bridge. It was like thunder. "You go back and tell someone. Let them deal with this."

But then I'd have to explain what I was doing way out on the bridge alone.

Are you enjoying this, Max? I mean, if I've let you read it. If I did, I hope to hell you're enjoying it, because I'm already sweating, drops of sweat darkening the encyclopedia pages. Right now I feel like that awful day on the bridge. I could stop now. I could turn back now. I could. I won't, but I *could*. Doesn't matter. I'll keep writing, Max, and you'll keep reading.

I kept walking. I didn't turn back, like a smarter girl would have done. A smarter girl who understood it was more important to tell the olders what I'd found than to worry about getting in trouble for being out on the bridge. There was a strong gust of wind, warm from the south, and the dust on the bridge was swept up so I had to partly cover my face with my arm. But I could see the tiny brown devils swirling across the road.

Right after the wind, while the dust was still settling, I came to an especially wide crack in the roadway. It was so wide and deep, and when I looked down, the bottom was hidden in shadow. It didn't go all the way through, or I'd not have been able to see down there. I had to climb over the barricade into the eastbound lane, into the lane with the car, to get around it. I haven't mentioned the crumbling plastic seagulls I kept finding. Well, I figured they'd been seagulls. They'd been birds, and were big enough to have been seagulls. They littered the bridge, birds that died twelve years ago when I was four. Once I was only, I don't know, maybe twenty-five yards from the car, I stopped for a minute or two. I squinted, trying to see inside, but the windows were tinted and I couldn't make out anything at all in there.

The car looked so shiny and new. No way it had been sitting out in the weather very long. There weren't even any pieces of the plastic girders lying on it, no dents from decayed and falling GOO, so it was a newcomer to the bridge, and I think that scared me most of all. By then, my heart was pounding—thumping like mad in my chest and ears and even the tip ends of my fingers—and I was sweating. Not the normal kinda sweat from walking, but a cold sweat like when I wake up from the nightmares of this day I'm writing about. My mouth was so, so dry. I felt a little sick to my belly, and wondered if it was breathing in all that dust.

"No point in stopping now," I said, maybe whispering, and my voice was huge out there in all the empty above and below and around the Mathews Bridge. "So when they ask what I found, I can tell them all of it, not just I found a car on the bridge." I considered the possibility that it might have been rovers, might be a trap. Them lying there in wait until someone takes the bait, then they ask for supplies to let me go. We hadn't seen rovers—looters—in a year or so, but that didn't mean they weren't still out there, trying to get by on the scraps of nothing they found and whatever they could steal. Lower than the sneaks, the rovers. At least the sneaks never kill anyone. They just slip in and rob you when no one's looking. Ma'am Shen says they're all insane, and I expect that's the truth of it. I wished I'd brought a knife (I have a lock-blade I keep in my footlocker), but that was dumb, 'cause rovers carry guns and bows and shit. What good's a knife for a fifteen-year-old girl out on her own, so exposed she might as well be naked. No chance but to turn around and run if things went bad.

I shouted, "Anybody in there?" At the very top of my voice I shouted it. When no one answered, I shouted again, and still nobody answered me. I hadn't thought they would, but it didn't hurt to try.

"You don't need to be scared of me," I called out. "And I ain't got nothing worth stealing." Which I knew was dumb because if it was rovers they wouldn't be after what I *had* on my person, but what they could *get* for me.

No one called back, and so I started walking again.

Pretty soon, I was close enough I could make out the plates on the front of the vehicle—Alabama, which we all thought was another LOST PLACE, since that's what the Army guys had told us. On the map of what once was the United States hanging on the wall in the library, Alabama was colored in red, like all the LOST PLACES (which is most of the map). But here was a car from Alabama, and it couldn't have been sitting on the bridge very long at all, not and still be so shiny and clean. Maybe I counted my footsteps after shouting and not getting an answer, but if so, I can't remember how many I took.

There was another southerly gust, and more swirling dust devils, and this time the bridge seemed to sway just a little, which didn't make my stomach feel any better.

Then I was finally at the car. Up close, it was a little dirtier than it had seemed from far away. There were a few dents and dings, a little rust, but nothing more than that. None of the tires were even flat. I stared at the tinted windows and waited for rovers to jump out and point their weapons at me, but that didn't happen. For the first time, I considered the possibility that the doors might all be locked, and I didn't even have anything to break out the windows. I looked past the car at the ruins of Arlington, and considered just sticking to my plan, forget the car for now, poke around over there a bit, then head home again. And yeah, tell the olders about the car and take whatever punishment I'd have coming.

I leaned forward, peering in through the glass, but the tinting was too dark even right up on it like that. I gripped the driver's side door handle, and it was very hot from the Florida sun. It was hot enough I almost pulled my hand back, but only almost. Instead, I gave it a quick twist to the left, and the tumblers clicked. Which meant it wasn't locked after all.

I took a deep breath and pulled up on the door. It came open easy as pie—like the olders say. It lifted, rising above my head, above the roof. The hinges didn't even squeak. There was only a soft whoosh from hydraulics and pistons. Scalding air spilled out of the car.

You know exactly what I found in there, Max? It seems wicked to write it down on these "borrowed" encyclopedia pages. It seems wrong, but I'll do it anyhow. Just in case you're right, because yeah, I want the dreams to stop. Dead people don't have dreams. Dead people probably don't have anything at all, so it's stupid me worrying like this, hesitating and drawing it out.

The door opened, and there were two people inside.

There was what was left of two people.

Like the might-have-been seagulls, THE GOO had gotten to them, and they were that same uniform shade of bluish green all live things go when the nano-assemblers get hold of them. I stepped back immediately and turned my head away. I even thought I might puke. It's not that I'd never seen a person who'd died that way; it's just I hadn't seen any in a long, long time, and you forget. Or I'd forgotten. I covered my mouth, not wanting to be sick and have to see my half-digested breakfast spattered all over the road at my feet. I leaned forward, hands on knees, and took deep breaths and counted to thirty. Someone taught me to do that whenever I'm afraid I might be about to throw up, count to thirty, but I can't remember who it was. Not that it matters.

When I felt a little better, I looked again. The woman was sitting with her back to the door, and her arms were wrapped tightly around the girl. The woman's fingers disappeared into the girl's hair—hair and hand all one and the same now. I figured they drove as far as they could, drove until they were too far gone to keep going. It takes hours and hours for the infected to die. Like the seagulls, the weather hadn't been at them, and the woman and the girl looked like they'd just been popped fresh out of a mold, like the molds they use in the machine shop to turn non-GOO plastic into stuff we need. Every single detail, no matter how fragile, was still intact. Their plastic eyebrows, each hair, their eyes open and staring nowhere at all. Their skin was almost exactly the color of Ma'am Lillian's teal-zircon pendant. Only completely opaque instead of translucent.

Their clothes and their jewelry (I noticed the woman's silver earrings), those hadn't changed at all. But it didn't strike me odd until later, like the car being okay didn't really strike me odd, though it should have.

I still felt dizzy even if the first shock of seeing them was fading. Even if I was just *seeing* them now, not seeing them and wanting to run away. I reached inside the car and touched the back of the woman's neck. I shouldn't have, but I did. It was just a little bit tacky from the heat, a little soft, and I left fingerprints behind. I thought, You leave them out here long enough, shut up and baking inside that car, they'll melt away to shapeless globs long before the plastic has a chance to get brittle. I thought that, and pulled my hand back. I was relieved to see none of the PVC had come off on my fingers. But I rubbed them on my jeans anyway. I rubbed until it's a wonder my skin didn't start bleeding.

They looked like dolls.

They looked almost like the mannequins in the busted shop windows inside Sanctuary.

But they'd both been alive, flesh and bone and breathing, and it couldn't have been more than a few days before. A week at the most. I stared at them. I wondered which of them died first. I wondered lots of stuff there's not much point writing down. Then I glanced into the backseat. And right then, that's when I thought my heart my might stop, just stop beating like the girl's and the woman's had finally stopped beating. There was a cardboard box in the back, and there was a baby in a blanket inside the box. I don't know how the hell it was still alive, how it had been spared by THE GOO or by the heat inside the car, but it *was* still alive. It looked at me. I saw it was sick, from the broiling day trapped in the automobile, but goddamn it was alive. It saw me and began to bawl, so I rushed around to the other side of the car and opened that door, too. I lifted the cardboard box out careful as I could and set it on the bridge, and then I sat down next to it. I screwed the lid off my canteen and sprinkled water on its forehead and lips. I finally pushed back the blanket and took the baby in my arms. I'd never, ever held a baby. We don't have many in Sanctuary. And the ones we do have, the dozen or so, not just any kid can go picking them up. Just the mothers and fathers, the nurses and doctors. The baby's face was so red, like she'd been roasting alive in there, so I sprinkled more water on its cheeks and forehead. It's eyes were glassy, feverish, and it didn't cry as loudly as I thought it should have been crying. I sat there and rocked it, shushing it, the way I'd seen people do with babies. I sat there trying to remember a lullaby.

No need to draw this part out, Max.

The baby, she died in my arms. She was just too hot, and I'd come along too late to save her from the sun. Maybe me sprinkling the water on her had been too much. Maybe just seeing me had been too much. Maybe she just picked then to die. And I wanted to cry, but I didn't. I don't know why. I knew I ought to, and I still know I ought to have, but I just sat there holding her close to me like she wasn't dead. Like she was only asleep and was gonna wake up. I sat there staring at the blue-green plastic people in the front seat, at the sky, at the car.

In my bad dreams, there are wheeling, screeching gulls in that blue-white sky, and it goes on forever, on out into space, into starry blackness, down to blue skies on other worlds without women and men and youngers, where none of these things have ever happened and where THE EVENT hasn't occurred and THE GOO will never reach. Where it's still THE BEFORE, and will never be THE AFTER.

God and Jesus and angels and a day of judgment of wicked men, they all live and breathe inside the Reverend Swales's black book, and in the songs we sing on Sundays. Many other gods and devils live in other holy books. But on the bridge that day, there was no god. In my dreams, there is no god. And I don't pray anymore. I don't think much of those who do.

You're saying, Now that's not what happened, Cody. I can hear you, Max. I can hear you grumbling, plain as day, "Cody Marlene Hernandez, you're mixing it all up, and you're doing it on purpose. That wasn't the deal, you welcher."

Fine, you win.

I scrounged about and found a couple of other things inside the cardboard box. I hardly looked at them, just stuffed them into my pack. Carrying the dead baby in her blanket, I walked back across the bridge, quickly as I could, quicker than I'd come. It was a lot harder getting over the fence with her in my arms, but I managed. I didn't drop her. I'd have fallen before I ever dropped her.

I spent a week in quarantine, just in case. Five men went out onto the bridge and brought back the plastic woman and the girl and buried them in the cemetery. They buried the baby there, too, after Doc Lehman did his autopsy. No one ever scolded me or yelled or revoked privileges for going out there. I didn't have to ask why. You get punished, you don't have to get punished all over again.

WHAT I'M WRITING DOWN LATER

Me and Max sat between the crimson river and the NOW | HERE wall, and I let him read what I wrote on the back of the torn-out encyclopedia pages. He got pissed near the end, and just like I thought he would, called me a welcher.

"The baby always dies in my dreams," I told him, when he finally shut up and let me talk again.

"I didn't say, 'Write what's in your dreams.' I said, 'Write what happened.'"

"It seemed more important," I told him, and tossed a piece of gravel at the river. "What haunts me when I sleep, how it might have gone that day, but didn't. How it probably *should* have gone, but didn't."

"Yeah, but you went and killed that baby."

"No I didn't. My nightmares kill the baby, not me. Almost every time I sleep, the nightmares kill the baby."

He chewed his lip the frustrated way he does sometimes. "Cody, I just ain't never gonna understand that. You *saved* the baby, but you go and have bad dreams about the baby dyin'. That's stupid. You waste all this energy gettin' freaked out about something didn't even happen except in a dream, and dreams ain't real. I thought writin' the truth, *that* would make you better. Not writing down lies. That's what I don't understand."

"You weren't there. You didn't hold her, and her so hot, and you so sure she was already dead or would be dead any second."

"I just won't ever understand it," he said again.

"Okay, Max. Then you won't ever understand it. That's fair. There's a lot about myself I don't understand sometimes. Doesn't matter the dreams don't make sense. Only matters it happens to me. It's all too complicated. Never black-and-white, not like SWITCH ON and SWITCH OFF, not like THE BEFORE and THE AFTER. I fall asleep, and she dies in my arms, even though she didn't."

He glared at the pages, chewing his lips and looking disgusted, then handed them back to me.

"Well, you don't win," he said. "You don't get any more than kisses 'cause you didn't even talk about the map or the book, and because you killed the baby."

"I don't care," I replied, which was true.

"I was just trying to help you."

"I know that, Max. Don't you think I know that?"

He didn't answer my question. Instead, he said, "I'm going home, Cody. I got chores. So do you, welcher." I told him I'd be along soon. I told him I needed to be alone for a while (which is when I'm writing this part down). So I'm sitting here throwing gravel at the sludgy crimson river people used to call the St. Johns River.

WHAT REALLY HAPPENED (FOR MAX)

Outside my dreams, the baby didn't die. The olders figured the car had only driven through Arlington and out onto the bridge the night before I found it. They guessed the girl and the woman got sick a couple of days before that, probably before they even got to Florida. They figured, too, the baby would have died of heat prostration and thirst if I hadn't found it when I did. "You did right," Ma'am Shen whispered in my ear when no one was watching or listening in. "Even if that wasn't your intent, you did right." We never found out the baby's name, so they named it Cody, after me.

The olders found something in the baby's blood. It's like SWITCH OFF, they say, but it's different. It's like SWITCH OFF, but it works better. You breathe it out, and it shuts off the nano-assemblers all around you. Maybe, they say, that's why the car didn't change, and why the woman and the girl's clothes and jewelry wasn't converted, too. But these new bots, they can't turn stuff back the way it was before.

And yeah, there was a map. A map of the United States and Mexico and Canada. Most of the cities had big red X's drawn on them. Montreal, up in Canada, had a blue circle, and so did San Francisco and a few little towns here and there. A red line was drawn from Birmingham, Alabama all the way to Pensacola. Both those cities had red X's of their own. I found the red pencil in the box with the baby. And I found pages and pages of notes. In the margins of the map, there was a list of countries. Some in red, some in blue.

Turns out the woman was a microbiologist, and she'd been studying when the sanctuary in Birmingham was breached. That's what she'd written in her notes. They read us that part in class. "The containment has been breached." I also know the notes talk about the nanites evolving, and about new strains the SWITCH OFF doesn't work on, and new strains of SWITCH OFF that shut down THE GOO better than before, like what kept the baby alive. They know the scientist also wrote about how THE EVENT isn't over because the bots are all evolving and doing things they weren't designed to do.

Of course, they also weren't designed to eat up the whole world, but they did.

Saul Benedict still frowns and asks his questions, and he says everything's even more uncertain than it was before I found the car.

But me, I look at that baby, who's growing up fine and healthy and breathing those new bots out with every breath, and sometimes I think about going out onto the bridge again with a can of spray paint and writing *HOPE HERE* in great big letters on the side of the car. So if maybe someone else ever comes along, someone who isn't sick, they'll see, and drive all the way across the bridge.

YOU WON'T FEEL A THING

BY GARTH NIX

It started with a toothache.

The Arkle had it, in one of the great hollow fangs at the front of his mouth, that would have been simple canines before the Overlords changed him, in the process of turning him into a Ferret. Not that The Arkle was entirely a Ferret. He'd escaped from the dorms when he was eleven, so he still looked mostly human. A very thin, elongated human, with his face and jaw pushed out so that it wasn't quite a snout but you could tell it would have been one if he hadn't gotten away.

The Arkle also had a taste for blood. Not the full-on bloodlust the Ferrets had, because he could control it. But when the Family killed a chicken to roast, he would cut its throat over a bowl and drink the blood down like a kind of pre-dinner cocktail. Sometimes he put parsley in the cup, as a garnish. Or, as he said, for those extra vitamins. The Arkle didn't eat a lot of greens.

He was one of the younger members of the Family. He'd come out of the city four years before, more dead than alive, his body covered with sores and his gums receding from malnutrition. He'd lasted almost six months on his own after escaping from the dorms, which was no mean feat, but he wouldn't have lasted much longer if he hadn't been lucky enough to have been found by Gwyn, on one of the latter's last foraging expeditions into the city fringe.

Gwyn was the first to notice The Arkle behaving strangely. They were working together, moving one of the portable henhouses to its new location, when The Arkle stopped pushing and pressed his fingers into his jaw, using the middle knuckle so he didn't slice himself with his talons.

"What are you doing?" asked Gwyn, annoyed. As always, he was providing most of the muscle, and though The Arkle's participation was mainly for show, the henhouse wheels *were* stuck in the mud, and even a slight amount of assistance would make it easier for Gwyn to free them.

"Toothache," muttered The Arkle. He stretched out his jaw and ground it from side to side. "Annoying me."

"Doc had better look at it right away," said Gwyn. He'd had a toothache himself a few years back, and there was still a hole at the back of his mouth where Doc had pulled out a big molar. But that was better than what could happen if it was left to rot. Gwyn had seen that too, in other survivors. And Ferret teeth were certain to be trickier than more nearly human ones.

"It's not too bad," muttered The Arkle. He winced as he closed his mouth, though, and tears started in his eyes.

Gwyn set down the chicken house and lumbered around, towering over The Arkle. Gwyn was the big brother of the Family, and the second oldest. He'd been thirteen when the Change swept through, disappearing everyone over the age of fourteen. Like most of the surviving children, he'd then been caught up by the suited figures driving their centipede trains, and taken to the Dormitories. Big for his age and well-muscled, he'd gone straight into the Myrmidon track, fed alien steroids and exercised to the limits

GARTH NIX

of torture, but like The Arkle, he'd managed to escape before the final conversion in the Meat Factory.

Even so, he was seven feet tall, measured four feet across the shoulders, and had arms roughly the same diameter as the massive logs he split for the winter fire, wielding a woodchopper that most of the others couldn't even lift.

"Go and see Doc now," ordered Gwyn. Like the few other almost-Myrmidons who got away from the dorms, his voice was high and reedy, a byproduct of the chemical infusions that had built his muscle, while also effectively making him a eunuch.

But high voice or not, The Arkle knew that when Gwyn spoke, he meant what he said.

"All right, all right, I'm . . . ow . . . going," he said. "You sure you can move this by yourself?"

"I guess I'll manage somehow," replied Gwyn.

The Arkle nodded sheepishly and trudged back through the sparse forest where the five henhouses were arranged. At the edge of the trees, he climbed over the old rusted fence with the sinuous grace of a true Ferret, pausing to tip a finger at Ken-Lad, who was on sentry halfway up the ancient tree that served as the western lookout post. Ken-Lad made a ruder gesture back, before resuming his steady, regulated gaze, staring up at each quadrant of the sky.

The Farm lay in a deep valley, more than a hundred kilometers from the city. The creatures had never come to fight their battles there, and even the Wingers never flew overhead. But very occasionally, one of the Overlord's flying machines did, and that was why the sentries watched. The Family could not afford to have a curious Overlord sweep down and see free humans, for the creatures would surely come then, correcting whatever oversight had kept the valley secret for the eight years since the Change.

The Farm had been a giant dope plantation before the Change, and the camouflage nets were still in place over a good thirty acres

321

of land. The Family had poked a few holes in the nets, here and there, to let in a little more light for the much smaller portion they had under cultivation. That provided vegetables, and the chickens provided meat and eggs, and there was hunting for wild game as well. There had been a lot of tinned and dried food earlier on, but it was mostly saved for special occasions now, since it was too risky to venture toward the city and the riches that still awaited there.

Doc Carol had found the Farm almost five years before. She'd never told the others whether she'd known it was there, or had simply stumbled upon it and then worked out that it was safe from the creatures.

She never told anyone how she knew so much about medicine and healing, either. Gwyn probably knew, and some of the older ones, but they never talked about anything the Doc said or did. All the others knew was that she had been a day short of her fifteenth birthday when the Change came, a day short of being old enough to go wherever it was that most of humanity went. If they went anywhere, as opposed to simply ceasing to exist.

The Arkle spat as he remembered the caterpillar train that he had willingly climbed aboard. He'd been seven years old at the time, and his mother had vanished in front of his eyes, and he'd been desperately afraid. The train had looked a bit like the one at the fairground, and it was already loaded with children. He even knew some of them from school.

So he'd got on, and it had taken him to one of the first established dorms. A tracking and ID device had been injected beneath the skin of his wrist, and he'd been subjected to a series of tests at the hands of those silvor-visored, faceless, suited humanoids. The tests had said "Ferret," and from then on, everything he did or that was done to him was designed to make him both less and more than human.

The Arkle looked at the strange purple welt on his wrist as he loped through the high grass that surrounded the main house. They cut the grass occasionally, using scythes, just to reduce the risk of fire, but never enough that it would look new-mown.

The tracking device in his wrist had been removed by Tira, a girl in the dorm, though The Arkle didn't know exactly how she'd done it. She simply touched her finger to the lump that showed where the tracker lay under the skin, and there had been a moment of pain so terrible that The Arkle had blacked out. When he'd come to, there was no lump. Just the purple welt.

Of course he knew that Tira had used a Change Talent of some kind. He had one too, only it wasn't as useful. Or at least it was only useful for one thing. The Arkle grinned as he thought of that, then grimaced and almost sobbed as the pain in his tooth came back, darting from his mouth up into his head, savaging him right behind the eyes.

The pain in his tooth was even worse than that remembered pain in his wrist.

Tira had taken her device out too, and they had run together. Only, she never made it over the perimeter wire. Tira was the one who had first called him "The Arkle." He didn't know why, but he'd kept the name just to remember her, his truest friend from the dorms.

Greenie was on the verandah of the house, carefully potting up seedlings of some plant or other that The Arkle didn't recognize. She looked at him with her head to one side, and he could tell she was wondering why he had come in early. But even then, most of her mind was probably on the plants. Greenie had a Change Talent too, and though like all Change Talents, hers was very weak down in the valley, she still had a special empathy for vegetable life. Greenie could always tell when a plant needed water, or more shade, or sun, or was being strangled by its neighbors.

"Got to see Doc," said The Arkle. He tried to smile, but it hurt too much, so he waved instead and hurried on inside.

The Arkle could see Doc Carol through the small square window that was set high in the inner door to her lab, even though the thick glass was smeared all around with sealant. Doc was clearly cooking up something fairly toxic, since she was wearing a gas mask and an ex-Army NBC suit.

The Arkle hesitated, then knocked on the window. He didn't want to disturb Doc, but his tooth was getting worse, a lot worse. The pain had been around for weeks, coming and going, and hadn't ever got too bad. Then a few days before it had suddenly escalated, ebbing occasionally but never going away, and when it hit full force he could hardly think or see, and he just wanted to smash his face into something hard and destroy the bastard tooth. Only, he didn't because he knew it wouldn't work.

Doc looked over, her eyes just visible through the round lenses of the gas mask. Doc had weird eyes. They were kind of violet, and bigger than normal. The Arkle had heard that up out of the valley they shone in the dark, and the Doc had to wear sunglasses all the time. He'd never seen it, but he believed it.

"That you, The Arkle?"

Her voice was muffled through the mask and the heavy door, but clear enough.

"Yeah. Can I come in?"

Doc was almost the only person in the Family who called The Arkle by his chosen name. Most of the others called him Arkle, or Ark, or Arkie, which he hated.

"Wait a minute," called out Doc. "This stuff won't do you any good. I'll be out in a minute. Go into my office."

The Arkle retreated through the outer door. Doc's office was the biggest room in the old house. She slept there, as well as worked. Her bed was behind the desk. The Arkle looked at it and wondered what it would be like to share it with her. He'd slept with nearly all of the women and at least half of the men on the Farm, because his Change Talent was for seduction, and even the pale version of it that worked down in the valley was enough to help out his natural charm. And since everyone had pretty much grown up in the dorms, there was no such thing as a normal human body anymore. So his snouty face and fangs and slimmest of waists was not a bar to relationships.

The Doc was the one closest to old human, and even then, she had those eyes. The Arkle had never dared try his Talent on her, had never even had a few minutes alone with her to see if it might be worthwhile adding that into the natural equation of liking and desire.

But he couldn't even begin to daydream about sex with Doc, not with the pain in his tooth. He lay down in the patient's chair, the old banana lounge that sat in front of the desk, and shut his eyes, hoping that this would somehow lessen the pain.

It didn't, and the sudden waft of a harsh chemical smell alerted him to Doc's presence. She was leaning over him, the gas mask off, her short brown hair pressed down in an unnatural way, showing the marks of the straps. Her violet eyes were fixed on his jaw.

"Your jaw is swollen," remarked Doc. She went behind the desk, put down her mask, and stripped off the suit. It gave off more chemical smells as she opened the window and hung it on the hook outside, ready to be hosed down later.

She was only wearing a pair of toweling shorts and a singlet underneath. The Arkle's eyes watered as he looked at her ruefully. The tearing up wasn't from the remnant chemical smell, but from the pain. A pain so intense he couldn't even appreciate his first real look at Doc without the white lab coat she nearly always wore inside—and there it was, slipping over her shoulders and getting done up at the front, far too swiftly for his liking.

"Is it a tooth pain?" asked Doc.

"Yeah," whispered The Arkle. He raised one hand and gestured toward the left-hand fang. "It's got . . . pretty . . . bad. Just today."

"That never got this bad in a day. You should have seen me when it first started," said Doc. She dragged a box over next to the banana lounge and sat on it. "Open wide."

The Arkle opened wide in a series of small movements because he couldn't do it all in one go, it hurt too much. Doc leaned over him, looking close but not touching. Some distant memory made The Arkle shut his eyes. For a moment, he was six again and in the dentist's chair, and his mother was holding his hand. . . .

"Keep your hands still," ordered Doc. "Stay there. Just lie quiet."

The Arkle heard the box slide back and Doc move. He opened his eyes and saw her go over to the door to the cellar. It had two big padlocks on it, and only Doc and Gwyn had the keys. The Family's hard-won pharmacopeia was stored in the cellar. All the drugs that had been found in scavenging expeditions in the small towns nearby, and in the outer suburbs of the city, plus the things that Doc had been able to make.

The Arkle shut his eyes again. It didn't really help with the pain, but it did seem to make it easier to bear. He didn't want to sob in front of Doc. He hadn't cried since Tira was killed, and he'd sworn he'd never cry again. It was hard not to now. This pain just went on and on, and it wasn't only in the tooth. It was all up the side of his face, and reaching deep inside his nose and into his brain.

"Ah, it's getting worse, it's getting worse," muttered The Arkle. He couldn't help himself. The pain was starting to make him panic, fear growing inside him. He'd been afraid before, plenty of times, felt certain he was going to die. But this was worse than that because the pain was worse than dying. He'd rather die than have this incredible pain keep going—

There was a sensation in his arm, not a pain, exactly, more like a pressure inside the skin. Something flowed through his arm and shoulder, and with it came a blessed darkness that pushed the pain away and carried it off somewhere far away, along with his conscious self.

Doc put the syringe back in the sterile dish and placed it on the table. Then she put a blood pressure cuff on The Arkle's arm, pumped it up and released it, noting the result. A check of his pulse followed, and a look at his eyes, gently raising each eyelid in turn.

Finally she opened his mouth, being careful to place her hands so that some involuntary reflex wouldn't put a fang through her fingers. Even more gently, she touched the top left tooth. Despite the sedation, The Arkle flinched. Doc curled back the young man's lip and looked at the gum around the base of the tooth. She looked for quite a while, then let the lip slide back, and stood up.

"Pal! You there?"

Pal came in a minute later. He was another of the oldsters, though unlike Doc, he'd spent time in the dorms. He had been destined to become a Winger, and was hunchbacked a little, and there were stubs on his shoulders where his wings had either failed to grow or been surgically removed.

"You called?"

Pal was the chief cook of the Family, and liked to pretend he was a particular butler, in some reference to the old time that only Doc and Gwyn understood. He always wore the same black coat, with long tails that hung down at the back.

"Go get Gwyn, will you? He's moving the chicken houses."

Pal looked down at The Arkle.

"Problem?"

Doc sighed.

"Big problem. Why don't they ever tell me when they first hurt themselves, Pal? A week ago this could have been sorted out with antibiotics. I mean, I've got enough broad spectrum stuff downstairs to treat a thousand patients, but it's got to be done early! Now . . ."

"Now what?"

"I'm going to have to cut out the tooth, and he's practically all Ferret in the jaw. Those teeth have roots four inches long, and nerve clusters around the blood-sucking channels . . . which I only know about in theory, since I never—"

She stopped talking suddenly.

"Since you never dissected a Ferret?" asked Pal.

"No," replied Doc. "Never a Ferret. At least a dozen Myrmidons and quite a few Wingers . . ."

"Which was just as well for me," said Pal. "All things considered. I suppose you want Gwyn to carry the boy up to the ridge?"

Doc looked at the floor.

"Yeah, I guess I was thinking that. It's the only way I can do it."

"Risky," said Pal. "For everyone. I thought we agreed no more trips out of the valley."

"What am I supposed to do?" asked Doc. "Arkle will die if I don't take out the tooth, and he'll die if I do it wrong. I have to be able to see inside!"

"You could try halfway up," said Pal. "Some of the Talents seem to work okay there. Gwyn's does."

"And mine doesn't," snapped Doc. "It kicks in at the ridgeline, never lower down. So can you go and get Gwyn now, please? I can't keep Arkle under forever. There's a big enough risk with what I've given him already."

"All right, all right, I'm going," said Pal. "I suppose you want to go alone, just you and Gwyn?"

"Yes," said Doc. "Better to lose two than any more."

"On that logic, better to lose just *one* in the first place," said Pal, inclining his head toward The Arkle. "That's what Shade would do."

"I'm not Shade," said Doc. "That's why I left Shade. You sorry you left, Pal?"

"Nope," replied Pal somberly. "I was just checking to see if you were. You had a mighty fine surgery back there, and those spider-robots of his to-be nurses and all. Yanking out a Ferret tooth there would be as easy as taking a piss."

"Maybe," said Doc. "But I reckon the Overlords have probably tracked down Shade by now, and whoever was dumb enough to stick with him, and the computers he lives in and the whole sub-marine and everything in it has probably been rusting away at the bottom of the bay for years."

"Could be," said Pal. "But I wouldn't be surprised if Shade is still going, even still looking for us. Another reason to be careful. Shade always did have his true believers, and he sends them far and wide. They could easily be more dangerous than the creatures."

"Just go get Gwyn," said Doc wearily. "While I get my kit together."

The Arkle came back to the world in total incomprehension. There was a terrible pain in his face, everything was on a strange angle, and he could see the sun in a very odd position. He groaned, and the angle shifted and the sun righted itself and moved away, to be replaced by Gwyn's broad face, up unreasonably close. It took The Arkle a few moments more to work out that it was so close because Gwyn was carrying him like a baby, across his chest.

"What's happening?" he croaked. It was hard to talk because

his mouth felt puffy and strange. His lips were swollen and too close together, his jaw wouldn't open properly, and there was this pain there, jabbing at him with every step Gwyn took.

"Stop for a moment," Doc said to Gwyn.

The Arkle blinked and tried to shift his head. Why was the Doc here? He vaguely remembered going to see her about something.

"Keep still, please, The Arkle," said Doc.

He obeyed, and something stung him in the arm.

"What is . . ."

The Arkle's words trailed off and he subsided back down in Gwyn's arms.

"He's not staying under as well as I thought he would," said Doc. "And I can't give him much more. We'd better hurry."

"Easy for you to say," said Gwyn. "You only got that case."

"You carried me a lot farther a lot faster once," said Doc. She could see the top of the ridge up ahead—the real top, not the false one that had famously fooled so many walkers in the old times, when there had been a popular trail that went along the ridge, weaving up and down on either side.

"Long time ago," said Gwyn. "You were lighter then."

Doc hit him on the arm, very lightly.

Gwyn laughed, a kind of giggling chuckle that sounded weird coming out of his barrel chest. Then he suddenly stopped, and his head snapped to the right, and he immediately crouched down, balancing The Arkle with his left arm as he drew his sword with his right. It was short but broad-bladed, and streaked with gold. Gold was good at disrupting creature circuitry, the augmentation stuff they put in at the Meat Factory, completing the transformation from child to monster.

Doc had ducked down too. Gwyn's Change Talent was an extra sense. He could feel other life-forms and track them, though he couldn't tell them apart. She drew her sword. Like Gwyn's, it was gold-plated, another relic of their service with Shade, the enigmatic computer personality who'd led what he liked to call the Resistance against the Overlords and their creatures.

"Where?" whispered Doc.

Gwyn pointed with his sword, across to a point below the ridge where the trees opened out and the undergrowth was not so thick.

Doc slid her sword back into its scabbard and reached inside her coat to take out a pistol instead. Since it was below the ridge-line, it was unlikely to be a creature.

Creatures were hard to kill with gunfire; the gold-plated swords worked better. But for a human, a gun worked fine.

And as Pal had said, Shade always did have plenty of true believers, escapees from the dorms who did whatever Shade told them to do without question . . . even if that might include tracking down and killing humans who Shade would undoubtedly have labeled traitors.

Particularly Doc, who Shade had labored over for so many years, tailoring educational programs and simulations to train her as a doctor. But not to help save human life. Shade had only wanted her trained up to help him with his research into the creatures, to dissect captured prisoners, to try to discover exactly how they worked, and how they were augmented by the strange energy that could be detected in the city after the Change. . . .

A low branch quivered and whipped back, and something loped down the slope. It came toward them for a moment, till it caught their scent and suddenly changed direction, even before Doc recognized it and decided not to shoot.

"A dog," whispered Gwyn. "Better make sure it's gone."

Dogs and cats were rare because the creatures killed them, as they killed anything that was not part of the complicated battles the Overlords played in the city—endless battles that soaked up the continuous production of the Meat Factory, and the dorms that fed it with their human raw material.

They waited for a few minutes, but the dog did not circle back.

"It's gone," said Gwyn. "Beyond my range, anyway. Let's go."

At the top of the ridge there was an old picnic station, an open structure with a galvanized iron roof and a single long pine table underneath. Gwyn set The Arkle down on the table while Doc laid out her instruments and drugs.

"Tie him down," she said, handing over a package of bandages. "I can't put him down deep enough he won't react."

Gwyn took the bandages. When he was done with the tying down, he looked over at Doc.

"Your eyes are bright," he said. "You seeing?"

"Yes," said Doc. She blinked and bent low over The Arkle's open mouth. Her violet eyes grew brighter still, and she stared down, looking through the tooth, through the bone, seeing it all. Her eyes moved, following the blood from the roots up along the altered circulatory channels. She saw the infection flowing with the blood, swirling across the boy's face, flooding into his brain, to join the pool of bacteria where it already dwelled and prospered.

Doc straightened up and looked across at Gwyn. Her eyes were shining still, but it was not with the light of her Change Talent.

"Too late," she said. "Just *too* late. It must have been hurting for weeks and he never said a thing; he never asked for help."

"They don't know how, the young ones," said Gwyn, who was all of twenty-one. "They just don't know how to ask."

The Arkle groaned, and one taloned hand fluttered under its restraint.

"Mom?" he whispered. "Mom?"

Doc picked up a hypodermic and plunged it deep, followed quickly by another. Then she took The Arkle's hand and held it tight, despite the talons that scored her flesh.

"It's all right, love," whispered Doc. "It's all right."

"You won't feel a thing. You won't feel a thing. You won't feel a . . ."

Author's Note

This story is set in the same world as my 1997 novel, *Shade's Children*, though it takes place about ten years before the events of that book.

THE MARKER

BY CECIL CASTELLUCCI

It was time for seeding, and I had finally reached the age of apprentice. This year I would join the other Paters, and I would observe and help Jas with the counting and with the machines. The machines would be my responsibility, and I was already nervous. I lay the batteries out, like I had been told, and let them soak in the sun. I turned each one on and off. I even tested one on myself by pricking my finger and putting the bead of blood on the machine. It took a moment. It whirred. It blinked three times. A green light came on for the first three codes, and the display showed the letters that I was meant to look for.

AGGCTTACACCG

GAATCACCTAGC

CTTGTAACCTGG

It blinked a fourth time and made an unpleasant noise and blinked red, but I ignored the letters. It did not matter. Three for Four of the sequence was what mattered. Everyone knew that. Satisfied, I switched the machine off and packed them all away. It would be a long walk to all the towns, and I wanted to rest in a bed before I would no longer have one to sleep in. I blew the wick out and shut my eyes. But I could not deny the truth. I was excited to leave Sandig and see the outside world.

I am interested in everything—the others in town make fun of me for this. But Jas doesn't. He turns a blind eye when I slip out of the gates and wander around the outskirts of Sandig. I am interested in the differences between home and away. I find things out there and add them to my collection of things. Things that are broken. Things that are from the past. Things that have no use. Things that interest me. Things that I take apart. Even the Romas, those who roam, the renegades, the outsiders who reject the Way, don't bother me. But the Romas know where I like to go. Out beyond the boundaries to stare and contemplate the strange signs of faces, with their tongues out, in the fields that surround Sandig, and to notice how many animals I can spot: now none, now more, now here, now there. Sometimes they leave me the interesting things they find in exchange for cooked food, dried fish and seaweed that I smuggle outside the gates. It is my secret trade. On occasion, if they find something they think is very valuable, they will wait for me and ask for things they need. I will show them items from my collection and they will pick something, like a knife or some thread to stitch with, good for caring for a wound.

But no matter how much the others may laugh, I like my things. I like to observe.

How the fields are always green in a different way and no one notices.

How mostly I have only seen a bird in an old book that I keep in my room.

How much we rely on the tech that the SciTexts left us from those that came before, to survive.

How when something breaks it cannot be fixed.

The Paters leave from Sandig four times a year. News, Ides, Fourth, and Remembrance. We leave our town in our bright red robes so that everyone may know who we are, and our yellow scarves so that everyone may know that we are from Sandig. Sandig is the most important town. We are the Paters who have the Counter. We keep the count for all that are left. When we walk on our journey to do our duty, even the Romas do not bother us. They watch out for us, escorting the way to the next town. We are that important to the world.

I am so excited to leave that I get dressed before the sun is up. I adjust my yellow scarf, which is stitched with blue and lavender. I have blue and lavender tattoo rings on both of my arms so that everyone knows that when I am a full Pater I may only go with green, brown, orange, and red. But since there are not many left that I can go with, I will become the next Counter.

There are twelve of us walking. The road is long and the work is hard. But we are special.

When we reach the first town, on the gate there is a blue, lavender, black, and green flag waving. That means two girls are ready for seeding. On the highest post, two white flags fly. That means two new babes. This town is growing. I will feast with the others as an honored guest while the two Paters who are called do their duty. Jas is one of them, and that means tomorrow at the counting, I will have to work alone.

"I'm nervous," I say to Jas.

"Don't be, Geo," he says. He hesitates, as though he is going to say something to me but then doesn't. Instead he says the Pater code. "Do your duty, for all. Three for Four count. Be swift."

I repeat it along with him. I know he is steeling me for what I must do. But I am restless.

Some of the Paters are complaining that the food was off, or not as good as last year. I do not understand why they are complaining, because I notice that most from my group do not eat much. Every year they seem to get skinnier. For me, the food seemed fine, and in all my years I have never seen so much food on a table. I know that every town feeds the Pater their best foods. I eat everything in front of me. Most of the others barely finish their first plate.

After the feast they all want to rest because their stomachs hurt. We are led to a cabin where we will all bunk, and almost everyone has to lie down. I never lie down after I eat, like the others do. I have been warned that I may feel ill from the different tastes, but my belly does not hurt and I do not have gas like the others. But even in our town, they complain and lie down after every meal, as they do here.

I stand at the door, looking out at this town, which is different and new.

"Shut the door," Dug says to me. He is lying on his bedroll, sweating and moaning. So instead of joining the others on the floor to rest, I go outside to roam. I have never been away from Sandig, and my eyes are interested in all that is before me.

The town looks nothing like our hometown, and yet parts of it seem familiar. Here, like us, they feast mostly on fish and seaweed. I can hear the water. The sound of it is comforting and familiar, and reminds me of home. As with us, the streets are still mostly paved, and the people live on the street with the most houses that are still standing. The houses from before, with glass windows and working doors. And some of the houses have the same names as we do; tarbu ks. Wal t, Donal 's. The houses go on, even past the large fence made of wood and metal that surrounds the town, and keeps its people safe. And outside, past the crumbling buildings, are of course those strange signs. The ones that scream danger. Now we know that there is not much out there, except for other barricaded towns and stretches of nothing. But after it all began, people needed to fight together to live. This town, Mesa, I know to be bigger than most but not as big as our home. I am warned that some other towns are very small. That is just part of the Way. And we do what we can to bring hope.

In the morning, when I wake up, it is time for the counting. It is the most important thing that our group of Paters do. We seed, like the other Paters, but our priority is the count. The village brings the babes that have been born since the last time we came. In this town there are two. I prick their fingers and the machines whir. They are both four for four. The town wants to celebrate with another feast. It is good news for them. Despite being a bigger town, their numbers were getting low. The two babes are boys. There is much to rejoice about that. Boys are rare, which is why most become Paters. But Jas has a schedule that he wants to keep, So he moves us along.

"We have many towns to go to," he reminds us.

As I am packing up my machines, a woman comes in and presses a shell necklace into my hand. When we file out of the town, more people come up and try to give us gifts. I take what I am given because I like the thought of adding things from my trip to my collection, but the other Paters wave the people away, as though they are irritated by the show of emotion.

"I think they were just trying to say thank you," I say to Jas.

"Geo, you'll learn that your pack will be too heavy if you take every piece of thank you that you are given."

"They were happy, that's all," I say. I am wearing my bead

necklace. And I have dried seaweed in my pocket. And a small metal box with the picture of a woman who is part fish.

Jas shakes his head. He is much older than me, and so he has wisdom, and I respect that. But when he talks to me like that, it makes me feel as though I am not an apprentice Pater, about to become a man, but still just a small boy with a silly love of collecting odd things.

"Come now, Geo, don't be sour," Jas says.

We walk on the road and head north, but we must stop a few times more than Jas would like because some of our group are sick. We slow down our pace, and that helps, but Jas worries that we will fall behind in our duty.

We pass another group of Paters from the North on the road. Their number is small, only five. We exchange news. Even though they do not mention it, I notice that most of their group is feeling sick, too. We camp together for the night before we part ways in the morning.

We pass by some more fenced-off towns. I think that we are going to stop at every single one, but Jas says there is no need. Sometimes there are no flags hanging, which means no counting must be done because no babes have been born. We only stop if there are white flags—to do the counting—or if there are colored flags—to do the seeding—and then, only if the colors of the flags mean that one of us is a good match. If there are no flags, it means there is no need, or some other Pater group has filled it. We are all in this together.

We come upon a town that needs us, and so we enter. Here, there are the cactus and the succulents. I notice that there are plots of land outside that people still water, although nothing pushes up through the ground except for weeds. I am surprised when, later at the feast, they put the weeds in everything. Many of our group are still feeling ill. Many in the town are too. But I have not lost my appetite.

"It tastes good," I say.

"Dandelions," a woman tells me. "I will pack some for your journey."

I continue eating my soup to avoid Jas's annoyed look, but I am glad that I will have a tasty snack for the long walks.

The next morning, in the room with the machines, the same woman enters with a bag of dandelions and a babe in her arms. She hands me the dandelions, and I am glad that Jas is still in the outhouse, taking care of his stomach because he is not feeling well, so I can put them in my pack before he sees me collecting another thing. I wait before beginning, for Jas, and he comes in and examines the babe. The babe has orange and brown tattoos. That is a rare combination, but not as useful since the babe is a girl. When I am a full Pater, and a seeder, brown and orange will be good for me to do my duty with. If there are any left. I heard Jas say that there are not many along the road of the Way.

The baby coos. The woman smiles. I distract the child when Jas goes to prick her finger. The baby laughs. The machine whirs. The first code comes up green.

AGGCTTACACCG

And then there are three red buzzes.

Jas looks at me. The woman looks at me. The baby coos again.

"Geo, why don't you give the litany."

He is teaching me how to do it because I am Apprentice Counter. I have never given the litany before. I stumble over the prepared speech.

"As we know in these dark times, it is important for all that only the strong be allowed to grow. Any of those without the sequence must go down for all to rise."

The woman looks at me. I feel terrible about the dandelions. I wonder if I should give them back. As is tradition, I take her hands in mine. I have not touched many hands in my life. Her hands are rough and cracked and dry. That is when I notice her birth marks. She has seven. On her *left* arm. Seven babes, all gone down. This will be her eighth to go down.

Jas has already taken the babe in his arms and put the poison on his finger for the babe to suck. In a few minutes the babe will sleep and never wake up again.

"Thank you," the woman says. Her eyes are hard, but mine are not. I am crying as she leaves the tent.

Jas moves close to me.

"The first one is always hard," Jas says. "It gets easier."

"How can it get easier?" I ask.

Jas shrugs. "It just does."

He leaves me to myself as I do my job of packing the machines. I try to remember that we are performing a kindness. No one, the Way says, except for those who are three or four for four, will live for very long. It is better for them to go down when they are young. It is less painful than to know them and then put them down.

"Orange and Brown is so rare, though," I say.

"Yes," Jas says. "Very rare."

"Why couldn't we have spared her for the orange and brown?"

"The sequence. Three or four for four. It is what we live by. It is our code. It is the law."

After one week, we arrive at the next town that needs us.

We are halfway through the feast when a man comes from a remote village. He has heard through the Romas that we were on the road. He comes to plead his case.

"We are a small town. Very small. We are new. We have only

two girls who are of age. We are prepared to give so much for just this chance. We are ready to join the Way."

Sometimes this happens. New towns form. The Romas get tired of wandering and fighting, and they settle down and make a town. In order to grow, they must join the Way. It is hard. The Romas take a chance by inviting the Paters in. The girls must be tested to see if they will fit into the Way. If they do, then Paters will be sent to them. If not, then they will not join the Way and the town will likely die.

Jas is the oldest. It will be him to decide. It will be him who will go with the man to visit the girls. He consults with the man. They look at me.

"Geo," Jas says. "They are desperate. The Way is their best chance. And they have birds." Birds are rare. My stomach and eyes delight at the thought of birds.

"Why don't you go?" I ask Jas. He should go. He is the leader. He is the Counter. I am just an Apprentice Counter. But then, as I look at him closely, I see that I don't have to have him give me an answer. I can see by the way he holds himself, as though it is with great effort to stand, by his paleness and by the way he has spent so much time by the side of the road, like the others. It will not be long before the fact that he is ill will be known to all. It seems as though many people in all of the towns are ill. But I have not weakened at all. The walk has made me stronger.

"I will do it for the birds," I say.

I will be gone a few days, and that will give the group a chance to rest and get better while I do our duty.

The man is so thankful, he pumps my arm up and down as though I will give water. It is shocking to be touched. But he is crying. And I try to remember that the Romas ways are not our Ways. He gives a sack of goods to Jas, with the promise for more upon my return.

I get my pack and find the man waiting by the gate. It is strange for me to leave on my own with a stranger. His accent is difficult to understand, but we make do with hand gestures and good will. We begin to walk. I can tell that he is sorry that I have to walk because it is far and the terrain is treacherous. And I am a Pater. I try not to let on that I am only an apprentice and have never seeded anyone, and that this is my first trip, and that after two hours my feet are in pain. I am his hope. I must always look like it.

We are walking up and up and up a mountain. As we turn on the path, the valley and the ocean spread out below us. The view takes my breath away. The water is silver, the sky is blue, and the ruins from two cities are in perfect view. I cannot help but wonder at the amount of people who lived there once. I cannot imagine the world without worry of extinction. The trip is worth it for this moment of beauty and sadness. My guide stops with me, and we both take a moment to ponder our fate, given to us by those who lived in those impossible buildings.

Jas has been slowly teaching me how to read the words of those from the ruined cities. He says that sometimes the answers to our questions lie in there. But the books are fragile and cannot stand the light. And many things that are written are confusing and incomprehensible. But I am always amazed at the things those people seemed to be able to do. Even everything in ruin seems more than what we are able to accomplish. I am amazed.

My guide nudges me, and I tear myself away from the view. I discover that I am close to crying, so I try to hide it, as though there is dust or sun in my eyes. I make a big show of adjusting my hat. But I think that my guide knows my heart. For he puts his arm around me and squeezes my shoulder in a sympathetic way. A way that says, "My heart is heavy for us all, too."

Just before sunset, we make it up to the village, if you can call it that. It is five houses and a well. Most of the few people here are old. Very old. These are Romas who are too tired to roam.

Here, in this village, there are two girls who are my age, in their sixteenth or seventeenth year. They have no tattoos. No one has tattoos. Romas don't have their line on their arms. They are outside of the Way. I look at the girls in a respectful manner, with my eyes down. Their features are different than the girls and women I know. One of the girls is shy. She looks at her feet and hides her face behind her hair. The other girl, who is more homely, comes up to me. She looks at me in my eyes, which makes *me* feel strange. As though she is looking right inside of me. No one looks at anyone like that. It is disturbing, but I take it to be another of the strange ways of the Romas. She motions for me to follow her, and she shows me to a small shack where I will sleep. From her pocket she pulls out a red thing. She polishes it on her shirt and hands it to me. Then she takes one out for herself and begins to eat it. I have never seen something like it. I sniff it and smell a faint pleasant perfume. I bite into it. It is not soft, but hard, yet it is juicy and it makes my tongue feel alive.

"Good?" she asks.

"Good," I say.

"Minerve," she says, extending her hand in what I know to be a Romas grip. It is a greeting among them. We of the Way usually do not touch one another, but I extend my hand and touch hers. It feels electric.

"Geo," I say.

She smiles. I notice that her eyes are green. I have never seen green eyes.

As she goes she closes the door behind me and leaves me to my preparations.

This town is so far out of the Way that there is no feast. Minerve comes back later and brings me a plate of food. Everything on the plate looks strange. Some of it I do not care for. But most of it is alive with flavor. When I am done eating, I feel full in a way that I have never felt before.

I begin my preparations. I will have to give them all a tattoo. I must choose a color and enter it into the book. I consult the charts. I notice that red has faded out a long time ago; it has not been used for more than fifty years. It makes me think that orange and brown will go that way soon, too, unless things change. But red has been gone for so long that it will be safe to give this town red. I am allowed to be with red. I like Minerve. Would it be wrong to make her a line that I can seed? I blush. But still, I settle down in my room to mix the color. If the girls are three for four, then I will give this town the color red.

The next morning, Minerve comes, and I am given breakfast. Once again there are things I have never seen before.

"What is this?" I lift up my food.

"Pan," she says.

"Pan," I say.

It is like eating a cloud.

A bell rings, and the other girl, the shy one, comes to my hut, along with all of the villagers. Everyone in town is outside my hut and the whole town amounts to no more than sixteen people. I understand now why the Counter has a ceremony and a script. It is too stressful to do this without a script. I take the first girl's finger and prick it. Everyone lurches forward to see as I put the blood on the machine. It whirs, it clicks. It buzzes four times red. Everyone is still. We all breathe as one as I take Minerve's finger. I look up at her. I must look like hope. But I feel fear. A drop of blood blooms on her finger. I place it in the machine. It whirs. It clicks. The first code comes up green.

AGGCTTACACCG

My heart lifts. I touch her knee.

The second sequence comes up green. I smile at her. My heart feels warm.

The third sequence comes up red. I squeeze her knee. The whole town is holding their breath. It could still be okay; she might just be three for four, like me. If so, then Paters will come. She will be seeded. The town will be allowed to trade. With birds, they will likely be rich.

The fourth sequence comes up red.

No one speaks. Someone gasps. There is a sob. Even the Romas know what that means. They will not be a part of the Way. I shake the machine, as though if I shake it, it will become green.

The man who guided me up the mountain suggests that we all have a meal together that evening and a good night's sleep before we go back down so that I can join the others. The townsfolk disperse. Minerve stays.

"You should go," I say. "I'm tired."

"You are upset," she says.

I had optimistically mixed the color to tattoo the village. I had ignored the protocol of *wait and see*. I am still learning, and now I understand that these rules are made to avoid disappointment.

I do not want her to make fun of my emotions. I am tired of people making fun of my sensitivity.

"Is it so terrible to be upset?" I yell. I kick the color pot on the ground. I want to smash the machine. But instead I yell again.

"It's okay, Geo," Minerve says. "We will go on as before, without the Way. It will just be our way."

But we all know that the Romas numbers are dwindling. That is why in the past ten years Romas are trying to make towns and join the Way.

She comes over to me and touches my tattoos. She traces them with her fingers.

"Beautiful," she says.

I go over to the pot. There is still some red in it. I take the needle from its pouch and I tattoo a red mark on her. I just want to see how the red will look on skin, since I have never seen it. When I have done a large enough circle on her shoulder for it to be noticeable, I stop. I cover it up with a bandage. She puts a hand on my cheek.

No one will be able to see the mark unless she is not wearing a shirt. I have not given her a false line. I have just given her a decoration that will be our secret.

I am suddenly very tired. I go to the corner and lay down on the bed. Minerve comes and lays down next to me and puts her arms around me. No one has ever held me. It is the most me that I have ever felt. I hold her like something known but long forgotten. I fall asleep.

A bell rings and the meal begins. It is modest, not a celebration. There is no pomp and glamour. I do not feel like wearing my red robe and yellow scarf. I wear my simple underclothes, and they make me feel more at home than in Sandig. There is a bird for a meal and a husk. I watch as the others open their husks. I have seen these kinds of husks before, but no one bothers with them. Where I am from, there is no part of it to eat. Just a white cone. But these husks are different: I notice that there are yellow insides. Minerve shows me how to bite into it, and it is sweet and earthy. When the yellow is eaten, all that is left is the white cone that I have seen before.

Later, as the town sleeps, I lie awake. I think about the babe in the town that we put down. I think about how if Minerve had been in the Way, she would have been put down too. I think about the birds. I think about the husks. I think that this town has something more than the sequence, more than our code, and that it must be saved. I cannot sleep. I want to wander outside and find Minerve. I want her to hold me again, but I know that is wrong. I close my eyes, my mind abuzz. When I do sleep, my dreams are vivid and wild. I dream of Minerve. I dream of the birds. I dream of the husks and the green.

In the morning, before dawn, my guide comes to get me. I notice that Minerve is with him. He is carrying a pack. He opens it to show me that it is full of gifts that he promised to Jas for my time: strange plants, dead birds, small pots. I nod in thanks. Our business done, Minerve then steps up to me and puts a small bag into my hands. I open it. It is the dried yellow parts from the husks we ate. I told her of the land near Sandig, where the fields are full but there are only empty cones inside.

"Will you walk with me?" I ask.

"I am glad to," she says.

On our way down the mountain we talk of everything and anything we can think of, because it will be our only conversation. We stop and stare at the ruined buildings, and I am glad that she reaches for my hand. Outside of the gates of the town, Minerve and the guide stop and converse. She takes the pack from him, and he stays while Minerve walks me all the way to the gate. Once there, I put my arms around her. I wish I could say that I will see her on the next walk, but I know I won't.

Jas and the others know by my face that the town will not join the Way. We gather our things to leave. This time, it takes us longer to get to the next town. Jas is so ill that he tells us we should cut our trip short and head back to Sandig. By the time we reach home, three of our group have died. People are sick everywhere. They eat, but most people are pale and thin. I am never sick. Neither are a few others.

When the time came for Ides, half of the Paters are dead. Jas is so weak that he does not think he could even make the walk. Also, word has come that many towns on the coast are having trouble. No one can figure out the sickness, or where it comes from. We start to call it the Waste. We do not go to Count for Ides or for Fourth. Jas insists that we follow the rule of quarantine.

But I am well. I am restless. After a few months, I begin to escape the town gates at dawn and roam, as was my way. I notice that I am more healthy than I have ever been, as though my body has more energy, more vitality. I notice more birds than the year before. I notice things that fly from tree to tree. I notice that none of the Romas are ill.

One of them seeks me out. He's found a machine that still works. A rare find indeed. It is one that I have been looking for, to replace the one that helps us to determine illnesses. He wants to trade. But nothing that I had will do.

He shakes his head at everything I've brought.

"I have nothing left," I say. "Everyone is ill. I've been quarantined for months."

"No," he says, poking at all the objects I've laid out before him. Then his eyes fall on Minerve's bag. He opens it, and out spills the hard yellow seeds into his hand.

"It's worthless," I say. "They are dry. I tried to eat one, it nearly broke my tooth."

But the truth is that I want to keep the bag that Minerve gave to me with those yellow pieces from the husks. They are from her, and I want to keep them close to me.

"This," he says, and pushes the machine toward me. He takes the bag and walks away.

Jas is happy when I come back with the machine. I am not scolded for breaking quarantine. But the machine does not reveal any sickness. If we are sick, it is from something that we do not know. It is beyond the understanding of the machines.

Time goes on, and yet more people die. But not me. As they thin, I grow fatter and stronger.

When News comes around, Jas had succumbed to the Waste, and although I am not yet considered a man, I am now the head Counter. I wait till Ides to make my decision to go on a walk without the other Paters. I will go Count. I will go see the towns. But I will not put the other Paters in danger. I teach one of the young boys how to use the machine in case I don't come back. I put on my red robe and my yellow scarf and begin the walk north.

So many villages are depleted of people. In some villages, everyone is gone. In one village, there is a babe. Since we had not come for so long, it is almost a year old. It is fat and round and healthy. When I prick its blood and put it on the machine, the machine comes up two sequences green, two sequences red.

I prepare the poison, as I was taught. I take the mother's hands and recite the script. She bows her head and says thank you. I dip my finger in the poison and hold the babe in my arms. I looked at the babe. Two sequences green, two sequences red.

Two sequences green, two sequences red.

I turn to the mother, my finger in the air. I deviate from the script.

"What is your code?"

She looks startled.

"Your code?" I ask. "Your sequence? Are you four? Or three?"

"I am three," she says. "I'm sorry, I am only three."

I look at her. She is healthy. She is round and well-fed and full of vitality. So is the child.

Two sequences green, two sequences red.

Jas was four sequences. Everyone who has died was four sequences. I was three code sequences green. One red.

I hand the mother back the babe. I wash my finger of the poison. She understands what I am about to do. That I will not put the babe down. We do not speak of it. She is afraid that if we do, I will change my mind. I have broken the only law of the Way that has been understood to be unbreakable.

As I go from town to town, doing the count, I ask every healthy person what their count is. They are all three for four. I make a decision to pass all babes no matter if they are red or green. With no one to stop me, since I am alone on the road and I am the Counter, none went down.

Something is wrong. The sequence is wrong. The code is wrong.

When I get back to Sandig, I am now the lead Counter. There are only four Paters left.

"What do we do?" they ask me. The ones that are left, Pat, Dug, Jig, and Mel are older than me, but I am now the one to look up to.

"In the texts, there are sometimes answers."

I went into the SciTexts. I go all the way back. To the beginning.

Some pages crumble at my touch. Some pages are like Jas said, incomprehensible. But one day, some parts of different pages make sense together.

Due to mass transgenic cross-pollination and the insertion of genes into the genome of food crops, unintended effects have begun to express themselves in the human host, and the way that mutations affect the function of the crops own genes are unpredictable. . . . We have reached a tipping point, and the development of unknown toxic components make it impossible for humans to properly metabolize proteins in the following crops: corn, soy, alfalfa, wheat. . . . Many other food stuffs may have been affected. The amount of cross-pollination is at 98% in all crops. . . . As of this date, within twenty-five years, we expect a mass population loss of five billion+ due to famine from the inability of humans to digest and process these food crops. . . . Research indicates that genotyping those with markers for the novel mutations TFDE109, TFDE110, TFDE111, and TFDE112 and crossbreeding the remaining human survivors with the aim of ensuring that those born have a minimum of three, preferably four, mutations, should allow for human survival. . . . Short-term solution includes breeding for the mutations. . . . Signs indicating the toxicity of crops until correct mutations have been expressed is an option. . . . Literacy cannot be counted on as a means of communication. . . . Note: There is, however, a high probability that, in the future, there will be a shift back, and at that time the mutations TFDE109, TFDE110, TFDE111, and TFDE112 will be detrimental to human metabolism. . . . The timescale of this process cannot be estimated, since projections cannot be made due to the inability to control crossbreeding of plant species in the wild.

I have my answer. I walk out of the room. I walk to the gates and I open them.

"What are you doing, Geo?" people ask.

"Close the gate, Geo," people say.

"The Romas will come!" people say.

I go to each field on the outskirts of Sandig and I pick what was there. I ignore the signs and take the things that grow that we have believed are poison. The things that the Romas ate all the time and sometimes lived and sometimes died. I put them in my pack and I bring them back to the town.

I will make everyone try to eat everything.

I will make sure that no more babes are ever put down again.

I will find Minerve and be with her.

I will spread the word.

And that will be the new Way.

AFTERWORD

BY **TERRI WINDLING**
AND **ELLEN DATLOW**

DYSTOPIAN LITERATURE FOR YOUNG ADULT READERS IS enjoying a surge in popularity these days—which, in turn, has prompted a veritable flood of newspaper and magazine articles attempting to explain *why*. Some people argue it's because today's teens are inheriting a world plagued by problems of a global scale unknown to previous generations. A taste for dark, dystopian tales, they say, is simply a natural response to growing up amid the great disasters of our age: 9/11, Hurricane Katrina, the Indian Ocean tsunami, the Japanese and Haitian earthquakes, the BP oil spill, the melting of the polar ice caps, etcetera, etcetera.

But other people point out that this is nothing new; *every* generation has its disasters and apocalyptic fears. The two of us grew up, for example, with "duck-and-cover" drills in elementary school to "prepare" us for nuclear attack . . . while *our* parents lived through childhoods shaped by the ravages and aftershocks of World War II. For as long as dystopian books have existed, generations of readers have been devouring them—although in the past, when the Young Adult publishing field was a whole lot smaller than it is today, teens usually had to raid the Adult fiction shelves in order to find it.

Of all the explanations proffered for why teen readers respond so strongly to dystopian/postapocalyptic tales, we like Scott Westerfeld's the best. Scott, of course, is the author of the Uglies series—which are books that, along with Suzanne Collins's *The Hunger Games*, deserve a large slice of credit for establishing YA dyslit as a genre to be reckoned with. In an essay for "Dystopia Week" on the Tor.com Web site, Scott said:

"Teenagers' lives are constantly defined by rules, and in response they construct their identities through necessary confrontations with authority, large and small. Imagining a world in which those authorities must be destroyed by any means necessary [as per dystopian fiction] is one way of expanding that game. Imagining a world in which those authorities are utterly gone [as per postapocalyptic fiction] is another."

If you're a longtime reader of dystopian fiction, you're probably already familiar with the genre's history, but for those of you who have just discovered the field—perhaps through *Uglies*, or *The Hunger Games*, or another YA dystopian book—you might be interested in knowing a bit more about where this type of fiction comes from.

The history of dystopian fiction begins with its polar opposite, *utopian* fiction: tales that envision a better world and more perfect society. The word "utopia" itself (from Greek roots meaning "no place" or "good place") first appeared as the title of a fantasy novel (or so it would be called today!) by Sir Thomas More, the great writer, philosopher, statesman, and Catholic martyr of sixteenth century England. More's *Utopia* is the story of a traveler to an imaginary island country where private property is unknown, women are educated alongside men, and religious tolerance is, if not perfect, then at least more advanced than it was in More's own time: all radical ideas that were safer to couch as fiction than to espouse in real life. Although utopian texts existed long before

More coined his famous name for them (such as Plato's *Republic* from the third century B.C.), it was More's book that went on to inspire the great utopian tales of the nineteenth century (which critics have dubbed "the utopian age"): *Erewhon* by Samuel Butler, *Looking Backward* by Edward Bellamy, *Gloriana* by Lady Florence Dixie, *News from Nowhere* by William Morris, and many others. These, in turn, directly inspired the birth of the *dys*topian genre.

The first recorded use of the word "dystopia" (derived from Greek roots meaning "bad place") comes from a political speech by John Stuart Mill in 1868, who used the word to describe utopia's opposite: a place where attempts to create an ideal society had gone badly awry. (He was talking about the English government's land policy in Ireland.) When we turn from politics to fiction, although we can find dystopian elements in a number of early texts, dystopian fiction as a *genre* does not begin until the nineteenth century, where it emerged in reaction to those utopian books so beloved by Victorian readers. Distrustful of the bright, lofty visions conjured by Bellamy, Morris, and the other utopianists, writers such as Anna Bowman Dodd, Ignatius L. Donnelly, Eugen Richter, and H. G. Wells published popular books in the opposite vein: dark, satiric, cautionary tales of utopia gone wrong. Most of these writers are forgotten now—except, of course, for the great H. G. Wells, for it was Wells who established the dystopian genre as literature (and not just polemic) with now-classic books like *The Time Machine* (1895) and *When the Sleeper Wakes* (1899). The prolific Wells also wrote utopian novels—such as *A Utopian Tale* (1905) and *Men Like Gods* (1923)—which had only mixed critical success and are rarely read today. Aldous Huxley, in fact, disliked *Men Like Gods* so much that he sat down to write a parody of it, producing his now-classic dystopian novel *Brave New World* (1932), set in a futuristic land of consumerism and technology pushed to soulless extremes.

Although less well known than the novels of Huxley or

Wells, *We* by Yevgeny Zamyatin (1924) is another classic of early dystopian literature: a chilling tale set in a bleak totalitarian society inspired by the author's experiences during the Russian Revolution of 1905. Zamyatin's novel, in turn, profoundly affected a young English writer and journalist named Arthur Eric Blair, who would go on to become the most widely read dystopian writer of all time. We know him better under his pen name: George Orwell, author of the dystopian masterpiece *Nineteen Eighty-Four* (1949)—a book so terrifying, powerful, and prescient that it's been embraced by readers of every generation since, despite the fact that the year 1984 has long since come and gone.

After Orwell (and perhaps because of him), from the 1950s onward, the dystopian genre grew exponentially, with a dizzying number of excellent books found both on the mainstream literature shelves and on the science fiction shelves (where teens were especially likely to spot them), including *Fahrenheit 451* by Ray Bradbury (1953), *Lord of the Flies* by William Golding (1954), *The Chrysalids* by John Wyndham (1955), *Harrison Bergeron* by Kurt Vonnegut (1961), *Make Room! Make Room!* by Harry Harrison (1966), *Stand on Zanzibar* by John Brunner (1968), *The Lathe of Heaven* by Ursula K. Le Guin (1971), *Flow My Tears, the Policeman Said* by Philip K. Dick (1974), and *The Handmaid's Tale* by Margaret Atwood (1985), to name just a few. (If you're unfamiliar with *any* of these books, please seek them out. You'll be glad you did!)

In the 1980s and 1990s, a new form of dystopian fiction emerged: tales written specifically for young adult readers, adding younger protagonists and coming-of-age themes to a genre that many teens had already embraced in its adult form. Recommended early works of YA dyslit include *The Green Book* by Jill Paton Walsh (1981), *Futuretrack 5* by Robert Westall (1984), *The Devil on My Back* by Monica Hughes (1984), *Children of the Dust* by Louise Lawrence (1985), The Obernewtyn Chronicles by Isobelle

Carmody (begun in 1987), The Giver Trilogy by Lois Lowry (begun in 1993), *Shade's Children* by Garth Nix (1997) . . . and too many other fine books for us to even begin to list them all. (Google "Young Adult Dystopian Fiction" and you'll find many good lists of these older works.)

By the early years of the twenty-first century, YA dyslit was well on its way to becoming the exceptional field that it is today, with a wide variety of authors exploring dystopic themes in many, many different ways. The explosive growth of the field has been helped, of course, by the commercial success of books by M. T. Anderson (*Feed*), Paolo Bacigalupi (*Ship Breaker*), Malorie Blackman (*Naughts and Crosses*), Suzanne Collins (*The Hunger Games*), Cory Doctorow (*Little Brother*), Nancy Farmer (*The House of the Scorpion*), Patrick Ness (*Monsters of Men*), Carrie Ryan (*The Forest of Hands and Teeth*), Scott Westerfeld (*Uglies*), and other best-selling authors. But some of the new up-and-coming dyslit writers, too, are producing good work that promises to push the field into new directions in the years ahead—including some of the lesser-known writers published in this book, whose novels we encourage you to seek out.

Of course, when any field enjoys popular success, speculation promptly begins on just how long such a "fad" will last—with the doomsayers insisting it will all soon be over, or is over already. Here's our prediction: modern dyslit is not disappearing anytime soon because it's not a passing fad, it's a literary form. And it's a form that is still evolving—that is not even *close* to finding its limits yet—as it shapes itself to the hopes, fears, dreams, and nightmares of each new generation.

ABOUT THE CONTRIBUTORS

Richard Bowes has published five novels, two collections of short fiction, and over fifty stories, winning two World Fantasy Awards, the Lambda Award, the International Horror Guild Award, and the Million Writers Award. Recent and forthcoming stories appear in *The Magazine of Fantasy and Science Fiction*, *Realms of Fantasy*, *Icarus*, *Bewere the Night*, *Naked City*, *Nebula Awards Showcase*, *Supernatural Noir*, *Wilde Stories*, and *Blood and Other Cravings*. Rick lives in New York City, and can be found online at www.rickbowes.com.

Sarah Rees Brennan was born and raised in Ireland, by the sea, where her teachers valiantly tried to make her fluent in Irish (she wants you to know it's not called Gaelic), but she chose to read books under her desk in class instead. She began working on her debut novel, *The Demon's Lexicon*, while doing a Creative Writing MA and library work in Surrey, England. Since then she has returned to Ireland to write and use as a home base for future adventures. Her Irish is still woeful, but she feels the books under the desk were worth it. Her most recent books are *The Demon's Covenant* and *The Demon's Surrender*; she also contributed to *The Girl Who Was on Fire: Your Favorite Authors on Suzanne Collins' Hunger Games Trilogy*. You'll find her online at www.sarahreesbrennan.com.

Cecil Castellucci is the author of YA novels including *First Day on Earth*, *Rose Sees Red*, *Beige*, *The Queen of Cool*, and *Boy Proof*, and *The Year of the Beasts* (forthcoming). She has published a picture book,

Grandma's Gloves; two graphic novels, *The Plain Janes* and *Janes in Love* (illustrated by Jim Rugg), and numerous short stories published in *Strange Horizons*, *Teeth*, *The Eternal Kiss*, *Geektastic* (which she coedited), and *Interfictions 2*, among other places. Cecil also writes plays, operas, makes movies, does performance pieces, and occasionally rocks out. You'll find more information on Cecil and her work at www.misscecil.com.

Carolyn Dunn is an American Indian writer of Cherokee, Muskogee Creek, and Seminole descent on her father's side, and is Cajun, French Creole, and Tunica-Biloxi on her mother's. Primarily a poet and a playwright, Carolyn began telling and writing stories at a very young age, being exposed to storytelling traditions from all aspects of her very Southern and very Western background. Her books for adult readers include *Through the Eye of the Deer*, *Hozho: Walking in Beauty*, and *Outfoxing Coyote*. She has also published YA short fiction in *The Green Man*, and a book for children, *Coyote Speaks*. Her plays have been produced all over the country, the most recent being *The Frybread Queen*. Carolyn and her family live in a redwood forest in California, where she's at work on a dystopian novel related to the story in this anthology. To learn more about her books, plays, poetry, and music, visit her online at www.carolyndunn.com.

Carol Emshwiller grew up in Michigan and in France and now divides her time between New York and California. Her stories have appeared in literary and science fiction magazines for over forty years, and have been published in a number of critically acclaimed collections—most recently, *The Collected Stories of Carol Emshwiller* and *In the Time of War & Master of the Road to Nowhere*. Carol's work has been honored with two Nebula Awards and the Lifetime Achievement Award from the World Fantasy Convention.

She's also been the recipient of a National Endowment for the Arts grant and two literary grants from New York State.

Jeffrey Ford is the author of the novels *The Physiognomy, Memoranda, The Beyond, The Portrait of Mrs. Charbuque, The Girl in the Glass*, and *The Shadow Year*; and his short fiction has been published in three collections: *The Fantasy Writer's Assistant, The Empire of Ice Cream*, and *The Drowned Life*. He has won the World Fantasy Award, the Nebula Award, the Edgar Allan Poe Award, and the Gran Prix de l'Imaginaire. Formerly a college teacher in New Jersey, Jeff now lives in Ohio with his wife and two sons, and writes full-time. You can learn more about his work at www.well builtcity.com.

Steven Gould is the author of the novels *Jumper* (which was made into a feature film), *Wildside, Helm, Blind Waves, Reflex, Jumper: Griffin's Story, 7th Sigma*, and the upcoming *Impulse*. His story for this anthology is set in the early days of the metal bug infestation detailed in *7th Sigma*. Steven is the recipient of the Hal Clement Young Adult Award for Science Fiction, and his short fiction has appeared on both the Hugo and Nebula ballots, but his favorite "honor" was being on the American Library Associations Top 100 Banned Books list 1990–1999. He lives in New Mexico with his wife, writer Laura J. Mixon, and their two daughters. His blog, An Unconvincing Narrative, can be found at http://eatourbrains.com/steve.

Nalo Hopkinson was born in Jamaica and has lived in Canada since 1977. She is the author of five novels (*Brown Girl in the Ring, Midnight Robber, The Salt Roads, The New Moon's Arms*, and *The Chaos*), one story collection (*Skin Folk*), and has also edited several anthologies. She is a recipient of the Warner Aspect First Novel

Award, the Ontario Arts Council Foundation Award for emerging writers, the John W. Campbell Award for Best New Writer, the Locus Award for Best New Writer, the World Fantasy Award, the Sunburst Award for Canadian Literature of the Fantastic, the Aurora Award, the Gaylactic Spectrum Award, and her work received an Honorable Mention in Cuba's *Casa de las Americas* literary prize. Visit Nalo online at www.nalohopkinson.com.

N. K. Jemisin is a Hugo and Nebula nominee for her debut novel *The Hundred Thousand Kingdoms* as well as for her short fiction, and has been published in such diverse venues as *Postscripts*, *Clarkesworld*, and the Escape Artists podcasts. "The Trojan Girl," published in *Weird Tales*, was set in the same dystopian milieu as "Valedictorian"; and she is (slowly) working on a young adult novel also set there. Her fourth and fifth novels, *The Killing Moon* and *The Shadowed Sun*, will be published in mid-2012. She lives in Brooklyn, New York, and can be found online at nkjemisin.com.

Caitlín R. Kiernan is the author of several novels, including *Low Red Moon*, *Daughter of Hounds*, and *The Red Tree*, which was nominated for both the Shirley Jackson and World Fantasy awards. Her latest novel, *The Drowning Girl: A Memoir*, will be released by Penguin in 2012. Since 2000, her shorter tales of the weird, fantastic, and macabre have been collected in several volumes, including *Tales of Pain and Wonder, From Weird and Distant Shores, To Charles Fort, With Love, Alabaster, A is for Alien*, and *The Ammonite Violin & Others*. In 2012, Subterranean Press will release a retrospective of her early writing, *Two Worlds and In Between: The Best of Caitlín R. Kiernan*, vol. 1. She lives in Providence, Rhode Island, with her partner Kathryn. She is currently working on her next two novels, *Blood Oranges* and *Blue Canary*.

Matthew Kressel's fiction has appeared in *Clarkesworld* magazine, *Interzone*, *Beneath Ceaseless Skies*, *Electric Velocipede*, *Apex* magazine, *GUD* magazine, and the anthologies *The People of the Book*, *Naked City*, and *Steam-Powered: Lesbian Steampunk Stories*, as well as other markets. He runs Senses Five Press, which publishes the magazine *Sybil's Garage* and published the World Fantasy Award-winning *Paper Cities: An Anthology of Urban Fantasy*. He cohosts the long-running Fantastic Fiction at KGB reading series in Manhattan. And he has been a longtime member of the Altered Fluid writers group, where he regularly builds and shatters worlds. His Web site is www.matthewkressel.net.

Katherine Langrish is the author of several young adult fantasy novels inspired by folklore and legends, including a trio of historical fantasies set in the Viking age: *Troll Fell*, *Troll Mill*, and *Troll Blood* (republished in 2011 in an omnibus version as *West of the Moon*), and *The Shadow Hunt* (UK title: *Dark Angels*), a tale of ghosts and faeries on the Welsh border in the twelfth century. Her latest book, *Forsaken*, is a short reimagining of Matthew Arnold's classic poem "The Forsaken Merman." Katherine lives in Oxfordshire, England, and is at work on a YA dystopian fantasy featuring the characters and world of "Visiting Nelson." You can visit her Web site at www.katherinelangrish.co.uk or join the chat about fairy tales on her blog, Seven Miles of Steel Thistles, at http://steelthistles.blogspot.com.

Gregory Maguire is the author of several dozen books for adults and children. His best known titles for children include *What-the-Dickens* and *Leaping Beauty*. His adult novel, *Wicked*, inspired the Broadway musical of the same name, and was followed by two *New York Times* best-selling sequels in the Wicked Years sequence,

Son of a Witch and *A Lion Among Men*. The final volume in the series, *Out of Oz*, was published in November 2011. He has also written and performed pieces for NPR's "All Things Considered" and "Selected Shorts." Gregory lives in New England and in France with his husband, the painter Andy Newman, and their three children.

Garth Nix is the award-winning author of fantasy novels beloved by young adult readers (including the Old Kingdom series, the Seventh Tower series, and the Keys to the Kingdom series), and the YA dystopian science fiction novel *Shade's Children*. His story for this anthology is set in the universe of *Shade's Children*, and takes place about ten years prior to the events in the novel. Garth's books have appeared on the bestseller lists of *The New York Times*, *Publishers Weekly*, *The Guardian*, *The Sunday Times*, and *The Australian*, and his work has been translated into thirty-eight languages. He lives in a Sydney beach suburb with his wife and two children. Visit him online at garthnix.com.

Before writing her *New York Times* best-selling novel, *Life as We Knew It*, **Susan Beth Pfeffer** didn't know what a dystopian novel was. She still doesn't know how to spell dystopian, but that hasn't prevented her from writing two more novels, *The Dead and the Gone* and *This World We Live In* in the same genre. Her most recent book, *Blood Wounds*, is a realistic YA novel, perhaps because she has no trouble spelling realistic. She lives in New York State, and you can fine her online at http://susanbethpfeffer.blogspot.com.

Beth Revis's debut novel, *Across the Universe*, is the first book in a science fiction trilogy for young adult readers. Like her story for this anthology, the novel explores life on the spaceship *Godspeed* under Eldest rule. The second book of the trilogy, *A Million Suns*, is forthcoming. Beth lives in rural North Carolina with her husband and dog, and believes space is nowhere near the final frontier. You'll find her online at www.bethrevis.com, and on the dystopian blog, The League of Extraordinary Writers (http://leaguewriters .blogspot.com).

Carrie Ryan is the *New York Times* best-selling author of several critically acclaimed short stories and novels, including *The Forest of Hands and Teeth*, *The Dead Tossed Waves*, and *The Dark and Hollow Places*. Her first novel was chosen as a Best Books for Young Adults by the American Library Association, named to the 2010 New York Public Library Stuff for the Teen Age List, and selected as a Best of the Best Books by the Chicago Public Library. A former lit-igator, Carrie now writes full-time and lives with her husband, two fat cats, and one large dog in Charlotte, North Carolina. You can find her online at www.carrieryan.com.

Genevieve Valentine is the author of *Mechanique: A Tale of the Circus Tresaulti*. Her short fiction has appeared in *Clarkesworld*, *Strange Horizons*, *Fantasy Magazine*, *Lightspeed*, and others, and in the anthologies *Teeth*, *The Living Dead 2*, *Running with the Pack*, *Armored*, *The New Adventures of John Carter of Mars*, and more. Her nonfiction has appeared in *Lightspeed*, *Tor.com*, and *Fantasy Magazine*, and she is the coauthor of the pop-culture book *Geek Wisdom*. Her appetite for bad movies is insatiable, a tragedy she tracks on her Web site, genevievevalentine.com.

Jane Yolen, winner of two Nebulas and a bunch of other awards, just counted up her books published—and under contract to be published—and the astonishing number is over 330. Of course if you counted her single poems, the count would be much higher. Her first love has always been poetry. The poem in this book was written on a gray day in Scotland (or as they write it there, "grey"), about the aftermath of some unnamed worldwide disaster. Though of course, even on extremely gray/grey days in Scotland, everything is green. Jane lives in Massachusetts and Scotland, and can be found online at www.janeyolen.com.

ABOUT THE EDITORS

Ellen Datlow has been editing science fiction, fantasy, and horror short fiction for over thirty years. She was fiction editor of *OMNI* magazine and *SCIFICTION* and has edited more than fifty science fiction, fantasy, and horror anthologies for adults, teenagers, and children, many of them with Terri Windling. She has won multiple Locus Awards, Hugo Awards, Stoker Awards, International Horror Guild Awards, World Fantasy Awards, and the Shirley Jackson Award for her editing. She was named recipient of the 2007 Karl Edward Wagner Award, given at the British Fantasy Convention for "outstanding contribution to the genre," and in 2010 she was given the Life Achievement Award by the Horror Writers Association.

Ellen lives in New York City, where she co-hosts the long-running reading series Fantastic Fiction at KGB. More information can be found at www.datlow.com or at her blog, http://ellen-datlow .livejournal.com.

Terri Windling is an editor, artist, essayist, and the author of books for both children and adults. She has won nine World Fantasy awards, the Mythopoeic Award, the Bram Stoker award, and the SFWA Solstice Award for outstanding contributions to the speculative fiction field. She has edited more than thirty anthologies of magical fiction for children, teenagers, and adults (many of them in collaboration with Ellen Datlow); she created the Bordertown series (a pioneering work of urban fantasy: www.bordertownseries.

com); and she's been a consulting editor for the Tor Books fantasy line since 1986. A former New Yorker, Terri now lives in small country village on Dartmoor, in the southwest corner of England, with her husband, daughter, and a dog named Tilly. Visit her on the Web at www.terriwindling.com, or on her blog, The Drawing Board, at http://windling.typepad.com/blog.